WOMEN IN PRACTICAL ARMOR

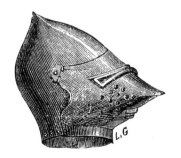

EDITED BY
GABRIELLE HARBOWY
AND **ED GREENWOOD**

Published by Evil Girlfriend Media, P.O. BOX 3856, Federal Way, WA 98063
Copyright © 2016

Cover image by Nneirda
Cover design by Eloise Knapp

ISBN: 978-1-940154-13-8

FROM THE EDITORS

Our deepest thanks to Katie Cord and Evil Girlfriend Media for believing in this project, and to Scott James Magner, Ann Shilling, Rena Watts, and our legion of Kickstarter backers for showing such a great demand for this book to exist. You put trust in us to deliver a great and anthology that celebrates female empowerment without disempowering anyone else to do so.

We were overwhelmed by the number of submissions we received, and we'd also like to acknowledge the talented writers whose stories didn't *quite* make it. The more difficult it is to pick the final roster, the happier we are, because it means we've got a lot of great fiction to choose from. By our count, we read over 750,000 words of it before ultimately choosing the stories you see here. We read all submissions blind, so that we would not be swayed by friendship or fame. As a result, we greatly appreciate the assistance of Fanny Darling, who stripped identifying information out of many, many files so that Gabrielle and Ed could read without bias.

As a result, you'll see some familiar names from our previous anthologies, some authors we're fans of but have never worked with before, and some debut authors celebrating their first professional fiction sale in these pages. We hope you've found old friends and new favorites here, as we have.

Thank you all—writers, readers, family, fans, and friends.

TABLE OF CONTENTS

ATTRITION

BY JUDITH TARR

The women had done it to themselves.

She was dead, the Queen: fallen in battle against the unending waves of invaders from the west. They came in their armies, drawn by tales of a land where the men were weak and slow, and war was the province of women. They came for the gold and for the fighting: an easy conquest, they told each other, and rich beyond imagining.

Women were weak, they said. Men were strong, unless women weakened them. War was men's glory; women had no place in it.

They said it over and over, year on year, in war after war. It was a lie, and as lies will do, it rose up above the truth and drowned it.

The Queen, the Penthesilea, lay in her grave outside the last camp of the people. There was no heir to heap the earth into a barrow over her body; no Queen to rule after her. Any who might have claimed the diadem was dead, or had succumbed to the Lie.

The one who had sold them all stood beside the foreign captain. She held her head high, even while she clung to his burly arm.

He liked a woman to cling, and to talk in a child's voice, and to mince beside him with tiny steps, as if she had no strength or will to stride out like a proper person. Kallisto played his game well, and thought she had won the war with it.

Charis leaned on a stick, watching in bleak silence. The war-club that had shattered her leg had saved her life. Otherwise she would be dead and buried with the rest of her sisters, or wrapped in soft wool and bound with ribbons and turned into a plaything for an outland raider.

She wore armor to honor the Queen, the only woman there who dared such a thing. The invaders slid eyes at her and muttered among themselves.

"She's not dangerous, is she?"

"That one? What can she do? She can barely hobble across the street."

That was true. But she could still ride and shoot and fight. If there had been anyone left to ride with, or any fight left in the people. They were all worn down. There was no Queen any longer, to give them hope.

Charis turned away from the grave and the dead thing in it. She hardly saw who moved aside, or cared why they did it. Her heart was still and cold. There was nothing left of her but a deep and abiding anger.

Strangers came often to the camps of the people, even in these darkened days. This one rode from the east, mounted on an ugly-headed, shaggy-coated, undersized pony.

People mocked it as she rode by. "Where'd you find a saddle to fit a dog?"

"Is that a horse or an old rug?"

"Who's carrying whom? You or the pony?"

The rider ignored them all—but not for lack of understanding. Charis saw how her narrow black eyes grew narrower, and her lips tightened into a thin line.

Charis had been tending horses. They were notably taller than the stranger's pony, and considerably prettier. But as she took the measure of the beast, she suspected that none would be its match for toughness.

The pony halted in front of her. The woman on its back peered at her as if nearsighted, or as if she had stared too long into the sun.

"Good day to you," Charis said, not particularly amiably.

The stranger frowned. "Good day," she said slowly. Her accent was less abominable than Charis might have expected. "This is the land of the women. Yes?"

"It was," Charis said.

She reached for the pony's bridle. The beast lunged, snapping. Charis sidestepped it, caught the rein, dealt it a sharp and quelling blow, all in a single swift, unthinking movement.

The pony squealed. Mare, Charis thought. It could not spin and kick while she had a solid grip on its headstall, though it did its best to try.

"Apologies," she said, without letting go. "I was presumptuous."

"So is the horse," the stranger said with the flash of a grin that transformed her plain, severe face.

She swung neatly out of the saddle, dodged a kick that had the air of ritual, and retrieved the reins. The pony stood with flattened ears and glaring eye, until she laughed at it. Then one ear came grudgingly up.

"Bitch," the stranger said lovingly. Then, flushing, as Charis' brows went up: "Not you! Oh gods. You must think I'm the rudest thing alive."

"I've known worse," said Charis.

The stranger bit back another grin. "My name is Birti," she said. "I came to serve your Queen."

Charis' heart contracted. She had begun a smile; it lingered wanly, all but forgotten. "Charis," she said. "My name is Charis."

"Charis," said Birti, sounding it carefully, as if she committed it to memory. "May I be presumptuous one last time? Will you tell me where to find the Queen?"

Charis pointed with her chin, mutely. There were still people lingering around the grave. The captain and his men had left long since, but a few women still cared, or pretended to care, for the customs of the people. They would keep watch for nine days, and dance and sing and make offerings to the Queen's spirit.

Charis should be with them. Instead she sent this stranger from the east on a fool's errand, and found herself entrusted with the care of the stranger's devil-pony.

That was just, in its fashion. Charis unsaddled and groomed and fed the pony; the pony offered one serious kick—barely evaded—and a lunge-and-snap that left a throbbing remembrance on Charis' arm. Thereafter, having observed the amenities, the pony settled to the serious business of eating, rolling, and making eyes at the stallion.

He was no fool. He kept a respectful distance.

So had men been once, before the world changed beyond hope of mending.

Charis lay on her blanket beyond the outermost edge of the camp and watched the stars wheel overhead. Far off she could hear the men roaring and singing inside the walls that they had built to keep the women in and each other out. At that distance it sounded no more human than the howling of wolves.

"She's dead."

Charis had heard Birti coming. She was soft-footed in the grass, but Charis' ears were unusually keen.

"The Queen is dead," Birti said, dropping cross-legged beside Charis. Her voice was raw with weeping. "They say there is no heir. There's a captain, but everyone says he'll be calling himself a king now there's nothing in his way. How can that be? This is the land of women!"

"Not any longer," said Charis. "We're all dead now, though some of us can't seem to stop walking and talking and acting as if we're alive. The men wore us down. There's nothing left of us."

"No," said Birti. "I didn't come all this way to find a broken people."

Charis shrugged, though Birti could hardly have seen it in the dark. "Maybe if we'd had you, we'd still be holding on."

"You'd need a hundred of me," Birti said. She flung herself flat on the grass, chin on folded arms. "What happened?"

"Time," Charis answered. "Invasion after invasion. Each time we drove one back, we lost more warriors; and too few were born to take their places. Too many listened to the men that they captured, fell prey to their promises, believed them when they told tales of women who lived among them in beauty and in luxury. No need to get their hands dirty. Certainly no obligation to defend their people in war, to buy with blood and pain what peace they had. They could live safe and protected inside of walls, and men would take on the tedium of danger."

"That's not true," said Birti.

"Of course not. But what does truth matter when a woman wants to believe a lie?"

"I came here for truth," Birti said. "I grew up in a city of traders. I heard the tales of your people; I learned the language you speak, and studied such of your customs as anyone knew. I heard the lies that men tell to their women, that always seemed to win advantage for the man and bind the women more tightly in servitude. I knew that there was no lie here. That in this place, women could see the truth."

Charis shook her head. She had nothing to say that this stranger would want to hear. She turned her back on Birti and pulled her blanket up over her head.

The captain did not even wait the nine days of the late Queen's funeral rite before he took on himself the title of king. Kallisto thought to sit beside him on the high seat. He suffered her to walk with him from the house that he had half-built already, but as they approached the sacred stone, he extricated his arm from her grasp and handed her into the care of two burly warriors. While she stood gaping, he went up alone to claim what should never have been his.

"Why is there no uprising? Why does no one speak?"

Birti held her tongue through the ceremony, with Charis' help: a hand over her mouth and a firm grip on her belt. She broke loose after the men had gone to feast and the women were left to stand about, ignored and forgotten.

The sweep of Birti's hand took in the lot of them. "You look like a flock of drunken sheep! Where is your strength? Is there a spell on you? Have you forgotten what you are?"

"What can we do?" Xanthippe said. She had been a war leader not so long ago. Then she had a pair of sons with the same man, and he convinced her that they were better served if she was the one to raise them.

She had a daughter in her arms now, nursing noisily, and the exhaustion of the new mother written deep in her face. She was still saddled with the sons, who should have gone to the father as soon as they were weaned, and made to look after the house and wait on the man.

"We're strong," she said, "but they're so many, and they never stop coming. There's no room in the world for us any longer."

"It *is* a spell," Birti said: "a curse of despair."

"Are you a witch or a priestess, then?" Charis asked of her. "Can you break the spell?"

Birti's high defiance tumbled down somewhat, but that only made her angry: she glared at Charis. "I'm a woman who left her tribe because the men had grown too arrogant, and went looking for the land of the women. I've come too far to find nothing but hopelessness."

"You are fierce," Xanthippe said. "I was like you once, I think. Before the world's weight fell on me."

"Fling it off," Birti said.

The child in Xanthippe's arms began to fuss. Xanthippe thrust the nipple in its mouth, but it twisted away. Its voice rose up in a full-throated wail.

"This child is the world to me," Xanthippe said over it. She still had that much of her old self: a voice that could carry above the roar and clash of a battle. "Would you have me cast her off?"

"Strap her in a sling and bring her with you," Birti said.

"Where?"

For that, Birti had no answer.

It was Charis who said, "We've always been wanderers and hunters across the steppe. Somehow we managed to forget that; to settle in or around cities and to limit our hunting grounds to those within reach of a camp or two, summer and winter. West now are lands full of vaunting men. What of the east, Birti? Is it still as empty as the stories say?"

"I rode from summer to winter and into summer again," Birti answered, "and after I left the farthest hunting grounds that our people know, I found nothing more than a tribe or two—and those were small and shy and not inclined to challenge even a lone rider."

Time and hard blows had taught Charis to trust no one, but in Birti's eyes she saw only truth. "And the hunting? Was it good?"

"In some places better than others," Birti said, "but yes. Mostly good. Sometimes more than good."

Xanthippe's eyes had widened. Through the dullness of exhaustion, her old self shone—dimly, but it was clearly there. "You're not thinking—"

"What is there for us here?" Charis said. "What have we been reduced to, that we could want to stay? What is there for us here?"

"It's home," Xanthippe said, but hesitantly.

"Home? Our home is the backs of our horses."

"If we still remember how to ride." Leuke had been listening, with a growing handful of others. She was big with child; two of her daughters hid behind the skirts that her man made her wear.

Daughters hiding, shy and subdued, as if they had not been born to rule the world—that was a slap in the Goddess' face. Birti's temper had struck a spark. In Charis' heart it roared into flame.

"I'm going," she said. "As soon as I can pack a saddlebag and fetch my horses, I'm heading eastward. Who's with me?"

"I wish," said Xanthippe, "but…" She tilted her head at her daughter, who had finally stopped squalling and gone for the breast.

"Bring her," Charis said. "We'll all bring our daughters. Those that can ride, can ride. The rest we'll carry."

"And our sons?" said Xanthippe.

"Leave them," Charis said. "Let their fathers raise them."

"No." Leuke's fair cheeks flushed as they all turned to stare at her. "Not all of them. It's the raising that twists them. Any that's still at the breast, bring him. We'll teach them the right way, just as we teach our daughters."

Charis nodded slowly. Then she held her breath. Someone would object; someone would, Goddess help them, go running to the men.

But no one did. Of all who had come to listen, not one woman spoke against this madness.

They were still the people after all. Birti had forced them to remember it.

As eager as Charis was to escape, she yielded to sense. They all agreed to finish out the day as if nothing had changed. Tonight would be a moonless night. In the dark, in silence, they would go.

She was certain to the bottom of her gut that it could not happen; that the men would stop them. But the day passed without incident, and night came softly, with wisps of cloud across the stars. The wind from the east had a faint scent of rain.

Rain was the Goddess' blessing. As the men finished their nightly round of drinking and dropped where they sat, one by one the women gathered their bits of belongings, their children and their horses, even such armor as they still had, hidden away in clothes chests or buried under rugs and tent poles, and drifted toward the eastern edge of the camp.

Charis waited there with Birti. So did Xanthippe with her baby in a sling, astride her grey-browed old stallion and leading the three sturdiest of his mares. She had found her heart and her courage after all. Her face in the starlight, though worn and thin, looked years younger.

The rest came, claimed their horses, mounted and fell into the old formation: each in her place, as she remembered, or as her sisters reminded her. Charis counted three twenties—enough to make her heart swell and her eyes fill with tears. She had hardly dared to hope for a dozen, and there were five times that.

Last of all, even as the tribe began to move, came one on a stout grey mare. She was dressed in tunic and trousers and her old corselet of leather and steel, and armed with bow and spear, and her hair was caught up in the long tail of the old warrior sisters. It caught the freshening breeze and streamed out behind her as she came face to face with Charis.

"Kallisto," said Charis. Her voice was as cold as her heart. "So. Where are they? Waiting beyond the hill? Ready to haul us back in chains, and bind us till we die?"

"Drunk or drugged so deep they'll sleep past morning," Kallisto said.

Her tone was as cold as Charis', but there was fierce heat beneath.

"All of them?"

"Every Goddess-damned one," Kallisto said.

"I don't believe you."

"So don't," said Kallisto, turning the mare on her haunches and taking her old place just behind Charis, on her right hand. Where the shield-sister belonged. Where she had always been until she cast her lot with the conquerors.

Charis' brows were up and her suspicions with them, but she could hear nothing in the camp but a distant chorus of snores. Even if they were feigning it, they would have to get up and dress and find their horses—and she had thought of that already.

She nodded to the two youngest and wildest of her old warband, Themis and Glauke. They nodded back, with a white flash of grins, and rode off knee to knee, with the tribes' pack of herding dogs circling and dancing around them.

As they passed the horses that would stay behind, a handful of dogs darted in among them. So likewise with the goats and the sheep, and the men's precious cattle. Well before Charis topped the eastward hill, the herds had begun to move, scattering to the winds—all but the east.

The dogs knew what to do, and Themis and Glauke would hold them to it. They would drive the herds as far as their feet and their stomachs would take them.

That, by morning, would be a long way. The men would be a long time finding them, and even longer bringing them back.

They still might choose to go after the women first. But the cattle were more valuable. That was the gamble the sisters had taken, and it was good—whatever came of it.

It had been a wonderfully long while since Charis felt what she felt now. It rose up out of her belly and swelled in her breast and her throat, and made her deliriously dizzy. After a while, as her tribe cantered down the long hill onto to eastern plain, she remembered what it was called.

It was joy.

NO BETTER ARMOR, NO HEAVIER BURDEN

BY WUNJI LAU

My boy might be a wastrel, but even so, stabbing him is a sure way to get my boil on.

I had no inkling it was him when the trouble started. Townsfolk running nigh and yon, screaming about soldiers in the tavern, Marshal Bregg nowhere to be seen, and never a thought entered my head of an angry boy who'd not messaged home in two years.

It's Laric, the steelsmith, who halts my advance toward the old tavern, just long enough to whisper, "Rose, have a care. Leians. Soldiers. Don't know why, but they've got Zaian at swordpoint."

He rushes away, shepherding children off the street. He has his own problems, and I can't blame him. He's the only one in town who knows I had sons, and why a woman my age might be running toward a fight, when everyone else is heading opposite. I'd rather it stayed that way. This is the best place for me.

The town is dusty and ramshackle, square walls built from mud bricks and held up with wood beams the settlers brought with them. No trees grow here, in the shadow of the Blacktooth. The Vault is strange here. Elsewhere in Ara, the world's ceiling is lit in predictable cycles, hot for months, then cooler, bright by day, glistening with excess energy by night. Here, the sky roils and pulses with red and angry purple, sometimes blazing with heat, then coal black and frozen for weeks. The town is far enough away that the changes are tolerable, but even a few miles closer is enough for a curtain of unnatural darkness to fall.

Some say it is because here, there is no Pillar to hold up the Vault. Blacktooth, shattered a thousand years ago, spreads a thousand feet wide at its base, rises miles into the sky and then shears off into a jagged tip. No howlers nest in its heights, nothing grows in the black mist that shrouds its feet. Thousands of other Pillars dot Ara, glowing gently and keeping the Vault in its place. Blacktooth is charred and cold. There are no others like it anywhere in Ara, and no one knows what could shatter an object whose surface can't even be scratched.

People, though, will live anywhere. Those who dislike other people will live in places that dislike everyone. I'd thought my sons lucky to have left. Farming in dust shouldn't be their lot. Sending them away was the best way to protect them.

The tavern building is old, layers of new brick on ancient stone. It has stood while the rest of the town has fallen and risen a dozen times. Its foundation may predate Blacktooth itself, for all I know. And yet, for its age, it's comforting, in that it manages to look just like every other tavern that humans have built. Among the timeless memories of our race, amid wild hunts, glorious discoveries, and religious fevers, there must also be, painted on the walls of the soul, the floorplan of a beerhall.

The front door gapes, and I slip through into the empty mainroom. I hear Zaian before I see him. He has twenty years and more, but now, I hear him as he sounded when he first fell off his own feet. That sound once made me run to hold him. Now it blurs my mind with fury.

I've little on me. Today isn't market day, so I was just walking through. A spear, on a back burdened with four decades and spare years. A gun, fearsome to locals and wildlife, but not to a warrior. Boiled leathers, good for riding and scuffling, bad for battle. It's a poor start to any day to have to rely on old age and wits.

There's two of them standing over him, hefty and glowering. Steel armor on the both of them, gleaming white, laced with glowing sigils, blazoned with the Steersman's Wheel. Why the holy orders of Leias have ridden this far into the wilds to start a barfight is a question I'll want answered, but not from these two.

The girl, laughing over the sound of screams, has her sword pierced through Zaian's thigh; she needs to go first. The other one, male, hairless and dull, is poking his blade here and there, drawing pricks of blood; his attention will be drawn away soon enough.

I don't have time for mercy and inquiries. They both outweigh me by at least four stone, not counting the armor, and their years combined wouldn't match mine. The armor, powerfully infused, makes them fast, strong, nearly immune to bullets and blades. With a word, it can repel, burn, or perform any number of wonders. Raised in the church, they'll have been taught to use the infusions in the armor instinctively, reacting instantly and by rote to any danger. It's the only weakness I can use.

I am granted a moment of surprise. They expect no one to resist them. What fool would? With one hand, my spear is raised. With the other, I sweep up a jug of wine and hurl it at the girl's head. The jug shatters harmlessly over the invisible mage barrier protecting her skull, but the liquid inside sloshes over her blonde hair and soaks her face, passing right through an automatic enchantment that can't tell rain from wine.

The girl turns to face me, laughter melting into shock, then anger, then amusement, all in the space of the moment that it takes her to die. She pulls her sword free with one hand, and with the other, gestures casually. In response, the barrier enchantment resets, pulling the wine from her hair, drying her face, wicking the liquid off to the side, and leaving the barest sliver of a break between magic shield and steel neckguard, no more than an inch. Enough for a spear tip.

Arterial blood spurts, and the armor, knowing no better, fulfills its owner's last command, diligently cleaning her dying face and keeping it pretty and pristine for her god.

The boy is just now registering my presence. He's young, younger than Zaian. Shame to kill him, but he's already swinging his blade, a glowing magesaber two arms long and able to cleave boulders. If I falter, he'll set this building alight or worse, accidentally decapitate my son.

I know the acolyte sword kata. Not as well as this young thing, but well enough. I dance the dance, duck, sidestep, step in. I draw my gun. I pass in front of the boy's increasingly confused look, and then I'm behind him, close on his back. It's nearly as dangerous here as in front; the armor has elbow spurs, and a better-trained user would impale me with a single swift tuck. This boy isn't such. He panics, forgets his place in his trained sword pattern. He stumbles forward to put distance between us, his nine stone of steel plate keeping all its momentum, no matter how magic might grant its wearer haleness or haste. I help him along with a kick to the rear.

Off-balance, he has no time for magical hand gestures. His head is still protected, but every armor has its gaps. I jam the gun's muzzle hard into the space between plates at the small of his back. By the time he finds his footing, I've pulled the trigger six times, and he's falling again.

The floor shakes from the impact and smolders from the dying sword-fire.

"Genira avenges, thief," he mutters, and dies.

It's been only moments, but it's done. Beer on the sword to silence the sizzle, a quick check of both bodies to make sure of them, and then I turn to see to my wounded blood.

The face I haven't seen in two years looks up, grins, and says, "I love you, Mama."

I remember liking the sound of those words so much better before his bollocks dropped.

Marshal Bregg is a competent man for keeping order and some form of rough law here, but his noble masters are far away, uninterested in this backwater, and just as happy to hear nothing from him as they are good news. Real trouble, with foreigners running about with military arms, is far beyond his purview. Until today, his job was easy; no one here has much worth fighting for aside from their solitude. He's not taking the change in pace well.

"Rose, you can't stay here," he simpers. He's my age, clearly once a fit figure, but given over to drink and soft chairs. Bregg can still win a fight with any two people in town, which earns him and his office enough respect, but he knows when he's up over his height.

Bregg doesn't know me well, no better than anyone here would care to know an old homesteader. He came in, though, on a room with two dead mage-warriors and a woman with a bloodied spear and empty gun, so he's finding out more about me than either of us would like.

Now that the danger is over, Bregg's deputies are suddenly models of professional efficiency, keeping the crowd outside at bay, stalling the understandably anxious tavernmaster, wrapping the bodies in canvas and even wiping the floors.

We're off near the bar, clear of the mess and out of general earshot. Bregg stands near, letting me finish treating Zaian's wound. The stab is through the meat, but not through the major vessels. The acolyte boy had infused poultice in his pouch, a valuable possession in these regions, useful for everyone. Zaian won't walk easy or run anytime soon, but there will be no infection, and in time, he'll heal.

Bregg continues in low tones. "You've put yourself to some trouble, stuck out your neck for a stranger, and I'm sympathetic to that, but that one," he gestures at Zaian, "says there's more coming." Zaian leans back against the bar, hiding worry and pain behind folded arms and a slight smile.

He looks as well as he did when last I saw him. Straight black hair, from me. Light skin and green eyes, from his father. The hint of tilt and sharpness at the edge of the eyes, again from me. Most palefolk are found more to the logward of Ara, but certainly not unheard of where I grew up, where more than a few children are born with colored hair and eyes. I've not traveled anywhere that such things aren't considered attractive, or at least fascinatingly different from a sea of black hair, black eyes, and dusky skin. It's especially so, here in the wilds, and part of the reason I told him and his brother to avoid coming here; they stand out.

"Just one," Zaian protests. "I led most of them wrong days ago, so only those two and their Evangeline, that Genira woman, managed to stay with me, and she went off to search the farmsteads."

"That's little better, idiot," Bregg shouts, startling the deputies milling about the mainroom. He composes himself. "One Evangeline is one too many. She'll hear of this soon enough, and then I'll have an angry priestess burning my town down and singing to her god while she does it. With who knows how many more to come in days, or sooner. Even if I hand you over, stranger, they'll be wanting who killed their warpriests, and I won't have them executing a local in my town square. Even if she did have a hand in the murders."

Zaian's eyes flash to me, and he suddenly looks far less composed. I purse my lips at him. "I ended the fight Marshal. I didn't start it. The acolytes should have come to you to ask for a binding, not gone sword-mad in a public house. The town will bear that much witness to it."

Bregg shrugs.

"I know, and that'd be enough for me to judge the matter as even." He pauses. "Maybe. But it's not up to me anymore, and do you think the word of Blacktoothers is enough to talk down that holy woman?"

There's no reason to think this Genira won't be as fair a judge as most of her faith, but anyone can be blind to the failings of their own kind. She likely won't believe her acolytes broke their code and started the fight, and that's the only part of the story that might keep her honor-bound from laying steel over anyone involved. Wouldn't be the first time this town has burned unjustly, nor the first time a far kingdom looked the other way and let it happen.

Bregg sees my hesitation.

"Didn't think so. So thank you, stranger, for killing my town." He does seem fond of calling Zaian "stranger."

Two deputies grunt nearby, lifting the girl's steel-clad body and stumbling toward the back door. Another deputy hauls the acolytes' swords, a wrapped packaged taller than he is. The weapons are dark, dull and useless to anyone without the training to activate them. Worse, in this situation, they're contraband. Bregg watches the deputies and their burdens thoughtfully, then turns to me, starting to speak.

"I was lucky," I interrupt. "They were drunk and stumbling. They practically fell down on their own."

He doesn't quite believe me, and he'd be a fool to. There are no more than a dozen guns in town, of poor make at that, and until now, I'm sure he assumed mine, though of unfamiliar craft, was simply a farmer's small-gauge varmint-popper. Even the Marshal's posse only has a few old long guns, and no money to buy metal to make more. He's probably never been this close to an automatic in his life.

"Then you should have left them be. Wasn't our fight, nor yours."

I shake my head. "Couldn't leave my boy."

"This one is your son?" Bregg's brows rise. His lip trembles and his pupils widen. He's surprised, which is expected. He's also fearful, which isn't. A little odd, but understandable.

"None of this was planned or expected, Marshal. I don't know why he's here any more than you do," I say, trying to reassure him. "But I do aim to find out." In the corner of my eye, Zaian shifts on his feet and looks studiously into a corner. I'm angry with the boy, but I'd certainly rather he be alive and a fool rather than wise and dead. He had troubles, ran to me for help, and I can't say he was wrong to do so. Shame about the acolytes, but they forced the situation. Killing them was the best way to protect him.

"Well, that's an explanation of some use, I suppose. I'd still like to know more, but not now. You, boy, whatever of their laws you broke, I don't care, but you're not my problem. You get out of town, with or without your ma." He turns to me. "Rose, I've had no trouble from you these years, and I've nothing against you, so I'll not," he pauses, glancing at the exiting corpses and clearly trying to pick his words carefully, "lay any stricture on you, but I'm asking if you'll consider what happens here."

He doesn't need to ask. I'd already decided when I came in the tavern, and I've just been looking for a way out of the conversation since.

"I'll take him with me, but even if we go, there's no guarantee that the Evangeline won't cause trouble here. No offense, Marshal, but you're not likely to stop her."

"I guess you'd know, wouldn't you?" he asks, leading, prompting. I meet his gaze evenly, and keep silent.

He barks a sad laugh. "You're right, I won't take that bet, Rose. But these holy folk aren't unreasonable. We'll tell her you stole daihorses and ran to Blacktooth. She'll follow or give up chase, and either way, there'll be no fire on these people here. I don't know if she'll believe her acolytes were drunk and unruly, but we'll say it. Might make for a fair argument for your actions, if she catches you."

"If she's not unreasonable."

He nods, not meeting my eyes. He's a man who wants only what he has, for whom knowing too much is a sure path to ruin. I'll be sad to leave the town, but not its rulers.

As we leave, I say to Bregg, "Tell her we rode away from Blacktooth."

We leave out the back, collecting a pair of the Marshal's daihorses and a wagon for the corpses, which he insisted we take with us. We pass a few shacks and buildings on the way out, where curtains are pulled just wide enough for fearful eyes. I didn't know most of these people, and they don't know me, yet I'm sorry for the worry I've brought them.

Well, to be accurate, it's my son who brought the trouble.

He breaks the silence. "Mama, thank you—"

I cut him off.

"What do they want with you?" I ask, keeping my voice even. "What did you steal?"

He adjusts his seat gingerly. He's riding sidesaddle on account of the wound, and he's unused to the posture or the discomfort.

"I stole nothing," he grouses.

"'Nothing' doesn't make a soldier ride twenty days to torture you in a bar." I motion back at the wagon and its stiffening cargo.

"I don't know why they were murderous. I thought they were bound to capture me for trial."

"Trial for what?" I ask again, growing exasperated. My temper's only chink is family, it seems.

"I don't know." He throws up his hands in frustration. When they came after me in the city, there was just shouting, and a dozen of those armored priests, and I ran. I've been running ever since. There was no help elsewhere, so I came here, a fortnight's hard ride. Those two in the tavern, they didn't say anything about a crime or a trial. They just threw me down to kill me. It's all gotten out of hand. I just wanted them to stop chasing me. I didn't think they'd, or you'd," he trails off, expended.

"Well, you come to your Mama for protection, that's what I'll do. As best I see fit." I look over at him. "Damned lucky I was in town, not at the farm. You stopped at the tavern to ask directions, didn't you?"

He rolls his eyes at me, like a boy half his age. "You told us how to write to you, not how to find you."

He's hiding something, but still, there's no doubt those soldiers were out to kill an unarmed quarry, which is an overreaction under any civilized law. I know my son's no killer, so whatever crime he's committed, imagined or not, can't justify what happened in the tavern. That's my hope, at least, else I'm not only a killer, but a murderer.

We ride on in silence, over low hills and scrubby growth, toward the grey wall of mist from whose center Blacktooth rises into the clouds. We see a few animals, wild dogs and the like, but they'll want nothing to do with a pair of healthy daihorses with riders. I've ridden this way before, and it's never a pleasant journey.

"Seen your brother?" I ask, partly to break the silence, partly to prod.

He shakes his head.

"He's well," I say, and leave it at that. To describe how well, or where, that's a sure road to more resentment. They were born on the same day, but even so, their talents differed. I didn't mean to encourage one more than the other. Every mother has her expectations, and what's the wrong in that, I've told myself. Daily.

"And you, living in Leias these past years?"

He looks up at me, then quickly away. "I met someone," he says.

I force a smile. This could go many different directions.

"That's good," I say, cautiously. "Infused?" He nods. "Two infused people together, I can see why the Church would be angry—"

"It's not like that," he interrupts, rolling his eyes again. "He's infused, but we're in the Scripter's Guild. No fathering laws there, so the Church doesn't care."

That, I understand. Only a few guilds in Leias are comfortable for genderlikes who are magically attuned. Most of the large guilds, influenced by the church, demand that the attuned pair with mundanes, in compliance with the doctrine of the Shared Burden, and the most devout of them demand children of attuned members, with compulsory gendercross pairings with mundanes. For the greater good, it's frowned upon for attuned to consort with attuned; the Leians don't want the kind of elites I grew up with.

Still, I'll want to know more about this Scripter beau of his, eventually. Must be persuasive, to bring an educated and highly attuned boy into the profession of hobbled academics. At least he's in honest work. I'd half feared he was living in the sewers and cutting purses. Still, such potential, spent on copying schoolbooks.

"You could have been a warsmith."

"I'm no killer," he blurts. Sheepish, he adds, "But I'm thankful one of us is. I didn't mean to sound ungrateful. But, I couldn't follow your path, and the Leians' way of war, it just seems so," he pauses. "Artless."

It sounds like something I would say, and he knows it. He snorts. "I suppose some ways of thinking run in the family after all."

My feelings aren't hurt. I raised the boys to avoid a life of violence, and I'm happy at least one of them managed to stay unbloodied. This one, well, I'm happy at least he's alive.

As we've been riding into the mists, the air has grown colder and grayer. In the space of a few minutes, everything is shrouded in darkness. The temperature drops to a chill, our breaths steaming outward in the dimming light.

We're still miles from Blacktooth itself, and this is more than near enough for me. The daihorses don't like it here, and growl their discontent. The ground is rocky and broken, so I pick a clear spot at the base of a ridge of rocks, and dismount to let them feed. There's no meat for them, so they try to make do with the sparse scrub and dry cactus, scraping and crunching the needles beneath their hooves to get at the softer green cactus flesh. A night spent here will be fine, but not much more before they get too hungry to be easily manageable. I can't afford to let them roam free and hunt, so best not to ride them too hard now, in case we need them later.

Zaian leans against a rock to keep the weight off his gimped leg. I reach into the cart, find a relatively blood-free canvas tarp, and throw it over him for warmth.

"We need to keep moving," he says, peering into the darkness, back the way we came.

I shake my head. "We'll set ambuscade here," I say.

He splutters.

"Marshal Bregg was scared, unreasonably so," I say by way of explanation. "You didn't see it?"

He shakes his head. I sigh. Warrior or scribe, being able to read people well is a useful skill. His brother is quite good at it.

"Scared men don't hold out long or lie well," I say, trying not to be pedantic. "He said he'd send her off with misdirection, but he, or his deputies, pointed her our way for certain. I'll bet she's right on us, just waiting for noise or light to give us away. Either they want her to kill us and leave them alone, or they want me to kill her and hide the body so Leias won't send more after her. Either way, best to deal with this now."

I start unwrapping the acolyte girl's corpse.

"What are you doing?" Zaian asks.

"Getting this armor off her. She doesn't need it anymore, and I do."

As he realizes what I'm planning, his voice starts to quaver. "Mama, I'm sorry I got you into this, but please, we can run, find safety." He's near tears. "She'll kill you, Mama."

It's my turn to roll my eyes. It feels good, actually.

"Well, at least you and your brother have that in common." He looks confused. I glare at him. "Neither of you have any faith in your Mama."

I work feverishly, using Zaian for what help he can provide. I haven't worn Leian armor before, but the basic principles of mass-produced armor are similar to those used for the artisanal suits of my experience. In battle, breaking through mage armor is a puzzle, a game between both the warriors and the armorers. If the crafter is a master, the armor is clever as well, and one never knows quite what to expect. These new suits, granting the power of Risen savants to the commoner, are marvels of human efficiency, a grand herald of changing times... and tragically repetitive.

Even without the chausses and boots, the armor is achingly heavy. It's not attuned to me, so I have to bear its full weight. It's too big for me, but the minor enchantments inside will pull its lining snug around my torso and waist, making the discomfort tolerable. The joints are oiled, so movement is smooth, if cumbersome. It will not blaze for me as it did for the acolyte girl, but I don't need the frippery. I just need its enchanted toughness to protect me from a few solid blows.

Before sealing myself in, I rummage through the girl's tunic, avoiding the ragged hole below her chin, and pull free a small charm at her neck. The charm glows gently in the darkness, and I breathe a sigh of relief. If I believed in their god, I would thank the Steersman for the use of his symbol—and apologize for the unseemliness of that use.

Zaian watches me shoulder the white steel pauldrons, grasp a coil of rope, and start carefully tying a series of intricate knots.

"I should have written to you," he says. It's a poor excuse for apology, but I didn't expect it, which makes it feel somewhat better to hear.

"Yes, you should have."

I can't be angry now. Prodigal or not, he's here now, and only I can shield him from the world.

"Don't worry," I tell him. "It's all well. Things will be well, son."

The trap is simple. The clearing at the base of the ridge is wide open. Zaian sits in the middle, next to the cart, lit by torchlight, feigning ill. I wait above.

From the darkness, sounds of hooves, dismounting, steel being drawn. Her voice rings out with a preacher's authority. "Zaian Mallory, you cannot run forever. Give yourself to my judgment, and be unburdened in fair punishment. I, Genira of the Evangel, compel you." In the clearing, Zaian shifts uncomfortably, clearly wanting nothing more than to get up and flee into the night. Genira continues her pronouncement. "Rose Mallory, you killed two acolytes of the Church. I come to avenge them, with merciful swiftness. Be not afraid. There will be no pain."

That's odd. Something isn't right there. She knows the mother's deeds from the son's? Unexpected, but I push the thought aside. Losing focus now might make the difference between risking death and meeting it.

I see the glow of her armor first, ghostly red in the inky mist. She steps into the torchlight and stops at the edge of the clearing. Tall, probably an inch or two over me. Armor of white, like the acolytes', but with a high helm protecting all but her face. Strong cheeks, smooth tan skin, as all priests strive to be, beautiful for their god. Her sword is massive, three arms long at least, and she grips it one-handed, made strong by the armor of her faith.

The Evangeline peers at Zaian, notes the cart and the shrouded bodies, sweeps her gaze over the clearing, and then abruptly spins and walks away. Now that, I expected. No fool, this one. She expects a trap, and is looking for its layer. From the shadows, I watch her gaze turn upwards, to the ridgetop above the clearing.

She makes a precise set of motions with her hand, and the armor's glow intensifies. Up the rocks she bounds, each step thundering, mancleaver raised, sigils aflame. On the battlefield, ranks of trained soldiers have broken before such a sight, rather than stand fast for a nation's cause.

My cause, though, is greater. (A stupid, stupid son who can't be bothered to write home once in a while.)

Genira tops the ridge. The ground crackles where her white sabatons touch. She looks over the length of the rock, seeking archers and gunmen.

On cue, Zaian plays his one part. From below, he shouts, "Run, you idiots. She's coming for you."

Adequate. A moment of distraction, just enough to force her to react instead of think. Hopefully.

Genira takes two steps forward, eyes focused ahead for triplines and fleeing shapes. In that moment, I strike a match and charge out of the shadows, to her side, closing the distance at a dead sprint.

The girl's armor digs into my shoulders, neck, hips, drawing blood with every weighty step. The acolyte sword bounces in its scabbard, clanking against my side. The heat of fire is hot on my cheeks, crisping my hair. I've used lamp-oil to set the sigils alight; a cheap fakery, but hopefully enough. All I need is for Genira to believe, just for a few moments, that she's facing an armored mage warrior, and not an old woman wearing a glorified tin barrel.

She's fast, as fast as I expected. She takes a perfect defensive stance, sword guarding her body, left hand raised and ready. She sees the armor, the flame, and the empty gauntlets, and acts accordingly. Empty gauntlets suggest a magical attack, so her hand draws out protective shapes, shielding her from a psychic assault.

I get within sword-reach before she realizes there is no magical onslaught. She drops her blade to impale me. With all my strength, I step to the side, not slowing my charge. The blade, searing hot, plunges into the left side of the breastplate, impaling it front to back. The breastplate, made for a woman much larger than I.

Inside the armor, the blade has missed me, but it melts the steel and burns my skin. It's expected, but still agonizing now, and will be worse in a few moments, when the shock wears off. Another moment of confusion, as Genira realizes she must pull her blade free. Time enough to tug the knots I've tied at the armor's back, releasing every enchanted catch at once. The catches are meant to let a warrior undress themselves or escape from water. Here, they serve as another distraction, a clatter of flaming armor falling at Genira's feet.

Fear of fire is instinctive, even when it's harmless. The lamp oil won't so much as dull her armor's sheen, but wary nonetheless, she motions with her hand and commands all fires near her to vanish. The flames on her armor smother themselves, and she is safe to touch.

The last piece of my armor falls away, leaving me free to tuck, roll, and close the final gap into her arms, inside her reach, our faces inches apart, my gun drawn.

The dueling step is an old one, meant for nimble fighters to use clever wrestling to disarm a foe and prevent magic use. It is useless against an armored enemy, so for all Genira's skills, it's not a move she expects. When Makanite mages dueled in her lands, she wasn't even born yet.

She realizes her error, at the same time she feels the muzzle of my gun on her lips. The armor's magical bubble still encloses her head, protecting it from all contact—except for the necessary devotional act of kissing the Steersman's holy symbol, currently chained at the end of my gun.

I am very lucky that the Church has not, in the last several years, lost any of its unwarranted confidence and adjusted its manufacturing to account for inventive behaviors. Or perhaps I shouldn't be surprised.

My finger tightens on the trigger. Same as before, no time for mercy. She'll kill me the instant I hesitate.

And yet, hesitate I do.

Breaths seep by, my gun in her face, her fingers ready to twitch the command to incinerate me. We are both very still. Being prepared to die is not the same thing as wanting to.

Murmuring through pursed lips, Genira says, "Your Marshal was right. I should have killed you first, then talked."

There it is. I knew something was wrong. Below, in the clearing, Zaian has hobbled to his feet and watches the impasse, clever enough to stay silent and still.

"Genira," I mutter quietly, "what is my son accused of?"

She can tell something is off now, too. Her eyes flick to the side, toward Zaian.

"Transporting stolen goods. Weapons," she says, loudly enough to carry.

I sigh. Genira raises an eyebrow.

"Zaian?" I shout. The effort sends pain shooting through the burns on my ribs.

"Yes, Mama?" comes the reedy answer. I know that tone. It's the same squeak he used to give when caught cheating on his schoolwork.

My finger stays on the trigger, but I do my best to soften my tone.

"Genira, did the Marshals happen to offer blood recompense for your acolytes?"

Unable to nod, she grunts assent. "They did. A thousand guilders each. A fair offer the Church would accept, but I deferred."

"To see if you could catch me on your own first?"

"For faith and honor," she states. I have to try very hard not to laugh at the woman who turned down two thousand republic coin to run into the night and get shot in the face, for faith and honor. For her part, she has the sense to show contrition. "I begin to see I've been deceived."

"Both of us have," I say, shooting a glare down at Zaian. I look carefully into Genira's eyes. "Evangeline, if I step away, will you kill me?"

She thinks it over. If either of us has a finger twitch, this could still end badly, and my hands threaten to begin shaking from the ever-increasing pain in my side. "You'd believe me?" she asks.

"I'll trust your word on that Steersman you serve."

She snorts. "I'm from the Liminals, edgeward of the republic. We call him Allmother there." I want to shake my head in annoyance. Why my son chooses to live among these folk…

"I don't care what you call your god, only that you'll swear by him."

She is clearly insulted, but neither of us is in any position to be easily offended.

Genira's word is good. She even helps me down from the ridge. My charred ribs pulse with agony, but poultices and charms must wait.

Zaian meets us in the clearing, wary of Genira's height and blade. I drop to the ground near the cart and vent my ire at him.

"Nothing, you said. Nothing."

"I didn't steal them," he says, insistent. "That was true. I was just asked to scribe a waybill for a cart bound for Blacktooth, and then leave the cart outside the town. That was all, before the Church set a whole phalanx of holy knights on me."

Genira stands over us, sword at rest, watching for more tricks from me. She is as dangerous as ever, and she thinks the same of me. Good.

"And yet you ran," she accuses. "The guilty always run."

"So do the frightened," he retorts. He gestures at the two dead acolytes. "Was I wrong to be afraid for my life?"

I turn to Genira.

"If he was told to leave the weapons, then someone else was meant to pick them up. And if the Marshal has thousands of Leian guilders to spare, he's told no one in town. I imagine he's headed there this moment to collect, expecting me to be dead and you headed back home. He told you far more than he had good reason to, for a man willing to spend money to send you on your way."

She is nodding before I finish. "It's possible. It was I who gave the order to track you here rather than take you in the capital. So these two," she waves toward the cart, "could have been associated with the sale at the other end. They wouldn't have expected you to seek shelter in the exact spot their buyer was in. If that's so, then they would rather silence you and the Marshal before either of you exposed the scheme, once I inevitably caught you. They volunteered to search the town without my guidance. Intentionally, it seems."

I am relieved she seems to be seeing what I see.

"Someone in your Church is selling church arms to a wildlands townmaster, and using my boy as a mule."

She narrows an eye at me. "I'll not deny that it's a plausible interpretation. One of many."

"But one that you'll need to sort out?"

She nods slowly. "Yes. I'll withhold judgment for the killings you've done, and grant consideration to your boy for possibly having been a duped simpleton rather than a hard criminal."

Zaian opens his mouth to reply. I silence him with a look.

"You should have told me everything," I tell him. "I didn't have to get set on fire today. Or fight a holy knight, whom I would have killed—"

"—might have killed—" she interjects.

"—if I had thought she was even a little less honorable."

Genira cocks her head. "Thank you?"

I take a deep breath and turn to Genira.

"You can take him."

"What?" he shouts.

I continue. "And I'll ride with you."

"What?" she says, incredulous.

"I can't go back to town," I point out. "I don't know how many the Marshal has in on his scheme, nor who he might harm if cornered. You don't know who in your church corrupted those two acolytes, or how many more there are. I'm coming with you. You've had plenty of time to kill me or my son, so I'm satisfied you're the person least likely to do either, which makes you the only safe option for us."

Genira is having none of it.

"You blasphemed an acolyte's armor and sigil, and assaulted me. I'll not travel with you. I'll take your son, but you ride alone."

I shuffle to my feet, hand on holster. "Well, you can try to kill me again. For faith and honor."

It's a bluff, and we both know it. Yet, after a long moment, she nods, without irony or mockery.

"You ride ahead of me. Unchained, for now."

Zaian limps over to me.

"Mama, what are you doing?" he asks, glancing nervously at Genira. He really has no faith in me.

"Protecting you." Perhaps not the kind of aid he'd have wanted, but we make do with what defenses we have.

"You said things would be well," he keens. Genira, listening in, snorts. I shrug.

"Well enough that you're not dead, son." I grin at him, happy to have him, happier to be able to tell him so.

We ride into the darkness, Genira watching my every move, Zaian muttering under his breath, and the pain in my side returning in dizzying waves. I've no home now, a woman who hates me for a guardian, and surely a price on my head. But Zaian rides behind me, so I'll be in front, come what may.

ARMOR THE COLOR OF WAR

BY DAVID SZARZYNSKI

In a large manor, there was a small room. It was dusty, dark, and mostly forgotten. It was full—full of the sort of things that didn't get thrown out but never are used: a slightly broken broom, a pair of boots that could really use new soles, wooden crates that would surely get filled sometime, a box of old apples so shriveled they might actually be corks.

And residing on a wooden rack, there was a suit of armor—a *harness*. Such armor! It was a clever thing, made of many fine plates of delicate metal all nestled next to each other to fit a body. What's more, it was a very peculiar color: not quite red, not quite black, maybe blue, or perhaps all of these.

It was actually the color of war, which is a color only enjoyed by those who don't recognize it. And quite possibly the armor was magic, although whether with more than the normal magic found in beautiful things is hard to know.

But this harness was, like the boots and broom, more than a bit broken. All of it was scarred and rent. The chest plating was pitted and cracked, with a square hole at the bottom of a deep dent right above the heart. It was the relic of a deadly blow and if anything, it made the harness look deeply guilty.

RING.

      RING.

            RING.

twrang.

"Shit."

"Ay. That's a pisser," she said, all grumpy anger and resignation. Her mouth twisted sour. Held at the end of tongs, a strange metal plate was bent and folded badly by the last blow.

With a long sigh she tossed the piece into the corner with a crash. It wasn't alone. In a crude rusting heap against the daub walls there was a pile of steel compost, slowly turning metal into red dust. Like a spreading blush, the floor and walls nearest it were already stained and the dust slunk slowly away around the room.

The other side of the dirty forge had a collection of open crates. She kicked them all over. Only one didn't move. She shifted through it, tossing straw around the room as she dug. The box was empty except for a single grey bar.

"Ay, now *that's* a pisser," and glumly she picked up the heavy bar one-handedly, the other hand full of tongs.

The doorway coughed impolitely.

She spun, and the bar slid from her fingers as her right hand flashed to the left side of her waist. With a startled grunt, she snapped forward with the tongs and grabbed the bar inches above the floor. Her feet parted, and one slid smoothly in front of the other as she dropped into a balanced stance.

Standing in the doorway was a riot of colors: crimson slashed and pointed shoes, tight slender party-colored hose that ran way up to a short doublet in purple and trimmed in ermine, and topped with a tam o'shanter. Inside all of it was a man, holding a clout of napkin over his mouth and nose and sneer.

"Miss Salewkir?" His voice was much bigger than it had any right to be, a voice that leapt from beneath his napkin, and it filled the small space.

"Nay, nay. But *Lady* Heathwiln, ay," she said tiredly. She turned and pushed bar and tongs into the small pile of charcoal in the forge. She gently pulled at the bellows, and after some creaking and leather complaints, the room filled with the sound of rushing air and a hot crackle. "And *Lady*

Kittlesfarrow." She paused. "And I think *Lady* of Far Side of the Rain. Mayhaps."

From behind her, he continued.

"Yes, well, I am Koulhas, herald to the Right Reverend Abbot Onfroi." He coughed more politely.

"I don't take commissions, Colors," she said rotely.

"Abbot Onfroi knows! This is no commission. No, it's—"

"I don't do heroics."

"This is, it's, it's—mercy!"

"Ay? I don't do mercy. Especially not for abbots."

"Abbot Onfroi is *here*, my lady. And he demands to speak to you!"

Lady Heathwiln's eyebrows shot up.

"Well, if he *demands*, then so be. Show the Father in?"

Koulhas quailed. "In here! A smithy?"

"The good Father gets me as he finds me."

Abbot Onfroi was a man who'd long ago gone to seed, then up and sprouted. Although dressed in the demure robes of his station, fox and squirrel fur peeked through the slashes in his sleeves, and like a miser hiding his money, cloth-of-gold lined the inside so that he flashed when he moved.

But the Abbot was clearly a man suffering. His face was haggard and drawn, there was a tremble in his hands as he picked up a cup of wine, and a impressive bruise bloomed across his left cheek and eye. When he was brought in he could barely stand, and quivered as he walked.

His entry into the smithy was preceded and postceded by lay-servants who set out a chair, draped it in blankets, brought the father in and set him down, put his feet up, poured wine into his cup, and were closing the door "to stoop up a chilling draft" until the servant saw the Lady's threatening eyebrows.

It wasn't until his second cup of hippocras that Abbot Onfroi could even speak.

"You look sore used, Abbot," she began, questioningly, when the father's face had taken on a rosier tint.

"You do not know, my daughter!" he muttered over the top of his cup. "You do not know!" He shuddered and pulled another draught.

"Ay," Lady Heathwiln began slowly. "Ay, but I do know what a mailed hand does to a face. Who be punching the good father in the face, Father?"

"That villain! That heathen scoundrel! That *blackguard*! Sir… Sir Robert Knolles!" he said with a gasp and his face flushed to match the bruise.

"What, in his person?"

"No. No! His band of thugs. They came during service, and rushed the door! They smote down brother Jerome and stole his cassock. They snatched the holy articles right off the *altar*! They tortured the brothers into saying where the holy treasures were hidden! Where the pence of the faithful were stored!"

"Ay. And they nay believe when you told them you were poor friars."

"No!" cried the Abbot, and drank more wine from his golden cup.

"And why didn't yeh defend yourselves?"

The Abbot's face looked, if anything, more appalled, and he shrank in on himself.

"Against Knolles' men? Oh no. No no. We're just monks. We are men of peace, Lady. Against Knolles? He'd kill us. He'd burn the abbey to the ground!"

"Ay. Well, he is well known for that."

The father drank wine, and Lady Heathwiln ground at the dust with her toes. Eventually, with the courage of wine, he spoke again. But now he didn't look at her, and spoke to her feet.

"I know that we haven't, perhaps, always agreed. But if you could help us, we would remember it." He took a small leather case from a servant and opened it. Inside there were documents in florid Latin. "These are for you," he smiled. "Signed by his Holy Father," he added in helpful encouragement. Seeing the confusion on her face he continued. "Indulgences and a pardon of your sins. In exchange for your help now."

Genuine surprise bloomed on the Lady's face.

"Yeh pronounce the anathema against me. Every year. On the anniversary of my return. " She stared at the squirming Abbot. "Yeh told my people they needn't keep their oaths to me. Or pay me rents. That I was damned."

"And all that can be forgiven if you support the Church and my abbey at this time of great need."

"Oh, ay? And what do I need be doing?" the Lady clipped back through a clenched jaw.

Now it was the Abbot's turn to be surprised.

"Do? Do! Raise your men! Come to the abbey! Defend us! Do your duty, Lady, given to you when you were given these lands. Have you no mercy for us?"

"No mercy? I have *no men*, Father. And why defend the abbey now? Knolles has taken all your gold, treasures, and robbed you poor friars of your cassocks. He'll nay come back. Why not go get your altar back?"

The Abbot spoke to her like a man speaking to a child.

"My daughter, Knolles has a *thousand men*. Apparently you have none." He gestured to his servants to get him up and out of the chair.

But Lady Heathwiln had cocked her head to one side.

"Just a thousand men, Father? Be you sure?"

"A thousand, two, ten thousand? It hardly matters," and taking his things, and his wine, and his gifts of indulgence, the Abbot left the Lady.

But she sat for a while after they were gone, staring at her hands and the forge around her.

"Ay. It matters."

The door to the small room opened inwards, and the Lady Heathwiln stepped inside just slowly enough to miss being clipped by the broom as it fell. She spoke softly, hesitantly, into the floating dust.

"Ay, hello." She coughed a little. "It's been a bit. A while. I'm…" She crossed carefully, past the apples, over the boots, to the stand, and reached out with a slow hand to trace a dirty line on a vambrace. "Ay, a long while.

I'm sorry. It be terrible dusty here." A circuit around the room; she poked at the box of once-fruit.

She opened her mouth, closed it again. "I've been trying. Every day, I've been trying. It's all I do. Every day." At the foot of the armor, she sank to the floor.

"I'm no Weylan Smith. But I've been swinging the hammer years and I, just, I, thought I could do it. But I'm out of metal. And coal. And you're not fixed yet."

She snorted. "All I have is the hammer and tongs now. Even the anvil is gone wrong. I be knocking in dents I can't take out."

She just sat. Dust settled and a square of sunshine crawled across the floor.

"I'm sorry. But I have a plan now. I just need a bit of help."

It was getting late by the time she slowly stood, her knees creaking, and lit a stub of candle. Then, with a loud sigh, and squared shoulders, she pulled the top off a crate nearby. She took off her leather apron, her scorched lines, and threw them aside. Her skin was a web of scars, growing out of a solid knot on her chest. As she flexed and bent, the scars didn't. They clung hard and sullen to her skin. Stiffly she bent down and reached inside the crate.

Out came a silver doublet of fustian, lined with stained gold satin and cut full of holes. She slipped it on with long-practiced motion. Next, a pair of fine hose of worsted wool, and slender pieces of silken blanket that she put about her knees. Finally, a pair of delicate shoes of dark leather, with many tough cords attached at toe and middle. These were the hidden skeleton for armor, and like the armor, they were artful things. Dusty, stained, but beautiful and fey by candle.

She took the sabatons up from the foot of the stand and tied them in place with the small cords on her shoes. Then, the greaves went on her legs, the cuisses on her thighs, and breeches of mail around her middle. The tonlets went above the breeches and though wickedly bent they at least fit, but when she lifted the breastplate and put it in place, snug against her chest and square above the scar, she let out a short hiss as it pressed into place. The dent dug into her skin, and the silver of the doublet shone through the hole.

She set the sallet helm down next to her, and took up from the box several coats, all with her arms emblazoned on them in muted color. The first had lions of fading gold crouched upon a field of dirty green. The second was four different quadrants of color all around a red cross slowly fading pink. They were dusty, but this dust was old and worked into the very fabric.

But the last one, that one was different.

At first it looked like it might be silver, pure and brilliant. Then again, it might be black. Then perhaps it was grey. But not some dead grey, made of white and black poorly mixed. If it was grey, it was the grey of a midday storm not quite gone.

But it was not, in fact, grey. It was the color of rain, seen from the other side. And, for the first time in a long time, the Lady of Far Side of the Rain put it on.

It was not hard to find Sir Robert Knolles, or his army. Armies are not hidden. Knolles' army had its own court of attendants, fawning courtiers, mistresses, and servants. The fighting men under Knolles lived alongside clerks, who drew up the contracts they made with terrified towns, priests who forgave them their sins religiously, merchants who bought their stolen furs and plundered plate, and prostitutes, who gave them something to confess. Like locusts, the whole seething mass could barely travel eight miles a day, and thoughtlessly stripped the land around it bare when it rested.

And, like any man in the business of ransoming castles back to desperate chatelans who rather wanted their roof back more than their money, Knolles always had a different one to live in each week. Yet everyone hurrying on the road knew where he was.

Lady Heathwiln was discomforted to discover that Knolles was only some thirty miles away. At least he only bothered to plunder the homes of those with something to plunder.

Armies only notice other armies. A single knight errant was as a fly on a horse and so the Lady passed through gate after gate, through camps, camp smoke, and past men lounging, laughing, drinking, and carousing. It was a fine day. Armored men on horse are common sights in the service of Knolles.

But the men at the gate were different. They were brash and young, fiercely loyal to Sir Knolles, envious of his deeds, and as proud of his victories as if they were their own. Tasked to watch the inner gates up to the center donjon, they were zealous, and equally fond of cards. As Lady Heathwiln trotted up, they put down their hands and shielded their eyes.

"I see a Sable coat with nothing, Johan!" shouted one to another.

"Your eyes are sick, old man. I see a field Argent. And a fine Azure harness, Auguste!"

"Your eyes are dead! The harness is a wonderful Gules! Hold, Sir Knight. Who are thee?"

"Heathwiln," the Lady replied.

"No" shouted the one named Johan. "Heathwiln is two couchant lions Or, on a field vert! And Heathwiln is a Lady who never leaves her door, Sir Knight! A poor choice for a lie."

Lady Heathwiln stripped off her helm. "I am she," and her voice carried. "I am here to see Sir Knolles."

At this the men fell to talking amongst themselves and after hurried conversation, Johan turned back to her.

"He may see you," conceded Johan, "but I must warn you. He's already happy with his wife and happier with his mistress! Can I tell him which one you're here to contest?"

"I am here," she replied with a smile as the men fell about laughing, "for the treasures taken from the Abbey Onfroi."

"Oh," said Auguste, "he won't be happy about that."

Not all bandit kings, captains of free companies, and knights are as large as men as they are in story. Sir Robert Knolles was lively, slender, and quick of the face and hands. When Lady Heathwiln was led in, he was the first to usher her to a chair, the first to press her to take wine and he ordered breads, cold meats, pies, and preserves up from the larders. He inquired solicitously of her health, of the bounties of her fields and herds, and after the happiness of her people. He mixed her hippocras himself and smiled with self-pleasure when she told him it pleased her. He wore daggers on his belt next to his prayer book, and a garland of flowers on his hair. When they'd both broken bread, Knolles began to talk seriously.

"Lady Kittlesfarrow. I've heard the stories of you," said Knolles, with his feet up and his hands behind his head.

"Ay? From whom?"

Knolles shrugged expansively. "Old soldiers. Young troubadours. Far travelers; the men who talk. They tell stories. Great and terrible stories. About men who have only one foot and hop as fast as the wind. About snakes who love music so much they stop up one ear with their tails."

Lady Heathwiln raised an eyebrow. "Silly stories."

"Stories about a woman who became a Lady, then left and one day returned. With strange harness and title. I listen to stories, my Lady.

"At least," Knolles added thoughtfully, "when they're about me. Now, my men say you've come for the gold of that rich Abbey."

"Ay, Sir Knolles. I have."

"At the behest of the Abbot?"

"Oh no," she said. "He didn't want that at all."

"We're neighbors of a kind, then! I'll give you the altar cloths, as a gift. They are cloth-of-gold and richly appointed."

"Nay, Sir Knolles. I'll take it all, please," she said.

His expression hardened, his eyes narrowed, and his lip curved ever so slightly into a sneer. The thin veneer of knightly brotherhood had peeled back to reveal the natural lout under the satin and silk.

"You come and eat bread and salt at my table, but in harness like someone expecting battle. In your nastily colored armor." He stood, his eyes wide in fury, pressed both hands on the table and leaned forward. "Yet where is your sword, my Lady? I've heard of it in the damn'ded stories. Where is your shield? Your shield is missing."

"I do not need them," she said quietly.

"And your armor? Your armor is broken."

She said nothing, and stared back at Knolles till he sat back down.

"You can leave. Now. I'm letting you leave," he said, dangerous and low.

"Nay."

"I have two thousand men-at-arms here. Fighting men. Warring men. Can you kill two thousand men?" And he waited then, for her reply. It came after a long moment.

"No."

Knolles spread his hands and nodded, but then she continued. "But can you make do with just half of them?"

Johan and Auguste were playing hazard when Lady Heathwiln emerged. She had, along with her palfrey, a loaded mule, and they called out to her as she went by.

"Lady! You'll be going back to the abbey, then, with Sir Knolles generosity and kindness?"

"Oh, nay."

Lady Heathwiln looked back at the mule.

"I'm taking this home."

THE BLOOD AXE

BY MARY PLETSCH

Agrona never knew, when she walked into a village, whether to expect a celebration in her honor or the doors and windows barred until she left. She knew she made for a terrifying sight, with her ruined eye and an Imperial battle axe as her blood weapon. Reluctantly, she looked down at her blood-splattered chest plate, her stained leggings, and the little bits of viscera slowly drying on her bracers, and wondered if she should have done a better job of cleaning her armor after eliminating the Imperial scouts she'd met on the road.

It was too late to go down to the river now if she wanted to reach Sarnagat before nightfall. Hopefully her own home town would be able to welcome her as just another kinswoman, and not the Devas' Wrath.

Agrona was coming forty, and her short-cropped black hair was brindled with iron and steel. Most other women her age had borne their first two or three children in their mid-teens, left them at their family hearth, and gone to war in their twentieth year. Those who survived a decade of combat could look forward to coming home, guarding their village, and raising their grandchildren.

Agrona envied them. High Priestess Sionne had spoken: from the moment Agrona crawled into Sarnagat dragging the blood axe behind her, she was bound for war. There could be neither reprieve nor retirement for the Devas' Wrath incarnate. She would fight until she died.

If she were very lucky, she might find a few days of peace in Sarnagat.

Lost in thought, Agrona felt a sudden chill of warning. Immediately, instinctively, she centered her consciousness, held out her hand, stabbed her palm with the sharp iron talon she wore on her fourth finger, and manifested her blood axe. Gripping the weapon's shaft, she wheeled towards the source of danger.

The main road where she stood was narrow and uphill but well-worn with the passage of feet and carts. The road to the left was overgrown with long grass and a few young saplings, swaying in the mountain breeze. The signpost had fallen over. Agrona stood in the crossroads, hands on her weapon, her feet on the road to Sarnagat, her face towards Vonn, the place where she had been born.

The danger she felt lay three decades behind her, receding further into history with each breath. Agrona had dreamed of Vonn during the long hot nights when her guts had burned with fever. She did not want to believe that she had lived her whole life in the shadow of a village in flames.

She turned away from Vonn and resumed climbing. Her belly twinged with pain, tender from the exertions of her hike. The surgeon had been cunning, and Agrona had survived the kind of wound that killed most others, but the injury bothered her still. She reminded herself it was not her first narrow escape.

But the first time she had been six years old, and surviving the blow that had taken her left eye had almost convinced her that she was immortal. This stomach wound made for compelling evidence to the contrary. It had changed her.

It was time to settle her affairs. To see her sister Gardia, the Chiefess of Sarnagat, and Gardia's son Niall—the last family Agrona had left. To ascertain whether she could have any greater legacy than a trail of Imperial corpses in her wake.

She would not live forever, and it was no longer enough for her to be merely the Devas' Wrath.

Traces of red and orange smeared the western sky before Agrona reached Sarnagat. The town was positioned high in the foothills, blessed with plentiful game, lush meadows and sweet rivers. The mountains guarded Sarnagat's back, a natural rampart. The treacherous, rugged track that Agrona had just travelled was the only approach to Sarnagat.

But the Imperials had taken that same road to Vonn. Agrona pushed the thought from her mind, but it did not retreat far. It lingered in the back of her skull with all its kinsfolk, casting a dark pall over her heart.

She passed through the palisade that guarded the town, ignoring the shouts of the surprised guard. Well-fed oxen and plump hogs grazed in the town common, ringed all around by colorful houses. The heart of the village was the stone circle erected in the center of the common, and Agrona noticed that there was activity at the circle this evening, though the moon was not quite full.

A group of girls, perhaps twelve to sixteen years of age, sat in a cluster in the middle of the ring. An elder in a priestess' headdress stood before a smoking fire, gesturing to the dagger on her hip. Agrona guessed that these were the girls of the village who had experienced their first moon-blood in the year past. They were training with the priestess to undergo the Rite and receive their blood weapons.

One of the younger girls looked about idly, and when she glanced towards the gate her gaze locked with Agrona's. The youngster elbowed a bigger girl sitting next to her, whispering excitedly. Soon the whole group was gawking at the bloody, one-eyed stranger rather than paying attention to their lesson. The priestess lifted her head, followed her charges' line of sight, and shot Agrona a cold glare.

Agrona recognized Sionne, the priestess who had sent her off to war all those decades past. Perhaps coming here had been a mistake. The line between champion and scapegoat was thin indeed, and these past seasons the war had not gone in the Free Tribes' favor. The priestesses would be looking for someone to blame and who more visible than Agrona? They might not be willing to confront the Devas' Wrath, but her sister's position as Chiefess was an elected one.

Agrona lowered her head and walked quickly away, cursing her own sentimentality. She should have known that the best thing she could have for her family was to stay away. She should have remembered how incensed

Sionne had been when she had seen a girl of six with a ruined face and the enemy's axe for a blood weapon. Agrona had dared to ask the Devas' blessing directly, without the intermediary of a priestess, and as a result she had been immediately sent to war. There was a price to pay for challenging the priestesses' power.

Agrona left the way she had come, hoping she had not done irreparable damage already. The shadows gathered strength as the sun dropped behind the mountains. Much to Agrona's surprise, she saw another person ahead of her on the road: a small, slight figure in a loose-fitting dress who appeared to be no older than the girls in the stone circle.

It made no sense for a child to be out alone in the hastening dark, not with Imperial soldiers in the vicinity and vicious animals in the woods. The girl was armed with a dagger in one hand, a bow in the other, and a quiver of arrows on her back, but her arsenal told Agrona that the girl had not yet manifested a blood weapon. If she had, she would not need to carry so much gear.

It wasn't unheard of. Some girls were never touched by the moon, never bled. The priestesses said that these women had been scorned by the Devas. They were barren fields, rejected by their own deities. But Agrona knew better than most that the link between moon blood and the blood weapon was a custom, nothing more.

Even if the child was not one of the Scorned Ones, she had to be an outcast of some kind. Her worn, patched dress had been cut for a curvaceous woman; it sagged on her frame. This girl was tall and slender, her body straight like a reed, her limbs gawky like a young calf.

The girl heard Agrona's footsteps behind her and stopped, turning to see who pursued her. Agrona lifted her head, intending to walk past without acknowledging the outcast. The priestesses had cautioned her that the Devas' Wrath must be entirely without pity. She had done enough to provoke their anger just by being here instead of in the wars where she belonged.

"Aunt Agrona," the girl said.

Agrona was aunt to one person only: Gardia's son Niall. She had met him a handful of times in the forests, hunting with the other men of Sarnagat. He had been quite skilful with bow and arrow, Agrona recalled, and yet Gardia had expressed disappointment that Niall would rather sing with the girls than learn swordplay with the boys.

"I don't," Agrona began coldly, but the girl did not back down and then Agrona glimpsed a trace of familiarity in that upturned nose so like her own, those freckled cheeks, and the ease with which that hand gripped the bow. "Niall?" Agrona demanded.

The sound of his own name caused her nephew to flinch.

Agrona halted, remembering how often Niall had performed in front of the hearth dressed in women's clothes, singing the soliloquies of priestesses and chiefesses. He had acted out battles like all the other boys, but always with a prop representing a blood weapon in his hand. Gardia had berated him for his odd behavior and Agrona had told her there had been no harm, it was only a game.

Agrona looked at Niall now and realized this was no game.

"Niall," Agrona repeated. "What is the meaning of this?"

Niall could not meet her eyes, and Agrona remembered how it had felt to kneel before the priestesses, six years old and unable to think of any defense that could explain the blood axe in her hands. The weapon spoke for itself, and so, Agrona realized, did Niall's clothing.

"It is who I am," Niall admitted. "I wish it were otherwise. I wish I could say to you, the Devas' Wrath, that I have become someone who would make you proud… but I am a blasphemy to the priestesses and an embarrassment to my mother."

Agrona did not consider herself to be a nurturing person. How could she, when she was taught to kill with the blood axe while still too young to cook or to heal? She wondered if it was Niall's loneliness she recognized, or just a reflection of her own rage at Sionne's callousness.

"Neila," Agrona said.

Her sister's child met her gaze. "What?"

"Neila. Like Niall, it means champion. But Niall is a name for a boy, and Neila is a name for a girl."

Neila's smile blossomed briefly before crumpling and collapsing. "I will never be recognized for a girl unless I bear a blood weapon."

And Agrona realized, with the force of a lightning strike, why the Devas had called her to Sarnagat. "Neila, I can offer you a choice. I can give you a blood weapon of your own."

A flicker of hope illuminated Neila's features, and Agrona could read in that expression a lifetime of wanting to be like any other girl. Then the light faded, an ember turning to ash.

"Sionne would call it evil sorcery, or a trick." Neila curled her hands into her fists. "You don't understand. You were gone for the years when I put away my skirts and tried so hard to be a man. The other boys, they can tell I'm not like them. I'm not a boy, not a girl, not *anything*." She drew in a shuddering breath. "You don't understand what it is to be…"

"Something they call unnatural?" Agrona ran her talon across her palm. The great battle axe manifested across the distance between them, the huge head cradled on Agrona's shoulder, the shaft laying across Neila's.

Neila swallowed her accusation. "Yes."

"Then know I can give you a blood weapon that will not be denied." The words were no sooner out of her mouth than she regretted her impulsiveness; the only thing she was good at was killing. But now Neila's face reflected genuine hope, and all Agrona could do was issue a warning. "If it is successful, you will never be anything other than a warrior like me. If it is unsuccessful, you will die."

"I will never be anything other than a warrior anyway," Neila said defiantly. "If I bow to Sionne and try to live as a man, I will go to war with the rest of the village men, carrying a man's weapon, a sword I can barely use."

"Then will you risk your life for the sake of something you would have done anyway?"

"You may think me unworthy of becoming a warrior now," the girl whispered, "but I will not lie to you. When I met you on the path, my intention had been to go down to Vonn, to the village of slaughter, and end my life."

Agrona bit her lip, tasting her own blood in her mouth. She could take Neila away with her, guard her, protect her. But the weight of the blood axe lay heavy on her shoulder and she knew that her side was no place for a non-combatant.

Agrona hefted her axe, driving its butt into the dirt. What she was about to do would infuriate Sionne, and perhaps cost Agrona her own life, but as she looked at Neila she realized that there was little point in being a warrior if not to fight for something that mattered. "Then come to Vonn with me, and I will teach you what I learned in that place, a mystery even the priestesses do not know."

"Tell me," Agrona said as she turned left at the signpost, wading through the long grasses under the wan light of the rising moon. "What do you know about where we are going?"

"The ruined village." Neila shrugged. "We used to sneak off there as children to play in the empty houses."

The confession sent a chill up Agrona's spine. "What did you find there?"

"Cookware, tools, blankets, clothes. We'd play at being grownups." She mumbled her confession. "I found this dress in one of the houses."

Agrona felt aghast; an emotion unbecoming a warrior. Her tongue was sharper than she intended when she spoke. "Gardia let you…"

"It was forbidden. I meant what I said: we had to sneak off." Neila added with sudden insight, "You're talking about the bones."

I am talking about my grandmother and your aunt Lealla and my childhood friends.

"We found many bones." Neila's voice broke. "The bards in my village, they say Vonn was the spark for the Devas' wrath-fire. The beginning of the turning of the war."

Agrona cradled her axe, not trusting herself to speak.

"Though lately the war has turned again, and this time it turns against us." Neila looked up at Agrona. "Is Vonn a holy place, where blood weapons are free for the taking?"

"Vonn is a place of desperation." She glanced down at her niece. "A place where tradition gives way to necessity."

For the next while the only sounds were the wind in the boughs of the forest around them. Then Agrona thought she saw a square shadow in between the trees. A little further on, the crumbled remains of a wall struggled to reach above the grasses. Agrona's vision seemed to shift; abruptly she recognized that they were in the former village common, ringed in by the charred remains of houses with rotting timbers and hollow doorways, empty as skulls.

And Agrona, who had faced down Imperial legions, who had long ago learned to control the fear in her heart, felt an unspoken terror deep in the marrow of her bones. It was as though a skewer of ice had pierced her empty socket and lanced her spine. With every drop of blood in her veins screaming for her to run, she forced herself to lower her axe into a resting position, blade on the ground.

The axe blade bounced off an object covered by the long grasses. Grasping the hilt, Agrona moved closer, hand over hand, afraid to let go of her weapon, her power.

"What is it?" Neila inquire unafraid.

"The stone circle." In the cold light of the moon Agrona glimpsed the tops of a few other stones peeking out of the underbrush.

I am the Devas' Wrath, your child come home at last, Agrona thought, and the clouds scudded across the moon, casting darkness, then light, then darkness. She patted the stone beside her. "Lay down your weapons, sit on this rock and I will teach you a song."

Neila set down her bow, quiver and dagger. She clambered up onto the stone where she sat cross legged, her skirts arranged around her. Agrona sang, and after only one line, Neila joined in.

"You know," Agrona marveled. "You know the words of the Blood Rite."

"I am a performer," Neila said, shrugging self-consciously. "The talecrafters and music masters were less quick to judge me. From their daughters I learned the words of the Rite; from their instruments I learned the tune."

"Then this is the truth hidden within us all: it is not just moon blood that can enable you to summon a blood weapon."

Neila's eyes widened.

"The blood weapon is created by your imagination, drawn from your life force, and manifested by your will. Moon blood, the blood that feeds a baby in the womb, is a symbol meaning the life-force itself. Since it is a symbol, a woman does not need to be menstruating to call her blood weapon. You have seen the older warriors call theirs at will when they cut themselves with their talons."

"But they menstruate during their first Rite. Is that not necessary?"

"The first time a woman needs to combine the Ritual song with lifeblood and her will." Agrona leaned closer. "There is more than one way for lifeblood to fall."

Neila reached up her arm and placed her fingers over Agrona's shattered cheekbone and empty socket. The girl's touch was but a whisper through the gnarled armor of scar tissue. Agrona's good eye watched as Neila pieced together the mystery. "This village. The Blood Axe," Neila breathed. "The priestesses say you manifested your weapon early. Too early."

Agrona nodded. "I was six."

"The Imperials put their weapon through your face."

"And my world became axes and vengeance and I put mine through theirs. Then I crawled to Sarnagat, uphill, pulling the blood axe behind me."

Neila lifted her hand. "How did you know to summon it?"

"My middle sister, Lealla, was preparing for her Rite. I learned the words from her as she practiced. When the Imperials sacked Vonn, I sang as my life's blood fell freely, and I called forth my weapon."

"How did you survive?"

"The conclusion of the Rite heals you. Somewhat."

"You meant it when you said I could lose my life."

"I did." Agrona hesitated as a noose of fear tightened around her neck.

"I meant it when I said I intended to come here and die." Neila raised her chin. "I have nothing to lose and everything to gain. I would rather die than continue to live in this limbo, a woman in a man's form."

Agrona recalled her blood axe, drawing the huge weapon back into her body, into her soul. She wrapped her right hand around the handle of Neila's bow, her left around the shaft of an arrow. Rising to her feet, she notched the arrow on the string, drew it back, and aimed.

If her intentions failed there could be no forgiveness.

"Do it," Neila said, as though she sensed Agrona's fear. "It is my turn to fight for the truth of my own self, but I need you to guide me. I will sing as you sang in this place, and the Devas themselves will pass judgment upon me."

Agrona bit down on her back teeth. It was not enough to merely be a warrior, but she had not expected being a mentor to be more terrible still.

Neila sang, sang with perfect trust, waiting for Agrona to help her accomplish what she could not do alone.

Devas guide my hand.

"Think of your bow," Agrona said, and she let the arrow fly. She wasn't half the archer Neila was—a lifetime of training to master the axe had seen to that—but perhaps the Devas had heard her prayer. Her aim was true.

Her arrow took Neila in the heart.

Agrona's niece gasped in the middle of a verse as her mouth filled with blood. Her left hand curled around the arrow's shaft, where a dark rosette pulsed through her shabby robes. Agrona dimly remembered a talecrafter here in Vonn, singing a story of a chiefess who threw away her crown, descended into the world of the dead, claimed the seed of a new spring, and rose again. This truth had been hidden inside the women of the Free Tribes for longer than Agrona had realized.

The light dimmed in Neila's eyes. Agrona held out her hand. "Call your weapon," she urged.

Too soon? Not soon enough? Agrona wished she had a priestess's experience, but truly the only Rite she had ever seen performed had been her own, seen through her only remaining eye. She knew nothing of magic or faith; all she remembered was how it had been to look up at the smirking Imperial soldier who had buried his axe in her skull. Her world had shrank to pain and blood and hatred, and in one last act of defiance she had stretched out her hand at her enemy. The world flashed white, and then she been standing with a blood weapon through her enemy's head and a flash-healed scar where her left eye had been.

Neila raised her palm. Her fingers scrabbled at air. She reached the final note of the song, held it.

You killed her.

Horror strangled Agrona's throat. She had felt true terror once, here in this place, and now once again she knew the unspeakable fear of having something valuable to lose. Agrona prayed as she had never done in all her life of war, that the Devas might judge Neila fairly.

Agrona's vision flashed away in a pain-bright flare of light. She staggered back, rubbing her dazzled eye. At first she could see only shapes and then the shadows solidified into Neila, sitting on the stone, holding a blazing crossbow in her hands.

Neila's lips curved into a triumphant smile.

Agrona found herself laughing giddily in the ruins of Vonn, glad, for the first time in her memory, to be alive.

They slept the night in the stone circle, and in the pink glow of morning Agrona and Neila hiked up the path to Sarnagat. Neila danced along at Agrona's side, but her merriment faded away when they arrived at the village and found everyone awake, armed, and readying for a siege.

Gardia stood just inside the town's main gate wearing the chiefess' torque of authority around her neck. She bellowed orders at her people, who dashed about stockpiling provisions and gathering weapons. Archers climbed rickety ladders onto the palisade ramparts while lancers readied their spears. Agrona and Neila broke into a run, barely making it to the gate before it closed.

"Niall!" Gardia chided, "where have you been, and with…" When she saw Agrona her face took on a conflicted expression. Her eyes sparkled with welcome, but her mouth hung open in dismay. Gardia closed her jaw just as Sionne approached.

"You should have shut them out," Sionne hissed venomously. "Remember, we are threatened now because of the Blood Axe's doing."

Agrona leaned forward, ready to fight, until she heard the villagers voicing agreement with their priestess. Shocked, Agrona took a step backwards, turning to Gardia for an answer.

The chiefess shook her head. "Agrona, was it you who ambushed an Imperial patrol on the mountain road?"

Agrona looked down at the blood still on her bracers and felt her stomach sink. Her fears had come true, though not in any way she'd suspected. No matter what she did, she brought disaster with her.

"The Empire is holding Sarnagat responsible for the massacre," Sionne said coldly. "They sent a runner to tell us that we are to surrender for punishment or see our town razed, our children slaughtered. Even now a full phalanx is on its way here with cannons and shot."

So it was her fault. Agrona squared her jaw. "So turn me over to them. Let the punishment fall upon me."

Gardia folded her arms, glowering at Sionne. "I am not surrendering my own sister to the Empire. Agrona would not have killed them if they had not been trespassing on our land, threatening our people. I would have done the same had I met them on the road. Who is to say they would not raze Sarnagat anyway, as once they razed Vonn?"

Sionne touched the chiefess' arm. "Her suggestion has merit, though. She is a willing sacrifice." She gave Gardia a simpering smile.

"Do you really think the Empire will be satisfied with one warrior?" Gardia retorted. "Do you really think they will take her and leave?"

"Surely the odds are better than our odds if we should fight?" Sionne said.

"No."

The word cut through the air like a slap on Sionne's cheek. "Who dares?" the priestess snarled, and then her eyes fell on the speaker. "You!"

Neila had clambered up on the palisade fortifications to join the female archers. She stood defiantly on the rampart, her tattered robe streaming in the wind, even as the other women scowled disapprovingly at her.

Gardia sighed. "Get over to the left wall with the other men, Niall, take up a sword, and leave the order-giving to women."

Neila rested her hands on her hips and spoke defiantly. "My name is Neila, niece of Agrona, and the Devas themselves have judged me the woman I have always claimed to be."

Gardia paled. "What do you mean?"

Next to her, Sionne reddened with fury. Agrona moved quickly, climbing up the ladder to stand next to Neila. If anyone tried to do the girl harm, they would have to face her blood axe.

"Aunt Agrona," Neila whispered. "I can fight but... where do I aim?"

The other archers had backed away. Gardia, torn between protecting her only child and enforcing the Tribe's rules, scrambled up the ladder in pursuit. Sionne, unable to match Agrona hand to hand, was shouting for warriors to cut down the blasphemer. Many balked, afraid of drawing arms on the woman called the Devas' Wrath.

With one final glare of warning to the other archers, Agrona gazed out over the valley below. She could see the Imperial phalanx approaching, its banners streaming, its soldiers marching in tidy lines along the narrow road at the base of a rugged cliff. At the front of the columns, Agrona identified the commanders on horseback, followed by a covered horse-drawn cart and two pair of oxen straining at their harnesses, hauling cannons behind them. Those long guns would splinter Sarnagat's wooden palisades in minutes.

Except.

Agrona said to Neila, "Do you see that horse-drawn cart?"

The girl nodded.

"It is filled with gunpowder for the cannons. If you took a flaming arrow, could you hit it from this distance?" The enemy was still a fair climb downslope, but not out of range for a skilled archer with a crossbow.

Neila smiled.

Agrona jabbed her talon into her palm, manifesting her blood axe. Then she pulled the bladed jewelry off her fourth finger and slid it onto Neila's. "Call your weapon."

Agrona turned to address the village, stopping Sionne's lackeys in their tracks. "Halt, and listen well, for as I am the Devas' Wrath, Neila is this day named the Devas' Judgment."

With her back to her niece, Agrona did not see the girl's crossbow manifest. She saw, instead, the stunned shock on the faces of Sarnagat's villagers, and the slow hopeful smile on Gardia's lips as she topped the ladder. Agrona smelled the pungent smoke of a blazing arrow. She heard the zing of the bow as Neila fired.

The arrow flew while all else hung suspended. Agrona's heart beat once, twice. Then a sound like the land itself applauding split the silence and sent the mountains ringing. A moment later, the archers broke into cheers, and after that, the entire village.

Agrona turned her head in time to watch as a cascade of rocks tumbled down the cliffside, sweeping away the enemy formation. The Devas had indeed made their judgment, and it had been final.

Neila lowered her bow and went down on one knee before her mother. "I beg your forgiveness, my Chiefess," she said, "but the Devas have seen fit to send a landslide to bury the enemy, and it will take some time for us to clear the rocks from the mountain road."

Gardia laughed. "We will clear them tomorrow. Tonight we celebrate. Rise, my daughter, Neila, the Devas' Judgment."

Agrona allowed herself a moment to observe Sionne retreating in disgrace before she slipped down the ladder and into the crowd. It was possible that some of the Imperial soldiers had survived the explosion and, if so, the Devas' Wrath had tidying up to do.

She paused at Sarnagat's gates, just long enough to raise her blood axe in salute to her niece, before she headed downslope alone. Despite her solitude, she no longer felt dissatisfied. She knew she was leaving something of value behind her.

FIRST COMMAND
BY CHRIS A. JACKSON

Charging pikes. Not my favorite thing. You stand a solid chance of losing your horse, and I've always liked horses. Granted, the one I was riding—He'd earned the moniker Ill-Tempered Beast—would sooner bite your nose off and kick your spleen out as look at you, but he probably thought the same about me. I could almost hear his thoughts as our phalanx broke into a canter and topped the rise.

Heavy, tin-plated bitch, just as soon run you into a wall of pikes as put a saddle on your back.

The thought brought a smile, but still, I didn't wish Ill-Tempered Beast any harm. All we were both trying to do was stay alive and break the Morrgrey line. My lord's lance dipped, and mine followed with his other squires'. The phalanx kicked into a gallop with a hundred yards to go. Something clanged against my helm, a stone or arrow. My ears rang, but I held steady. I watched an arrow fix in my mount's shoulder near my knee. It had punched right through the barding and probably hurt like hell, but he didn't even lose his stride. It wasn't enough to kill him, and anything that didn't kill this one-ton mountain of war-trained insanity generally just pissed him off.

That was fine. I needed him pissed off.

Fifty yards and I made sure my shield was seated against my saddle. Surviving a charge against pikes is a lot more about your shield than anything else. This wasn't some silly joust. A good steady pikeman could put the tip of his weapon exactly where he wanted it to go. An inexperienced one might put it into your mount's eye or heart. If they did, they wouldn't see another cavalry charge. If a pikeman killed Ill-tempered Beast, I'd kill him in the next instant, then try to unseat my dead horse before he crushed me. The better strategy is to go for the rider.

Pikes are longer than lances, so if they kill you before you kill them, they might survive. But that meant getting past your shield, or getting really lucky and putting the tip of their pike through the slit in your visor. Pikemen were trained to aim just over the horse's shoulder at the inside rim of the shield. If the tip of the pike struck true, the lancer's shield would only turn the blow far enough to strike the right side of the breastplate. If it didn't shatter, the head of the pike would run the knight through and pluck him or her right out of the saddle. The horse might trample through the line, but that was better than being skewered by a knight's lance.

I wasn't a knight, just a squire, and I could count the number of times I'd charged pikes in combat on one hand, but I was still alive. I was Lord Fornish's second squire, and I intended to make knight someday. That meant staying alive today.

Arrows whistled over our heads at the enemy, our longbowmen softening up the line. The pikes wavered, and we lunged forward over the last twenty yards.

Shield steady, lance braced, pick your target… steady.

Something hit my visor, and pain lanced across my skull. Blood blinded my left eye.

Steady… you heavy, tin-plated bitch.

Ill-tempered Beast grunted with every lunging stride now, foam flecking his muzzle, platter-sized hooves trampling the sod with a vengeance.

Pick your mark…

I lowered my lance at the chest of a dark-faced Morrgrey. The tip of his pike wavered and aimed to my right, toward my lord. I jinked, nudging his white-coated charger over to ruin the dead-man's aim.

The pike hit the outer edge of my lord's shield and another hit mine squarely. A blinding moment of impact, the instant of death unstoppable, Lord Fornish's shield flung aside by the impact as another pike I had not seen struck him. His mount was half a stride ahead, and I saw the pike head dent the back plate of his armor from the inside before the shaft shattered.

My lance spitted the Morrgrey, and I let it go, even as my lord sagged in his saddle. I was screaming. There was a sword in my hand. My sword. There was blood on it. Ill-tempered Beast bit through a man's shoulder as I kicked him into a turn, his rear hooves lashing out like scythes. My lord's horse, staggered, a pike through its body, trying to stay up, but without any signals from its rider. I charged back as it fell, Fornish toppling like a metal ragdoll. A Morrgrey footman raised an axe above my fallen lord and looked up at me an instant before I rode him down, Ill-tempered Beast's hooves churning through flesh like soft sod. I reined in hard and kicked him into another turn. He crow-hopped and thrashed, but complied.

"To me!" I snatched my dagger and cut my saddle straps. "Squires, lancers, defend your lord!"

Never dismount in a battle. Your odds of survival plummet. I wasn't thinking about survival. I was thinking of the man I loved like a father bleeding out on the turf. I landed hard on a Morrgrey corpse and fought to my feet, blinking away blood and laying about my fallen master with sword and shield. My throat raw, blood and steel were all my eyes beheld.

Heartbreak would come later.

"Camwynn! Stop!"

I blinked, and realized that my blade had left a crease in a shield bearing my own coat of arms. I turned, looking for black hair, dark eyes, ringmail, and green and black, not Fornish's scarlet and gold or the blue and white of Tsing. The field of battle was ours. The enemy was in full retreat, our lancers and the arrows of our longbowmen chasing them into the wood.

I dropped my sword and tore at my shield straps, staggering back to my fallen lord. "Milord!" I knelt beside Tamrey, my friend and co-squire, third under me and Utar, our senior. I flipped up my visor and wiped blood from my eyes. "Milord!"

"Tam…" The voice came out reedy, but alive. "Cam…" An arm moved reaching up. "I can't… see."

"Here, milord. Let me." Tamrey cut the chin strap and eased off Fornish's helm, his salt and pepper hair and beard streaked with blood and sweat.

He drew a ragged breath and coughed blood, blinking up at us. I wrenched my helm off and shared a glance with Tamrey. The pikestaff was broken off at our lord's breastplate, just left of center. It must have missed his heart, but only just. A lung had certainly been pierced, and from the amount of frothy pink blood oozing from beneath his gorget, there was nothing we could do. I looked around desperately.

"Healer!" I searched for one of the white robes, anyone who could help, but the battle still raged far afield. I saw our standard, Utar commanding a phalanx against the Morrgrey flanking maneuver. I held my lord's head and looked down into his dark eyes. "Easy, milord. The field is ours. We must wait for aid to move you."

"Don't... lie to me... Camwynn." Blood flecked his teeth, a grimace or a smile, I couldn't tell. "I told... you. Shield. Mine got knocked, and I paid for it."

I remembered my jostle and wondered if I'd killed him. "I'm sorry, milord. I nudged your horse to deflect a pike."

"Never... apologize for rendering aid, Cam..." He blinked and looked to Tamrey, at the tears rolling down the young man's beardless cheeks. "Follow her orders, Tam. She's... in—" His lips pulled back in a rictus of pain, and he coughed blood.

I wiped his mouth and held him. "Be still, milord. Help will come."

"No." The muscles of his jaw clenched, and he swallowed. His hand gripped mine, for a moment as strong as ever. "Listen! You, Cam... must take command. Not Utar. Do... you hear?"

"I..." I stared at him, and glanced at Tamrey. "Milord, I cannot! I'm second."

"Don't disobey my final... order, Camwynn." He smiled then, and the strength slipped away from his grip. "Promise... me."

"I promise on my oath to you, milord!" I could do nothing else. He was my lord. "I'll take command."

"Good." His eyes fluttered closed. "Now... let... me..."

Tamrey and I watched the last breath leave him, felt the last beat of his heart in his grasp.

"Camwynn?"

I eased my lord's head down to the turf and lurched up to my feet. The ground around us was a mire of blood and churned earth. Astonishingly, Ill-tempered Beast stood only yards away, stomping and pawing, his muzzle bloody, and the arrow still sticking out of his shoulder. He was breathing hard, but looked hale. I went to him, and damned if he didn't stand perfectly still as I cut the barbed arrowhead free. From my saddlebag I recovered a pot of ointment, a water skin, and my cloak. The former I applied to Beast's wound and the cut over my eye. The latter I draped over my lord's corpse.

"Camwynn!" Tamrey stood there gripping the hilt of his sword. "What will you do?"

I drank deeply from my skin and handed it to Tam. "Mourn, eat something, drink a skin of wine, tend this ill-tempered beast…" I patted his massive shoulder, and he turned to gnash his teeth at me, but only half-heartedly. "…and follow my lord's last order."

"Utar won't like it." Tamrey waved to the approaching foot soldiers and the rest of the scattered lancers. "He'll pitch a fit like he always does."

"Probably." I thought about Utar. Yes, he would throw a fit. "I don't care. You heard Lord Fornish's order. I'm to take command."

"I heard it, and I'll back you, but it's not going to go smoothly." Tamrey wiped his sword and sheathed it. "There'll be all nine shades of the hells to pay."

"Then I'll pay it."

The stretcher bearers arrived, staring down in shock at my fallen lord.

"See to the wounded first! The dead can wait. We'll take Sir Fornish back. Help me, Tam."

Tamrey and I lifted our fallen liege to the back of my horse and walked back to camp. We'd won the battle, but at a horrible cost, and there was a war yet to be fought, but not the one I was thinking of.

"I'll not stand aside and let you steal this from me, Camwynn!" Utar clenched his massive hand on the hilt of his broadsword and glared at me openly. "I'm Fornish's senior squire! Command is mine by default!"

"No, command is mine by our lord's final order." I girded my temper and kept my thumbs hooked in my belt. I wasn't afraid of Utar. He wouldn't strike without warning. Such a cowardly act was beneath a squire of Tsing. "Tamrey witnessed it with me. Lord Fornish ordered me to take command and I won't disobey."

"The troops won't follow a half-trained squire!" Commander Dask pounded his fist on the map table in emphasis. He was regular army, experienced and hard as a twenty penny nail, but he was also wrong.

"You suggest we cede the field of battle because my lord fell, Commander?" I glared at him, willing him to hear my thoughts. *Don't go there you idiot. You'll lose.*

"I suggest nothing of the kind! Utar should take command as is his right."

"If eight years means half-trained, most of your officers have less, and Utar is as *half-trained* as I am, Commander!" If you counted fighting through a dozen other squire applicants and street fights before that, I had more training than Utar. "Fortunately, Lord Fornish saw to our training in arms and in tactics. We are *both* quite capable."

"But you're a…" His eyes flicked down to the undeniable bulge of breasts beneath my tabard, then back up to my face.

My temper flared and I ripped my gloves from my belt. "If the next word out of your mouth is 'woman' I will call you out this *instant*, sir!"

Female soldiers were rare in Tsing, perhaps one in twenty, but about one in ten squires were women. Contrary to the filthy scuttlebutt among common soldiers, we aren't recruited to warm our lords' beds. I'm a trained soldier, master-at-arms, military tactician and strategist, and I've rarely had to beat those facts into anyone. I hoped that I wouldn't have to do so with Dask; he was a valuable commander and the troops respected him. My beating him might earn me their enmity.

"It wasn't." The lie only shone in his eyes, and I was grateful for it. "You're young, that's all."

"My age is irrelevant. Lord Fornish was your commander," I looked back to Utar, "and it was his last order that I take command."

"I will not relinquish it!" Utar glared. He didn't hate me, but he also wouldn't back down. I could see it in his eyes.

"It is not yours to relinquish, Utar." I squared my shoulders. "I was ordered by *your* lord to take command."

"So you *say*."

"I was there, too, Utar!" Tamrey stepped forward, his smooth jaw writhing with his clenching teeth. "You call me a liar?"

"I call you a teat-suckling whelp, boy!"

Tamrey lunged, regardless of propriety or that Utar out-weighted him by half. I caught his arm and hauled him back. My gloves were already in my other hand, which made it easy. The stout leather slapped across Utar's bearded cheek. He didn't flinch, but just grinned at me.

"Ahorse or afoot, Camwynn?"

"We don't have time or resources for this nonsense!" Dask glared at us both. "We're at war, for the love of the Gods."

I didn't take my eyes off Utar. "The Morrgrey are reforming on the other side of the wood, Commander. We have a day, perhaps two, to reposition. Our business will be concluded at first light on the morrow. I'll give you my orders for deployment then."

"Arrogant bitch!" Utar's lips curled back from his teeth.

"You're half right, Utar." I grinned back at him. If he was trying to goad me as he had Tamrey, he'd have to do better. "But it's *confidence*, not arrogance."

"Ahorse or afoot?"

I had a better chance of winning astride Ill-tempered Beast, but the army could ill afford losing mounts on a squire's challenge. Utar knew that. What he didn't know was that I had much more interest in following my lord's final orders than I had in taking command. I would fight my best, and win if I could, but I would follow Utar's commands or die with honor if I lost.

"Afoot."

"Dawn."

"Dawn." I turned to Tamrey. "Be my second, Tamrey."

"It would be my honor." He nodded, still glaring at Utar. "And if you don't kill this fat bastard, I will!"

Utar just laughed at Tamrey's threat and walked out of the command tent. Tamrey stormed out, swearing like a sailor on shore leave.

"Do me a favor, Squire Camwynn." Dask leveled his flint grey eyes at me.

"If it's in my power, I will, Commander."

"Don't kill him, and don't get killed yourself." He tapped the map table as if to remind me of the greater issue. "We're *still* at war, and Tsing needs you both."

"I'll do my best on both counts, Commander." I nodded respectfully and left the tent.

I made good on my claim: I tended Ill-Tempered Beast—his halter had been tied to a deep stake, so he couldn't bite me, but he did try to kick me, so I knew he was hale—ate a meal, and finished half a skin of wine, but my thoughts on how I would fight Utar wouldn't congeal. I'd also spent two hours paying my respects to my lord, trying to reconcile his loss in my mind. I needed to think, and to sleep, and the wine wasn't helping. After pacing my tent for another hour, I decided to go for a walk.

Utar would be a problem. Heavier and stronger than I, though not any more skilled at arms and certainly no quicker, we were a close match. Beating him without killing him would be the true challenge. I doubted that he had any similar compunction. Utar didn't generally see the bigger picture. Nothing beyond the tip of his lance, Fornish used to say. I wondered if that was why he ordered me to take command. I did see the bigger picture, long-term goals, how to achieve them at least cost, sparing the most lives, burning the least forest or cropland.

I wondered if our differences were due to our sexes, and dismissed the notion. Not all men are short sighted hot-heads. My lord had been a brilliant tactician, disciplined but not unkind, hard when he needed to be, and jovial when it served him better. Could I be that?

Yes. You're just doubting yourself.

I knew my conscience was right, but I didn't know how to calm my tumultuous thoughts. Grief, worry, anxiety, and determination all swam in my head in a maelstrom, and I was a boat caught on that torrent. I needed to sleep, and I didn't know how I was going to achieve it.

Yes you do.

I blinked and realized I was in the section of the camp reserved for the camp followers. I heard laughter and music, the jingling of hand cymbals and strum of a lute. I espied a circle of firelight, a woman dancing with gold in her hands, moving like a serpent. Men and women clapped and sang to the music. My feet turned to join them.

Dark eyes flicked toward me as I entered the light. A man stood, his white teeth flashing against olive skin, beautiful dark eyes, and hair made to clench in my trembling hands. I blinked and saw the startled gaze of the Morrgrey I'd killed that morning. I wondered if this beauty was a distant relative, and suddenly felt like apologizing.

"May we be of service, lady." He bowed fluidly, waving a hand at the firelight, the dancing, the smiles, and camaraderie.

"Are you Morrgrey?" I asked. I didn't know why I even needed to know.

"No, Lady. We are Jesti. Travelers, singers, dancers… and tellers of tales." He bowed again. "You are troubled. Join us if you will."

I wondered how he knew, and realized that it didn't take a fortune teller to know I was upset. My emotions were writ large on my face, no doubt, and the news of Fornish's death had reached all corners of the camp. I wore his livery. The man was observant as well as beautiful.

"Would you like a cup of wine?" I asked him.

"We have wine, lady."

"I'm not a lady." Technically true; a squire isn't a noble. "Would you like a cup of *my* wine?"

One dark eyebrow arched, and those clean white teeth flashed again. "I would be honored to share your wine, Sir Camwynn."

That he knew my name surprised me, but the premature title more so.

"I'm not a knight."

"In time." That smile again.

"Come with me." I turned and gestured back to the camp and my tent. He fell into step beside me. "I need to know your name."

"Veshka Li Predaluru Kepatushka."

Music…

His fingers found my hand, a light caress. "Please, call me Vesh. My friends all do."

"Vesh." I liked the sound his name made in my mouth. I entwined my fingers in his. "Thank you."

"Thank me on the morrow, lady." He chuckled, and I felt my thoughts moving away from the maelstrom into the sweet bliss of this beautiful man.

Sometimes my conscience is truly brilliant.

I woke to the light of my lamp burned low. Some noise, the clank of a pot, the crow of a rooster, had snapped me out of my blissful sleep. I knew without looking outside that it was time to rise. Vesh stirred beside me, his tousled black hair a dream, the smell of him… a memory… oh glory of the Gods, what a memory.

My mind was clear, my thoughts orderly, the day's tasks lying before me like a pile of wood needing to be chopped. Simple.

Thank you.

I slipped out of the nest of furs and blankets and knelt mother naked before my tiny altar to Eloss the Defender. A quick prayer, a splash of icy water, clothes, boots, padded gambeson, bread and cheese, and a swallow of the wine we'd never touched the night before. I reached for my sword belt, then looked back to my nest of furs and Vesh. I knelt and brushed his shoulder with my callused fingers. He stirred, and rolled to look up at me blinking.

"I have to go." I smiled and ran the backs of my fingers over his wonderful lips. He kissed them. "Wish me luck."

"You need no luck, beautiful Camwynn." He smiled with those lovely teeth and I felt a shiver, wondering if I'd ever see him again.

"Here." I fished a pouch from my things and handed it to him. "Buy your sisters something pretty."

"I will." He took the pouch and sat up, knotting his fist in my short hair to pull me into one more lingering kiss. "And I will sing your song tonight."

"Thank you." I stood and left him, strapping on my sword on the way out. Dawn was coming.

Outside the tent I found Tamrey pacing in front of our arms rack. The junior squires had seen to my things, bless them, and everything gleamed in the wan light.

"Sleep well?" Tamrey grinned at me and I wondered if he knew how I'd spent the night.

Probably so. Tents offer little privacy, and his was right next to mine.

"I did." I surveyed my things, and my strategy congealed. "Mail and breastplate only this morning."

"I thought so." He lifted my mail and helped me into it, fastening the clips, then my chest armor, cinching the straps tight. "Full face, or visorless?"

"Visorless." He picked my open helm from the stand and I put it on, adjusting the straps as he fitted greaves. Twisting to check the fit, the weight, and the straps, I surveyed my weaponry.

"You know he'll be in full plate."

"He better be. I'm counting on it." I picked a flanged mace, a better weapon against plate armor than a sword, especially if you were interested in keeping your opponent alive. I wore sword and dagger as well, just in case I lost my weapon.

"Do me a favor, Cam." Tamrey cinched my shield straps tight and glanced up at me.

"If I can."

"Kick his fat ass." He grinned and punched me in the chest as hard as he could.

I laughed at his antics, hoping he hadn't hurt his hand. "Am I getting odds from the wagerers?" I waved toward the practice field, and he fell in beside me.

"Even money." He shrugged. "Not many people betting."

"Well, the rank and file probably don't care who wins. One squire commander's as bad as another in their eyes."

"You're wrong." Tamrey pointed to the grounds as we rounded the mess tent. "They care, and there's quite a disparity of opinion, but nobody's fool enough to bet when they don't have a clue who's going to win."

It looked like about half the camp had turned out, and more were on the way. "Great."

The crowd of soldiers parted, and a few cheers went up. Inside a chalk circle Utar stood ready, Balric, another of our lord's junior squires standing as his second. As I'd hoped, my opponent wore full plate armor, helm, visor, and shield. I'd hoped he'd wield his broadsword, but he held a hooked axe in his hand. That could be a problem. The spike on the back of the axe would pierce my mail if he got a stroke in.

Tactics shifted in my mind like water flowing around rocks in a stream. I took my position, and Commander Dask stepped between us.

"This is a bout of honor between *allies*." His gray eyes fixed us both in turn. "Do either of you cede prior to trial of arms?"

"Do you name me commander as is my right as senior squire?" Utar's voice was muffled from behind his helm's venttail, but clear enough.

"I do not. Do you name me commander as our lord ordered, and offer apology for insult?"

"I do not."

"Very well!" Dask glared at us both again. "This bout will proceed until one contestant cannot continue or yields to the other. Mercy is to be given if asked. Striking a senseless or defenseless opponent is prohibited. Do you both agree to these terms?"

"I do," we both said.

"Then let's get this done before the Gods-be-damned Morrgrey attack!" Dask raised an arm, and dropped it. "Commence!"

Fights generally last only seconds. This one didn't.

Utar and I knew each other. We'd sparred thousands of times over the years, and knew each other's tricks, strengths, and weaknesses. He was stronger, and I knew it. I was quicker, and he knew it. His left shoulder had been broken once, and he tended to lower his shield when he was tired. I had suffered a spear through my right knee, and couldn't lunge to full extension. Consequently, the contest dragged on, both of us feinting, striking and dodging, deflecting and trying for a lucky trip. My shield arm grew numb from the force of his axe blows, and he limped from where I'd struck his right knee once solidly, but neither of us was hurt.

He was breathing hard, and his shield began to drop between clashes. I hoped I had enough left to exploit it.

Now! the voice inside my head insisted, the pattern of his movements clicking into place.

I deflected an axe blow and feinted low. The shield dropped to guard the injured knee. I spun and lashed out at his head. My mace struck squarely, ripping the venttail off his helm in a spatter of blood and broken teeth. How he stayed on his feet, I don't know, but he spun with the blow, and lashed out with his axe. I raised my shield to take the blow, ignorant that he'd shifted his grip to lead with the pick instead of the blade.

Four inches of steel pierced my shield and my forearm. Numb already, there was no pain, but a bone might be broken, and I couldn't rely on that arm any longer.

And his weapon was stuck.

I brought my mace down at his head, but he shifted and took the impact on his pauldron. The plate buckled, and I knew his collarbone was broken. He wrenched hard on his axe, jerking me forward. The crest of his helm sent stars exploding through my eyes as it met with my nose guard. My back hit the ground before my senses returned, and his axe was coming down toward my face.

I raised my weapon and caught the haft of his axe, stopping the spike an inch before my eyes.

The bastard's trying to kill you!

I don't know where my conscience got the notion, but I knew I only had one tactic left. Flat on my back, probably with a broken arm, head spinning, ears ringing, his next stroke would probably finish me. I kicked him as hard as I could right in his injured knee.

The joint folded with a screech of metal as the poleyn hinge snapped. He fell forward, his axe burying haft deep in the turf beside my head. I dropped my mace and drew my dagger, rolling on top of him and placing the point under his chin.

"Yield, or I'll pith you like a toad!"

"I yield!" At least his answer came right away. I'd have hated to kill him.

Tamrey was there before I could even cut my shield free, pounding me on the back hard enough to send more stars exploding behind my eyes and hauling me to my feet. There were faces all around, cheering and laughing as if we'd not nearly murdered one another. They rolled Utar onto a stretcher, and four men-at-arms lifted him. His knee was still bent the wrong way.

"Wait!" I stumbled over. They'd removed his helm and washed some of the blood off. It looked like I'd broken something in his face. "Sorry about the leg, but I thought you were trying to kill me."

He blinked, and his swollen lips peeled back from broken teeth. "Thorry about the arm. And I wath trying to kill you… thir." He saluted me; my first.

The healers were there, insisting they see to his leg immediately.

"Get him on his feet! I need his fat ass in the saddle by tomorrow!" That earned me another round of cheers from the soldiery.

A healer examined my arm, but the spike of Utar's axe had miraculously passed between the two bones without breaking either. Dumb luck.

Maybe Vesh had wished it on me when I wasn't looking.

"Orders, Squire Commander?" Dask saluted me, his face grim. "Your nose is broken, sir."

"Is it now?" Tamrey helped me off with my helm and I felt the lump of smashed meat on my face. "Well, I'll have to fix that, I suppose, but I need to speak to you about deployment."

"Yes sir." He waved toward the command tent. My tent.

I sat astride Ill-Tempered Beast and kicked him into a canter. "Forward!" He snorted and capered, complaining as always. The phalanx around me broke into a chanter, Utar to my right, Tamrey to my left, and we lowered our lances, a wall of steel on three tons of pissed-off horse.

We were charging pikes again. Never my favorite.

THE BOUND MAN

BY MARY ROBINETTE KOWAL

Light dappled through the trees in the family courtyard, painting shadows on the paving stones. Li Reiko knelt by her son to look at his scraped knee.

"I just scratched it." Nawi squirmed under her hands.

Her daughter, Aya, leaned over her shoulder studying the healing. "Maybe Mama will show you her armor after she heals you."

Nawi stopped wiggling. "Really?"

Reiko shot Aya a warning look, but her little boy's dark eyes shone with excitement. Reiko smiled. "Really." What did tradition matter? "Now let me heal your knee." She laid her hand on the shallow wound.

"Ow."

"Shush." Reiko closed her eyes and rose in the dark space behind them.

In her mind's eye, Reiko took her time with the ritual, knowing it took less time than it appeared. In a heartbeat, green fire flared out to the walls of her mind. She dissolved into it as she focused on healing her son.

When the wound closed beneath her hand, she sank to the surface of her mind.

"There." She tousled Nawi's hair. "That wasn't bad, was it?"

"It tickled." He wrinkled his nose. "Will you show me your armor now?"

She sighed. She should not encourage his interest in the martial arts. His work would be with the histories that men kept, and yet…"Watch."

Pulling the smooth black surface out of the ether, she manifested her armor. It sheathed her like silence in the night. Aya watched with obvious anticipation for the day when she earned her own armor. Nawi's face, full of sharp yearning for something he would never have, cut Reiko's heart like a new blade.

"Can I see your sword?"

She let her armor vanish into thought. "No." Reiko brushed his hair from his eyes. "It's my turn to hide, right?"

Halldór twisted in his saddle, trying to ease the kink in his back. When the questing party reached the Parliament, he could remove the weight hanging between his shoulders.

With each step his horse took across the moss-covered lava field, the strange blade bumped against his spine, reminding him that he carried a legend. None of the runes or sheep entrails he read before their quest had foretold the ease with which they fulfilled the first part of the prophecy. They had found the Chooser of the Slain's narrow blade wrapped in linen, buried beneath an abandoned elf-house. In that dark room, the sword's hard silvery metal—longer than any of their bronze swords—had seemed lit by the moon.

Lárus pulled his horse alongside Halldór. "Will the ladies be waiting for us, do you think?"

"Maybe for you, my lord, but not for me."

"Nonsense. Women love the warrior-priest. 'Strong and sensitive.'" He snorted through his mustache. "Just comb your hair so you don't look like a straw man."

A horse screamed behind them. Halldór turned, expecting to see its leg caught in one of the thousands of holes between the rocks. Instead, armed men swarmed from the gullies between the rocks, hacking at the riders. Bandits.

Halldór spun his horse to help Lárus and the others fight them off.

Lárus shouted, "Protect the Sword."

At the Duke's command, Halldór cursed and turned his horse from the fight, galloping across the rocks. Behind him, men cried out as they protected his escape. His horse twisted along the narrow paths between stones. It stopped abruptly, avoiding a chasm. Halldór looked back.

Scant lengths ahead of the bandits, Lárus rode, slumped in his saddle. Blood stained his cloak. The other men hung behind Lárus, protecting the Duke as long as possible.

Behind them, the bandits closed the remaining distance across the lava fields.

Halldór kicked his horse's side, driving it around the chasm. His horse stumbled sickeningly beneath him. Its leg snapped, caught between rocks. Halldór kicked free of the saddle as the horse screamed. He rolled clear. The rocky ground slammed the sword into his back. His face passed over the edge of the chasm. Breathless, he recoiled from the drop.

As he scrambled to his feet, Lárus thundered up. Without wasting a beat, Lárus flung himself from the saddle and tossed Halldór the reins. "Get the Sword to Parliament!"

Halldór grabbed the reins, swinging into the saddle. If they died returning to Parliament, did it matter that they had found the Sword? "We must invoke the Sword!"

Lárus's right arm hung, blood-drenched, by his side, but he faced the bandits with his left. "Go!"

Halldór yanked the Sword free of its wrappings. For the first time in six thousand years, the light of the sun fell on the silvery blade bringing fire to its length. It vibrated in his hands.

The first bandit reached Lárus and forced him back.

Halldór chanted the runes of power, petitioning the Chooser of the Slain.

Time stopped.

Reiko hid from her children, blending into the shadows of the courtyard with more urgency than she felt in combat. To do less would insult them.

"Ready or not, here I come!" Nawi spun from the tree and sprinted past her hiding place. Aya turned more slowly and studied the courtyard. Reiko smiled as her daughter sniffed the air, looking for tracks. Her son crashed through the bushes, kicking leaves with each footstep.

As another branch cracked under Nawi's foot, Reiko stifled the urge to correct his appalling technique. She would speak with his tutor about what the woman was teaching him. He was a boy, but that was no reason to neglect his education.

Watching Aya find Reiko's initial footprints and track them away from where she hid, Reiko slid from her hiding place. She walked across the courtyard to the fountain. This was a rule with her children; to make up for the size difference, she could not run.

She paced closer to the sparkling water, masking her sounds with its babble. From her right, Nawi shouted, "Have you found her?"

"No, silly!" Aya shook her head and stopped. She put her tiny hands on her hips, staring at the ground. "Her tracks stop here."

Reiko and her daughter were the same distance from the fountain, but on opposite sides. If Aya were paying attention, she would realize her mother had retraced her tracks and jumped from the fountain to the paving stones circling the grassy center of the courtyard. Reiko took three more steps before Aya turned.

As her daughter turned, Reiko felt, more than heard, her son on her left, reaching for her. Clever. He had misdirected her attention with his noise in the shrubbery. She fell forward, using gravity to drop beneath his hands. Rolling on her shoulder, she somersaulted, then launched to her feet as Aya ran toward her.

Nawi grabbed for her again. With a child on each side, Reiko danced and dodged closer to the fountain. She twisted from their grasp, laughing with them each time they missed her. Their giggles echoed through the courtyard.

The world tipped sideways and vibrated. Reiko stumbled as pain ripped through her spine.

Nawi's hand clapped against her side. "I got her!"

Fire engulfed Reiko.

The courtyard vanished.

Time began again.

The sword in Halldór's hands thrummed with life. Fire from the sunset engulfed the sword and split the air. With a keening cry, the air opened and a form dropped through, silhouetted against a haze of fire. Horses and men screamed in terror.

When the fire died away, a woman stood between Halldór and the bandits.

Halldór's heart sank. Where was the Chooser of the Slain? Where was the warrior the sword had petitioned?

A bandit snarled a laughing oath and rushed toward them. The others followed him with their weapons raised.

The woman snatched the sword from Halldór's hands. In that brief moment, when he stared at her wild face, he realized that he had succeeded in calling Li Reiko, the Chooser of the Slain.

Then she turned. The air around her rippled with a heat haze as armor, dark as night, materialized around her body. He watched her dance with deadly grace, bending and twisting away from the bandits' blows. Without seeming thought, with movement as precise as ritual, she danced with death as her partner. Her sword slid through the bodies of the bandits.

Halldór dropped to his knees, thanking the gods for sending her. He watched the point of her sword trace a line, like the path of entrails on the church floor. The line of blood led to the next moment, the next and the next, as if each man's death was predestined.

Then she turned her sword on him.

Her blade descended, burning with the fire of the setting sun. She stopped as if she had run into a wall, with the point touching Halldór's chest.

Why had she stopped? If his blood was the price for saving Lárus, so be it. Her arm trembled. She grimaced, but did not move the sword closer.

Her face, half-hidden by her helm, was dark with rage. "Where am I?" Her words were crisp, more like a chant than common speech.

Holding still, Halldór said, "We are on the border of the Parliament lands, Li Reiko."

Her dark eyes, slanted beneath angry lids, widened. She pulled back and her armor rippled, vanishing into thought. Skin, tanned like the smoothest leather stretched over her wide cheekbones. Her hair hung in a heavy, black braid down her back. Halldór's pulse sang in his veins.

Only the gods in sagas had hair the color of the Allmother's night. Had he needed proof he had called the Chooser of the Slain, the inhuman black hair would have convinced him of that.

He bowed his head. "All praise to you, Great One. Grant us your blessings."

Reiko's breath hissed from her. He knew her name. She had dropped through a flaming portal into hell and this demon with bulging eyes knew her name.

She had tried to slay him as she had the others, but could not press her sword forward, as if a wall had protected him.

And now he asked for blessings.

"What blessings do you ask of me?" Reiko said. She controlled a shudder. What human had hair as pale as straw?

Straw lowered his bulging eyes to the demon lying in front of him. "Grant us, O Gracious One, the life of our Duke Lárus."

This Lárus had a wound deep in his shoulder. His blood was as red as any human's, but his face was pale as death.

She turned from Straw and wiped her sword on the thick moss, cleaning the blood from it. As soon as her attention seemed turned from them, Straw attended Lárus. She kept her awareness on the sounds of his movement as she sought balance in the familiar task of caring for her weapon. By the Gods! Why did he have her sword? It had been in her rooms not ten minutes before playing hide and seek with her children.

Panic almost took her. What had happened to her Aya and Nawi? She needed information, but displaying ignorance to an enemy was a weakness, which could kill surer than the sharpest blade. She considered.

Their weapons were bronze, not steel, and none of her opponents had manifested armor. They dressed in leather and felted wool, but no woven goods. So, then. That was their technology.

Straw had not healed Lárus, so perhaps they could not. He wanted her aid. Her thoughts checked. Could demons be bound by blood debt?

She turned to Straw.

"What price do you offer for this life?"

Straw raised his eyes; they were the color of the sky. "I offer my life unto you, O Great One."

She set her lips. What good would vengeance do? Unless... "Do you offer blood or service?"

He lowered his head again. "I submit to your will."

"You will serve me then. Do you agree to be my bound man?"

"I do."

"Good." She sheathed her sword. "What is your name?"

"Halldór Arnarsson."

"I accept your pledge." She dropped to her knees and pushed the leather from the wound on Lárus's shoulder. She pulled upon her reserves and, rising into the healing ritual, touched his mind.

He was human.

She pushed the shock aside; she could not spare the attention.

Halldór gasped as fire glowed around Li Reiko's hands. He had read of gods healing in the sagas, but bearing witness was beyond his dreams.

The glow faded. She lifted her hands from Lárus's shoulder. The wound was gone. A narrow red line and the blood-soaked clothing remained. Lárus opened his eyes as if he had been sleeping.

But her face was drawn. "I have paid the price for your service, bound man." She lifted a hand to her temple. "The wound was deeper..." Her eyes rolled back in her head and she slumped to the ground.

Lárus sat up and grabbed Halldór by the shoulder. "What did you do?"

Shaking Lárus off, Halldór crouched next to her. She was breathing. "I saved your life."

"By binding yourself to a woman? Are you mad?"

"She healed you. Healed! Look." Halldór pointed at her hair. "Look at her. This is Li Reiko."

"Li Reiko was a Warrior."

"You saw her. How long did it take her to kill six men?" He pointed at the carnage behind them. "Name one man who could do that."

Would moving her be a sacrilege? He grimaced. He would beg forgiveness if that were the case. "We should move before the sun sets and the trolls come out."

Lárus nodded slowly, his eyes still on the bodies around them. "Makes you wonder, doesn't it?"

"What?"

"How many other sagas are true?"

Halldór frowned. "They're all true."

The smell of mutton invaded her dreamless sleep. Reiko lay under sheepskin, on a bed of straw ticking. The straw poked through the wool fabric, pricking her bare skin. Straw. Her memory tickled her with an image of hair the color of straw. Halldór.

Long practice kept her breath even. She lay with her eyes closed, listening. A small room. An open fire. Women murmuring. She needed to learn as much as possible, before changing the balance by letting them know she was awake.

A hand placed a damp rag on her brow. The touch was light, a woman or a child.

The sheepskin's weight would telegraph her movement if she tried grabbing the hand. Better to open her eyes and feign weakness than to create an impression of threat. There was time for that later.

Reiko let her eyes flutter open. A girl bent over her, cast from the same demonic mold as Halldór. Her hair was the color of honey, and her wide blue eyes started from her head. She stilled when Reiko awoke, but did not pull away.

Reiko forced a smile, and let worry appear on her brow. "Where am I?"

"In the women's quarters at the Parliament grounds."

Reiko sat up. The sheepskin fell away, letting the cool air caress her body. The girl averted her eyes. Conversation in the room stopped.

Interesting. They had a nudity taboo. She reached for the sheepskin and pulled it over her torso. "What is your name?"

"Mara Halldórsdottir."

Her bound man had a daughter. And his people had a patronymic system—how far from home was she? "Where are my clothes, Mara?"

The girl lifted a folded bundle of cloth from a low bench next to the bed. "I washed them for you."

"Thank you." If Mara had washed and dried her clothes, Reiko must have been unconscious for several hours. Lárus's wound had been deeper than she thought. "Where is my sword?"

"My father has it."

Rage filled Reiko's veins like the fire that had brought her here. She waited for the heat to dwindle, then began dressing. As Reiko pulled her boots on, she asked, "Where is he?"

Behind Mara, the other women shifted as if Reiko were crossing a line. Mara ignored them. "He's with Parliament."

"Which is where?" The eyes of the other women felt like heat on her skin. Ah. Parliament contained the line she should not cross, and they clearly would not answer her. Her mind teased her with memories of folk in other lands. She had never paid much heed to these stories, since history had been men's work. She smiled at Mara. "Thank you for your kindness."

As she strode from the room she kept her senses fanned out, waiting for resistance from them, but they hung back as if they were afraid.

The women's quarters fronted on a narrow twisting path lined with low turf and stone houses. The end of the street opened on a large raised circle surrounded by stone benches.

Men sat on the benches, but women stayed below. Lárus spoke in the middle of the circle. By his side, Halldór stood with her sword in his hands. Sheltering in the shadow by a house, Reiko studied them. They towered above her, but their movements were clumsy and oafish like a trained bear. Nawi had better training than any here.

Her son. Sudden anxiety and rage filled her lungs, but rage invited rash decisions. She forced the anger away.

With effort, she returned her focus to the men. They had no awareness of their mass, only of their size and an imperfect grasp of that.

Halldór lifted his head. As if guided by strings his eyes found her in the shadows.

He dropped to his knees and held out her sword. In mid-sentence, Lárus looked at Halldór, and then turned to Reiko. Surprise crossed his face, but he bowed his head.

"Li Reiko, you honor us with your presence."

Reiko climbed onto the stone circle. As she crossed to retrieve her sword, an ox of a man rose to his feet. "I will not sit here, while a woman is in the Parliament's circle."

Lárus scowled. "Ingolfur, this is no mortal woman."

Reiko's attention sprang forward. What did they think she was, if not mortal?

"You darkened a trollop's hair with soot." Ingolfur crossed his arms. "You expect me to believe she's a god?"

Her pulse quickened. What were they saying? Lárus flung his cloak back, showing the torn and blood-soaked leather at his shoulder. "We were set upon by bandits. My arm was cut half off and she healed it." His pale face flushed red. "I tell you this is Li Reiko, returned to the world."

She understood the words, but they had no meaning. Each sentence out of their mouths raised a thousand questions in her mind.

"Ha." Ingolfur spat on the ground. "Your quest sought a warrior to defeat the Troll King."

This she understood. "And if I do, what price do you offer?"

Lárus opened his mouth but Ingolfur crossed the circle.

"You pretend to be the Chooser of the Slain?" Ingolfur reached for her, as if she were a doll he could pick up. Before his hand touched her shoulder, she took his wrist, pulling on it as she twisted. She drove her shoulder into his belly and used his mass to flip him as she stood.

She had thought these were demons, but by their actions they were men, full of swagger and rash judgment. She waited. He would attack her again.

Ingolfur raged behind her. Reiko focused on his sounds and the small changes in the air. As he reached for her, she twisted away from his hands and with his force, sent him stumbling from the circle. The men broke into laughter.

She waited again.

It might take time but Ingolfur would learn his place. A man courted death, touching a woman unasked.

Halldór stepped in front of Reiko and faced Ingolfur. "Great Ingolfur, surely you can see no mortal woman could face our champion."

Reiko cocked her head slightly. Her bound man showed wit by appeasing the oaf's vanity.

Lárus pointed to her sword in Halldór's hands. "Who here still doubts we have completed our quest?" The men shifted on their benches uneasily. "We fulfilled the first part of the prophecy by returning Li Reiko to the world."

What prophecy had her name in it? There might be a bargaining chip here.

"You promised us a mighty warrior, the Chooser of the Slain," Ingolfur snarled, "not a woman."

It was time for action. If they wanted a god, they should have one. "Have no doubt. I can defeat the Troll King." She let her armor flourish around her. Ingolfur drew back involuntarily. Around the circle, she heard gasps and sharp cries.

She drew her sword from Halldór's hands. "Who here will test me?"

Halldór dropped to his knees in front of her. "The Chooser of the Slain!"

In the same breath, Lárus knelt and cried, "Li Reiko!"

Around the circle, men followed suit. On the ground below, women and children knelt in the dirt. They cried her name. In the safety of her helm, Reiko scowled. Playing at godhood was a dangerous lie.

She lowered her sword. "But there is a price. You must return me to the heavens."

Halldór's eyes grew wider than she thought possible. "How, my lady?"

She shook her head. "You know the gods grant nothing easily. They say you must return me. You must learn how. Who here accepts that price for your freedom from the trolls?"

She sheathed her sword and let her armor vanish into thought. Turning on her heel, she strode off the Parliament's circle.

Halldór clambered to his feet as Li Reiko left the Parliament circle. His head reeled. She hinted at things beyond his training. Lárus grabbed him by the arm. "What does she mean, return her?"

Ingolfur tossed his hands. "If that is the price, I will pay it gladly. Ridding the world of the Troll King and her at the same time would be a joy."

"Is it possible?"

Men crowded around Halldór, asking him theological questions of the sagas. The answers eluded him. He had not cast a rune-stone or read an entrail since they started for the elf-house a week ago. "She would not ask if it were impossible." He swallowed. "I will study the problem with my brothers and return to you."

Lárus clapped him on the back. "Good man." When Lárus turned to the throng surrounding them, Halldór slipped away.

He found Li Reiko surrounded by children. The women hung back, too shy to come near, but the children crowded close. Halldór could hardly believe she had killed six men as easily as carding wool. For the space of a breath, he watched her play peek-a-boo with a small child, her face open with delight and pain.

She saw him and shutters closed over her soul. Standing, her eyes impassive, she said. "I want to read the prophecy."

He blinked, surprised. Then his heart lifted; maybe she would show him how to pay her price. "It is stored in the church."

Reiko brushed the child's hair from its eyes, then fell into step beside Halldór. He could barely keep a sedate pace to the church.

Inside, he led her through the nave to the library beside the sanctuary. The other priests, studying, stared at the Chooser of the Slain. Halldór felt as if he were outside himself with the strangeness of this. He was leading Li Reiko, a Warrior out of the oldest sagas, past shelves containing her history.

Since the gods had arrived from across the sea, his brothers had recorded their history. For six-thousand unbroken years, the records of prophecy and the sagas kept their history whole.

When they reached the collections desk, the acolyte on duty looked as if he would wet himself. Halldór stood between the boy and the Chooser of the Slain, but the boy still stared with an open mouth.

"Bring me the Troll King prophecy, and the Sagas of Li Nawi, Volume I. We will be in the side chapel."

Still gaping, the boy nodded and ran down the aisles.

"We can study in here." He led the Chooser of the Slain to the side chapel. Halldór was shocked again at how small she was, not much taller than the acolyte. He had thought the gods would be larger than life.

He had hundreds of questions, but none of the words.

When the acolyte came back, Halldór sent a silent prayer of thanks. Here was something they could discuss. He took the vellum roll and the massive volume of sagas the acolyte carried and shooed him out of the room.

Halldór's palms were damp with sweat as he pulled on wool gloves to protect the manuscripts. He hesitated over another pair of gloves, then set them aside. Her hands could heal; she would not damage the manuscripts.

Carefully, Halldór unrolled the prophecy scroll on the table. He did not look at the rendering of entrails. He watched her.

She gave no hint of her thoughts. "I want to hear your explanation of this."

A cold current ran up his spine, as if he were eleven again, explaining scripture to an elder. Halldór licked his lips and pointed at the arc of sclera. "This represents the heavens, and the overlap here," he pointed at the bulge of the lower intestine, "means time of conflict. I interpreted the opening in the bulge to mean specifically the Troll King. This pattern of blood means—"

She crossed her arms. "You clearly understand your discipline. Tell me the prophecy in plain language."

"Oh." He looked at the drawing of the entrails again. What did she see that he did not? "Well, in a time of conflict—which is now—the Chooser of the Slain overcomes the Troll King." He pointed at the shining knot around the lower intestine. "See how this chokes off the Troll King. That means you win the battle."

"And how did you know the legendary warrior was—is me?"

"I cross-referenced with our histories and you were the one that fit the criteria."

She shivered. "Show me the history. I want to understand how you deciphered this."

Halldór thanked the gods that he had asked for Li Nawi's saga as well. He placed the heavy volume of history in front of Li Reiko and opened to the Book of Fire, Chapter I.

In the autumn of the Fire, Li Reiko, greatest of the warriors, trained Li Nawi and his sister Aya in the ways of Death. In the midst of the training, a curtain of fire split Nawi from Aya and when they came together again, Li Reiko was gone. Though they were frightened, they understood that the Chooser of the Slain had taken a rightful place in heaven.

Reiko trembled, her control gone. "What is this?"

"It is the Saga of Li Nawi."

She tried phrasing casual questions, but her mind spun in circles. "How do you come to have this?"

Halldór traced the letters with his gloved hand. "After the Collapse, when waves of fire had rolled across our land, Li Nawi came across the oceans with the other gods. He was our conqueror and our salvation."

The ranks of stone shelves filled with thick leather bindings crowded her. Her heart kicked wildly.

Halldór's voice seemed drowned out by the drumming of her pulse. "The Sagas are our heritage and charge. The Gods have left the Earth, but we keep records of histories as they taught us."

Reiko turned her eyes blindly from the page. "Your heritage?"

"I have been dedicated to the service of the gods since my birth." He paused. "Your sagas were the most inspiring. Forgive my trespasses, may I beg for your indulgence with a question?"

"What?" Hot and cold washed over her in sickening waves.

"I have read your son Li Nawi's accounts of your triumphs in battle."

Reiko could not breathe. Halldór flipped the pages forward. "This is how I knew where to look for your sword." He paused with his hand over the letters. "I deciphered the clues to invoke it and call you here, but there are many—"

Reiko pushed away from the table. "You caused the curtain of fire?" She wanted to vomit her fear at his feet.

"I—I do not understand."

"I dropped through fire this morning." *And when they came together again, Li Reiko was no more.* What had it been like for Aya and Nawi to watch their mother ripped out of time?

Halldór said, "In answer to my petition."

"I was playing hide and seek with my children and you took me."

"You were in the heavens with the gods."

"That's something you tell a grieving child!"

"I—I didn't, I—" His face turned gray. "Forgive me, Great One."

"I am not a god!" She pushed him, all control gone. He tripped over a bench and dropped to the floor. "Send me back."

"I cannot."

Her sword flew from its sheath before she realized she held it. "Send me back!" She held it to his neck. Her arms trembled with the desire to run it through him. But it would not move.

She leaned on the blade, digging her feet into the floor. "You ripped me out of time and took me from my children."

He shook his head. "It had already happened."

"Because of you." Her sword crept closer, pricking a drop of blood from his neck. What protected him?

Halldór lay on his back. "I'm sorry. I didn't know… I was following the prophecy."

Reiko staggered. Prophecy. A wall of predestination. Empty, she dropped to the bench and cradled her sword. "How long ago…?"

"Six thousand years."

She closed her eyes. This was why he could not return her. He had not simply brought her from across the sea like the other "gods." He had brought her through time. If she were trapped here, if she could never see her children again, it did not matter if these were human or demons. She was banished in Hell.

"What do the sagas say about my children?"

Halldór rolled to his knees. "I can show you." His voice shook.

"No." She ran her hand down the blade of her sword. Its edge whispered against her skin. She touched her wrist to the blade. It would be easy. "Read it to me."

She heard him get to his feet. The pages of the heavy book shuffled.

Halldór swallowed and read, "This is from the Saga of Li Nawi, the Book of the Sword, Chapter Two. 'And it came to pass that Li Aya and Li Nawi were raised unto adulthood by their tutor.'"

A tutor raised them, because he, Halldór, had pulled their mother away. He shook his head. It had happened six thousand years ago.

"'But when they reached adulthood, each claimed the right of Li Reiko's sword.'"

They fought over the sword, with which he had called her, not out of the heavens, but from across time. Halldór shivered and focused on the page.

"'Li Aya challenged Li Nawi, saying Death was her birthright. But Nawi, on hearing this, scoffed and said he was a Child of Death. And saying so, he took Li Reiko's sword and the gods smote Li Aya with their fiery hand, thus granting Li Nawi the victory.'"

Halldór's entrails twisted as if the gods were reading them. He had read these sagas since he was a boy. He believed them, but he had not thought they were real. He looked at Li Reiko. She held her head in her lap and rocked back and forth.

For all his talk of prophecies, he was the one who had found the sword and invoked it. "'Then all men knew he was the true Child of Death. He raised an army of men, the First of the Nine Armies, and thus began the Collapse—'"

"Stop."

"I'm sorry." He would slaughter a thousand sheep if one would tell him how to undo his crime. In the Saga of Li Nawi, Li Reiko never appeared after the wall of fire. He closed the book and took a step toward her. "The price you asked… I can't send you back."

Li Reiko drew a shuddering breath and looked up. "I have already paid the price for you." Her eyes reflected his guilt. "Another hero can kill the Troll King."

His pulse rattled forward like a panicked horse. "No one else can. The prophecy points to you."

"Gut a new sheep, bound man. I won't help you." She stood. "I release you from your debt."

"But, it's unpaid. I owe you a life."

"You cannot pay the price I ask." She turned and touched her sword to his neck again. He flinched. "I couldn't kill you when I wanted to." She cocked her head, and traced the point of the blade around his neck, not quite touching him. "What destiny waits for you?"

"Nothing." He was no one.

She snorted. "How nice to be without a fate." Sheathing her sword, she walked toward the door.

He followed her. Nothing made sense. "Where are you going?" She spun and drove her fist into his midriff. He grunted and folded over the pain. Panting, Reiko pulled her sword out and hit his side with the flat of her blade. Halldór held his cry in.

She swung again, with the edge, but the wall of force stopped her; Halldór held still. She turned the blade and slammed the flat against his ribs again. The breath hissed out of him, but he did not move. He knelt in front of her, waiting for the next blow. He deserved this. He deserved more than this.

Li Reiko's lip curled in disgust. "Do not follow me."

He scrabbled forward on his knees. "Then tell me where you're going, so I will not meet you by chance."

"Maybe that is your destiny." She left him.

Halldór did not follow her.

Li Reiko chased her shadow out of the Parliament lands. It stretched before her in the golden light of sunrise, racing her across the moss-covered lava. The wind, whipping across the treeless plain, pushed her like a child late for dinner.

Surrounded by the people in the Parliament lands, Reiko's anger had overwhelmed her and buried her grief. Whatever Halldór thought her destiny was, she saw only two paths in front of her—make a life here or join her children in the only way left. Neither were paths to choose rashly.

Small shrubs and grasses broke the green with patches of red and gold, as if someone had unrolled a carpet on the ground. Heavy undulations creased the land with crevices. Some held water reflecting the sky, others dropped to a lower level of moss and soft grasses, and some were as dark as the inside of a cave.

When the sun crossed the sky and painted the land with long shadows, Reiko sought shelter from the wind in one of the crevices. The moss cradled her with the warmth of the earth.

She pulled thoughts of Aya and Nawi close. In her memory, they laughed as they reached for her. Sobs pushed past Reiko's reserves. She wrapped her arms around her chest. Each cry shattered her. Her children were dead because Halldór had decided a disemboweled sheep meant he should rip her out of time. It did not matter if they had grown up; she had not been there. They were six thousand years dead. Inside her head, Reiko battled grief. Her fists pounded against the walls of her mind. *No.* Her brain filled with that silent syllable.

She pressed her face against the velvet moss wanting the earth to absorb her.

She heard a sound.

Training quieted her breath in a moment. Reiko lifted her head from the moss and listened. Footsteps crossed the earth above her. She manifested her armor and rolled silently to her feet. If Halldór had followed her, she would play the part of a man and seek revenge.

In the light of the moon, a figure, larger than a man, crept toward her. A troll. Behind him, a gang of trolls watched. Reiko counted them and considered the terrain. It was safer to hide, but anger still throbbed in her bones. She left her sword sheathed and slunk out of the crevice in the ground. Her argument was not with them.

Flowing across the moss, she let the uneven shadows mask her until she reached a standing mound of stones. The wind carried the trolls' stink to her.

The lone troll reached the crevice she had sheltered in. His arm darted down like a bear fishing and he roared with astonishment.

The other trolls laughed. "Got away, did she?"

One of them said, "Mucker was smelling his own crotch is all."

"Yah, sure. He didn't get enough in the Hall and goes around thinking he smells more."

They had taken human women. Reiko felt a stabbing pain in her loins; she could not let that stand.

Mucker whirled. "Shut up! I know I smelled a woman."

"Then where'd she go?" The troll snorted the air. "Don't smell one now."

The other lumbered away. "Let's go, while some of 'em are still fresh."

Mucker slumped and followed the other trolls. Reiko eased out of the shadows. She was a fool, but would not hide while women were raped.

She hung back, letting the wind bring their sounds and scents as she tracked the trolls to their Hall.

The moon had sunk to a handspan above the horizon as they reached the Troll Hall. Trolls stood on either side of the great stone doors.

Reiko crouched in the shadows. The night was silent except for the sounds of revelry. Even with alcohol slowing their movement, there were too many of them.

If she could goad the sentries into taking her on one at a time she could get inside, but only if no other trolls came. The sound of swordplay would draw a crowd faster than crows to carrion.

A harness jingled.

Reiko's head snapped in the direction of the sound.

She shielded her eyes from the light coming out of the Troll Hall. As her vision adjusted, a man on horseback resolved out of the dark. He sat twenty or thirty horselengths away, invisible to the trolls outside the Hall. Reiko eased toward him, senses wide.

The horse shifted its weight when it smelled her. The man put his hand on its neck, calming it. Light from the Troll Hall hinted at the planes on his face. Halldór. Her lips tightened. He had followed her. Reiko warred with an irrational desire to call the trolls down on them.

She needed him. Halldór, with his drawings and histories, might know what the inside of the Troll Hall looked like.

Praying he would have sense enough to be quiet, she stepped out of the shadows. He jumped as she appeared, but stayed silent.

He swung off his horse and leaned close. His whisper was hot in her ear. "Forgive me. I did not follow you."

He turned his head, letting her breathe an answer in return. "Understood. They have women inside."

"I know." Halldór looked toward the Troll Hall. Dried blood covered the left side of his face.

"We should move away to talk," she said.

He took his horse by the reins and followed her. His horse's hooves were bound with sheepskin so they made no sound on the rocks. Something had happened since she left the Parliament lands.

Halldór limped on his left side. Reiko's heart beat as if she were running. The trolls had women prisoners. Halldór bore signs of battle. Trolls must have attacked the Parliament. They walked in silence until the sounds of the Troll Hall dwindled to nothing.

Halldór stopped. "There was a raid." He stared at nothing, his jaw clenched. "While I was gone… they just let the trolls—" His voice broke like a boy's. "They have my girl."

Mara. Anger slipped from Reiko. "Halldór, I'm sorry." She looked for other riders. "Who came with you?"

He shook his head. "No one. They're guarding the walls in case the trolls come back." He touched the side of his face. "I tried persuading them."

"Why did you come?"

"To get Mara back."

"There are too many of them, bound man." She scowled. "Even if you could get inside, what do you plan to do? Challenge the Troll King to single combat?" Her words resonated in her skull. Reiko closed her eyes, dizzy with the turns the gods spun her in. When she opened them, Halldór's lips were parted in prayer. Reiko swallowed. "When does the sun rise?"

"In another hour."

She turned to the Hall. In an hour, the trolls could not give chase; the sun would turn them to stone. She unbraided her hair.

Halldór stared as her long hair began flirting with the wind. She smiled at the question in his eyes. "I have a prophecy to fulfill."

Reiko stumbled into the torchlight, her hair loose and wild. She clutched Halldór's cloak around her shoulders.

One of the troll sentries saw her. "Hey. A dolly."

Reiko contorted her face with fear and whimpered. The other troll laughed. "She don't seem taken with you, do she?"

The first troll came closer. "She don't have to."

"Don't hurt me. Please, please…" Reiko retreated from him. When she was between the two, she whipped Halldór's cloak off, tangling it around the first troll's head. With her sword, she gutted the other. He dropped to his knees, fumbling with his entrails as she turned to the first. She slid her sword under the cloak, slicing along the base of the first troll's jaw.

Leaving them to die, Reiko entered the Hall. Women's cries mingled with the sounds of debauchery.

She kept her focus on the battle ahead. She would be out-matched in size and strength, but hoped her wit and weapon would prevail. Her mouth twisted. She knew she would prevail. It was predestined.

A troll saw her. He lumbered closer. Reiko showed her sword, bright with blood. "I have met your sentries. Shall we dance as well?"

The troll checked his movement and squinted his beady eyes at her. Reiko walked past him. She kept her awareness on him, but another troll, Mucker, loomed in front of her.

"Where do you think you're going?"

"I am the one you sought. I am Chooser of the Slain. I have come for your King."

Mucker laughed and reached for her, heedless of her sword. She dodged under his grasp and held the point to his jugular. "I have come for your King. Not for you. Show me to him."

She leapt back. His hand went to his throat and came away with blood.

A bellow rose from the entry. Someone had found the sentries. Reiko kept her gaze on Mucker, but her peripheral vision filled with trolls running. Footsteps behind her. She spun and planted her sword in a troll's arm. The troll howled, drawing back. Reiko shook her head. "I have come for your King."

They herded her to the Hall. She had no chance of defeating them, but if the Troll King granted her single combat, she might escape the Hall with the prisoners. When she entered the great Hall, whispers flew; the number of slain trolls mounted with each rumor.

The Troll King lolled on his throne. Mara, her face red with shame, serviced him.

Anger buzzed in Reiko's ears. She let it pass through her. "Troll King, I have come to challenge you."

The Troll King laughed like an avalanche of stone tearing down his Hall. "You! A dolly wants to fight?"

Reiko paid no attention to his words.

He was nearly twice her height. Leather armor, crusted with crude bronze scales, covered his body. The weight of feast hung about his middle, but his shoulders bulged with muscle. If he connected a blow, she would die. But he would be fighting gravity as well as her. Once he began a movement, it would take time for him to stop and begin another.

Reiko raised her head, waiting until his laughter faded. "I am the Chooser of the Slain. Will you accept my challenge?" She forced a smile to her lips. "Or are you afraid to dance with me?"

"I will grind you to paste, dolly. I will sweep over your lands and eat your children for my breakfast."

"If you win, you may. Here are my terms. If I win, the prisoners go free."

He came down from his throne and leaned close. "If you win, we will never show a shadow in human lands."

"Will your people hold that pledge when you are dead?"

He laughed. The stink of his breath boiled around her. He turned to the trolls packed in the Hall. "Will you?"

The room rocked with the roar of their voices. "Aye."

The Troll King leered. "And when you lose, I won't kill you till I've bedded you."

"Agreed. May the gods hear our pledge." Reiko manifested her armor.

As the night black plates materialized around her, the Troll King bellowed, "What is this?"

"This?" She taunted him. "This is but a toy the gods have sent to play with you."

She smiled in her helm as he swung his heavy iron sword over his head and charged her. Stupid. Reiko stepped to the side, already turning as she let him pass.

She brought her sword hard against the gap in his armor above his boot. The blade jarred against bone. She yanked her sword free; blood coated it like a sheath.

The Troll King dropped to one knee, hamstrung. Without waiting, she vaulted up his back and wrapped her arms around his neck. *Like Aya riding piggyback.* He flailed his sword through the air, reaching for her. She slit his throat. His bellow changed to a gurgle as blood fountained in an arc, soaking the ground.

A heavy ache filled her breast. She whispered in his ear. "I have killed you without honor. I am a machine of the gods."

Reiko let gravity pull the Troll King down, as trolls shrieked. She leapt off his body as it fell forward.

Before the dust settled around him, Reiko pointed her sword at the nearest troll. "Release the prisoners."

Reiko led the women into the dawn. As they left the Troll Hall, Halldór dropped to his knees with his arms lifted in prayer. Mara wrapped her arms around his neck, sobbing.

Reiko felt nothing. Why should she, when the victory was not hers? She withdrew from the group of women weeping and singing her praises.

Halldór chased her. "Lady, my life is already yours but my debt has doubled."

He reminded her of a suitor in one of Aya's bedtime stories, accepting gifts without asking what the witchyman's price would be. She knelt to clean her sword on the moss. "Then give me your firstborn child."

She could hear his breath hitch in his throat. "If that is your price."

Reiko raised her eyes. "No. That is a price I will not ask."

He knelt beside her. "I know why you cannot kill me."

"Good." She turned to her sword. "When you fulfill your fate let me know, so I can."

His blue eyes shone with fervor. "I am destined to return your daughter to you."

Reiko's heart flooded with pain and hope. She fought for breath. "Do not toy with me, bound man."

"I would not. I reviewed the sagas after you went into the Hall. It says 'and the gods smote Li Aya with their fiery hand.' I can bring Li Aya here."

Reiko sunk her fingers into the moss, clutching the earth. Oh gods, to have her little girl here—she trembled. Aya would not be a child. There would be no games of hide and seek. *When they reached adulthood, each claimed the right of Li Reiko's sword...* How old would Aya be?

Reiko shook her head. She could not do that to her daughter. "You want to rip Aya out of time as well. If Nawi had not won, the Collapse would not have happened."

Halldór brow furrowed. "But it already did."

Reiko stared at the women, and the barren landscape beyond them. Everything she saw was a result of her son's actions. Or were her son's actions the result of choices made here? She did not know if it mattered. The cogs in the gods' machine clicked forward.

"Are there any prophecies about Aya?"

Halldór nodded. "She's destined to—"

Reiko put her hand on his mouth as if she could stop fate. "Don't." She closed her eyes, fingers still resting on his lips. "If you bring her, promise me you won't let her know she's bound to the will of the gods."

He nodded.

Reiko withdrew her hand and pressed it to her temple. Her skull throbbed with potential decisions. Aya had already vanished into fire; if Reiko did not decide to bring her here, where would Aya go?

Her bound man knelt next to her, waiting for her decision. Aya would not forgive Reiko for yanking her out of time, anymore than Reiko had forgiven Halldór.

His eyes flicked over her shoulder and then back. Reiko turned to follow his gaze. Mara comforted another girl. What did the future hold for Halldór's daughter? In this time, women seemed to have no role.

But times could change. Watching Mara, Reiko knew which path to choose if she were granted free will.

"Bring Aya to me." Reiko looked at the sword in her hand. "My daughter's birthright waits for her."

PRIDE AND JOY
BY ERIC LANDRENEAU

"**S**hit, you're an even uglier bitch than they said!"

I look up from the shield-strap I'm adjusting to see Regana leaning against the door-frame. She's wearing a quilted, padded subarmallis set; vest, leggings, soft boots, arm bands. And her belt, of course. Ten years running and no-one's taken it from her. My heart skips a beat, but I don't show it. The scar across my mouth pulls my face off-kilter, so my smile looks like a sneer, or a snarl. I've learned to use that. "Each scar's a story, and there's a dead Dhrastli at the end of every one."

She looks at me like a maggot in her rice. "So you think having killed a few heathen spear-slaves has given you the chops to take me down in the Arena?"

I set my shield down, shifting as I do so to obscure the carapace on the bench behind me. No fun in spoiled surprises. Then I look right at her, displaying more confidence than I actually feel. "You do. Else you wouldn't be here trying to shake me up before we meet on the rusty sands."

Tall, hard, mighty Regana arches one beautiful, golden eyebrow and crosses her arms. Only the lowest clasps are fastened on her vest, and Pride and Joy crowd into the breach. "I've held my title for over ten years," she says, "by right of might alone. I don't need tricks. I'm just here to look you in the eye before I gut you for the masses. See if you're worth respecting."

I shrug. "I should feel honored?"

Regana's face darkens. I guess I'm not groveling enough. Never was good at that sort of thing. "You should," she says. "This city worships me. This time tomorrow I'll reign as I do today, and the Mad Boar will be just a memory."

I sigh. "Wish I knew where that damn name comes from. Since we're being all cordial, you should know my given name is Elaine. And the future will be written by blood, not your words."

She laughs, and my eyes lock onto the heavy cleft between her heaving breasts. I taste blood, and look away. Regana is too busy composing her speech to notice. "Bold words for such stumpy, ugly fresh meat! And true! But it's your blood'll be the ink, and my blade the quill!" She leans over me, hair cascading over her broad shoulder in a perfumed wave, vest falling open. "I'll give you credit for climbing this far. You've got—" She finally realizes that I'm fixated on her Pride and Joy, and breathing hard. I lick my lips as the airy, coppery taste of blood dances across my tongue and up my throat to tease my scarred nose. Her eyes narrow and her lips pull into a mocking, satisfied smile. "You're sly, aren't you? I shoulda known. You've got the thick, dumpy body of a dyke. Here."

She yanks her vest open and stands up straight. She hefts Pride, then Joy, arches her back and caresses them. Then she snaps her vest shut and glares at me.

If I could adequately describe the look on her face, I'd have long ago abandoned the hammer for the quill. Haughty, yes. And victorious. Her face expressed the exact quantity of loathing I should feel for my pitiful self, and how high above me I should perceive her to be. I'd seen others try to wear such an expression, but I think Regana was born with it on her face.

She hmphs in a self-satisfied way as she fastens the clasps. "A gift. A chance to witness perfect beauty before I hack you apart for sport."

She turns, triumphant, and strides back to her prep quarters (much bigger than the closet I've been given) to don her armor and prepare for the fore-mentioned hacking.

I breathe again as the taste of blood fades, reach back, and trace my fingers over the contours of my carapace. It'll be over soon, one way or another. She thinks she'd won a victory, thrown a dyke off-balance with her distracting bosoms. But she'd read me totally wrong. True, I have a bit of a preference for women, but it's not her Pride and Joy that had me so riveted. I'd touched them before, not that she'd remember. No, I don't give a used moon-rag about her stupid tits. It's that soft, breakable plate of cartilage between them that's got my blood up today.

Regana and I last met almost ten years ago. I was then an unscarred girl just budding into womanhood, not particularly pretty, already showing that I'd inherited more of my father's physique than my mother's. Regana, however, was taller and stronger than most men, beautiful, powerful, every inch of her somehow perfectly balanced between athletic muscularity and womanly allure. (Many suspected black magic.) She'd taken the champion's belt—and kept it for over a year by then—without taking a single wound. No one could touch her, she was so quick and agile. And she had plenty of brawn to match—it was no easy thing to cut a man in half, yet it was getting to be expected of her by the time we met. A signature move.

So it is no wonder one as famously elevated as her didn't recognize me. Who would recognize a mule one once passed on the road from any other?

Regana came into our smithy, unannounced, and the world stopped. I gaped at her, an impossible dream standing under our roof, breathing in our smoky air. Father glanced up from his work to tell her he'd be a moment, then brought his hammer down. I couldn't believe it. There she was—she, She! The most famous gladiatrix in Baygonne—the only one called, simply, the Gladiatrix—and my father was making her wait. He struck again, then again, inspected, shifted the piece on the mold, braced, then struck again. Finally he inspected, nodded, and cooled the piece in water. He set the hammer down and moved around the anvil. "Beggin' your pardon," he said with a bow. "Delayin' would have ruined it."

Regana said, "Hmph," and looked around our shop. People stopped in the street, held back by her litter-bearers, and stared in through the open front of Father's smithy. They were as stone-cold stunned to see her as I was. She wore a light, floor-length gown of material so airy it might as well have not been there, cinched tight at the waist by her broad championship belt with its heavy gold medallions. The furnace made it sweltering in Father's smithy, and the gauzy fabric stuck to her.

Seeing Regana's body was not unusual—the way she flaunted it was already a legend, even then. She only wore armor in the arena when she thought she might need it. The less she thought of an opponent's mettle, the less she wore. It got to the point that opponents would piss down their greaves if they saw the Gladiatrix step onto the sands wearing nothing but a helm and sword-belt—quite the opposite of the expected reaction. The crowd loved it—horny men and idolizing women alike, and me somewhere between the two.

So it is no wonder that, turning around and finding my idol, my goddess, a scant few feet away, I was rendered helplessly stupid.

Father smacked me in the back of the head. "Oi! Din' ya hear me girl? Fetch the lady summin' cool. Can't you see she's sweating?"

Oh, I saw all right.

I scrambled back into our apartments behind the smithy, carved deep into Baygonne's Cliff. Furthest back was our pantry, always cool, even as the arid world outside baked. I unstoppered an amphora of precious white wine, poured a cupful and knocked it back. Then I filled it again. The wine went a long way to blunt my jangly nerves. But then I thought of the impending contact between Regana's lips and the very cup which mine had just kissed, and my heart roared back to full speed. I waited, breathing deep for a few minutes, letting the wine's magic further saturate my blood, until I was composed enough to bring the Gladiatrix her refreshment.

She didn't even look at me as she took the cup from my shaking hands and gulped down half of it.

She and Father were talking shop.

"You're looking for something less mundane?" he asked.

"Quite. Won't do for me to wear a common soldier's armor anymore." She tapped a finger on the glazed earthenware cup. "That is unexpectedly fine wine."

My father inclined his head. "While I live modestly, I do understand and prize quality in craftsmanship."

There was a slight relaxation of her lips and the set of her shoulders. "So says your reputation. That's why I'm here. The 'Young Master,' you're called among the Guild Armorers. A Master of every sanctioned technique and design, and an unmatched innovator. I seek to be armored, without hiding an inch of my beauty." She stood taller, pulling the sheer gown distractingly tight. "I need an innovator, not a hidebound master."

"Hmm..." Father moved to a worktable and scribbled notes in chalk on a slate. "You've an aggressive style. Movement is your sharpest weapon. So light weight and flexibility will be paramount." His eyes flicked from her to the slate as the chalk snicked and scratched. "I've never actually seen someone land a proper blow on you."

Regana scoffed and rolled her eyes. "If I were foolish enough to think myself invincible, I wouldn't be here. My fame will grow. Greater challengers will come to me. One day someone will manage to knock me down. Your job is to ensure that I am still alive to get up and kill them."

"Sensibility. That's your first layer of armor right there. So, when you *are* hit, we can expect the blow to be hard, and well-aimed. I'll draw up an estimate. Some of the metals are quite rare, but worth—"

She waved his worries away. "Send your bills to my manager. They'll be taken care of."

Father shrugged. "As you say." He gestured to a curtained alcove. "If you'll follow my daughter, she'll take your measurements."

Regana scowled. "What are you, pious? I'm to trust your child to measure me well?"

Father snorted. "Religion's got nothin' to do with it. Elaine's my apprentice. She takes all measurements, men and women. Sews all the subarmallis, even yours. An' her sweat an' blood'll be right there in the metal with mine. Her measurements are never wrong. Might even be a better metalworker than me one day."

On any other day I would have wept to hear such praise from Father, but on that day I was too starstruck, too focused on staring and not staring at the living goddess before me.

The Gladiatrix eyed me. "Very well."

My heart sank as she disappeared from view behind the curtain. Then my father grunted harshly, snapping me out of my daze enough to remember that I was supposed to follow her. I snatched up my knotted measuring cord and scampered in behind her.

Regana's gown was already wadded up on a bench when I entered. She responded with mute boredom as I instructed her to hold her arm like this, her leg like that. She was entirely unimpressed with her own nakedness, but my hands shook as they maneuvered my knotted cord here and there across her body. My breath caught. I sweated. My heart's thunder roared in my ears. Time and again the chalk flew from my clumsy fingers, and my notes were childlike and crabby. Meanwhile she just stood there, oblivious to me as anything more than a nuisance she had to endure.

For weeks we toiled, Father and I. Metals with astounding properties and exotic names drifted into our smithy from across the Empire and beyond. We hammered, folded, melted, bound layers of different metals with works of chemistry, alchemy and wizardry to create segments of unparalleled durability and lightness.

When each day's smithing was done, I worked on her subarmallis while Father wrote in his journal. Bloody, abraded fingers marked my learning curve with the strange materials Father had ordered—black silk from iron spiders, incredibly resistant to penetration (and a bitch to stitch, even with orc-gut thread and a needle of pure titan-metal) stuffed with chameleon wool to wick away sweat.

During one evening of quiet work, the needle caught on a bind in the fabric. I pushed, pushed and, without warning, it gave. "Shit!" I dropped my work and pulled the needle out of my finger.

Father looked up from his journal. "You all right?"

I wrapped a rag around my finger and nodded. "My hands are just tired from the metalwork. I was impatient, pushed too hard."

Father nodded. "It's hard, creating something new. Every step is a foreign country. That's why I keep this journal. For you. You see and feel every step of the work, but the details matter. Materials, ratios, temperature, proper timing for imbuing the spellcraft. I keep it all in here. Every experiment, every failure, each success. When this work is done, I'll take up sewing at night, and you will begin studying this." He thumped the book. "You will repeat everything I've done, and thus learn all I know."

My eyes watered. "I— That—"

He smiled. "The guild is already reviewing my petition to grant you true apprentice status. I said you would surpass me, and I meant it. "

A fire filled my heart and hands from then on, an echo of the involved passion I'd seen written on his face before, which I had never understood. When we took to the forge the next day, I saw the work differently. It was not something I was helping Father with. It was also, now, mine.

Finally the day came, Father and I exhausted but ecstatic as Regana approached with her entourage, knowing that our greatest work lay arranged and shrouded on the workbench.

Regana's servants beat back the crowd as she came in. She looked us each in the eye, with a soft nod to my father, then handed her belt to a waiting servant. Not wasting any time, she shucked off her airy gown and stood there in the middle of our smithy in nothing but the briefest cache-sexe. "Well," she said. "Let's see what you've wrought."

Father inclined his head to me. "Elaine, the subarmallis."

I hardly breathed as I dressed her, wanting to burn the experience into my memory. If I'd only known, I would have choked her till she was dead and blue, but instead my mind and other parts heaved as I clasped the arming vest shut across her famous bosom and below her groin. I pulled on sleeves and individual leggings, fastening each to arming points on her vest, protecting the extremities while leaving the vital joints of hip and shoulder unencumbered.

She was stunning already. When I describe the subarmallis as quilted, don't think of the heavy blankets of the far cold south, or the bulky horsehair-stuffed subarmallis you may have worn as an infantryman. No, this padding was as good as armor itself, yet it fit Regana like a second skin, a wash of shimmering black in breath-stealing contrast with her golden hair and skin. Yet this would disperse the weight of her armor, the force of a mighty blow, and never tear or wear. I'd out-done myself. She moved, flexing the outfit, muscles rippling across her back, unimpeded by the subarmallis.

Regana turned to my father, the trace of a scowl marring her delectable brow. "It may serve."

Pride and relief washed across Father's face. "The finest subarmallis ever stitched by either my daughter or myself, and designed to perfectly support the finest armor ever crafted in my shop and, I dare say, in all of Baygonne."

With a flourish Father pulled the shroud from the table. Arrayed like the crown jewels on display, the armor gleamed. Greaves and vambraces, sabatons, skirt of linked scale, sweeping helm with glaring brow, pauldrons fluted to deflect blows, the joints and clever hinges as supple as silk. The Empire worships a vast pantheon, most of them gods of war in one aspect or another. The sigil of a different god marked each segment of the armor, bringing divine protection to each god's favored body part; Rynno's might to the thigh, Crafty Anz marked the helm, Kar Kee Wat the Cleaver of All graced the pauldrons, and so forth.

Chief of all segments was the carapace. A work of genius, and I'm not too humble to say it. The sigil of Ainwug Who Stands, the Victor at the End of Time, hovered over the sternum. Raised ridges radiated from the sigil, swooping below the arm or above the shoulder, following Regana's sublime contours, so that any blow taken on the torso would deflect away from the body.

Scenes of Regana's greatest feats were etched across the breast, filled in colors that would never fade. And on the subject of breasts—though the carapace covered from neck to hip, there was no loss of femininity in the shape. The armor would fit tight across waist and belly, crafted in overlapping lames to allow for supple core movement. The main carapace swelled from the narrow waist upward to encase Pride and Joy—indeed, the very size and shape of Regana's legendary bosom had inspired the force-deflecting shape of the armor.

I tore my eyes from our beloved masterwork, and my world turned black. Father's eyes followed mine soon after, found Regana's face, and his blood retreated to his feet.

"What the fuck is this?"

"Er, it's your…" I'd never seen my father lose his confidence until that moment, and it never came back. "You are displeased?"

"Displeased?" She rounded on him. "I'm fucking furious, you ill-wanked little cum-stain of a man! You useless wad of tripe!"

"But-but My Lady Regana." His hands shook as he approached her, fingers open as if he would grasp her garments and beg. "You have not even tried it on."

Oh, the thunderheads that roiled in her eyes then. "*Try it on?* I'd sooner armor myself with shit than wear this garbage." She loomed closer with each word, breaking my father's spirit as she pressed him deeper into the smithy. "I poured my gold into your shop on the reputation of your abilities, I suffered the awkward groping of that retarded lesbian you call daughter, only to find you cannot count?"

"Wha, what?" Father gaped as if the air had left the room. "Regana, Gladiatrix, I—"

"One, two!" She grabbed his hands, placed one on Pride, "One!" and the other on Joy, "Two!" He tried to pull away, but she held him for an uncomfortable moment as he struggled, then released one hand and slapped him so hard he staggered against a table. "One!" She punched him with her other fist, laying him out flat. "Two!"

Father held up his hands, cowering, a different creature than the man I'd always known. "I don't understand!"

Regana stood over him. "'Make me beautiful,' I said. 'Do not hide me.' And yet you expect me to stand in the arena with a single, protruding lump, like a camel, like the prow of some lumbering cargo ship?"

Father blinked up at her, utterly baffled. "You… you wanted… discrete cups?"

"Of course I did, you cupful of bloody flux! A fortune I poured into your idiot pockets, and there it sits." She pointed an accusing finger at the table of untouched armor. "Wasted, lost, hideous."

"But, the inverted ridge—"

"Silence!" She stomped one foot onto his chest to pin him down, snatched one flailing hand, and wrenched it too far about. Bones snapped in her grip. Father shrieked.

I finally broke from stunned shock and charged, snarling. I didn't know what I would do when I reached her. I knew nothing of combat. It didn't matter. This was family.

She straight-armed me without even looking, checking my rush and knocking me down. She hauled Father up by his ruined hand, grabbed him by the ear and pulled his face close to hers. She hissed, "I'll not send good money after bad, con-artist. Falsifier. Boaster. Someone else will prove capable enough to armor me as I desire. You're finished. Best sell that rubbish fast—you'll be expunged from the Guild by sundown."

She dropped the broken wreck who'd been my father, then attempted to tear off the subarmallis. When it did not rip, she popped the fasteners and yanked the pieces off, dropping them on me, and added a kick to the gut for good measure. She dressed, kicked over the table of fabulous armor, and left us in ruins.

Regana was as good as her word. The Guild may hold the reins of power in Baygonne, but it is the gladiators who hold the hearts of the people. Once The Gladiatrix smeared Father's name, the Guild had no choice but to revoke Father's membership to spare themselves from the plague of public disfavor. Without Guild membership, Father could not smith anywhere in the Empire.

And she'd mangled his strong hand, anyway.

The consequences of her intrusion into our lives came swift and brutal. My sad, broken sack of a father took what jobs a one-handed pity case could find. There weren't many. We sold half-finished pieces for scrap. I hid his journal and Regana's armor away. Father raged when he discovered them, then shortly drank himself into forgetting. Stayed drunk after that. We sold our tools, sold our home. Shortly thereafter, Father washed rat poison down with about a gallon of hooch, leaving me an orphan.

I joined the army rather than Baygonne's horde of prostitutes—they were happier to have a brawny girl like me than any john would have been. Thus began nearly a decade of constant warfare, marching from frontline to frontline. I learned to fight, to kill. Cohesion, discipline and formation didn't come to me so easily, so they slotted me into the Berserker Corps. If you've never seen the Imperial army in combat, then think of it this way: the infantry with their rigid formations and synchronized spear-thrusts were like a sword and shield; cavalry could be swift arrow or shocking war-hammer as needed; and the Berserker corps were the dagger you shoved into the other's neck when you were so close his blood would pour over you. We moved behind the infantry, a restless, twitchy pack, waiting for them to close. When the infantry broke open the enemy line, they parted and we poured through. We fought dirty. Heel, elbow, shield, helm, thumb, blade, haft, stone, stick, I learned to kill with all of them, and more, a savage let loose behind enemy lines.

The army put firebrands like me into the Berserker Corps to use them up. I wasn't expected to go on living. But I did—I just saw Regana's face on every Dhrastli that came screaming at me, and found the motivation to do them before they did me.

Most nights, while other soldiers drank and snored and rutted around me, I studied Father's journal. Father's words and diagrams forged a smithy in my mind. It wasn't the guided apprenticeship I'd been promised, but I hammered away anyway, imagination and memory serving as paltry surrogates for a real forge.

I returned to Baygonne after my service was up, skin toughened, tanned and scarred, my wounded, sorrowing spirit transfigured by time and blood into something hard and hot.

I shacked up with Gath, a blacksmith of little consequence—classified by the guild as suitable for little more than forging farm implements and hardware for saddles and such. I didn't care a damn about his skill, or him. What mattered was that he had a forge, way down-canyon from central Baygonne, with few neighbors. We had a simple arrangement. He could tell people I was his wife, his whore, or whatever he wanted, so long as he didn't tell them what I worked on, and didn't meddle.

You can squirm and judge, and then you can go right to hell. I needed access to a forge, and there was no way I could ever secure guild membership for myself. Ten years in the army had scoured away the frilly dressings girls learn to put on sex. Fucking's nice, if done well, and it's an honest means to an end. You don't split hairs with social niceties when you're bound to get a spear through the guts the next day. Sometimes offering a quick favor was worth it for extra rations. Sometimes a hard ploughing before sleep was the only thing that'd help me not wake up screaming.

Gath tried to turn my offer down—funny how even men like Gath, whose face looked like a donkey's ass warmed over and who received more amorous advances from dogs than women—funny how even men like him try to be picky and hold out for pretty women. I broke into his home that night, proved that the scars meant nothing in the dark, and changed his mind for him. The next morning I rolled his snoring ass off me and conscripted him for a treasure-hunt.

The dried-up well where I'd hidden Regana's armor from my father had crumbled, but a bit of grunt work had it cleared enough to reach down and yank out the loose stone. A line was tied to an eye I'd anchored in the brick, hidden from above. It took two of us to haul up the bundle. Carapace, helm, subarmallis, even the special needles and leftover materials had all weathered the decade well. I'd stashed it all, knowing even then, as a grieving, heart-wounded girl, that I would return.

I went to the Arena that afternoon, decked in my Berserker's kit, armed with shield and hammer, and signed on to the bottom of the Gladiator lists. There were two ways onto the Arena sands. The most common was as a prisoner of crime or of war. The Arena chewed through hundreds of prisoners each feastday. It was cheaper than maintaining jails. Voluntary Gladiators like me joined the lists for prize purses. The game-makers moved Gladiators on to tougher bouts with fatter purses so long as they kept on living, eventually admitting them to the rounds of single-combat against other proven Gladiators.

Thus began weeks of toil. I slept through the mornings while Gath banged away at his plough-blades and infantry pots. Each weekly feast-day saw me in the arena, slaughtering fools for the pleasure of the shrieking masses. I worked on the armor through the nights, after Gath banged away at me for about three minutes and passed out. Didn't lead a complicated life, that Gath.

Re-fitting the armor to myself was not easy. I am not built the same as Regana. Not even if you're slobbering drunk with a concussion and one eye swollen shut would you mix up the two of us. Journal or no journal, I didn't have a fraction of Father's knowledge. I'd worked out all the details over the decade, planned every step I'd have to take to make the armor fit me. Almost every plan was wrong. Making the carapace fit my shorter, broader torso took most of the time I had, and that was after compromise after shameful compromise. I did not have the skills, the familiarity, the tools or the time to complete most of the alterations I had planned. So I cut corners.

I left out the cuisses and upper-arm segments altogether, knowing it would be years before I'd be able to replicate father's clever hinges. Better to re-fit the greaves and vambraces without them, and hope the pauldrons and skirt would hang low enough to close the gap. I didn't even think about trying to alter the complicated gauntlets and sabatons. Hot battles after long marches taught me the value of good boots—mine were broken in so well they were part of me, and I wouldn't dare wear anything else. Same for my leather gloves with the steel plates sewn on the back. Those pieces looked tawdry next to Father's wonderful armor, but fashion was my last priority. All that mattered was that Regana see me, and remember.

For my first few bouts in the Arena, the game-makers pitted me against Dhrastli prisoners in the early rounds of the day—the crowd-warmers. I butchered them easily. I moved up with each feast-day, facing off against wolves, gunny-orcs, frenzies, and worse.

Regana, reigning champion of champions for ten years and more, fought each holy day, and I always stayed to watch. To study. The years had not blunted her a bit—much the opposite, rather. She was a monster, inhuman, godlike. After wetting her out-sized cutlass on a dozen or so armed and armored prisoners—often unarmored herself—she faced off against anyone who'd climbed high enough in the Gladiator lists to challenge her. Sometimes she donned her new armor, sometimes she didn't. Sometimes the challengers stayed home, content to retire as second-best, and stay alive. Most often they didn't, sure they'd be the one to take her down.

It amazed me, even after so long at the front, just how much human meat our Empire could grind through. How much screaming death this world had room for. They kept coming—not just prisoners, but voluntary Gladiators and Gladiatrixes full of bravado and swagger, sure that they'd be the ones to take Regana's belt. They didn't. Digging mass graves was costly, but Baygonne had a seething volcanic caldera nearby that served as a perfect dumping-ground for the Arena's used meat. Baygonne's Stock-pot, we called it.

Three weeks after I entered the arena, I was placed in a three-fighter team and pitted against a Gladiator. I killed each of my cohorts, then cut the Gladiator down myself. That's when the game-makers let me into the Gladiatorial tourney. I began clawing my bloody way to the top, and picked up the name "Mad Boar" along the way.

Each night I continued my work on the armor in Gath's smithy, altering it to fit me as best as I could manage. While Regana caroused in the taverns bare-chested and doused in wine, using people up and throwing them away at will, I prepared myself to humiliate, then kill her.

"The time is close, Boar."

I look at the runner—a comely, unblemished boy, so out of place here below the arena—and nod. I don't need him to tell me. I hear the crowd well enough, swelling and roaring as Regana finishes off a handful of prisoners.

He runs off, and I buckle on my re-fit armor, piece by piece. I take up my shield, and my battered war-hammer. The bladed spikes on the top and trailing edge are in good shape—I don't use them much, but keep them clean and sharp just in case. But the blocky, triple-wedged hammerhead is nicked, scarred, and tarnished almost black. I'd seen Regana's face on every foe this hammer had smashed in a decade of hard soldiering. It wasn't fancy, but it was well-made, and suited me perfectly.

Maybe tomorrow I'll look up the maker. I don't know much about weapon-making. Maybe he would share what he knew. Or at least I could thank him.

But before tomorrow comes today. I'll worry about tomorrow if I ever see it. I march through the tunnels to my gate as the roar of the crowd heaps up.

The gates open on cue, and I step onto the rust-stained sands. The sun burns down, turning the arena into a kiln. A forge. Sandy-red statues of our major war gods rise from the rim of the arena, watching along with the thousands of citizens crammed into the boxes, the cheap stands, hanging from balconies in Baygonne's cliff-wall where it overlooks the hot sands. The people's mouths are open, each a little black gate to hell. Some few scream my name.

"Mad Boar! Mad Boar!"

But most scream hers.

"Regana! Regana!"

"Gladiatrix!"

"Champion!"

The war gods stay silent, their eyes cold and pitiless.

The gates slam shut behind me.

I ignore it all.

Regana stands across the sands, outside of the opposite gate. She wears her armor—so, she has not discounted me.

I taste blood.

I smile.

The gong strikes, and we move to the stone markers of our starting positions. Heat waves shimmer off the sand, bringing with them the stink of death. Here and there lie leftover bodies and bits. Shield high before me, I prowl, circling right toward my marker, matching my foe step-for step as the crowd grows hushed.

This is Regana at her most beautiful. Long hair billowing from below the rim of her helm. Polished black armor chased in bright gold, hugging every contour, amplifying every curve with perfectly formed metal, flawless articulation, sweeping ridges and flanges. Her massive cutlass—as large as any bastard sword, but single-edged, the hilt shaped in a motif of lion skulls, the back edge a jagged sawblade, with a cutout grip a handspan below the tip—her cutlass hangs at an angle across her back. The lion-skull motif is repeated on Pride and Joy; after ruining my father, my life, the Gladiatrix had found a smith willing to shape the armor for each breast separately, as she wished.

She moves languidly, almost neglectful of my presence, a haughty lioness. Joints and nested lames move fluidly as she steps forward, a living statue of Beauty and Menace, a new War Goddess for our pantheon.

So the armor is pretty, and moves well. The armorer has some skill, but I already know him for a fool.

Just before we near our respective markers I lower my shield, exposing my breastplate. There is the slightest hitch in her stride, and I fancy I see a glimmer in the shadowed eye-slit—eyes opening wide in shock.

She recognizes the armor. Ten years on and she doesn't know me from a brick wall, but she recognizes my father's handiwork, even altered as it is for my figure.

Her stride recovers, and she plants herself on her marker, a stone slab one meter across, half-buried by wind-blown and foot-churned sand, identical to mine. She draws her blade, plants her feet, and waits. I raise my shield up to a ready position, war-hammer held low behind me. I can see the waves of menace pouring from her helm's eyeslits, sense it in the tighter set of her shoulders. There is a quiet, windy moment, then the crowd begins stamping. One foot, then the other. One spectator, then the next, then the next, until the entire arena thrums like a giant war-drum.

The gong is struck.

My legs bunch, as do hers, and we fly right at each other. The spectators scream in an ecstasy of bloodlust, but all my attention is locked on her, the black-and-gold object of my wrath. I've got over a decade of pent-up hatred fueling this moment.

She strikes down hard from my left. I take the blow on my shield, not absorbing the impact—I'm strong, not stupid—but turning to deflect the force down and away. I spring to the right, pushing against the force to land to her exposed left. I swing.

This close, I am reminded just how tall she is, how short I am. A wolf-hound and a bulldog. She looms over me. Cracking her skull would overextend me, so I aim for her elbow.

Unable to bring her blade around in time, she wrenches the cutlass across pommel-first, bashing the hilt into my hand, knocking my strike wide. The blade scrapes across the face of my shield.

We both spring back and circle. I'm close enough now to see the dark fire in her eyes.

"You!" she says.

I nod. "Me."

I attack.

We say no more. There's no time for the language of breath and lips. We speak at the speed of steel. I begin aggressively, pressing in with one blow, then the next, knowing that I have no margin for hesitation against her. She parries each strike, feet sure, shoulders ducking this way and that, and within a handful of strikes she's taken the momentum of the fight and turned it back on me. I give ground, parrying and blocking with the shield.

She's good, incredibly good.

Idiot. Of course she's good; she's held her championship for over a decade.

I catch a pattern in her attack, an instinctual recognition deeper and quicker than thought, and use it. I catch and deflect her next blow off of my shield, and am already swinging my hammer, up from behind me, turning and bringing it across into the gap in her defense.

I'm too slow.

She swings to parry my warhammer. I change direction, bind her blade in the crook between haft and head, and jab the edge of my shield for the gap below her helm. She dips her head and takes the minor blow on the cheek-guard. She twists her blade and yanks it downward. I dance backward, the blade just skimming past my fingers. I plant and lunge right back at her, capitalizing on the wide gap in her guard.

I see, this time, as she snaps her sword around. I see it, but don't understand how she manages. There should been too much momentum in that heavy blade, dragging it down and outward, for her to reverse it so swiftly. But she does. Her wrists dance, and the blade of that massive cutlass levels at me like a javelin, her body perfectly aligned to strike. She snaps open like a spring, thrusting for the center of my chest. I'm already committed to my attack, lunging forward and unable to dodge.

One does not normally thrust a cutlass at an armored foe. But Regana's strength coupled with my forward momentum add up to an abnormal amount of force. I have only a moment to prepare for death.

Father is with me.

The force of the blow spreads across my entire torso—an endurable agony. The tip of the sword is pushed to the side of my breastplate, and I slide up its length to bash against her extended arm. I bring the hammer down to smash the back of her crown. She elbows me back and my strike scrapes along the front of her helm instead, skewing her eyeslits but doing no real harm.

As I stagger back, she yanks her sword up, and strikes for my head. I duck down and to the left. Her sword bites into the side of my helm, ripping it off and flinging it away. I barely get my shield up in time to meet her next strike. The shield holds, and somehow my arm doesn't snap, but the force of that blow knocks me down onto my knees.

The toes of my rearward foot catch against the lip of one of the stone markers.

Regana's shadow falls across me.

"A pitiful attempt at vengeance." The sun is behind her. I cannot see the sneer on her mouth, but I can hear it well enough.

Her shoulders shift. She plants her feet. She is going to cut me in half. I'd seen her do it before. I let my shield droop, set my face in a mask of terror. I let the word "Mercy" babble from my bloodied lips. She sees all that, and so does not notice as I brace my right foot against the marker, does not see the leg coiling under me like a snake ready to strike.

She raises her sword high in both hands, smiling. Chopping beaten, unarmed foes in half is her favorite hobby.

I don't need my hammer.

I am a hammer.

I jump, heaving with every muscle from toe to spine, launching myself at her chest before she brings her sword down, my shield braced before me. I slam into armored Pride and Joy, the face of my shield bashing each peak simultaneously with all the force of ten years of hatred.

She staggers back, her cutlass swinging wide as she fights to stay on her feet. Her eyes are wide with shock, her lips gaping for air. She paws at her chest with her free hand. I land on my feet, crouching low, and study my handiwork.

Pride and Joy are dented, both buckled slightly inward, but Regana still stands. Those tit-cups are more stoutly-made than I'd expected.

I don't think, just charge in swinging before she recovers from my unexpected attack. I swing from the right—wham!—and clobber my hammer into the left slope of Joy, or Pride, or whatever the fuck she calls the left one. Cursed stupid thing to do anyway, naming your tits.

Crump!

The armor over her boob twists inward, and already I'm turning my wrist to bring the hammer against the other on the counter-stroke.

She lifts her cutlass, catching my hammer against its blade and bears forward, holding my weapon fast. I push back, eyes locked on hers, refusing to—

Explosion of white fire across the right side of my vision, just ahead of the agony and the realization I'm turning about. I never even saw her left fist—gauntleted—coming at me.

Carved, pitted stone. I'm on hands and knees, staring at the marker. What marker? Where am— War? Why then don't I hear the Dhrastli war chants? I can't open my right eye, can hardly see at all through the starbursts swimming across my left. I try to raise my left arm, but can't. It's too heavy. I wrestle it from the dented shield and reach for my aching head.

Regana's shadow falls across me from behind, and she drops her blade over my head—one hand on the hilt, the other on the grip cutout near the tip. She yanks the serrated rear edge back for my throat as she presses into my back with one knee. I catch the blade on my vambrace, press with everything I've got to keep it from my throat.

Now I remember—I'm in the Arena. Her sudden punch must have spun me completely about, so I'm on my knees before the marker. Regana's trying her second favorite hobby out on me: dull saw beheading.

She leans in, pressing her knee against my back, groaning as she wrestles to bring her blade to my throat. I can't move my head—it's pinned between the lower armored slopes of mounts Pride and Joy. My left arm is braced between the blade and my throat, and my right hand is next to hers, just above the hilt.

I hear the crowd again. I'd been deaf to them. But now, as my arms weaken and the serrated reverse of her cutlass crushes closer to me, I hear them again.

"Gladiatrix! Gladiatrix!"

"Take 'er head!"

"Kill! Kill! Kill!"

The whole of Baygonne, screaming for my blood.

I won't give it to them. I won't give it to her.

I hear, also, a wheezing, pained quality to her breathing. I pull strength from that.

My head is wedged, locked under Pride and Joy. But braces hold both ways. I tense the muscles in my neck for the coming load and rise, taking her weight across my back, lifting her by the tits. I get one foot under, then the next, and rise further. She squawks in surprise as her feet leave the ground. She is unbalanced, without leverage. She reflexively tries to lower herself to the dirt.

In that moment as her arms relax I rock forward to throw the balance of her weight over me. Muscles in my side and belly tear, but I don't let up. I snap shut at the waist like a terrified pillbug. I push with both arms at the same time, throwing her sword up and away from my neck.

The bitch is too dumb to let go, too freaked out by her sudden unmooring. She slides forward off my back, belt and knee and toe clanging against the back of my head, adding to my list of agonies. But every hurt is worth it.

Regana slams down onto the flat stone, spread-eagled and prone. She grunts as she hits, a pained, frightened sound. Already she is recovering, pulling one hand in to push herself up. With her armored weight off my back, a lightness enters me. My taut, bent legs spring, and I hurl myself up, forward. I spread my arms and legs wide, so that my torso will be the first to land. I trust in my father's armor.

I crash onto Regana's back, slamming her down under her own weight, my weight, and the weight of our armor.

Crunch. And then a wet, cracking sound. And then a gurgling cry.

For a few long moments I pant, paralyzed, feeling like there's a blacksmith for every bone in my body, working them between hammer and anvil.

I rise a little, enough to yank off Regana's helm and turn her head toward me. There is still life in her eyes. Bewilderment and life, ebbing away.

I get to my feet, and haul her up onto her knees for all to see. Blood pours out from under her carapace. The lion-skulls of Pride and Joy are flattened, the cleavage smashed inward.

Armored tits may look fetching, but a good armorer sees that distracting cleavage for what it is, from the inside—an axe blade, channeling the force of any blow to the chest right onto the sternum. That's what my father tried to tell her. "Cleavage," indeed.

I raise her up to get one last look at her beloved audience. The people of Baygonne are silent, stunned. Her eyes dart. She tries to move, but there is no strength left in her. She tries to speak, and coughs up blood. I unbuckle her champion's belt and throw it into the dirt. I say to her, "You deserve worse." Then I let go, letting her fall back onto her face to finish dying.

I strike while the metal is hot. Sparks fly, and the steel takes on a little of the curvature from the form.

I move the piece back into the fire and watch the glow return.

I quit the arena after killing Regana, sick of the stink of blood and the sounds of breaking bodies. I left the belt in the sand, let the game-makers decide what to do with it. I used my champion's winnings to buy a smithy.

New champions also receive a boon—a request. Anything within reason. I could have had Regana's villa and servants. Instead I had Father's membership and standing in the guild restored, And I had the game-makers lean on the Guild until they granted me the rank of junior smith.

I move the piece back, holding the curve of metal pinched in tongs. I turn it this way and that, settling it over the form. Hot air shimmers over it, smelling of steel, mingling with my own sweaty stink, reminding me of my father.

The piece finds the right place on the form. I brace, and I strike. It is raw still, untempered, unadorned, no scalloped ridges to channel strikes away from the body. No sigils of war gods. But the shape is right. The foundation is strong. Father designed it. I tested it in battle. I am perfecting it.

Nothing I could ever have done would have changed the past. But I have reclaimed what I could, and will forge what I can from it.

VOICE OF THE TREES
BY GABRIELLE HARBOWY
AND ED GREENWOOD

A tree takes a long time dying. It's a quiet thing; slow. It buds fewer leaves each spring, to reserve its water and energy. Then with a silent sigh, when even a single leaf is too much to give, the long thirst begins. It is a subtle drying. A hollowing. A turning inward. There can be many passes of the seasons from the first weakening to the final, thunderous crash to the forest floor.

Acoria was one with her tree. She knew the signs.

"Shall we talk about your malaise?" she asked, in the language of leaves and wind. He answered with a shrug of branches, unseating a flock of birds to startled murmuration.

"There is an odd taste to the water and I do not care to drink," he answered. "Have you not noticed it?"

"The water has tasted odd before," Acoria replied. "After the fire on the mountain, or that spring when the land slid and the streams changed."

"This is worse. It is not char, nor mud, nor the rot that mud holds. This is… a wrongness."

"Coming from?"

Torian shrugged again, rustling. One of his curled and browning leaves left him and drifted down, a mere dried husk. "From beyond where I can see or taste."

"Then this is my work," Acoria said. She peeled away a sharp sliver of sapwood and thrust it into her heart, so she could travel afar and yet remain with her tree. Tingling life thrilled through her, even as the brief pain died away and the wound she had made closed over Torian's splinter.

That tingling comforted her through the wrench of forlorn loss she always felt when she stepped out of the comforting sphere of Torian's roots and canopy. Two steps away she turned, stopped, and stood gazing at her tree, old and huge and proud, judging him against his neighbors as she always did. As she always told herself she would not do, yet found herself doing again in an unthinking rush, every time. Rooting herself in what she saw, now that she was sundered from it.

"Do not leave me for long," Torian rumbled, sounding less calm than Acoria had ever heard him before. "And take care. Whatever the cause is… it is not to be taken lightly."

"I never take things lightly," Acoria chided.

"For a dryad," Torian said dryly, reminding her of how long he'd stood here; how many trees he'd seen fall, and their dryads with them. Withering away and rotting until the final crash. Or without their dryads, wasting away alone while worldly pleasures distracted their fae.

Acoria shivered and looked away from the two stumps that were nearest, thrusting out of the loam like a pair of gray and misshapen teeth among the soaring trees. She rushed back to Torian's trunk and embraced his rough outer bark, longing to melt back into him.

Instead, she slid around his great girth to his far side, where the mountain rose up against the sun and the forest marched on up its lower flanks, and whispered, "I go!"

She tore herself away, and went.

Torian said nothing at all, though she could feel his silent regard for a long while as she climbed, slipping barefoot between younger, lesser trees. His gaze was as loving as ever, but there were two new flavors to it that she liked not at all.

One was sadness.

One was fear.

From the plateau, Acoria walked until she reached the bank of the river. Here the scent of tainted water was stronger, and a finger dipped into the current told her the river itself had been sullied. Silent, flitting from the lee of one trunk to the lee of another, she went that way.

Half a day upstream, she found the cause.

Humans had made camp at a bend in the waterway, a goodly number of them by Acoria's untutored count. They were felling trees and collecting boulders, and mounding all of it into what seemed at first to be a bridge across the river—here no wider than a stream—but which at closer view revealed itself to be more of a wall.

What reason, even a strange human reason, could there be to build a wall across a river? It was not as though the rest of a human dwelling could easily follow. And when the spring floods came, not even a tall, stout fortress raised all of stone could stand in the river's path and not be swept away.

As that question hung unanswered, and Acoria truly saw all the felled trees, so many, and the size of the pile of split logs, she reeled.

Death, so much death …

She pressed her hand to her heart, over the splinter of Torian she carried, and made of it not just comfort, but armor against the darkness. And felt glad trees could not see through their dryads' eyes.

The smell of corruption grew stronger as she drew nearer. Were the humans making it? She must ask them about their odd wall.

Acoria strode along the riverbank in clear view. When a scout spotted her and shouted, she raised her hand in greeting, her open palm facing out in the human way, to show she bore no weapons.

"Intruder!" the human screamed. "Foul spirit, infesting our water and attacking our town!" He hurled his spear at Acoria.

His aim was remarkably true, yet his cast was long enough that she had ample time to simply step aside to evade it. After the spear thudded into the earth, Acoria wrestled it free and took it with her, holding it out butt-first to offer it back, that its keeper might use it again.

But it seemed humans were prone to take every gesture, no matter how gently intended, as a threat. For now *two* humans charged at her, swords drawn, and Acoria had to swiftly summon the flexibility of a sapling to bend herself away from the shining blades.

"Peace!" she called to them, and "Truce!" while evading their weapons and making no offensive strikes with the spear, but they pressed her in their ignorance, backing her to the edge of their man-made clearing. With a quick apology to the dryad within and to Torian, she took a step back, letting fall the spear, and merged through the bark of the nearest tree.

Its dryad was dormant, sleeping, and did not seem to notice Acoria's presence enough to wake. The tree made apologies for her, but did not try to rouse her. This distressed Acoria more than the humans' aggression. How was it a dryad could be so close to what was destroying her forest, yet retreat into melancholy slumber?

The swordsmen had halted their rain of blows to stand peering about in confusion, asking each other if they had truly seen a woman disappear into a tree, so she peeked her head out past the outer bark.

"If you'll just stay arms a moment," she said swiftly, "I'm not here to fight or to do ill. Only to talk."

One man warily lowered his sword. The other stood at the ready. Both glared at her.

Well, about as much of a truce as she'd expected.

"The water," Acoria asked, "what's happened to it?"

The men exchanged a look.

"The river," Acoria added. "Please, I won't harm you. I just need to know."

"It's you damned elves, as well you know already," growled the one still poised to strike. He spat toward the base of the tree. "It's you who've poisoned the river against us! Now we've got to block its flow before the poison reaches the base of the mountain. Our town."

"What poison?"

The other man eyed her. "You truly know not? Not all elves work together?"

Acoria gave him a shrug. "I know not. There've been no elves this side of the mountain since you humans came, and that was long ago."

Came and killed them, she did not say aloud. Humans seemed touchy about their butchery. Perhaps because they always did it so swiftly. Unthinkingly.

"Except you," the man who'd lowered his blade said accusingly.

"I'm no elf. I'm a dryad. We are of the trees."

The man's eyes narrowed, and his sword came back up. He and the other man both darted looks at the nearest trees as they hastily backed together a step or two. "So there's one of you hiding in every one of these trees around us?"

"No," Acoria said simply. "Not every tree." *Not anymore.*

The men seemed to relax a little.

"Saw no naked women when we were felling," the other man offered, to his companion. "All just wood, through and through."

Acoria tried a teasing smile, but could tell by their changing expressions that it had been taken as something of a challenge. "Can I be trusted enough to be told about this poison? I came here hunting its source. It sickens the trees, too."

The men traded glances again, then the one who'd dared to lower his sword growled. "Can't see it in the water, but it don't seem to harm the birds and the beasts, or make them not want to drink. We can taste it though, right enough, and it burns the belly. Sickens any man who drinks of it."

"How far up the river can it be found?" Acoria asked. Both men's eyes narrowed again.

"What're you planning, elf?" the one who'd raised and lowered his blade snapped.

"Dry-ad," the other man muttered.

"To go and find where the poison comes from, and do what I can to stop it," Acoria said simply.

"How many are there of you?" The man was still suspicious.

"Just me," Acoria told him. "And my name is Acoria. Acoria of Torian."

The two men stirred. Her naming had seemed to shake them, or shame them. Was the giving of names something special among humans?

"Tesker," the man whose sword rose and fell told her, grudgingly, jerking a thumb at his chest.

"Morlon," the other man muttered reluctantly. "Work no charms on us, now! In the name of Lothloan, Lord Of All, I abjure ye!"

Acoria blinked. "Work charms? I'm a dryad, not an elf." Then she swept aside her irritation, tried a smile, and said, "Morlon—Tesker—you have my word. Upon the roots of Torian, I'll work no charm on you. Ever."

Then she gave them the cupped rain-catching hand of farewell and turned away.

She did not look back until she was a good twenty trees away, far enough that no hurled spear could thread its way through. Far enough that they'd be able to see her, yet too far for them to tell just which trees she stood between. They were standing staring after her, but had not followed her a single step. Acoria gave them the weaponless wave and ducked behind a tree. It was a young smoothbark that would have no dryad.

So she went to the earth and crawled, running amongst the roots as dryads in a hurry could do. By the strength of the odor by the humans' wall, it was time for haste.

The roots told her where the river lay, so she could follow it but didn't have to travel alongside it; she could keep it afar to avoid any other humans that might be populating its banks. Occasionally she caught sign of their presence, distant echoes of chopping or hammering, or the unintelligible shout of one human to another.

She went closer to the river when she came to the falls, for humans often seemed to do things to falling water, constructing wheels and bucket-chains and the like.

And yes, it was at the falls, where the water tumbled down out of the rocks from the cliffs above, that the river's sickness was most pronounced. Beside and behind the plunging water, the land rose before her in a huge, jagged wall of rock, the rising side of the mountain. So it was to be a climb then, and one she was glad to have no humans to herd along with her.

Nimbly but with care, looking for signs of humans, Acoria clambered up the rocks, enduring the misty spray of the falls and their odd too-sweet flavor. She kept her mouth firmly shut, but tiny droplets beyond counting seeped into her skin, stinging like tiny spring flies.

At the top of the falls, the mountain went on up, back a ways—but crowning a great shoulder of rock right beside the river, she found a walled enclosure altogether different than the wall that forded the stream. A great square wall of stones, or rather two massive walls with some other sort of stone packed between, to make a barrier as unyielding as the mountain. Much heat and noise issued from inside. As a sheer face of human-piled stone was little different to her than a similar one built by the earth, she crawled up to its top and peeked over.

Within the wall rose a huge bare stone hump like a back of some great buried stone creature, where sweating humans with cloths bound about their lower faces stood coughing in endless snarling smoke, working with long rakes. They were reaching into shallow pits full of charcoal and dancing flames. They all stood downwind of the pits, which had been chiseled out of the hump of stone at an angle to catch the prevailing winds across the height. They were raking at the fire to feed its edges with fresh fuel, or to heap and reheap the charcoal to be hottest around and under open-topped stone molds that stood atop blackened boulders in the searing heart of the furnaces.

A few of them held not rakes, but long stone bars that they pivoted atop other boulders jutting up in the pits, to poke or shove or hook in pairs behind the molds, and so move them gratingly and ponderously in and out of the fires. A glowing liquid shimmered in the outbound molds, as pinkish-orange as some rocks Acoria had seen in distant places where only pracklepines flourished—and she thought she saw stony rubble of that same hue of stone in one mold that sat outside the pits, not yet heated.

Acoria crept along the edge of the wall, past a stretch of it where piles of empty molds were stored. She knew of molds; the dryads often made treats in them, pressing caked dirt or snow or acorn paste into decorative shapes, depending on the season. These empty molds, like the ones baking in the pits right now, were all the same: boulders with rounded, deep recesses chiseled into them. Any pinkish-orange metal melted in them would take the shape of round cakes.

Beyond the heaped empty molds, farther along the inside of the wall, a few smaller humans in rough garments were busily lining empty molds with mud. Beyond them, other humans were loading a small cart with used molds that had been emptied of their cakes, but were crusted with scorched and crumbling mud that had seen too much heat.

The cart was interesting, and by following it Acoria found a gate in the wall that opened for the cart. From the gate, a winding and rutted path that had seen much use ran down to the water's edge. There, two humans washed the molds in the river just above the falls, vigorously scrubbing with stiff brushes.

The scorched sand they were cleaning from the molds stained the waters a dirty gray-green. Its contamination, kicked up into spray by the falls, fell upon Acoria in a shower of fine, fine mist as she skulked along through the sorry-looking, wilted vines and bushes. Instantly, she felt pain and rawness wherever it touched her skin. *This.* This was the poison.

Steeling herself with a hard-drawn breath, she stepped out of the undergrowth, striding toward the two humans heavily as humans did, so her footfalls made noise. The men, their ears full of the noise of the river and their own work, did not turn. Acoria sighed.

"Hello," she called, her hand up in the no-weapons wave. "What is it that you are doing here?"

They looked up. They were astonished to see her, a bare and slender woman, but these two were young ones, mere saplings; they did not leap up to attack.

"We clean the forms we use to make the copper," the larger one told her, pointing at the one he was working on with his brush.

"Copper? Is that what you're scrubbing into the river?"

"This? Nah, this is what's left behind when we take the copper out."

"It is poisoning the river. Could you please stop?"

The sapling blinked at her. "Why would we stop because an *elf* tells us to? If you elves didn't want us to do it, then you shouldn't have taught us how."

Acoria opened her mouth to speak, but closed it again. Then she did it once more.

"Well? Are you an elf or a fish?" the other young human demanded. "Either help us with this, or leave us be. Plenty molds still to do." He pointed at the waiting stones with his brush.

"Stop," Acoria said again. "*Please.*" And she tried to take that brush.

The young man jerked it away from her, then gave her a fierce look and slashed it through the air at her like a woodcutter's axe, in clear menace. "Begone, elf!"

"You are poisoning the river," Acoria said pleadingly. "You *must* stop. Everything below here will die." She approached the other, larger human, and held out her hand in the thin hope he would surrender his brush.

The larger human snorted. "*Everything* dies, sooner or later. And if you want this brush from me, better come back with an army to try to take it! Murthrak hits hard—and holds back supper—if the molds aren't clean before he needs them again."

"Who is Murthrak?" It did not sound like an elven name.

"Lord of all this. Big, muscles, bristling beard. Loud. He's up there overseeing the smelting right now."

"He's not an elf?"

The larger human laughed; the smaller one snorted, and said, "He *hates* elves."

"You said elves taught you to do this. Why would they do that?"

The two men shrugged, and turned back to their cleaning. "They want the copper. They pay Murthrak in food and gems. Murthrak trades them more copper, and we all eat."

"This must stop," Acoria said, more to herself than to the two young humans. This time, only the younger one looked up, and it was to give her a sneer and the words, "Come back with an army."

Acoria stepped back, and then turned away. When armies marched, bad things happened for all. Yet if no army marched, the woods—Torian and herself with it—and the humans downriver would all sicken and die. Were sickening, already.

An army.

She said no more to the two saplings with their brushes. She had not the words, and that sneer had been hot and young.

It takes more than words to move a mountain.

Neither elf nor fish she might be, but Acoria was a dryad with answers. Owing the humans at the riverbend no loyalty, she returned first to her tree.

"Torian!" she called, running with all speed into the embrace of his canopy and throwing her arms around his trunk. "I've not left you too long, have I?"

"Not too long," he rustled warmly, "and your presence is clear water for my roots. What news?"

She slipped inside his bark and told him about the humans and their copper.

"Flamemetal," Torian said grimly. "Elves love flamemetal—they wear it, and make blades of it—but working it sickens them. That must be why they've made the humans get it for them."

"So what do we do? We can't fight humans *and* elves!"

"The way to beat elves," Torian said, "is to rouse the forest against them, beasts as well as roots. But the way to fight humans is with other humans."

"What do you mean?"

"We must deal with the elves."

"They will not come to you unless I bring them," Acoria said thoughtfully. "So that means *I* must deal with the elves."

"Elves do not like to be told what to do by anyone," Torian pointed out. "They will shoot you full of arrows. Copperheaded arrows."

"So I shall die right then, and all the trees and their dryads die after," Acoria said slowly. "We are doomed."

"We are doomed," Torian agreed.

They shared a long and gloomy silence as the sun went down and rested, ere he spoke again. "Unless you can withstand their arrows. They live on the plains, but all elves worship the forest they first came from. The forest, not this tree or that one. So if you tell them you speak for the forest, and invoke the name 'Breit,' they may obey you."

"Breit? Who is Breit?"

"Their oldest goddess. The One Who Shields Us Against Fire, they call her."

"And if they believe me not?"

Torian was silent again for a time, then told her, "We must scheme. It is what elves do, and humans do."

"Will it hurt?"

"Scheming always hurts someone. The trick is to let it be someone else."

"And how do we do that?"

"We trust in this Breit, and in Annyaea."

"And who is Annyaea?"

"Their goddess of good fortune. The luck we will need for this crazed scheme to have any chance of success."

While the sun rested, they fixed their plan. And so it was that as the next dawn broke, Acoria stole forth from Torian, bare as all dryads always went, but for one place: she wore a piece of his bark over her heart. It adhered to her skin as if it belonged there—had grown there.

"Get trees to yield it willingly, in lieu of their dryads going to war with you, and their bark will stick to you and grow upon you, too," Torian had told her. "Make sure you are armored all over, save for your fingertips and the soles of your feet—for the earth cannot send you strength when you are shod against it. That is the mistake humans make."

"Their only mistake?" Acoria had teased.

"Their *root* mistake," Torian had replied, and chuckled.

That slow, deep mirth warmed Acoria as she went from tree to tree, visiting only the oldest trees that had dryads, and roots near the river. As Torian had said, trees who at first were reluctant to give her a piece of their bark, even to end the sickening, parted with it almost eagerly to keep their dryad safe at home, if their dryad was curious enough to want to join Acoria in seeing humans fight humans elsewhere.

It took her an entire rise and fall of the sun to get enough bark that she was covered with widely-overlapping pieces of it, and she spent the resting of the sun that followed rooted in Torian's biggest taproot, drinking of his vitality until she swelled taller and wider, and the overlaps of bark were much smaller all over her.

When that dawn came, she was taller and thicker and fully armored in bark, all but the soles of her feet and her fingertips. She looked like a walking tree, and so walked right into the camp of the riverwall-building humans before they noticed her.

Whereupon they grabbed for their weapons amid much frightened shouting, and Acoria knew fear as swords were swung.

She swayed back, and flung up her hands and cried that she was unarmed, and then caught sight of one of the swordsmen she'd met here before—the one who'd lowered his blade—and went to him.

"You know me, yes? The dryad who came to you before?"

He eyed her warily. "Your face—what I can see of it—looks like her, but you're taller."

"It is my armor."

"So you go to war," he said, and peered hard at the nearest trees that had not yet been felled. "Where is your army?"

"I have no army. I am alone. I am Acoria, the dryad. I walk alone. Tesker, I told you that before."

That brought murmurs from the men who ringed her now, their swords in hand. Acoria turned to look at them all, and explained, "Tesker and Morlon were on guard duty, when first I came to find the source of the taint in the river. I asked them about it—and I swore upon the roots of Torian I'd work no charm on them."

"Who is Torian?" one man snapped.

"My tree. I am a dryad; I am bound to a tree."

"Go get Ulvair," Tesker ordered some of the younger men. Acoria waited in the ring of swords until an old man was brought to join the circle of men.

"What is this?" he asked gently, looking Acoria up and down. "An elf, going to war?"

"Hah! She told us she was a dryad! She lied!" one young man roared, and made as if to jab Acoria with his blade.

Ulvair threw up his hand, looking stern, and that blade stilled.

"We hear anyone before we hew them, Nathras!" he said sternly, then met Acoria's eyes, and added gravely, "You look like an elf, but also not like an elf. And the elves I know go to war with bows and knives and long slender swords, and your hands are empty. So where are your weapons?"

"I have no weapons."

"Magic?"

"Not of the sort that harms." Acoria offered that freely.

A bushy old eyebrow rose, then fell again. "So, Acoria, why are you here, come among us?"

"What taints the river and harms you, also harms me, and every dryad and tree that drinks of the river. I am here as the voice of the trees. We want the poison stopped, as you do. To learn how, is why I wander."

She took an entreating step towards Ulvair, and blades came up all around her, but he waved both hands fiercely, and they went down again.

She was close enough to touch the old man now, and she raised both hands to him. "This is what I have learned. Your wall cannot hold back what is killing you. You must stop the humans atop the waterfall from smelting copper and washing its leavings in the river. *That* is what poisons us all."

Ulvair frowned, but spoke gently. "Which humans are these?"

"I know not, but they are led by the one called Murthrak."

"Murthrak!" some of the men spat and snarled. "That mad, snarling dog! He—"

Ulvair held up his hand, and they fell silent. "Not in front of the elf."

"I am no elf," Acoria told him. "I am a dryad."

The old man peered at her. "The women of the trees? My father's father told tales of them. How they tease and trick men, and lie with them."

"I have done none of those things," Acoria replied. "Perhaps I am not a good dryad."

The old man snorted, in the way men did when it meant mirth. "Well said. I like you, dryad. What can you tell us of Murthrak?"

"He is loud and bearded—or so I am told, by his own folk. He trades copper to the elves, and gets food and gems in return. Those who work for him do this smelting in a stone place they have built, on the height beside the waterfall. If you end the smelting, the river will run clear again, and the sickening will stop."

"Their fort on the height we have seen. We followed the corruption there, but they told us it was none of their doing. *They* said it was fell elf magic."

"They lied," Acoria said simply. "It is something humans do."

The old man snorted again. "And if we march on the men of Murthrak, dryad, what will you do?"

"I will come with you," Acoria told him. "And then I will go, in my armor—" she waved down at the overlapping bark covering her, "—and try to stop the elves, and hope that this will be enough protection when they shoot me full of arrows."

"It is something elves do," the old man agreed gravely, and his eyes twinkled. "Will you bide here, dryad, while I muster all our men?"

"I will."

That was done; when they were gathered, Acoria asked curiously, "You have females, yes? Why do they not go to war?"

"They are the fiercest of us all," Ulvair replied, "so they defend our homes while we are away warring. Foolish is the foe who raids our places when we are away, thinking them undefended."

"Do humans make war often?"

"Aye. It is something humans do. Because, I fear, we are good at it."

The young men wanted to shout as they raced the walls and plunged down among Murthrak's men, but Acoria fiercely whispered that the panthers and wolves and all else that hunted the forest did so in silence, or they'd starve. "Go swift and quiet, and pounce."

"Dryads might fight so," one man sneered, "but—"

"But you will listen to her, and heed," growled Ulvair, "and we shall be silent until we are over their wall and among them. Do you *want* to greet hot coals in your face? Heed the dryad!"

And so it was that the men of the river poured over the stone walls like wolves, raising a ragged shout only when they were down among Murthrak's humans. Acoria ran with them, though a snatched-up fallen bough was her only weapon—and she used it not.

The surprise was complete, and although two men of the river were burned, they felled almost a score of men around the pits ere the rest fled. Murthrak came out of a tent outside the walls, sleepy and bewildered, in time to hear his fleeing men—who had seen Acoria in her armor, leading the men of the river over their walls—shout, "The elves! The elves make war on us!"

"Then they shall have no more copper!" Murthrak snarled, ere he joined them in running away, pelting away through the hewn-down waste of forest with the men of the river in hot pursuit.

"Kill them! Kill them all! Kill the poisoners!" the young men of the river cried, rushing through the trees hacking at anyone they could catch.

Ulvair, who lacked the wind for such work, was not among them. He stood amid the walls, looking around at the sprawled bodies, and the pits, and the molds, then said to Acoria, "Tell me of this. They will come back, or others will. What must we do to stop it?"

"Break these stones, these molds," she replied. "All of them. It will take much time to make new ones; stone is hard. That gives you much time to strike down or drive away whoever is making them. They cannot flee with their stones; too heavy. Break molds until they are tired of making them."

"You are wise, dryad," Ulvair said gravely, nodding, "I thank you. So where, exactly, came the poison from?"

"Through the gate and down the path, to the river above the falls they went, washing the mud out of molds that they put there to keep the flamemetal—the copper—from sticking. That mud holds the poison; it comes out of the copper somehow, when the copper is melted out of the rock."

Ulvair nodded, and waved nearer one old and suspicious warrior, who had been following Acoria about with his sword ready. "Dulvar, count these molds, here and along the wall and down the path to the river. I want them *all* broken, before Murthrak's humans can sneak back and make off with even one."

"What about *her?*" Dulvar demanded.

"Well, what about her? Acoria, where will you go now?"

"Down to the plains beyond the forest, where the elves are," Acoria answered. "For Murthrak's ire may fade when his empty belly grumbles. I must persuade the elves not to train new humans to make copper here."

"New humans like *us*," Dulvar growled meaningfully.

Ulvair frowned and shook his head. "No, Dulvar. Not if the sickening comes from the copper." He looked at Acoria again.

"And how will you persuade the elves?"

Acoria sighed. "I will tell them I speak for the forest, which they venerate, and bid them stop getting this copper, in the name of their goddesses."

"But you are not an elf. Will they believe you speak for their goddesses?"

Acoria sighed. "No. Not if their greed for this copper is too great. Hence this armor."

"Bark. Bark stops no arrows."

"You speak true," Acoria said. "But my armor is *living* bark, given freely from the trees. Elves revere the forest. They cannot knowingly harm the trees."

"So your scheme," Dulvar growled, "is one dryad with bark armor and a stick persuading all the proud elves of the plains. Your plan is doomed."

"True," Ulvair said, "but I do not think one dryad will have to do so. The elves, behind Murthrak and his ilk, are the cause of the sickening, so the elves are our bane. Acoria shall go to persuade them with all the men of the river marching with her."

Dulvar nodded slowly. Then his eyes narrowed again. "Will she not demand a price? There is always a price."

Ulvair turned to Acoria. "Well?"

Acoria drew in a deep breath. "Will you use no fire in the forest, and cut down only the trees I mark?"

"The ones without dryads?"

She nodded. "I go on this errand in the first place so that no more trees will die."

Ulvair nodded, spat into his hand, and held it out to her. Acoria had seen humans do this, and did the same. In such wise, with handclasps, did humans seal bargains.

Ulvair smiled at her. He did not have many teeth left, but it was a nice smile.

THE RAVEN AND THE SWANS

BY AMY GRISWOLD

The elf guards who opened the door of Carlin's cell were ungentle, grasping her by the arms to drag her out into the light. She came out with her head high, shaking back her hair although she knew it to be a rank and tangled mess snarled around the ravens' feathers braided there to mark her as a captain.

The unspeaking guards marched her down a bright corridor. Prisoned between two sweet-smelling men in clean tabards and shining mail, Carlin was all too aware that she stank like the end of winter, that her trousers were stained with blood and worse, that her own armor was gone the way of her sword and bow, and that there was filth under her nails that she hadn't been able to scrub away in cold water.

"I don't suppose your queen would let me take a bath before pronouncing her sentence upon me," Carlin asked. "My people prefer to wash their faces before they meet their doom." She expected no answer, and got none, only the tramp of heavy boots on stone.

Carlin's own doom waited behind two heavy bronze doors at the end of a corridor that reeked of roses. Beheaded blossoms were piled in great basins all along the hall. Some thrall's work, that would be, to mow down roses and pile them up to scent the air so that the elf queen didn't have to smell the muck of her own cells. She straightened her back even further, telling herself it was a good thing she'd put her sword through the elf queen's own brother. At least no one would suggest keeping her as a thrall to do the flowers.

She stepped through the doors as the guards opened them, and into a dream. White marble rose to a great vaulted ceiling hung with rich fabrics in every shade of blue, from the robins-egg color of the sky at noon to the berry-black of the sky just before sunrise. Blood-red roses spilled from urns and twined heavy on lattices against the walls, filling the room with their perfume. One wall was filled with leather boxes crammed side by side on shelves. They might have been books, if Carlin could believe there were so many books in all the world.

The elf queen Genevra stood at an arched window, looking out at the mountains that stabbed up knifelike at the sky. She wore a gown rather than going armed like a war chief of Carlin's own people, but such a gown as made it clear she was no ordinary woman, heavy rust silk embroidered in twining russet vines so intricate that Carlin's fingers ached to think of the hours of needlework it must have cost.

The queen turned, and three things struck Carlin at once; that she looked no older than Carlin herself, though she might be ages her elder; that she bore a strong resemblance to the man Carlin had recently stabbed through the gut; and that her face and her form were beautiful enough to wake a heat twisting in Carlin's belly.

Apparently certain parts of her had gotten the message that she was about to die, and had a last request. More sensible parts of her felt that being run through by a guard for making an indecent proposition to her mortal enemy was not the way she wanted to ensure a memorable death.

"You wanted me," she said instead. "I'm here."

"My brother was three days dying," Genevra said, apparently feeling they needed no more introduction.

"For what it's worth, I'm sorry for that," Carlin said. "I'd have killed him clean if I'd had the time." She'd taken a mace upside the head at that point, and woken dreamless hours later to find herself in a cell alone, her head aching and bloody. "Are the others dead?" she asked bluntly, wanting the worst first. Worse than her own death, to lose all those she'd been responsible for shepherding home.

"Your own men, you mean, those foolish boys with swan's feathers in their hair?"

"My sword-brothers," Carlin said. She'd pledged their lives to her cousin the war chieftain when she brought him the levy of men from her village, friends she'd known since birth, and he'd braided the raven feathers in her hair and raised her up as their captain. Harald and Martin, Rhys and Edric, Cormac and her merry Alaric, the youngest and her best-loved. "There were six who looked to me."

"I have six prisoners with swan's feathers in their hair," Genevra said, and Carlin felt a knot in her chest loosen, her breath coming easier. "The men you led to raid our lands and slay my brother from ambush."

"Your brother marched to war, to join his captains in trying to harry my people back to the hills where we may starve in the snow," Carlin said. "And the lands he was marching over are ours, for all that the sharpness of elf-swords argues otherwise."

"I expect you believe so."

"Have you decided yet how I am to be killed? I have a passing interest in the matter, you understand."

"Traditionally, regicides are hanged," Genevra said, as if it were indeed a matter of only passing interest. "If you hadn't killed a king, you might have died by the sword, but it's felt that the threat of being hanged as a common criminal and left for the carrion birds discourages this kind of thing."

Carlin shrugged. "It'll all be the same to me when I'm dead," she said, though to tell the truth her heart rebelled at the idea.

Genevra looked at her with her head to one side as if she doubted that. "I have written to your cousin to ask him to ransom you."

It was the last thing Carlin expected to hear, and she narrowed her eyes. "Why would you do such a thing?"

"Three reasons," Genevra said crisply. "First, because you have done me a service; my brother and I were not friends, and now he is dead and I am queen. Second, because your cousin is not rich, and every penny he pays for your return is a penny less to keep his army equipped and fed. And, third, because I take no joy in seeing foolish brave children hung up for the ravens' supper."

"I am no child," Carlin said.

"By the reckoning of your people, I am sure you are not," the elf queen said. She bent over a piece of parchment, rolling it up and sealing it with wax the color of a red rose's heart. "Tell me, can your cousin read?" she asked briskly without looking up.

Carlin wasn't certain, but something in her balked at saying so. "If the words are in our tongue." She was certain at least that there would be a priest about who could read it to him.

"Then I will have this sent to him at once, and see what kind of bargain we can make for your life."

"And the lives of my sword-brothers."

"I'm afraid I can't include them," Genevra said. It might have been real regret in her voice, though it didn't make her words any less bitter to Carlin's ears. "Your cousin might pay a few sheep for the lives of common men, but we have little use for sheep. And I must have someone to hang. How else can I show the sincerity of my grief?"

There was a dark humor in her eyes, and against her will Carlin felt an equally black humor kindled. "Half a cut onion will make you weep."

"Alas, my people shed no tears. So I must take more drastic measures."

"You may as well kill me too, then, and prove yourself entirely bereft."

"But I prefer not to," Genevra said. "You may lodge with your brothers if you enjoy hard floors, or you may be my guest until I have your cousin's reply. I set a somewhat better table than my prison guards."

It was on the tip of Carlin's tongue to say that her place was with her sword-brothers. But practicality told her that it was easier to contrive an escape when you had more to work with than a supper-dish and a handful of dank straw.

"You want me to give my parole?"

"Your promise not to harm anyone within these walls."

Carlin looked at her askance. "Not my word not to escape?"

"You will not escape unless you jump from the window, and that I cannot prevent, though I would regret it," Genevra said, and smiled almost kindly. "Now, what would you say to a bath?"

Carlin spent the next week in comfort the likes of which she had never imagined. Her feather bed was deep enough to drown in, even if she slept in it alone, and the cast-off gowns Genevra found for her use would have done for a war chief's wedding day. The food was plentiful, if odd, with the fruits tasting of salt and the meats sweet, and she could have stayed in the baths all day. At night the elf-lights gave a cool green light, like sunlight seen through pond water. It was a pretty prison, but still a prison, and Carlin spent long hours sitting in the arched windows looking out at the mountains on the horizon for some speck that might be her home.

Looking down was less of a comfort. It required only a single glance to see why Genevra was unconcerned about the possibility of her escape. The elf castle perched upon a jagged tower of rock jutting up from middle of a great chasm, with only a single span of stone running from the castle's gates to solid ground. From any other side, there was no escape except the plunge into the chasm. To cross the bridge under a hail of elf-arrows from the arrowslits above would be as sure a death for men without armor as to leap from the window into the chasm.

Genevra dined with her like a friend each night, a familiarity Carlin tried not to let warm her heart. One evening Genevra brought down one of the leather-bound boxes, which proved indeed to be a book, more richly illuminated than any Carlin had ever seen. "I want to show you something," she said, and opened the pages to a map.

"I am no reader," Carlin admitted, although under Genevra's eyes, she wished she had some other answer.

"Only use your eyes. Do you see, here, the boundaries that are marked?" They encompassed the lands the elves had recently invaded, up to the hills where Carlin's people had been driven. "This was our land, and so we agreed by treaty with your people, a thousand years ago. The war chiefs of the bird-folk promised us they would keep to the other side of the mountains and trouble us no more."

"Who remembers what was promised a thousand years ago?"

"Those of us who do not share your short lives," the elf queen said, sounding a bit impatient. There was a spray of freckles across her nose, Carlin noticed not for the first time, an imperfection that only improved her beauty.

"We have never lived beyond the mountains, not in my mother's mother's memory. And in our own lands, we have found a few crumbling ruins, and castoff elf-darts to prick the fingers of our children and poison them, but those things are old."

"We turned our attention elsewhere," Genevra said. "To lands we have now lost. We must have back what is ours. It is owed to us by your own people's word."

"Not my word," Carlin said. "We cannot live in barren land above the snowline to keep faith with a promise made so long ago no one remembers it. And across the mountains there are horsemen with sharp swords who mislike strangers."

"There can be no peace between us if you will not give us what is ours," Genevra said. She touched Carlin's chin and tipped it up, the lightest of touches, her fingers warm against Carlin's skin. "I think we could be friends, you and I. I would like for there to be peace between us."

"So would I," Carlin said, and knew there could never be.

A week was time enough to learn where her sword-brothers were lodged in the dungeons. The taciturn thralls who served in the baths told her that much, and when she begged leave to search for her old clothes for sentiment's sake, pointed her toward the laundry. She didn't have to ask them not to fetch her clothes themselves; none of them seemed the least bit inclined to put themselves out for her, which she supposed she wouldn't have been either in their place.

The laundry smelled of lavender so heavy that it seemed to drug the air, and the human thralls who moved between the steaming tubs moved slowly, their faces flushed and their eyes dreamy. Carlin slipped among them unnoticed, having taken off her rich gown in favor of the linen shift beneath.

She had hoped only to retrieve her boots, or perhaps her leather cap, and came instead upon the best sight she had seen so far: her mail shirt, lying under her discarded clothes, such a commonplace apparently among the elves that it might lie there until it rusted, rather than taking pride of place in an armory or being snatched up at once by a soldier who had only padded cloth to fend off blows.

Carlin wrapped up the mail shirt in a bundle of rags, and hastened back to her room with it. Thrust beneath her mattress she had some hope that it might lie unnoticed. She went to the window and looked down at the bridge, feeling temptation tug at her.

The castle doors were never locked. Genevra had taken pride in telling her so, and in the implication that locks were never needed. In the dead of night she might slip out, and clad in mail, might make it the length of the bridge. She remembered running-races as a girl, and the triumph of leaping across the finish line, and tried to tell herself that running with the hissing of elf-arrows about her ears would be no different. But it would mean leaving her brothers, and that she would not do, tempted or no.

On the seventh day, one of Genevra's thralls came to fetch Carlin to come and hear the queen's doom on her pronounced. She put on her mail shirt under her gown, and wrapped herself in a velvet cloak to hide its shape, uncertain of anything but that if she was to hear her doom, she would prefer to face it with her armor on. She found Genevra gazing out the window at the sun as it sank behind the distant peaks.

"I have no reply from your cousin," Genevra said without preamble. "Only the news that he marches on my lands with his host of shepherds and huntsmen. My guards have marched out to meet him, and should they turn him back, your position will become difficult."

"And if they fail?"

The queen shrugged. "Then you will become an even more useful bargaining piece. But I am afraid your men have outlived their usefulness in either case. I must have a hanging, to avenge my brother's death, before his friends begin to feel that I have outlived my usefulness as well."

For a moment she looked young, and afraid, and Carlin thought of the fear on her cousin's own face when his father had died and left him to lead their warriors, and felt a flicker of sympathy. This for the woman who meant to hang her friends, she thought, and snuffed that flame out.

"And will you leave their bodies for the carrion birds? Is that your friendship?"

Genevra's eyes shifted a little, as if the barb had gone home. "I will see them buried as is fitting among your people," she said.

"Then I must sew their shrouds," Carlin demanded. It was the custom, true enough, and it would give her time, precious time to wait for her cousin's army to draw closer to the walls. She held out no real hope that they could assail the fortress, but any hope was better than none. "If it is not done properly by one who knows the words to sing over the stitches, ravens will come to eat their souls."

"Your gods are merciless," Genevra said.

"They want their due."

"And they will have it from my hand. Whether you believe it or no, I still would be your friend. Perhaps when this business is done…"

"Perhaps," Carlin said, but turned her head away so that Genevra could not see her eyes.

Genevra led her to a room heaped high with linen, and gave her a case of sewing-needles and a blade short enough that it would not have harmed a child. "Take what you want, but I hope you are a quick seamstress," she said. "I can spare you three days, and no more."

"It will be time enough," Carlin said, and cast her gaze about the room. It was a lush bower draped with green silk, cave-like and quiet, and it was tempting to curl up among the great bolts of linen and give in to the urge weep. She hardly needed the time to sew. Genevra's soft fingers had probably never held a needle, but any seamstress worth her salt could sew a shroud in an hour, a shirt in seven.

A shirt, she thought, and fingered the linen. And it was coarse, which was all to the good. She kept her voice hard to hide any flicker of hope. "Once I begin, I must be left alone until my work is ended," she said. "Our songs of power are not for the ears of the elves or their thralls."

"I will have food and drink left for you outside the door," Genevra said. She looked for a moment as if she might say more, but then she shut the door and left Carlin in the cool green sewing-room.

She began cutting at once, and threaded her needle once she had the first shirt pieced out. There was no time to waste in hesitation. She sang as she sewed, not the grave-songs of her people, but battle-songs she had learned at her mother's knee. She thought about Harald, the oldest of her sword-brothers, lifting her up onto her horse when once, wounded, she had gone sprawling into the mud.

It was the ugliest of shirts when she had finished. She flipped another length of fabric atop it and cut the next shirt a fingernail's width larger, stitching each piece to the shirt beneath. Her needle flashed and her fingers ached, unaccustomed to such work. She had traded the distaff for the sword early, but the skills of girlhood came back to her at need, and she sang until her throat was sore.

When darkness came, the elf-lights lit themselves, shedding a greenish light through the room. She sewed on, and the sky was lightening when she added the last layer to the first padded jack, sewing on the last sleeve at the shoulder and the hood at the throat. Her eyes were swimming, and her fingers burned. She took her little sewing knife and plunged it through the fabric at the back. It pierced the first layers but not the inner ones, and she let out a held breath, daring to hope that the makeshift gambeson might turn aside elf-arrows.

She ate, and drank, and slept a few hours curled up among the bolts of cloth, and then began again.

The second padded jack went slower. Her fingers stung and burned and finally bled, and though she would not stop sewing, thinking of her sword-brother Martin coming home with a brace of rabbits slung over his shoulder for the pot, she could not force her fingers to move faster. It was past midnight when she finally finished, and although she promised herself she would only sleep a little while after she ate, it was dawn when she woke.

The third jack was for Rhys, who had twin girls at home who laughed when he swung them high in his arms. The fourth for Edric, who was court-ing a shy, freckled girl who had been white as death when he rode away to war. Her fingers were on fire, blood speckling the linen rust. She sang naming-songs, now, lists of the birds of the ground and the trees and the air, the sacred birds of fire and ash, the hunting birds of war.

The time was trickling away, the third day brightening toward noon. It was tempting to leave off a layer, but then she thought again of the rain of elf-arrows, and she stabbed her needle again through the thick linen. The fifth jack was for Cormac, a stolid boy who preferred laying about him with a stick to learning the art of swordplay. It was dark when she finished, but surely not too far past dark, she told herself. She had no way to count the hours, the elf-lights glowing steadily without the need for fresh candles or oil.

The last of the gambesons was for Alaric, barely out of boyhood, the brother not just of her oath but of her heart. He was merry and dauntless, a scamp with a quick fierce blade and no more eye for women than she had for men. The pain in her fingers and hands was nothing, the rasping croak of her voice as she sang was nothing. There was only the hammering of her heart as she glanced again and again at the sliver of sky outside the vine-hung window, praying she would see black and not the purple of coming dawn.

The sky was lightening despite her prayers, despite the songs she chanted now, raven-songs of death and darkness that needed no more melody than she could force from her hoarse throat. The last of the jacks was too thin, three layers only and no hood, one sleeve thin and missing a layer of cloth, but there was no more time. If they were to escape, she must go now.

She wrapped up the gambesons in a bolt of cloth, and slung it over her shoulder, a great ungainly sack. If she was seen with it, surely the most dull-witted of the elf queen's guards would know it was not shrouds. She dressed herself in her old stained clothes, and kicked off her delicate slippers, wrapping her feet instead in linen and knotting it tight. When she opened the door a cautious inch, the hallway outside was silent.

Down the corridor, and down the stairs to the dungeons, her lips pressed tight to prevent a betraying gasp of effort, and then she stood in front of the cell door. She used the little sewing knife in place of keys, twisting it in the lock with her bruised fingers until finally, on the edge of despair, the lock gave and the door swung wide.

They were all there, the six of them, and they crowded her like joyful wolves, thumping and embracing her until she nearly went sprawling.

Harald hauled the others off, making sharp signs for silence, and Alaric gave her a grin despite the bruises that marred his face.

She handed round the padded jacks, and the men slipped them on, pulling up hoods. She held back Alaric's until last, and started to pull off her own mail shirt. "You'll take this, and I'll wear what I've made," she said under her breath.

"I may be young, but I'm broader in the shoulder still than you," Alaric said, snatching the ragged gambeson from her hands. "This will suit me well enough." He saw her eyes go to the ragged sleeve and the missing hood, and gave her a quick smile, tossing his hair where a few bedraggled feathers still flashed white. "For what should we do if we lost you? Clearly without you we're little use."

"Now's the time to show your mettle," she said. "Out we go swiftly, and through the front gates, and then we run." The elves tamed no horses and followed no hounds on foot, and if only they could get across that bridge, she thought their chances in a running-race were good. "I've promised the elf queen I would harm none within these walls, but outside them all bets are off."

"And is she very fair, this elf queen?" Alaric teased against her ear as the rest filed out.

"Not as fair as our own green hills," Carlin said. "Which you will never see unless you step lively now and end your thrush's chatter."

The entry hall stood empty and the doors unguarded, though elf-lights blazed to sudden green light beside the doors when Cormac and Harald set their shoulders to them. Carlin nodded to urge them on, and the doors were open when two guards appeared in the entry hall.

"Out, out," she cried, and shoved the first man she could reach out into the moonlight. She fled after him, casting a single glance over her shoulder. Cormac was through last, and as the nearest guard reached for him, he tugged the man out through the door with him, and then flung him bodily from the bridge. "Now run!"

It was a footrace, only a footrace, her feet pounding against stone, her legs driving and her chest heaving. Her men were falling in before and behind her as she ran, and she could not spare the breath to curse them for it, when she was in mail and they only in padded linen. Arrows were hissing down at them now, and she felt the heavy thuds as they struck her shoulders and back, bruising but not penetrating the mail.

The arrows were turning on the padded jacks as well, though Edric stumbled and nearly went sprawling into the chasm when an arrow struck his hood. Harald steadied him and hauled him on when he seemed too dazed to know which way was forward.

She was sprinting next to Alaric, now, on his right and beginning to out-pace him, and she grasped his arm to shove him past her, where he would be in the shelter of her body. He stumbled heavily against her, crying out in wordless pain, and she saw to her horror that an elf-arrow had pierced his arm, standing out like a barb from his skin.

"Run," he said, his face white, the sweat coming out on his skin. She could see his hand going purple and then black, the arm shriveling as the elf-dart's poison spread though his veins. But he was running, his legs still working even if his arm was hanging helpless now, and she ran as well, until her lungs burned in the chill air, until she stumbled, finally, when her feet left stone and touched uneven ground.

They were across, but could not rest. She ran on, looking back only long enough to see that a few guards were pursuing on foot, and not gaining ground. None of them could sustain the breakneck sprint, and she slowed them to a hunter's jog, but dared not let them rest. Alaric was still on his feet, though he stumbled as he ran, and the arm the elf-dart had struck was stinking like old meat.

The pounding of her heart in her ears turned to a thunder, and then she realized it was the thunder of hoofbeats. Finally she let herself slow, and stumbled at once in exhaustion. Rhys steadied her, and then bent over his knees, gulping air.

"You'll see those girls of yours again," she said, and as the first of the horsemen neared them, the rider leaping off, braids flying, she let herself sit down, slow and easy like a swan coming to rest, and though she didn't mean to, she closed her eyes.

She woke to warmth, not the sinking softness of a featherbed but the scratchy wool of blankets piled round her. The sun was shining through the flap of a camp tent, and outside she heard the sound of feet and many voices too low for her to make out words, only the reassuring thrum like the sound of many birds flying.

Alaric ducked through the tent flap, and her eyes went wide to see him on his feet. "How long have I been sleeping?"

"A night and a day," he said. His face was haggard, and his eyes bright enough that she suspected his jaunty smile owed much to strong drink. A cloak of swan's feathers was flung over his shoulder, hanging loose enough that she knew there was no arm beneath it. "It was all withered away," he said when he saw her gaze. "The surgeons barely had to cut to get it off me. But it wasn't my sword arm, so I needn't learn how to plow at my advanced years."

"Nor would you make a good farmer's hand, as disobedient as you are." Carlin shook her head at him, and then leaned it back against the roll of blanket that served as her pillow.

"And what about you?" Alaric asked. "Any elf-darts pierce your heart?" He shrugged at her raised eyebrow, and said, "Our guards talked, a bit. Told us you were alive, for a kindness, and that you and their queen were getting on something fine. That wasn't meant for a kindness."

"I'm unscathed yet," Carlin said, though she knew that never again would her heart sing at the scent of roses. Heather and wild onion were good enough for her, she thought, and pushed herself resolutely up to her feet, to go take charge of her men and see what the day might bring them.

THE FAMILY BUSINESS

BY KRISTY GRIFFIN GREEN

The *clang* of hammer on steel is like a song, one Naomi learned a long time ago and still knows how to dance to. One arm stays stock-still, gripping the tongs and holding the metal steady on the anvil; the other swings the hammer again and again, drawing out the shape of the sword in steady, even strokes. It's almost hypnotic: the balance of power and control, the rhythm, the heat of the forge and the yellow-orange glow of the steel shuddering in front of her in the dim light.

It's the work of several hours to forge the blade, but that's okay—she likes the work. It's eventually going to be a replica of an eleventh century Viking sword; for now, it's a long piece of metal slowly taking shape under her hammer as she works on it one section at a time, drawing it to a point, hammering out the ridges, beveling the sides. For a long while there is nothing in her world but the heat and the light and the clang of the hammer.

Finally she's satisfied with the shape and moves the blade to the sword forge, burying it in coals until it glows red and no longer attracts the magnet she waves over it. Then she moves it to one side, turns off the forge, and finally leans back to wipe her sweaty forehead with a sigh of relief.

She hangs up the leather apron with tired, happily sore arms and takes off her hearing protection, turning to go back into the house—then stops, a smile slowly spreading across her face, at the sight of the lunch left out for her on the little chair, far enough back from the forge to avoid getting ash into the food. Ham and swiss on toast and a thermos of tomato soup. Her favorite.

The metal of her right leg taps on the floor as she moves upstairs, munching on the sandwich. She pauses at the entrance to Kerran's computer den, leaning against the doorframe, a soft look in her eyes as she watches her husband work. His hair is as grey as hers now, tight curls close-cropped like so much fuzz; his arms have become skinny old-man arms, and his belly's developed a paunch. But his skin is still smooth and dark as polished walnut, his features still fine, his eyes still merry and wise.

She remembers, at thirteen, thinking he was the most beautiful boy she'd ever seen. She'd rescued him from the Bandit King Ko and his mercenaries and claimed the reward, but at the time she'd thought that getting to ride back with him was reward enough. A year later he'd been the one to rescue *her*, when the Tilago Twins had lured her into their trap. She remembers a terrified teenager stammering spells to distract the twins, sending them off in opposite directions while he snuck in to cut her loose. He'd spent the next several years poring over tome after tome of arcane lore, painstakingly translating the incantations and memorizing the sigils. She'd stayed nearby, always, practicing her endless sword forms and watching him work. And she remembers that final battle against General Zandri—the two of them, back to back, holding off the invasion force with magic and steel there at the bottleneck pass, buying time for the reinforcements to arrive.

She smiles, even as the missing half of her right leg twinges at the memory. Some moments are worth the pain.

He hears her approach—he always does, her leg makes sure of that—but he doesn't turn. She can feel the little half-smile on his face, even though she can't see it—he always likes it, knowing that she knows that he knows that she's there watching him. She moves behind him, leaning warmly against his back, and wraps one meaty, soot-stained arm around him. "Hey there, lover," she says, and kisses the top of his head. "How goes the coding?"

"Not bad!" He leans into her without turning around. "I think I've got this bug finally figured out. It's a tricky one, but..." It had been the biggest sacrifice he could make, leaving his home behind and coming to a world without magic, just to be with her, but he'd made it without hesitation. His joy when he discovered computers—something his brilliant, meticulous mind could pore over and worry at and memorize and tweak, just as he'd done with the equally complex and arcane rules of magic—had been beautiful to behold. Certainly it was more profitable than her own profession, although even in her world there was still a market for hand-forged swords and other metal goods, if you knew where to sell them.

She lets him ramble happily on for a few minutes, just hugging him. She'd made a good-faith effort, years ago, to understand exactly what it was he did, and it had just given her a headache; these days she sticks to smithing. Steel doesn't care if you drop a bracket. But she loves listening to him talk about it, loves seeing how excited he gets.

Eventually he draws to a close; patting her arm and glancing up, he asks, "So how are things coming on the 'bending metal into interesting shapes' front?"

She grins. "Oh, pretty good. I'm ahead of schedule for the Medieval Festival, and I'm working on that custom order today. Damn, but the air conditioning feels good, though." Laughing, she leans back and takes another sip of her soup. "Thanks for lunch."

"Anytime." He smiles. "I know you, you get into your projects and forget to eat." He doesn't mention that he's just as bad. Sometimes it feels like they take turns taking care of each other in that area. *Some things never change.*

Finally she sighs, finishing the last of her food. "Well. I'll let you get back to it; I've got some other projects I can work on while this one cools." Bending over and leaning around him, she kisses him—tenderly, if not with the fiery passion of their youth—and heads back down to her forge.

The next morning, Simone bursts in.

Naomi looks up from where she's patiently grinding and filing the blade, refining the rough shape she hammered out yesterday into something more like the finished product, and her brow wrinkles in concern at the expression on the girl's face. Dark and beautiful as her grandfather—well, all grandmothers think their grandchildren are beautiful. But today those pretty features are contorted in panic. "Mimi!" she cries out, running into the dark forge. "*Mimi!*"

She sets aside the blade in a hurry, moving to wrap her arms around her granddaughter. Up close, Simone's eyes leak tears; the girl is gasping, barely able to speak. "Baby, what's wrong?" she asks, keeping her voice calm and steady. "What happened? Can you tell me?"

Simone gulps, pressing her face into Naomi's chest—noteworthy in itself; since becoming a teenager, Simone's been very conscious of the soot that usually covers her Mimi. "I don't know," she finally manages. "It's Bianca. Someone—I don't know—they jumped out, they *attacked* us, Mimi, they were hitting us and they—they *took* her!" She hiccups; she's shaking badly, and Naomi holds her tight, rubbing a large hand up and down the girl's back.

"Shh," she says, soothingly. "Shh. We'll fix it. We'll figure it out. Who took her? Where did they go?" She's met Bianca several times—shy and quiet and timid, with hair so blonde it's nearly white and a look about her like she might blow away in a bad storm. Still, she and Simone have been nearly inseparable for about two years now, so her granddaughter must have found a way to get through the reserved girl's shell.

Simone sobs harder. "You won't believe me," she gulps out, her voice suddenly bitter and despairing. "You won't believe me if I tell you, and you couldn't fix it if you did."

"Baby," she says, soft and gentle, "you have no idea how much I'm prepared to believe, and what I'm able to fix. Tell your Mimi."

Simone pushes back from her then and looks up at her with eyes made puffy and red from crying, ringed with soot. "Monsters," she spits out, watching her grandmother with wary eyes. "We were attacked by monsters, and they dragged her through a magic door and disappeared." Despite clinging to Naomi for comfort a moment before, now she looks poised to run the moment her grandmother laughs or yells or accuses her of lying.

Naomi reaches out, very gently, and places both hands on Simone's shoulders. "Baby," she says, "this is very important. What kind of monsters?"

The girl blinks. "Um." Startled, she takes a moment to rearrange her thoughts. "Um. They were. They were short? Just to my shoulders. Um. Greenish-grey skin. Big ears. They were—uh. They weren't fat, but they were kind of... thick? But skinny arms and legs. They smelled bad, and they had *teeth*." She shudders and closes her eyes, trying to remember more. "They—they had spears, I guess, but they didn't stab us, they just hit us with the stick part... and they were so strong..."

"*Goddammit*." That gets a reaction; even with all the other emotions, Simone draws back, shocked to hear her grandmother swear. "Goblins. Solneran goblins, that's them exactly, but they shouldn't be able to — Simone, can you find where they went through the magic door?" There's a note of command in Naomi's voice, one her granddaughter hasn't heard before. Without waiting for an answer, she grabs her hand. "Come on."

They run upstairs, Naomi's leg clunking as she pulls her granddaughter behind her. "Kerran!" she shouts as she bursts into his study, and he turns, startled. "We've got goblins," she barks. "They've opened a portal from Solnera—yes, I *know* it doesn't make any sense. And they kidnapped Simone's friend Bianca. Grab your gear; if we hurry we can make it through before it closes."

He jumps up, nearly tripping over his own computer cords, and although his eyes are wide he doesn't say a word, just hurries out of the room. Naomi can hear him pulling boxes out of the storage closet.

She's pulling out her own armor when she sees Simone reaching for a newly-finished sword. "Oh no," she says, "you don't get one. You stay put. Just you help me on with my armor and tell me where the door was, we'll bring her back."

Simone's eyes widen in outrage. "Mimi, I don't know what's going on, but I am not staying here! If you're going to find Bianca, I'm going with you!" Her voice is firm, despite the near-panic and confusion in her eyes.

Naomi sighs. "Baby, it is dangerous." Simone folds her arms. "And portals don't stay open very long. We don't have time—" *for this argument*, she realizes. Gritting her teeth, she sighs. "Fine," she says shortly. "Let's find you some armor that fits."

About half an hour later, they're standing at a bend in the country road that leads to their house, watching Kerran make an intricate cat's cradle with a fine silver chain from which dangles a bright blue stone. When he'd come clomping downstairs, legs stiff from too much sitting, his long robes and handcarved staff—both covered in runes—had only made him look like an elderly computer nerd kitted out for a LARP. Now, however, some of his former dignity returns as he focuses on the magic-dowsing web he's building.

Other than the few words it took to guide them here, Simone is silent. She watches her grandfather work now, her school clothes covered in a chain shirt that reaches nearly to her knees, held in place by a leather belt. A sword and scabbard hang from it, although Naomi warned her against actually trying to attack with it. "Use it to fend off any attacks, if you have to, but remember that you've had no training. It's a worst-case scenario weapon, nothing more." A shield is strapped to one arm, her hair tucked up under a helmet.

Naomi's armor is a little better—it was made especially for her, and she has the strength to bear it, though it doesn't fit quite as well as it did forty years ago. "Half of this is birthing three babies, and the other half is your Granddad's cooking," she'd grunted as Simone struggled to tighten the unfamiliar straps of her breastplate. "Nevermind. It's as good as it's going to get. I'll just have to trust in the mail underneath." Now she stomps around the road, impatient but knowing from long experience how useless it is to rush Kerran in these things. Her long-handled axe bounces against her back as she paces.

Finally, *finally* the blue stone starts to glow, reacting to the residual magic from the portal, and tugs slightly towards a clump of bushes. With a triumphant smile, one that makes him look at least twenty years younger, Kerran hurries towards it, pulling his fingers free from the web and making complicated gestures in the air. A shape like the outline of a door starts to glow, and he pushes at it, and…

…and oh god, there it is, it's Solnera, with the colors that are just a little more rich than her world and that scent on the wind like sunshine and heather and something she could never place, and Naomi's eyes fill with tears and just for a moment she feels twenty-five again.

Kerran can feel it too, she can tell, reading his wrinkled face like an old, favorite book; he steps back, blinking away tears, and makes a grand gesture. "Ladies first." Naomi takes Simone's hand, and they all step through.

They walk in silence for a while, and that's okay. Partly it's pragmatic; a band of goblins and a struggling thirteen-year-old do leave a trail, but following it while moving at speed still takes some concentration. Mostly, though, everyone is simply lost in their own thoughts: Naomi and Kerran in happy memories, and Simone…

Naomi steals glances at her granddaughter as they walk, trying to guess what's going on in the girl's head. She's bearing up well under the armor, Naomi notes with satisfaction; mail is heavier than most people believe, but years of soccer practice have left Simone sturdier than most thirteen-year-olds. Still, it's unusual for her curious, forthright granddaughter to be this quiet. Naomi smiles to herself. Simone is like her—they may not think fast, but they think *long*. The questions will come, once she's wrapped her head around everything.

And they do, about twenty minutes into the walk. "So," Simone says abruptly, not looking at either of them. "You've been here before."

Naomi nods evenly. "When I was your age," she says. "I fell through a portal—no one knows how it opened. Thought I'd gone crazy at first, or maybe I was dreaming—a world where magic was real? Where there were kings and queens, knights and monsters? Please." She laughs at the memory. "But it's hard to disbelieve it when you're *there*. I had a couple close scrapes, realized I wasn't half bad at fighting, and then by sheer accident wound up rescuing this prince who'd been captured by bandits…" She trails off, and shakes her head to come back to the conversation. In a quiet voice, she continues. "I spent, oh… more than ten years here."

"In a magic land," Simone says, her voice flat as only a thirteen-year-old's can be. "Doing magic."

"No, your grandfather did the magic," Naomi says, fighting not to smile. "I did *swords*. Well, and axes later," she amends. "When my arms got stronger."

Simone makes a noise. "And you never *told me*?" She pauses. "Does Mom know?"

"Believe it or not," Naomi says in a mild tone, "I wasn't in any great hurry to have our children or grandchildren believe we were delusional. Would you have believed me, before today?" She shrugs. "Besides, we'd made a new life for ourselves, and—"

It's Kerran who interrupts. "Simone," he says, holding up a hand, "does your friend wear glitter makeup?"

Simone presses her lips together, a stubborn look in her eyes; the reflex passes a moment later and she sags. "Sometimes," she admits. "When she can hide it from her dad. Why?"

He blinks, and a wide smile spreads slowly across his face. "Fairy dust," he chuckles. "She's leaving us a trail of fairy dust." He points to the ground; shimmering in the light is a dusting of glittery powder on a clump of leaves. "It started just a few feet back." He shakes his head. "I like your friend."

Naomi shoots him a look. "How does she know anyone's following her?"

It's his turn to press his lips together, the gesture remarkably like his granddaughter's when she doesn't want to say something. "Maybe a hunch?" he finally says, and shrugs. "Maybe she's just desperate and trying anything. Either way, grab any shiny leaves you see. If I get enough of the powder, I can make a sympathetic connection. If I can scry on her…"

"…Maybe we can find a shortcut, maybe we can get an idea of what we're walking in on," Naomi nods. *And maybe you'll get confirmation on whatever theory just occurred to you about the girl,* she thinks wryly, eyeing her husband with fond suspicion.

For a while they move in silence again, plucking glitter-covered leaves and handing them to Kerran, who painstakingly scrapes off as much powder as he can with a small knife, pooling the results in his palm.

It's Simone, again, who breaks the silence, her dark eyes taking in the too-blue sky, the too-green grass. In a hushed voice, she asks, "Why did you leave?"

In answer, Naomi pulls her jeans up to reveal her metal leg. It's beautiful, stainless steel scrollwork shining under Solneran skies—not as efficient as some of the high-tech modern models, but she made it herself and she's proud of it. "There was an invasion," she sighs. "I was good, real good. But there's always someone better. Or luckier." She pauses. "Maybe not that lucky; I went into a red haze after that, don't remember a lot of it but I don't think he walked away from it. Still." She shrugs, matter-of-fact. "The healers here can repair a lot, but that was beyond them. It got infected... well. I needed modern medicine," she says simply. "So they found a way to build a portal back, using me as a sort of... of focus point. But it was one-way; once I was gone, they wouldn't have a way to focus it and open another." She shrugs. "Your granddad came with me," she says, a world of meaning in the simple statement. "I found a hospital, got healed up, found my family... had to make up some real good excuses..."

She'd eventually wound up spinning a story about being drawn into a cult. Embarrassing, in retrospect, but it had worked. Her family, once they'd gotten over their initial shock, had been overjoyed to see her, and welcomed Kerran into the fold with chaotic, exuberant Filipino warmth. Her mother, she thought, always suspected there was more to the story, but she'd never pushed too hard, for which Naomi was forever grateful.

Simone watches her, and Naomi can see her piecing together the parts she didn't say out loud. Behind them, Kerran scowls and pokes at the small pile of shimmering dust.

The girl shakes her head. "Okay. So. These goblins. The ones that took Bianca," she says, her expression sharp. "What about them?"

Naomi sighs. "They're dangerous, at least in large groups. Smart and vicious, good grasp of strategy and tactics. You leave the fighting to me and your grandfather, just keep your shield up and stay out of their way. They—"

"Are right over there," Kerran interrupts, his voice tense. "They went the long way around this hill—short legs. The girl's mostly unharmed, they've got her bound and gagged but her legs are free, there's only a handful of them, if we run we can get them before they get back to their base—come on!" He breaks into a sprint at the final words; after a startled moment, Naomi and Simone follow.

Kerran and Naomi are decades older than the last time they charged into battle; Naomi and Simone are wearing heavy armor; Naomi's missing half a leg. Still, they move as fast as can be expected, under the circumstances. They catch sight of the goblins before too long; Naomi lets out a fierce battle-scream as she falls upon them, axe out and at the ready, as beside her white light already begins to form around Kerran's hands.

It's a massacre.

Naomi may not be as limber as she was in her youth, but her blacksmith's arms have lost none of their power, and she remembers the steps of this dance too. Her axe gleams as it slices through her foes. Kerran keeps close to her, shooting out arcs of light that shear through armor and flesh with devastating precision. One goblin runs at Simone and Naomi's heart nearly stops for a moment—but the girl sidesteps with a quickness learned on the soccer field, raising her shield-arm and deflecting the waving sword, and Naomi can breathe again. A moment later one of Kerran's bolts cuts the goblin down with pitiless wrath.

And then it's over, almost over, just one goblin left—one goblin with his arm around the tied-up Bianca, holding a knife at her throat. He hisses at them in the tongue that Naomi was once so close to learning but now can't make any sense of, but his tone and his posture and his knife send the message loud and clear. Bianca looks up at them with terrified eyes, and Naomi stops short.

While the goblin glares defiance at them, she exchanges a worried glance with Kerran. Behind them, Simone lets out a whimper. Naomi lowers her blood-spattered axe; furiously she searches her memory for even a few words of the goblin's tongue, but time and age and the heat of battle have driven them away. She sets the axe down by her feet and raises her hands in a placating manner, trying to indicate that they're willing to let him go if he releases the girl, but the goblin just snarls, tightening his grip on the knife.

The seconds crawl by as the stalemate stretches out; Naomi is on the verge of charging the goblin anyway, trusting that his sense of self-preservation will instinctively move the knife away from the girl's throat and towards her instead… when Kerran nudges her. She blinks, and looks more closely.

There's rage in Bianca's eyes now, mingled with the fear, rage at having rescue so close at hand and yet thwarted. And something else... a light, nearly a glow, in her pale skin...

Naomi barely has time to think, *So that's what he suspected!* before that white light bursts out of Bianca in an uncontrolled blast. It drives the knife away and sends the goblin staggering back, stunned. Without even stopping to think, her husband's triumphant laughter ringing in her ears, she ignores the axe and darts in, laying the goblin out with one well-placed, metal-coated punch.

And then turns just in time to see Simone rush forward, pull the gag away from Bianca's mouth... and kiss her, with all the fervent passion and relief her teenage soul can muster.

Naomi raises an eyebrow. *Ah.* Glancing at her husband, she shrugs. *Well, we were about that age...*

She limps over to him; as the adrenaline drains away, her leg complains loudly where it attaches to the metal. Wrapping him in a clanking metal hug, she listens to him and the girls exclaim over the adventure.

"...and I don't know, I just knew someone was looking for me, so I..."

"...yes, that'll be the latent magical talent, you've lived your whole life in a world without magic but now you're here, and..."

"...your face! Did they hit you, are those bruises..."

"...don't even know what I did, I was just so mad and..."

"...find you a mentor if you want, I mean I suppose I could..."

"...hit one with my shield, did you see? Teach him to mess with..."

She smiles and lets it wash over her... that is, until the sound of hoofbeats coming over the hill, and a commanding voice calling out, "Halt in the name of the queen!"

She sighs, and turns.

A company of Solneran knights, and her heart twists to see the regalia. The leader lifts his helmet. "We've been tracking this band of goblins for days now," he says sternly, "looking for the best plan of attack, and now the element of surprise is lost. Explain yourselves."

Naomi lifts her own helm. "Apologies," she says wearily, "but this raiding party kidnapped a child. We didn't mean to interfere in your mission, and we did take a prisoner if that helps, but we couldn't just..." She pauses. The captain's skin is a warm brown, lighter than Kerran's; it's familiar, somehow, as are his cheekbones and the straight line of his nose..."Beg pardon, Sir Knight," she says slowly, "but are you by any chance related to Sir Varalen?"

Behind him another knight urges his horse forward, lifting his own helm to reveal a face even older and more careworn than hers—but oh, so familiar. "My son," he rumbles. "Who's asking?"

Closing her eyes and smiling for a moment, she pulls off her helmet, running fingers through short, wavy hair—iron grey now rather than the coal-black he knew. "An old friend, Sir Champion," she says, her tone suddenly teasing.

It takes him a moment, then her old mentor's eyes go wide. "Naomi? Lady Naomi? *How*?" He gasps, recognition and affection flooding his face, and takes in the rest of her party. His gaze stops on her husband, scrawny but dignified in his wizard's robes. "Then this… *Prince Kerran*??"

Kerran wearily covers his face with his hand as the knights, as one, bow in their saddles. "Your Highness," Varalen says formally, "I believe your sister the queen would like to see you."

Leaning over to the dumbfounded Simone, Naomi whispers, "I told you I rescued a prince."

At Kerran's insistence, they meet Queen Taris in her private chambers rather than before the court.

She isn't much changed, Naomi notes. Older, of course. Skinnier—the thinness that had looked delicate in her youth now seems strong and hard, like aged dark wood. The hair that frames her face like a halo, wild and glorious as a stormcloud, is nearly white. But her back is still ramrod straight, her presence commanding, and her eyes still flash with pride and dignity—though not the impetuous wrath Naomi remembers.

She's been forged, she thinks, watching the queen with a blacksmith's approving eye. *Tempered by the heat of her crown.*

Behind her, she can hear the girls whispering. They haven't let go of each other's hands since Bianca was rescued; the knights, smiling under their helms, had obligingly ridden close enough together to let their passengers reach across to each other. They sound nervous, and Naomi doesn't blame them—Taris was intimidating enough forty years ago, when she was just the Crown Princess.

Her lips are pressed together sternly now, her default expression. It always makes her look like she's never smiled, like she doesn't even know how—until suddenly she does. She does now, and it lights up her face, transforming her. "Baby brother," she says warmly. "Welcome home."

The corner of his mouth twitches. "Before you ask, I swear I'm not here to steal your throne."

She actually laughs—a minor miracle in itself. "I actually said that, didn't I? Gods, I was such a child."

"You were," he agrees cheerfully. "But then you actually had to *take* the throne, so as far as I'm concerned, you've been punished enough." She sighs in exasperation at this, rolling her eyes—then laughs again, and steps forward to embrace her wayward brother for the first time in decades.

Then she turns to Naomi. "And Lady Naomi Bautista," she says with a smile. "I wasn't sure if we'd see you alive again. Welcome back." She pauses. "Although I suppose we should call you Princess now?"

"Just as soon you didn't," Naomi chuckles. She clanks forward, still in her armor, and drops to one knee, ignoring the spike of pain. The sound of steel on marble echoes through the chamber. "Just a humble knight, your Majesty. At your service as always."

"Always with the flair for the dramatic," Taris grumbles. "Get *up*, Naomi. And so help you, if you've cracked my tiles..."

"Ah... that may be easier said than done," Naomi admits with a sheepish smile. "Down is easier than up. These old legs aren't what they used to be, you know."

"Oh, for..." With a sigh, Taris steps forward to take one metal-clad arm and Kerran takes the other; nodding sharply at the two girls, the queen snaps, "Well, don't just stand there!" Startled, they move to help too.

Once they've gotten Naomi on her feet again, Taris leads them to a little table; Naomi sinks gratefully into a chair, her right leg aching, as servants begin to lay out a lunch. "So," the queen says, "Varalen says you came back... to deal with *goblins*?"

Naomi and Kerran explain as they eat, Simone chiming in from time to time. Bianca remains quiet, her eyes on her plate. "What I can't figure out is why—and *how*," Naomi finishes. "How did they manage to open a portal in the first place? That shouldn't even be possible, not without someone from my world to focus it! And why use it to kidnap one human girl?"

"How, I don't know. *Why*... to start a war, I think," Taris says grimly, studying Bianca. "The child is distinctive-looking. The only person I know of with hair so fair it's almost white is Princess Aina of Falleron. Princess Aina, who's about the same age as these two, and who's currently traveling through our lands on her way to study with the Sages of Comren."

Kerran's eyes widen. "The peace treaty..."

"With Falleron still holds, yes," Taris agrees. "But..."

Naomi closes her eyes. "But if a thirteen-year-old girl with white-blonde hair was found dead just inside your borders..."

"...then that would be more than enough justification to start a war..." Kerran adds slowly.

"...and by the time anyone contacted the Sages—who are *notoriously* hard to contact, especially when they've got a new student to focus on—and found out Aina was alive," Taris finishes, "it would be too late. The peace we fought so hard to win would be shattered."

Simone blinks, listening to this back-and-forth. "They were going to *kill* her?" she demands, protective fury in her voice as she glances at her girlfriend. "Because she looks like this princess, they were going to kill her?"

"They were going to kill her first," Taris corrects, sounding tired. "And then they were going to kill a lot more people."

"Who would want to destroy the peace, though?" Kerran asks, brow furrowed.

"The question is, who profits from it?" Naomi frowns. "What alliances would be redrawn, what trade routes would be disrupted? Who know goblins well enough to rebuild and recruit the Crimson War tribe?"

"And who's got the magical resources to scry out the girl *and* open a portal?" Kerran adds. "I can start asking questions at the Wizard's College and among the trade guilds, and if I can get the space to make a big enough sigil maybe—"

Taris lays a hand over his, interrupting him gently. "Baby brother. This isn't your fight." She shakes her head. "It's not your world anymore, remember? I've got wizards as we speak working on building another portal. We're going to get you home."

"I don't want to go home," Bianca suddenly says. All eyes turn in surprise to the quiet girl, but for once, she doesn't look shy. Her voice shakes, but there's a blaze in her eyes. "I don't want to go back to my father. I want to stay here. I have *magic* here! I want to learn magic, and fight goblins, and stop a war, and I *don't want to go back to my father!*"

Simone reaches over and takes her hand again, then looks at the adults. "I want to stay too," she says, and Naomi is surprised by the fierce pride she feels at the steel in her granddaughter's voice. "Mimi, you were my age when you learned how to fight. I want to stay. I want to learn who tried to kill Bianca, and I—I want to learn how to *stop* them! And if Granddad's a prince then aren't I—aren't I technically a princess? So it's even my responsibility!" She hesitates, then takes a deep breath. "And I don't want Bianca to go back to her father either," she adds quietly, meeting her grandparents' eyes steadily.

"Your mother—" Naomi begins, then stops. Her eyes take in Bianca's thin, nervous face, the way she hides behind her hair most of the time. She takes in Simone's hand on hers, protective. Loving.

"With three of you here," Taris says quietly, "I believe it would be possible to open a portal and send all but one of you back... and then open it again. Say, two hours later?"

So that we could come back, Naomi realizes suddenly. *We could say our goodbyes properly, explain where we were going... pack up our mementos...* She looks at Kerran, a question in her eyes.

"It's possible," he agrees, sounding stunned. "It's more than possible. We could… we could even go back and forth. We wouldn't have to choose."

"Stop a war and still make it home for Christmas," she says, shaking her head and laughing at the sheer, perfect ridiculousness of the idea. She wants this, she realizes. She wants exactly this.

Opening her eyes, she regards Simone and Bianca for a long moment, then slowly nods. "Well, girls," she says gravely, "welcome to the family business."

STONE WOKEN

BY CRYSTAL LYNN HILBERT

For weeks, Hjalli dreamt in the sound of dry scales rasping on stone-choked soil, the taste of still, damp air. Distant heartbeats fluttered, flame-bright mice in the periphery of her un-vision. She thought it an oddity, when she thought of it at all, but before long, the dreaming spread. Like spores on a cavern wind, it sunk into her sister-king.

Kvern dreamt of confinement. She dreamt of tight chambers and a writhing hunger, wide as open sky. Venom filled her cheeks each night, burnt her tongue bitter come waking.

In private, the two sister-kings worried. They scoured the sagas of old battles, combing for answers in the Archivists' songs of past catastrophes. Together, they spoke the names of ancient monsters into the loamy dark of their lower caverns and waited for the answer, the whisper of recognition from below. But though they spent weeks searching, no old horrors answered them. The shadows remained silent, their visions sprawling ever onward, until soon—too soon—even the mountain dreamt.

Knowing only permanence, only the slow tick of centuries aching past, the stones held no understanding of hunger. Struck wanting, gneiss and granite gnawed itself awake, twisting, kicking in its bed. Underground streams of magic overflowed their banks. Potential spilled outward from these ley lines, soaking into the soil and shale until ore melted in the earth. Gold dripped from the walls, blistering unwary boots. Iron bubbled in rivers through the halls.

Finally, desperate, the two kings spoke one last name into the earth—*Níðhöggr*, the Striker in the Dark, the World-Eater—and fell to their knees, copper pale, as the whole of the mountain shook.

They returned above in silence, shoulders squared and strides heavy as they walked through the living belly of the mountain. Though the floor still shivered beneath their boots, they held steel in their faces, teeth bared in axe-blade grins. Dread soaked Hjalli's stomach, flooded her bones, filled her mouth until she tasted it thicker than the citrine suck-stone between her teeth. But her people crowded the corridors—craftswomen watching from doorways, waiting with weighted spines, tools hanging half-forgotten from their callused fingers—so, steeling herself, Hjalli showed them strength.

She smiled, though she held her sister's hand tight enough to shatter diamond. She told them, "We know our enemy," like triumph, like pride, though the words sank claws into her throat.

Not quite a lie, she told herself, fingers numb in her sister's fist—and one of them was shaking, but Hjalli could not place which. She stepped closer to hide it, pressed her shoulder to her sister's so their people wouldn't see, wouldn't fear.

Used to the bright lamps of shops and workrooms, out here in the dimmer high-hall corridors, the women of the mountain saw only what their kings showed them. Caught up in the swell of confidence, they cracked hardened hands to stony breasts in the drumbeat of a coming war. They returned their kings' axe-edge smiles, teeth bared and glittering black in the crystal-lit halls, and saw nothing of the fear Hjalli hid behind her teeth.

From a distant chamber, an Archivist sang. Soon, her sisters joined her. Heroes rose in their shared voice, weapons high and bloodied. Grateful, gritty hope caking in her throat, Hjalli closed her eyes. She unclenched her fists, following the song-swept path of her ancestors and in the heavy foot-falls of her people, her fear cowered. With each heart-beaten boom, she chewed her grandmother's cunning victories, her mothers' careful negotiation, until she walked like a coming storm, her earthquake clenched between her teeth.

The mountain would not fall.

Hand in hand with her sister, Kvern wore bravery for armor. Raising her voice with the Archivists, with her sister-king, she bellowed the names of their ancestors into the rock and soil, claiming their homes, their strength, their history.

Let the World-Eater listen. It might thrash, but their people stood strong.

As long as they lived, the mountain would not fall.

Caught in the hopeful thrum of their earthen city, laden with the weight of their trust, Hjalli found her sister's eyes and read understanding there.

As long as they lived—

Gods, let them be enough.

Striding into their private war-oratory, Hjalli held her face proud and strong just long enough to see her safely hidden. When the heavy doors rocked shut, her calm king-mask shattered.

She strode for the walls, hands fisted and jumping, scouring the maps she'd hung here, but the heavy lines of distant ridges gave her nothing. The dragons' dens that necklaced the mountain range spoke of ancient, half-fledged alliances already frayed. Slender trade routes betrayed weakness. Human settlements on the spruce-pocked borders offered only frying pans and fires. If they fled the mountain, they'd find themselves embroiled in a second war, and still, *still*, a monster beyond legend gnawing from below.

Hjalli glanced to her sister, hoping for some epiphany there. She found little, Kvern pacing the wide encampment of heavy crates that encircled the oratory walls. Jaw tight, shoulder shale-sloped, she rooted through container after container of old missives and wayward gems, her mouth drawing tighter with each discarded leaf. Crossing the room, Hjalli joined her. She upended several smaller chests over the wide quartz table, raking her fingers through diadems and baubles, searching—both of them searching—and finding nothing.

An hour passed this way, silence prowling between them on needled feet, itching at Hjalli's throat, and the backs of her eyes. Finally, her sister sighed. She ran her fingers through her braids, the gold-stiff strands chiming with the passage of her earthen hand and murmured, "I must go below. Perhaps I can speak with it."

Hjalli stiffened, startled from a handful of spells and a litany of half formed plans. "What are you thinking? *No.*"

Once, she might have agreed. Kvern had charmed giants in her youth. She'd danced a careful line of flattery and threat, fashioned courting-gifts for warring kings, weaving peace between them with their mothers' spells and the precious snarls of her own hair. Given half a mind, her sister could tame dragons.

But Hjalli had spent days roaming the lower country of their mountain, hoping for the whisper of a name. And day after day, she'd watched an ocean of pale, eyeless creatures fleeing from their depths—strange beasts without name, without sight, moon pale and skin thinner than the cauls of shadow-blessed babes.

Driven by dreaming, by the monster whispering beneath, they clawed from the darkness, white bellies bloodied on the tunnel-spent shards of flint and gneiss littering the ground. Relentless, regardless, they dragged themselves onward, to the mouth of the mountain.

Hjalli did not know what they searched for, only what they found—crows, an army of crows, shatter-shard songs summoning their brethren to the feast.

Perhaps whatever madness sent them moving could not be passed to harder hosts. Perhaps. But Hjalli loved her sister too much to risk it.

"Not yet, at least," she amended, reading the determination in Kvern's eyes. "We need more time. We don't know our enemy."

"It knows speech. It can be reasoned with."

"It knows the sound of its name. It knows the sound mountains make between its teeth. You go below, it will know the sound *you* make between its teeth."

Kvern pursed her lips. "I am harder to chew."

"Your head, perhaps," Hjalli snapped. "This is madness. We need to consider, to organize our options."

Sighing, her sister-king slumped into a chair. She jogged the meat of her fist against the treasure-strewn table, eyes dark and restless. "What other option do we have? Old territory alliances with serpents that would sooner eat us? A fistful of human cities waiting for us to fall?"

"We have a mountain range of kin. We could raise an army, confront the monster in its den."

Kvern pursed her lips. "To what end?" she asked. "How can we march an army through a single mountain? We may as well abandon our home as try."

Irritation prickled Hjalli's nape; anxiety set her hands jumping. "And go where? Doing what? Don't be goatish, sister—I'm advising caution, not heresy."

"Then I will be cautious."

"You'll be cautiously eaten. Kvern—if you will not take an army, fine. But there *must* be another path." She flattened her unsteady hands to the table to still them, the scars over her knuckles yet another map in the fire-crystals' steady glow. "Give me time. I will find a way."

"I know you could. Given a month, two—my clever sister, I *know*," she snapped. "But there *is* no time. Our tubers rot in their beds, our chambered fields of night-grain fall fallow. Hjalli, I have to try."

"Fine! But let me try *first*. Give me a week—another *day*, even. Speed is well and good, but going in underprepared, armed with—what? Your charm? Mother's bones and grandmother's axe? Kvern, we'll be destroyed in the attempt."

Kvern nodded—nodded and shrugged, her head tilted as though they discussed fabric prices in a foreign city and not the fate of their own. "I understand," she said. "But rocks are never destroyed, only changed."

Sharper than a human spear, fear and fury lanced Hjalli's too-tight throat. Desperation sizzled in her gut, a high ledge and loose stones underfoot. She could not lose her sister to this beast. She *would not*.

"We are as much flesh as stone," she insisted, "and more flesh than our mothers ever were! Our grandmother-kings could gnaw the mountains into gravel, but we spend days on a single suck-stone. This beast grinds the mountain into sand. What hope do we have, us two against a leviathan?"

"No," Kvern said quietly, "not us two," and the light in her eyes shone like steel in sunlight, spell-fire on a spent breath.

Hjalli saw—of course, she saw—but she misread the determination in her sister's face for stubbornness.

"Who then?" she pressed, leaning forward. "How many women of how many mountains? Give me a number and I will raise you an army."

"No other mountains. No other *body*," Kvern said, holding so still, so barely breathing. "Just me."

Hjalli's heart seized—mudslide, cavern collapse—and for a long moment, she could not breathe. *Too late*, she thought, *too late*. The creatures' madness had caught already, flame to summer sedge.

"No," she said, for what she could, teeth vicious on the word, the citrine in her mouth rattling a warning on her teeth. "No. You are my sister. If you do this, I walk with you."

But Kvern only watched her, her eyes too bright, too hard. "If we go together—Hjalli, if we *fail*—who will lead?"

Hjalli fell back. Words crept away from her—sightless things, searching for a distant sun and an inglorious death.

Not an argument at all, she saw, but two roads to the same end. They had no time, no option, no greater future hope. They could not risk marching the women of the mountain without knowing what they'd find below. Nor could they ask another to scout the way, braving mountain-break and monstrous teeth.

Only a king could go—

And go alone.

Gently, Kvern caught Hjalli's hand. "I will return," she said.

Heart gasping, Hjalli had no choice but to believe her.

The mountain rang for Kvern's departure.

Scores of women pressed shoulder to shoulder in the lowest hall, a rough-hewn cavern, walls earthen and decorated with only a few disparate rune-marks of protection, strung rubies faceted in an ancient formula. Singing, swaying, the women pounded time with copper-shod boots, calling luck from the jade woven in their braids, protection from the jasper mounted in the tools of their trade. Incense hung heavy in the still air, cedar warring attorlaðe, loud as axe-crash, heavy as collapse.

Kvern stood at the head of the assemblage and though fear wedged a broken beam in the hollow of Hjalli's throat, pride bubbled in her stomach.

Tonight, her sister wore the stony hide of their great-great grandmother-king—so thick it took a diamond knife to part it when she passed—gnarled corundum outcroppings oiled to a shine. Her mother's bones caged her face, her spine, her legs. Several generations of women's braids fringed her shoulders and skirted her waist, a woven legacy of greats and grands and many mothers, tangible protection in their lengthy history. When she walked, tonight, Kvern's steps spelled war. When she bared her teeth, her people roared.

Hjalli knew better—knew her too well to be fooled by shining armor and a charming coal-black smile. As the Archivists anointed her face, as they blessed her boots and sang her strengths, Hjalli saw her sister's restless hands combing through the lengths of her mother's hair. Her fingers closed around a pair of beads, larger and less delicate than the others. Even from a distance, from her position guarding the tunnel's open mouth, Hjalli knew these beads. She remembered the scent of their baking, remembered weaving them into their mother's steel-strand hair, hot yet from the oven and their fingertips still soft enough to burn.

A gift—an old gift—and the precious memory of safety.

Around them, the singing swelled. The earth shook. Far beneath them, the World-Eater turned over in its darkness. But if it spoke, if it muttered in its hungry dreaming the words of ancient dragons, none here stood in witness.

The assembled pounded their boots to earth, their fists to breasts.

They shouted the names of older kings—ancient, distant mothers—summoning their blessings from the earth, calling forth their useful attributes. Their voices sank, blistering and deep, shaking the mountain—*claiming* the mountain—until their words became soil, until even the over-flowing ley lines of the mountain's root knew to whom they belonged.

Then, at last, they stopped. One by one, the echo of their voices flickered into silence.

Kvern said nothing. She bared her teeth to them—to honor, to victory—and knocked knuckles to her heart. Proud—love like a seam-fire in her stomach—Hjalli clenched teeth around her fear.

"Deep may you dwell," she whispered her blessing, eyes bright and voice loud in the empty breathing of the cavern chamber.

Kvern swallowed. Brave before her people, she pressed her lips in a firm line, met her sister's eyes. Hjalli saw her swallow again, saw her move her mouth to form words and find nothing left of speech. At last, she nodded. She flicked her fingers in the secret signs of their childhood—*I love you, I love you*—and turning away, one wayward palm sweeping her downturned eyes, she descended into the dark.

One by one, the women of the mountain dispersed. Hjalli remained.

She seated herself at the entrance to the under-mountain, a drum of quartz and goat between her knees, both flayed so fine shadows danced beneath the fabric of its face. Carefully, she sent her heartbeat down, down with the mountain's breathing.

May it light Kvern's path. May it see her safely home again. May their mother's bones carry her and their grandmother's skin protect her.

Let it be enough, Hjalli prayed, her heartbeat skipping against stone, into the deepest darkness—*come home, come home.* Hope and hurting scored her ribs, gnawed with every finger fall against the drum—

Come home, come home—

Come home whole.

And Kvern came home, after a sort.

Blind and staggering, she wandered into the circle of Hjalli's gem-fire, calm as a child as her legs buckled beneath her. In an instant, Hjalli found her feet, abandoned her drum.

"Kvern?" she called, reaching for her sister. "*Kvern.*"

But her sister sat somewhere past words, shoulders slumped and head bowed. Many of their mother's bones jutted in shattered cairns around her face and arms. The ledges of her shoulders lay bare, the woven curtain of their ancestors' hair torn away. Silver scrabbling marred the surface of the once-shined stone, marking the places claws searched and scored and found no purchase.

"What—?" Hjalli began.

Kvern lifted her head. The words died on her tongue.

Once, long ago, their mother showed them language in the lines of a goat's liver. Bent over its steaming belly in the snow, she pulled their fingers through the coils of its viscera, marking marriages and births, sorrows and success.

With shaking hands, Hjalli cradled the bloody wreckage of her sister's face.

She thought, perhaps, her mother would know what to make of this.

Though her heart sat in her throat, hotter than a hearthstone, Hjalli swallowed it down. She stood.

Carefully, so carefully, she carried her sister home.

Pale and grim, the healers tended their king. They dribbled betony broth between her battered lips, laced with linden for sleep, for peace. When she settled, when she stopped groping for the knife no longer at her side, stopped muttering half-words in an ancient dragon tongue, the women set to work.

Singing low, the healers washed the empty ruin of her eyes, bound them shut with linen soaked in bittercress and traded honey. With the memory of their own mothers, they stitched closed the gash along her cheek and lip, pried the shards of gravel from beneath her fingernails. They bathed her, the water scented and dark, and finally—when she lay as clean and whole as they could make her—quietly, the women left.

Hjalli remained. For days, Hjalli remained, staring at the same silvered tapestries, the same pelts on the same bed. Time slipped past, unmarked save for the tide of couriers ferrying word from the world beyond her sister's bedroom walls.

Still, blind and white-fleshed creatures fled the mountain.

Still, the crows screamed.

Still, the ground trembled, overwrought beneath their feet.

Hours crept along, days aching by, and yes, Kvern woke. She woke and walked, roaming her chambers, pacing over and over the same meaningless path, heedless of the contents of her room. She'd oil her hair when prompted. Hjalli could coax her into eating if she ignored the dripping dragon words, if she placed the food into her hands and brought them to her mouth. Kvern could even dress herself, after a fashion, in loose robes and careless boots.

She lived, at least. She lived.

But still, hours crept along and Hjalli spent too long in her sister-king's chambers, bleary-eyed in the firelight, her mouth filled with stones.

Holding vigil, she thought, when she thought of much at all.

Come home, her heart whispered in the silence, heavy and grieving. *Come home whole.*

If Kvern could hear it over the World-Eater's whispering, she did not attempt to say.

Word spread quickly through the mountain range, even to the low valleys. By week's end, though she left half a kingship behind her at the mountain's foot, Kvern's oldest daughter found her way home again.

As with all meetings between leaders, Hjalli received her in the Storied Hall. Here, the faces of their grand and mother kings peered down from andalusite walls, shadows dancing in the carved corners of their smiles, the deep onyx insets of their eyes. It was a hall for war councils, for treaties, for feasts. A hall for kings.

And they were all kings. Even Kvern, woke and walking, drifting through the hall, vague as ghosts.

It would have been better, Hjalli thought, to greet Lendi as any other journeyed daughter—to seat her before roasted meat and spiced mush-ale, to envelope her in family before presenting her with loss. But Lendi grew into her axes long ago. Though Hjalli's memory recalled a girl with bark-soft skin, leaping after goats on the ridge, the woman that stood before her today carried herself hard and proud as ancient lava flow. No protecting her now.

"What happened?" Lendi asked, her eyes fixed to her mother as she roamed, muttering half-formed words in a bastard dragon tongue. The valley king held her face still, her shoulders steady boulders, but her hands betrayed her, shaking, the weathered skin of her knuckles creaking over her clenched fists.

Sinking down at the head of the long spruce table, Hjalli searched for words to make this travesty sing a victory. But such word-weaving had ever been Kvern's art. When she groped for something clever, something comforting, speech crumbled to dust between her teeth. At last, she shook her head and sighed.

"She went into the depths to meet the World-Eater," she said, longing for her sister's silken skill. "She meant to end its thrashing."

Lendi held her jaw tight enough to crack. "She was unsuccessful," she said, and a dissonance rattled in the last word, a half-question still hoping.

"She is questing," Hjalli told her, to offer her what little hope she had, to chase the memory of her shattered face away. "She has not yet returned."

Of all things, this broke Lendi's resolve. Her king-mask slipped, lips pale and teeth bared, her whole body bent in pain.

"Did you go blind with her, Hjalli? Did your mind leave you, too? Questing? *Look*! Look at her!"

Unheeding, Kvern ran her hands down the wall bearing their mother's visage. But at the table, Hjalli stilled. Struck, quiet as cracking ice, she said, "I am looking."

Lendi shook her head, uncowed by the threat of avalanche in her voice.

"Then what is it you see?" she snapped. "She walked into the deep and it shattered her. My mother-king is dead."

All sharp teeth and hurt, Hjalli rose, fists clenched and a distant drumbeat throbbing in her ears. "Shattered? Perhaps. She knew the ley lines would require sacrifice long before she spoke with them. Shattered, yes— but shattered isn't *dead,* Valley King. When a stone breaks, is it less a stone?" she demanded. "Does it un-become?"

Lendi turned away. She watched Kvern roaming the room, empty eyes scouring the carvings, her fingers mapping the features of her ancestors. Once, this woman forged pieces of the mountain's spine into a fearsome blade, drove the humans from their mountain's foot with its howl on the air, with the boulders lifting in her roar.

Today, she hissed soft snake words, unformed as broken eggs. Blind, she roamed the room, not caring what she crashed into.

Quiet and small, the memory of a girl with a night sky of freckles, Lendi whispered, "She doesn't even know my *voice.*"

At this, Hjalli softened. She understood. Of course she understood— she had carried her sister bloodied and insensate from the bowels of the mountain. But whatever happened, whatever *changed*, she stood by Kvern. She *trusted* her.

"She can't hear us well," Hjalli said, naming a truth she knew in her bones. "She is far below, arguing with the World-Eater. She will return when she wins."

Lendi's half smiled, though it was the smile of a battlefield—the smile her mother wore as she promised to return. "You think she's winning?"

"She would not give the World-Eater a different choice," Hjalli told her. Pausing, she remembered Kvern in the war-oratory, so certain of her path. "Your mother is stone," she said, echoing her sister. "Stone cannot die, only change."

And she meant it for a comfort. She meant to spin for her the warmth and hope she offered all her people. But Lendi only looked at her, her eyes heavier than her boots.

She said, "All sand was stone once."

And what could Hjalli reply to truth?

In the night, Hjalli woke to the ley lines howling, the mountain's spine seizure-struck and shuddering. Crystals flaked from her ceiling, fluttering like the heavy snow of the high peaks. In its grate, the fire struggled and in its leaping light, Hjalli found Kvern seated on the floor of her chambers. She'd dressed herself properly, unprompted, in her grandmother's skin. Shadows caught in her mouth as her lips moved soundlessly, pebbles riding her teeth with the sound of a distant war.

Slowly, half dreaming, Hjalli freed her legs of pelts and loam, swung her feet to floor. But where she expected cool earth, her toes found instead the fabric of Kvern's blind, stained sticky with plant pitch and old scabs.

At the sound—flesh to fabric to floor—Kvern turned, and firelight danced against the deep-river stones lodged in the hollow sockets of her eyes.

Hjalli's breath caught. Crows scrabbled at the cage of her breast, scoring runes into her ribs, drowning out the drumbeat of her heart with their feasting cries. She felt cold, ice in her fingers, her legs somewhere miles beyond her.

Long ago, when she and Kvern were yet young and wild, hunting every interloper through the spruce and sedge that peppered their mountainside, the Archivists had composed a song to their basalt black stare.

A prophesy, perhaps. Or else the World-Eater had listened, and sought to prove it true.

Far beneath them, Hjalli felt through her feet as the ley lines leapt and lashed, spilling their banks. She heard words in the earth's groan, heard the mountain pleading as it wept. And her sister, wearing her war-skin, sitting

on the floor with stones in her skull—

A signal—and one Hjalli understood.

"*Enough*," she snarled—to the mountain, to the World-Eater slavering in its den—and rose from her bed, snatching the blind from the floor.

Kvern had asked for opportunity. For her sake, Hjalli gave it. But the time for bartering with dragons had passed. Bringing her bare foot down onto the packed earth of her chamber, Hjalli stomped with the weight of all her years and wars, her victories and her legacy. She pounded her name into the stone, her history, her strength, until water wept from the walls, until the crystals in the ceiling gnashed wildly and the mountain woke to meet her, labyrinthine corridors ringing a call to arms.

Though much of her walked elsewhere, Kvern understood this summons in her bones and in her blood. She rose from the floor, basalt eyes glittering in the firelight and grinned—grinned as though she'd been waiting for this.

Striding to the ancestor shrine in the far corner of her room, Hjalli threw open a heavy iolite chest and lifted out her own grandmother-king's skin. Where once her sister would have aided her to dress, now, Hjalli threw herself inside alone, spitting half-chewed spells to suture the closures and bind the clasps. From the bottom of the chest, she lifted a war-axe forged from her childhood—steel-soaked carnelian, pyrope laced and burning with a soul-gleam of its own—and now, when her foot struck earth, the whole of the mountain trembled, singing, "*War! War! The kings march to war!*"

When she turned, Hjalli found Kvern at her side. Without a word, she laced their fingers together. And hand in hand, the sister-kings walked from the chamber, armed and glittering as blood.

Around them, the mountain seethed with song, with foot-strike, with women taking up arms and voice and singing their own histories into the earth, calling on ancestors a thousand years deep.

Lendi met them in the open mouth of the gathering hall, a bone-gaunt pick propped against her armored shoulder. Behind her, the whole of the mountain stood gathered, glittering in their grandmothers' skins, firelight dancing down their ready blades.

"Where do we go, mothers?" Lendi asked, smiling. "Who do we hunt?"

Though crows kicked in her throat, Hjalli swallowed them down, blinking until the water left her eyes.

"The World-Eater," she answered, louder than the mountain, than the long history of their kind.

And her people—her warriors, vicious and bright—answered her in the overwhelming thunder of fists on breasts, feet on stone. Hjalli walked with Kvern between them, down to the depths, feeling the force of their love and pride like the open mouth of a raging forge, and she was steel, she was stone—

She might shatter, Hjalli knew, but these shards would find a dragon's throat, and she would be the deadlier for breaking.

In the lowest hall, Hjalli's quartz drum lay forgotten, abandoned on its side. Stray gravel littered the uneven floor, crumbs of ceiling flaking down beneath the thunder of their many feet. A living river, they filled the hall, flowing towards the deepest dark.

But as Hjalli lifted her axe and made to pass, her sister strode ahead. Kvern stopped, silhouetted in the open dark, blocking the passage. Spitting eggshell fragments of dragon tongue, her basalt eyes found Hjalli's at the head of the crowd. Her hands danced.

Go blind, she said, in the ancient language of their childhood. *Go blind*.

And her stance, her shoulders, solid as sugilite… Not madness or mourning, Hjalli understood, but *war*. Even far from herself, Kvern fought— had not stopped fighting—and Hjalli would not let her sister battle alone.

"Bind your eyes!" she called to the women assembled. "Bind your eyes or it will use your sight against you."

Without hesitation, Lendi tore the lining from her cloak, blinded herself with rabbit-felt. In a breath, the others followed. The sound of rending fabric filled the hall, becoming an instrument in their song. Hjalli turned to see. If she fell, if she failed and left her people leaderless, she wanted this— one last vision of their daughter, their clan, their *mountain,* standing solid at her back. But watching them, the fire in her chest blazing high, Hjalli knew only love, only victory.

Teeth bared, vicious and keen, she bound her eyes with her sister's own sap-stuck linen, belted a battle cry and sent her heartbeat to the shadows, battering the stones.

Her voice returned to her louder and alive, echoed in a hundred throats, no longer *come home* but *we're coming—*

We're coming, it sang, *and you will not survive.*

They did not go cautiously. They did not stop to plan or plot. The women of the mountain roared, axes drawn, and flew into the shadows. And here— deep may they dwell—their mothers, grandmothers, great-grandmother-kings watched from the earth and they could see where their daughters could not, so in the prayer of their names, they painted the chamber in living sound.

Dry scales rasped stone-choked soil. A searching tongue whispered in the still air. In Hjalli's periphery, the heartbeats of her warriors fluttered, a hundred flame-bright mice. Hefting her axe, she roared, her woman roared, until every bone, every scale, every pebble sang like struck crystal and the dragon could not hide from the thunderous din.

Together, they were steel, they were stone, and they fell heavier than a rockslide.

The World-Eater fought—of course, it fought—but what could it manage against so many? Its lashing tail met vicious daggers, its snapping jaws the teeth of maces.

When it lunged, Lendi's pick found its eyes.

When it swung its heavy head, it kissed the grinning mouth of Hjalli's axe.

When it reared, Kvern sank her knife into its breast.

And in a whimper, in a wheeze, the World-Eater sank to the earth and closed its ruined eyes.

Wrenching her blade free, Hjalli pulled down her blind. All around her, she watched women of the mountain doing the same, scattered through a vast and rough-hewn battlefield. Heart leaping in her throat, Hjalli turned to Kvern. For the first time in weeks, she recognized her sister in her face.

"Hjalli," Kvern breathed, arms outstretched and blood-soaked, smiling like coming home.

And in the cavern around them, already women wove together the song of their battle. A half-built tune filled the cavern, their victory thick with laughter, everyone cutting joints of dragon meat with fists full of their grandmothers' teeth, shaping promise, carving love—raw and hard and gleaming—into the heart of the mountain itself.

SERENDIPITY

BY STEVE BORNSTEIN

Cade let the door swing shut behind her and peered around the cramped little shop. The shelves were crowded with books and jars, with narrow aisles between them. Everything looked like it should have been covered with a layer of dust, but the air was fresh and as she slowly moved up toward the counter her finger couldn't stir a single mote of gray from one leather-bound tome. She wondered if every mage's shop looked like this, ancient but deceptively clean.

"Ahoy the shop," she called out, leaning a little to cast her call through the open doorway into the back. What sounded like a bird's frantic cheeping answered her, cut off by the sudden chop of a heavy blade on wood.

A refined voice, male, floated out of the doorway. "In the back, if you please." Cade gave the shop another cautious look, adjusted her bladesbelt, and slowly moved down a dimly-lit corridor toward the voice.

The corridor opened up into a workshop of sorts. The walls were lined with shelves holding more books, jars, and boxes, like a private smaller version of the shopfront. A double row of pegs held various tools above a long workbench against the back wall. One side of the workbench held a birdcage with a dozen colorful songbirds chirping and flitting about inside. The other side held a small pile of dissected songbird carcasses. Between the two was the unmistakable form of a Kin, his back to her. Cade was immediately struck by the improbable color of his long straight hair; it was the same platinum as her braids.

She'd seen Kin before, when they'd occasionally venture outside their Homelands, but had never been this close to one. They were notoriously private and even more notoriously aloof and pompous. Take the most perfectly beautiful human you could imagine, improve their looks even more, stretch them a full head taller, add between a splash and a torrent of innate mage affinity, and give them an arrogance to match. Most people suffered their presence because of the power and wealth they wielded, and the Kin knew it.

"Cade of Stonehaven, yes?" the Kin said, his back still turned. "Tildar at the Gold And Cups said you'd be coming by today."

Cade could see his willowy arms, so much thinner than hers, shifting in short precise movements accompanied by wet little sounds. Tildar had told her this Kin, Alcreagh, was paying top coin for a personal protection job, the very thing she specialized in, and he needed someone immediately. Kin rarely extended business such as this to humans, which only made the job more enticing. "Ser Alcreagh, I presume? Tildar didn't say anything about cleaning livestock."

She moved up to his side, boots clomping on the wooden floor. She had an idea of what she was about to see but it still took her a moment to take it all in. If you paid a bladesmith a month's wages to make a single cleaver, you'd end up with the tool Alcreagh was using to dissect these songbirds. It looked almost ridiculously huge in his hand but he wielded it like a surgeon, carving a tiny blob of flesh out of the bird's chest before tossing the headless carcass aside and grabbing a fresh bird. His fingers were covered in dark green blood from his efforts, which was surprising given how Kin were typically almost fussily clean.

Alcreagh chuckled as he worked, never taking his eyes off the squirming, squeaking bird in his hand. "I don't need help harvesting these afristine, thank you, though they are related to my goals—goals which will hopefully be our goals. I am in need of a discreet and accomplished bladedancer. Tildar tells me you have quite the reputation, from Asmara all the way here to Bradon." The bird's frantic cheeping was cut off with its head as the knife came down again.

A bright red feather from one of the bird's fluttering wings lifted off the workbench and landed on her broad shoulder, sticking pin-first into a link of her chainmail shirt. From anyone else, the bird show would have struck

Cade as unnecessary posturing. But Alcreagh was Kin, and most people never got so close a look inside their world. Maybe this was some kind of test to see if he could rattle her. If so, it was a test she intended to pass, if for no other reason than to see where this was all going.

She nodded, resting a hand on one of her blades and brushing the feather away. "Tildar said you had a week-long job and paid a good wage. What's your offer?"

Alcreagh chatted amiably as he worked his butchery, bird after bird calmly carved up and tossed aside. "I will be casting a ritual inside the lair of Karthys, during which time I will be unable to defend myself. I require your talents to make sure I am not interrupted."

Cade's mouth dropped open in spite of herself. "Karthys? The dragon? That Karthys?"

Alcreagh continued on. "I will pay you five thousand astrals upon our return to Bradon and you may keep anything you find in his hoard, though do keep in mind," he said, lifting a finger to make his point and flicking a droplet of green blood in the process, "that if I should perish, you will likely join me."

Cade stared at Alcreagh for a moment while she tried to put all this together. The Kin didn't seem to notice, immediately absorbed in carving up songbirds again. "You want me to fight a dragon," she deadpanned.

"Oh heavens no," the Kin chuckled, shaking his head. "Karthys will be away from his lair, but I've reason to believe he'll have left some sort of guards behind. They will be your concern."

Cade just looked at the back of Alcreagh's head. He was acting like they were going to take a stroll through a meadow, not violate the lair of one of the most powerful beings in the world. Still, if they managed to live through this, it would surely earn her a place in the Temple of Blades.

Alcreagh finished off the last afristine and used the knife to scoop his harvest into a small leather pouch, then wiped his hands clean on a small towel, turning it black. He turned to Cade, finally giving her a good look at his face. He had classic Kin features, regal and beautiful with cerulean eyes and an aquiline nose. He arched a perfect eyebrow, waiting.

Cade's eyes were drawn to the splat of dark emerald blood marring the smooth alabaster complexion of his cheek and had to stifle her snort. She wasn't sure what to make of this Kin, bizarre even by their own standards, or of his quest. Yet, if she didn't see it through to the end, her curiosity would kill her just as surely as dragonbreath. She cleared her throat and tapped a finger to her cheek before holding her hands out palms-up, showing the crossed-sword tattoos on each wrist, silvery ink proud against her chocolate skin. "Ser Alcreagh, on the honor of my blades, you have a deal."

Alcreagh blinked and wiped his cheek with a thumb, glanced at the greasy dribble on it, and licked it clean with an appraising hum, as if sampling a fine wine.

Nobody knew how long dragons lived. Cade had never heard of one dying of old age; until their war against the Scourge, it had been thought that they rarely died at all. Like the mountains they dwelled in, dragons had always been there, as far back as anyone could remember. Their lairs were well-known, but few dared to visit and fewer still ever returned. Finding Karthys' lair was the easy part; any map of the Shield Range worth its astrals would show the lair and the dragon's typical range around it. The details of any dragon's lair, though, had undoubtedly been bought with something red and wet rather than silver and shiny. Knowledge of a dragon's schedule was just as hard to come by, and Cade wondered just how Alcreagh had gotten any of it.

Alcreagh's research had been thorough, as far as she could tell: a map of the interior with locations of the most valuable treasures labeled. One particular cavern was circled in red ink, a dead end down a long passage. "This is where the ritual will take place," he'd said as they plotted over the counter of his shop. "I'll need several minutes to complete my work. Your charge is to defend me and hold off anything that may try to interfere with the ritual."

She'd done bodyguarding before, but only the sort of routine caravan and merchant lord jobs so easy to come by in this part of the world, where the cluster of trade routes from Asmara fanned out to the rest of the world. This was anything but routine. Luckily, she loved a challenge.

Bradon sat much lower in the mountains than Karthys' lair. It would be several days' travel to reach their goal. While their drays sauntered through the foothills of the Shield Range and lumbered up the slopes, the early morning fog curled around them, shrouding them from the sounds of the waking day.

"Tildar tells me you were a member of the Allies, yes?"

Cade's brow drew together at the mention of her former employer. "I was, yes," she said, her lips pressed thin.

They continued on for several silent minutes before the Kin finally chuckled, the sound almost swallowed up by the fog. "There is a story there, I think."

It wouldn't do to alienate her charge. He was paying for her time and expertise. If he wanted to make chit-chat for the next three days, so be it. But the bladedancer could dance around the issue he was driving toward. "I needed a change of scenery. I don't like the desert." She tried in vain to burn off the morning fog with her stare, to maybe give the Kin a distraction other than her company.

"The Allies are one of the most successful guardian contractors in the Barrens. They're the organization of choice for caravans north of Asmara."

He wasn't buying her curt replies and Cade felt the truth starting to boil in her belly. She prided herself on being professional, and that meant keeping private matters to herself, but Alcreagh's pointed questioning was quickly bringing it all to the surface again, churning like acid.

Maybe she could trust him. He certainly wasn't like any other Kin she'd ever heard of. Even the fog seemed to nudge her towards him, bringing their voices closer and blocking out the rest of the world.

The truth spilled out of her before she realized it. "The Allies are a sham," she blurted, immediately embarrassed by how loud her voice sounded. She cleared her throat and continued. "The smaller caravan runs are legit because they're not worth the trouble, but the upper echelon fakes bandit attacks on the bigger caravans. It's not enough to give the Allies a bad name because they made a big show of fighting the fakes off, but they always made sure to skim some product in the fighting. We were looting our own charges, just often enough to get away with it without making anyone suspicious or hurting our reputation."

Cade sagged a little in her saddle and found herself panting as if she'd just run a mile. There it was, out in the open. She felt like an immense weight had been lifted from her heart. She stole a glance at Alcreagh and found him looking sharply at her, one eyebrow raised. "And you kept that confidence all this time? Why not tell the caravan masters and put an end to the Allies?" he said.

Cade looked away, blinking strongly. "Because the shame was mine to bear," she muttered. "Even if I didn't know what I was a part of, I was still a part of it, betraying our charges like that. I realized what was going on after we were attacked one night and I tracked some of them back to their camp, saw their uniforms, and overheard them bragging about their spoils. As soon as we got to Asmara I cashed out and never looked back. The Sharp Lady expects better of me."

That was enough to keep Alcreagh quiet for the rest of the morning. It wasn't until they stopped by a burbling stream to water their drays that he broke the silence again. "You've not asked what my ritual is for."

She adjusted a saddlebag while her mount grunted and nosed in the creek. "Your business is your business. My business is keeping you alive." She pulled the strap tight and looked over at him, chin up.

Alcreagh walked around his idle dray towards her. Cade had no idea how he kept his ornate mage robes so clean out here on the trail. Even the gold thread still shined. He was intense now, his eyes alight with purpose. "The dragons are consolidating their power, bringing more cities under their purview. They've a plan and I aim to divine it."

Cade stopped and turned to look at him. Until now she'd mostly written him off as just another crazy Kin obsessed with whatever caught his fancy, but now he practically radiated power and menace. "Why are you telling me this?"

Alcreagh cracked a thin smile and gestured to the tattoos on her wrists. "Because your cause is my cause. The Sharp Lady bids you to protect those you take as your charge, and you perform that bidding in repentance of wrongs only you know. I am trying to protect us all, to right past wrongs as well. No good will come of the Draconic Combine, of that you can be sure." He raised a finger to emphasize his point.

The Kin's dray moaned and shuffled restlessly. Alcreagh swooped up into its saddle with inhuman grace. "And now we have shared our secrets," he continued, grinning wider. "I'd wager you never thought you'd confess your sins to a Kin. I certainly didn't expect to unveil myself to a bladedancer. And yet here we are, united by a common cause only separated by scope. It's interesting how the worlds unwind, neh? Shall we be off?" The mountain breeze caught his fine platinum hair, giving him a shimmery halo.

Cade stared up at the Kin for a moment, proud in his saddle. She felt… better? If not better, she at least felt understood. She may not have same the lofty goals as Alcreagh, but he knew why she did what she did, and that made doing it easier. A burden shared was a burden eased. Her mouth curled in a crooked smile and she hauled herself into the saddle, her leather trousers creaking as she tossed her leg over the dray's mottled back. "Hup hup," she called out, and steered her dray up the next hill.

Cade peeked out from behind a boulder at the cave entrance, a gaping maw at the foot of a sheer cliff. "It looked smaller in the picture."

"That's because the book was the size of your hand," Alcreagh said, gathering pouches from his saddlebag.

There were still times when that Kin attitude shined through. Cade shot him a dim look and went back to checking her armor, adjusting her chainmail to settle its weight squarely on her. Her fingers worked their well-practiced routine, moving from shoulders down to ankles checking the straps and buckles on her chainmail, heavy leather leggings and boots, and the twin curved swords on her hips. That done, she fished around in a saddlebag for her mechanika lantern. She wasn't sure what dragons used to light their lairs, but she wasn't counting on it to still be lit.

Alcreagh settled a satchel over his shoulder and glanced at the cave with narrowed eyes, then at Cade. "Ah, you'll not require that." With one hand, he sketched a quick sigil in the air before her.

Cade hesitated, then blinked as her eyesight shifted. Colors seemed to fade while edges became much cleaner, leaving objects in sharp relief but with muted vibrance. "What—"

"That's Allsight," Alcreagh said, unconcerned, taking another look inside his satchel. "You'll get used to it in a moment. It's better than trying to hold a torch and fight at the same time."

"Truth." Cade couldn't help but agree. That little trick alone could have saved her a lot of trouble, more than once. She tucked her lantern away.

Cade took a calming breath and drew her swords, crossing them flat against her forehead and closing her eyes. "Sharp Lady, I wield Your blades today, going forth to protect those in need of Your service. Make my wit sharp, body strong, eye quick, aim true, and heart pure. Glory awaits."

She opened her eyes to find Alcreagh watching her with a patient smile. "When you're ready, Guardian," he said, gesturing towards Karthys's lair.

Guardian. That's what she was now, here where the danger lay. Alcreagh's life was hers to protect or forfeit.

They walked together into the cave entrance, the daylight fading behind them but the cave darkening only slightly as the Allsight took over. Cade's arms swung in careful arcs, swords held ready for action. The cave's cool breeze wafted around her, smelling of nothing more than dust.

Cade had memorized their route to the ritual site and the passage unwound before them as expected, one branch after another falling behind them as they walked deeper into the mountain. Cade's ears strained for the tiniest sound but heard nothing beyond their own breathing and footsteps. The time for idle chatter was past.

She stole a glance at Alcreagh to find him looking much like he had back at the stream, gazing ahead and striding with intent, like a coiled spring ready to be unleashed. The thought of what he'd said about the Combine threat returned to her but was quickly put aside as the passage opened into a cavern.

The map had shown this cavern between the entrance and their destination, a minor section of Karthys' hoard. *Minor?* Even in the dim light of the Allsight, coins and jewels glittered like stars under the new moons. Piles of them here and there, bound chests locked shut, statuary so real Cade had to look twice to make sure they weren't people in disguise, weapons, all made by master artisans working in the most precious metals. She found her voice quiet with awe. "This is…"

"Obscene?" Alcreagh said, unimpressed. He came to a stop in the middle of the cavern and glanced around. "They do enjoy their collections, don't they? See anything you like?"

Cade's eyes fell on a pair of swords, crossed and mounted on a fine wooden rack. "Yes, I do." She walked over for a closer look. They weren't like any swords she'd ever seen. Their curved blades were mounted off-center from the grip, almost serving as a sort of handguard, and gleaming with precious filigree and inlays. They looked like they should be clumsy, but when she picked one up it felt almost weightless. The pair of them together practically whistled through the air, and a practice swing at the wooden rack left it cleaved in half.

"These are mine," she said, returning her own blades to their scabbards and walking back to her charge.

Alcreagh watched her, idly amused. "Those are Kin blades, laifhan. I wonder how he got those." The Kin shrugged with a delicate grunt. "Enjoy them, they'll serve you well."

Cade was a little surprised that he would let her take Kin property without resistance. Newly armed, she led the way toward their destination at the end of the passage.

This cavern was much like the previous one, differing only in the volume of its contents. It wasn't nearly as full of riches, and the middle of the floor was unobstructed. Alcreagh immediately walked to the center and began taking pouches out of his satchel. "It will take me a few moments to prepare. There are…" He lifted his face as if sniffing the air. "Three, perhaps four guards in the lair. I expect they'll arrive when they sense the ritual. You can expect a full-out attack."

Cade began pacing out the cavern, noting the paths between the stacks of treasure, the choke points and blind corners. "You seem to know a lot about dragons."

As Cade's path brought her back to him, she found him laying out colored powders in a pattern on the floor, dotting it at certain points with the little green gobbets he'd gotten from the birds. "You might say they're a particular interest of mine, yes." He gestured for her to move back and then laid down a line of red powder circling his mandala. "You'll need to make sure they don't break this circle. I will be inside of it. Everything and everyone else, including you, must remain outside."

Cade backed off several paces, took one last look around the cavern to fix it in her mind, then nodded. "Ready."

Alcreagh stepped into the middle of his circle, swung his arms wide, and brought his hands together in a fierce clap. The lines he'd laid down on the floor leapt into the air, the flat pattern suddenly a globe around him. Almost immediately Cade heard a surprised screech from down the passage.

Cade moved toward the mouth of the cavern and readied herself in the primary fighting position, the form that led to all others. Her new blades felt light as air in her hands as her focus narrowed and her senses reached out to the rapid skittering of talons on rock. Her dance was about to begin.

They looked like dragons but stood like men, a full head taller than her and much stockier. Any one of them looked like they could tear limbs from bodies without having to resort to the swords and shields they carried. They wore no armor, but Cade figured their scaled hide served the same purpose. She'd never seen anything like them, and three were running at her.

She heard Alcreagh shout something behind her and there was a flash of light that lit the faces of her opponents, followed by a strong breeze that began swirling around the cavern. She didn't know what was going on behind her, but the dragonmen were so fixated on it that they were going to run right past her. That gave her the advantage, one she sorely needed taking on three others by herself. As they swept around her to the right, she saw her opening. "For you, Sharp Lady," she whispered, and bounded forward to engage.

She ran at the closest dragonman. His shield was towards the other two, leaving his open side unguarded. He raised his sword and turned to her but she brought her left blade up, locking hilts with a sharp clang. He screeched and swung his shield into her side but she pushed off, using the locked blades as leverage to spin away and twirl with her right arm held out. The gleaming blade arced sideways and through the dragonman without stopping, cutting off his scream with a wet scrunch.

Cade braced her foot to bring her spin to a stop, coiling her body with blades in the ready-to-pounce form. The other two dragonmen had her in their sights now and were already rushing her, moving to either side of the steaming remains of their companion. She grinned, all teeth and malice, hot blood spray drizzling down her face. Now this was a fair fight.

She feinted right and dove left, trying to duplicate her first attack. Her target was ready for her, already bringing his sword down in an overhead swing. She tucked and rolled, the sword glancing off the back of her chainmail and crashing to the stone floor in a shower of sparks that glittered like stars in the Allsight. Cade came out of the roll with her swords to one side and spun again, bringing them around point-first and plunging them into the dragonman's back until their hilts stopped against his leathery hide.

She heard the third one scream and saw him dashing toward her so she pivoted, using his compatriot as a shield. Her victim gurgled once and then her attacker cut his head off, nearly scalping Cade in the process. She ducked the fountain of black blood and leaped away from the collapsing corpse before it could fall over and pin her.

The last dragonman barreled right over his brethren, charging with his shield. Cade dove left, out of the shield's swing, but her opponent was faster. Her right arm went numb as the shield smashed into her shoulder, her chainmail doing nothing to cushion the blow. She staggered away, the clatter of her sword on the stone floor ringing in her ears.

She panted through gritted teeth, trying to reach her old blade still in its scabbard. Her hand didn't want to take hold of it. She kept her remaining sword up in a guard as she circled to keep herself between the last dragonman and Alcreagh's ritual. She didn't dare take her eyes off her opponent but as she moved she got a brief glimpse of the Kin as he gestured at the colored shapes swirling around him. The breeze began to strengthen into a solid wind and there was another flash of light, this time accompanied by the beginnings of a shrill keen.

She was pretty sure her shoulder was dislocated. Her fingers felt numb and didn't even want to make a fist. The dragonman beat his sword and shield together and screeched, loud enough to be heard over the sound of the ritual. She took a deep breath and screamed back, then took a pair of quicktime steps before bounding toward him.

The dragonman curled behind his shield and rushed to meet her charge, his sword thrust forward. Cade's laifhan seemed to reach out on its own, deftly finding the tiny gap between the sword and shield to turn the dragonman's blade aside, slicing open his arm from wrist to elbow as Cade ducked his thrust. She went under him in a somersault and came out of it on her feet, already spinning back toward him. The bones in her shoulder ground together, sending sparks of pain across her vision and threatening her with vertigo.

She flipped her sword around in an underhand grip and swung wide, deflecting the dragonman's sword headed for her belly. The blades keened as they clashed off each other, the sound almost drowned out as the ritual gathered more momentum. It was like fighting in a thunderstorm without the rain, all flashing lights and ripping wind and deafening roar.

The dragonman pressed his attack, blow after blow deflected just in time by Cade's defensive stance. She slowly fell back through the piles of treasure, using his bloodlust to lead him away from the flashing, swirling globe of Alcreagh's ritual. The fight was a stalemate right now but he was beginning to wear her down. She needed to end this soon.

She slowly backed towards a teetering stack of chests she'd seen earlier. Her grip was beginning to go numb from blocking the dragonman's swings. She leaned in toward the stack, then aimed her sword to deflect his attack into it. His blade embedded itself in one of the chests with a meaty thunk. The dragonman screeched indignantly and wrenched it free, pulling the chest loose and toppling the rest of the stack on top of him. He staggered back and fell.

Cade took the opening, leaping and twirling her sword to shift her grip. She brought the glittering blade down point-first in a smooth arc, falling on top of the prone creature and pinning his head to the stone floor with her sword. Only once the life had left his eyes did she let go of the grip and roll off.

The chaos of the ritual ended with a tremendous thump, as if someone had slammed the door to a boisterous room. Cade was suddenly aware of herself panting for breath, and the stillness of the cavern brought the pain in her arm back to the fore again. She pushed herself to her feet and wiped ichor from her face, peering into the fading flashes of color as Alcreagh strode from the ritual circle.

"Every bit as impressive as Tildar promised," he said with a wide grin. He glanced at the way her arm hung at her side and curled his fingers through the air. "Brace yourself."

Cade opened her mouth to speak but instead gasped as her shoulder unceremoniously seated itself back in its socket. Stars sparkled across her vision again, but the pain in her arm settled to a dull roar. She blinked her vision clear. "Thank you, on both counts," she said, carefully flexing her fingers.

The Kin glanced around the cavern with a confident smile. "Karthys knows what I've done here today. No matter, we'll be far away by the time he returns."

Cade walked back to her last opponent and retrieved her blade, then walked to fetch the one that she'd dropped. She nudged the beheaded dragonman with a boot. "What are these things?"

"Draconids," Alcreagh said, picking up his satchel and settling his robes. "The dragons have created them as troops, to enforce the Combine's will."

Cade's eyes widened. "Troops?" She looked back down at the draconid's corpse. As far as she knew, the Draconic Combine was simply a glorified mutual defense pact. None of the dragons had said anything about having their own troops. This changed a lot of things. Maybe everything.

Alcreagh smiled grimly at the look on her face, then looked around at the three dead draconids. "As I said, no good will come of the Combine. You showed great spirit and ability here today. I have another proposal I believe you might be interested in."

Cade worked her injured shoulder. She'd set out on a remarkable job and achieved greatness here today. If this was leading where she thought it was, she might be able to bring even greater glory to the Sharp Lady. She tipped her head towards the cavern's exit. "You've got my ear. Let's talk about it on the way back."

RAVENBLACK

BY ALEX C. RENWICK

The Magicker's retinue was smaller but more richly dressed than Ravenblack thought they'd be. Her mount snorted and stomped, and Ravenblack's steward said to her, "Your horse feels your displeasure, Houndskeeper."

"Yes, Gart. The poor beast senses my reluctance to let Netta dress me for a formal dinner straight down through the bones of my arse."

Her steward coughed into his sleeve to hide his laugh as the over-mountain Magicker drew to a stop and waited for one of his dozen silent, dirty blond-mopped pages—hard to tell gender or age, they all were dressed so similarly and of such similar aspect, each as hunched and silent as the next—to kneel under his stirrup, a human step to assist his descent. The Magicker dismounted with a sweeping gesture of his arm that sent everyone but Ravenblack flinching. Hounds Keep didn't host over-mountain lordlings often and its residents didn't know much about sorcery, though all knew the stories of ancient battles, of fire called up out of the ground to engulf whole armies, of water crashing over desert in massive drowning tides to sweep war caravans into a vast and sodden common grave...

But this Magicker's gaudy gesture had been simply a flourish to show the man's cape to greatest advantage. It was a beautiful cape, flashing even in the anemic winter sun, embroidered with metal threads spun thinner than human hair and studded with flat hammered discs of what looked like gold. The dozen identical liveried pages dropped to their knees, adding to the man's air of majesty.

Watching through narrowed eyes, Ravenblack wondered if the Magicker's showmanship masked lack of substance, or celebrated its abundance.

The feast that night was fit for the Queen Herself, and not a mere lowland Magicker lordling of one of Her nine minor Houses. Ravenblack shifted on the wide stone bench worn thin in the middle by generations of restless houndskeepers over an aeon of boring feasts, resisting the urge to run a finger under her heavy gold torque as though it were the itchy collar of a new tunic. At least she had a ready excuse to leave early this particular night; the gryphound had swelled to the size of an overfed heifer and would surely whelp before another day dawned, or Ravenblack didn't deserve her title as Keeper.

Too late, Ravenblack reached to cover her cup with her hand before one of the Magicker's pages clumsily sloshed it full of lowland wine, a common gift from the over-mountain Houses. It was also customary for visiting retinues to lend serving staff to the host during a feast. In most households this was mere tradition and courtesy, but at Hounds Keep, on the wrong side of the pass and far even from the outer settlements, it was a necessity.

Glancing up at the soaring rough-hewn walls of the mountain hall, Ravenblack caught the eye of the portrait of her predecessor, Keeper Falkon. Reaching past her full wine glass for water, she raised her fist in silent toast, keenly missing the old man who'd rescued her from a filthy wineslop shop, a child whose head barely reached a gryphound's haunch, whose tongue couldn't form the guttural words of the mountain Houses and whose belly had never known a full meal.

Another scrawny, gaudily dressed Magicker page shuffled near. Not seeing Ravenblack's wine untouched, the child tipped the ewer over the cup's rim, so red liquid splashed across the Keeper's plate and lap. With the unthinking swiftness of one trained to the sword, Ravenblack caught the ewer in the split moment between the child dropping it in surprise and the thing hitting the stone floor.

The hall went silent. Ravenblack studied the cowering page—a girl, she could see now, the flat features and pale dirty sameness of hair and skin rendering her indistinguishable among the Magicker's retinue. Gart and the rest of Ravenblack's small household looked on with mild interest, probably as bored as she at feasting the tedious lowlander, and welcoming the distraction. The other lowland pages cowered as though they themselves had erred, and the Magicker looked… the Magicker looked *enraged.*

The lordling rose to his feet, one hand outstretched. The hearthfire crackled, its light glinting off countless tiny pearls sewn into cleverly folded pleats in the velvet, visible only when the man moved. The child gave a strangled wheeze, sinking to her knees on the stone as though in the grip of a mighty invisible hand. Once kneeling, only her eyes moved, rolling wildly as a wet gurgle escaped her throat.

The Magicker lowered his hand, slowly, slowly, and the girl flattened as he did, sinking the rest of the way to the floor.

"Stop!" Ravenblack slammed the dull silver ewer on the feasting table. Her steward and her other guests were rising to their feet, looking in wary confusion from the Magicker to their lordess.

The Magicker let his arm drop and the scrawny page struggled to her feet—gasping, gulping air—before wheeling to stagger from the hall. In three strides Ravenblack was at the man's side. His over-mountain height forced her to look up into his face, which she did not like. But his eyes flicked to the scabbard, scratched and worn and stained, buckled over Ravenblack's feasting finery despite her maid Netta's wails of protest, and that she liked quite well.

The Magicker was first to break their locked gaze. He swept low, velvets glinting in the hall's smoky dimness, eyes glittering with something Ravenblack couldn't name. "Apologies, Keeper," he said, "but these pages must be taught. They must see all the realm, they must master the arts, and they must learn to acquit themselves as befits their House. Those who survive will be toasted in the halls of the Queen Herself. Gryphounds cannot swim, and do not fight on land; the Houndskeeper will no longer be Her favorite once the over-ocean king and his armada reach our shore."

Dropping pretense of civility, Ravenblack said, "And the realm's Magicker will not be Her favorite once I remove his hands and he can no longer cast his spells. That's the punishment in this House for touching a child in violence, lordling."

Behind her came the whisper of a sword drawn: Gart, Queen bless him. Mountain folk were hardy and loyal, but generations of gryphounds keeping the snowy passes safe and clear of invasion from the southern lands had made them comfortable, and soft.

For a heartbeat Ravenblack thought the lordling might raise his hand against her, though it could mean his banishment or worse. The Queen had kept the Nine unified for generations; she had little tolerance for squabbling within the mountain-ringed shelter of Her realm. The only law in the land more sacrosanct than the Queen's was the law of a lord in his or her own House.

"I didn't touch her," said the Magicker. He must've sounded petty, even to himself. Ravenblack didn't hide her contempt as she turned her back on him and strode from the cavernous hall. Let Gart smooth things over; he was better at such statecraft anyway. The over-mountain bully wasn't worth Ravenblack spending even another moment away from her gravid gryphound.

With impatience, she ripped the gold torque from her neck and flung it into the black recesses of the rocky passage, well past the flickering glow of torches. She tore open the closure of her feasting tunic as she mounted the hewn stairs to her rooms, and listened with satisfaction to the soft pings of gold buttons ricocheting off hard rock walls, echoing in the tunnel behind her.

At least Netta wasn't lurking in her chambers. Ravenblack loved her ancient maid, but was relieved to avoid tuts and sighs over the state of her rent and wine-stained feasting clothes. And the buttons and torque belonged not Ravenblack of course, but to Hounds Keep. She already felt sheepishness replacing anger, imagining herself slinking back tomorrow through the ever-dark passageways, poking into rocky cervices looking for glints of gold.

The Keeper laced up her breeches and buckled a scuffed hard-leather cuirass over her undertunic, feeling truly herself for the first time all night; her stained fighting leathers were as much a part of her as her tight-coiled midnight braids, her short fat sword, her name.

And the gryphounds: they were a part of her too. The best part.

She tugged her boots back on and rose, suddenly eager for the straight-forward company of creatures less complicated and less troublesome than humans. In her haste to reach the rookery, she nearly strode right over the small figure crouched near her chamber's entry.

The Houndskeeper studied what she could see of the child's face past the dirty mop of hair. "You're far from the feasting hall," she said. Did her voice always sound like that? So stern? Not with the gryphounds, she was sure... at least, she hoped.

The Magicker's page held out both hands, one cupped upward holding several golden buttons, the other gripping Ravenblack's torque.

"Oh, I... Thank you." Ravenblack accepted the child's offerings and placed them on the small table inside her chamber's vestibule. When she turned back the girl was still there. Still silent, still staring up with inscrutable mute anticipation—though anticipation of what, Ravenblack couldn't imagine. It looked like the child who'd spilled the wine, but... too difficult to be certain under the Magicker lordling's ornate House livery and those filthy locks. Definitely a girl, though.

Coming to a sudden decision, Ravenblack said, "I'm headed to the rookery to check on an expecting gryphound. You can come if you'd like. It's not a sight many outside this keep ever get to see."

The page glanced back down the stony passageway in the direction of her master. Ravenblack imagined the battle raging under the child's carefully neutral expression, saw the slight tensing of her jaw and the determined squaring of her shoulders a split moment before her nod.

They wound up the steep spiraling passageway. Down led to kitchens, feasting hall, stables. Remembering what it was like to see the Keep for the first time, Ravenblack watched the child for sign of distress; lowlanders often found oppressive the dark rocky passages, the thick walls and the nearly tangible weight of the mountain bearing down from above.

On entering the rookery, a familiar peace settled into Ravenblack's bones. Though one wall was riddled with enormous openings to the sky, heavy tapestries had been hung across to seal in the aerie's natural warmth. Keep walls were warm to the touch from under-mountain hot springs. But the cliffs were dry, and sound, and unbreachable: home to gryphounds millennia before humans thought to scale the daunting peaks, to tame the narrow pass through mountains unnavigable much of the year. The Magicker and his retinue would be the last visitors until spring.

Before humans, an expectant gryphound would've been kept warm and fed by others of her colony until her brood was old enough to fly. Now it was just Ravenblack to keep her company, to care for her until her last pup took wing and left to patrol the realm's mountain border in a gryphound's solitary fashion, returning to its birthplace only to mate, to recuperate after injury or illness, to alert the Houndskeeper to potential danger, or to whelp.

Ravenblack placed a hand on the lowland girl's shoulder, holding her back. "Best stay here, child," she said. "Gryphounds bond to only a single human in a generation. Most trying to touch one are lucky to retreat with the hand still attached."

The young page studied Ravenblack's face, looking for… something. The Houndskeeper mentally shrugged and, deciding the girl understood more than she spoke, left her standing just inside the rookery to approach the rounded yellow mound of fur lying awkwardly in the fresh straw heaped against the far cavern wall.

As old Falkon had taught her, Ravenblack cleared her mind, smoothing the jumble of the evening's frustration and boredom and contrition and curiosity and emotional maelstrom of a human interior. She pictured her mind as a clear blue sky, her more chaotic thoughts and worries merely wisps of cloud dotting the distant horizon, recognizable but unthreatening.

Shifting, the gryphound met Ravenblack's gaze. Her rounded belly bulged between haunches powerful enough to launch from a mountaintop straight up into the air. The beast closed her eyes as Ravenblack stroked her pointed ears and ran a light hand down the feathery golden fur of her long neck, avoiding the sensitive wings sprouting from between muscular leonine shoulders.

Eyes still closed, the gryphound rolled her thoughts out to meet the Keeper's: a bank of stars glittering in a midnight sky blacker than the woman's braids. There was a subtle art to communicating with the creatures, both incredibly difficult and, at the same time, as simple as falling asleep. They weren't pets—were certainly not domesticated!—but they'd long ago adopted a role with the over-mountain realm, engaged in a sort of intangible bond with the humans of their choosing. Ravenblack often sensed in their nonverbal communications a nebulous paternal tolerance and distant affection for her and her people.

One of the gryphound's piercing golden eyes snapped open, and Ravenblack saw with alarm that the Magicker's page stood at her shoulder. But the gryphound's eye drifted slowly shut again, her breathing resuming its regular syncopation, panting brought on by the discomfort of her condition. The Keeper felt again the gentle intrusion into her mindscape, saw again the animal's projected field of stars, this time with snowcapped mountains a powdery white blur far below.

"She likes you," she whispered to the child, and was rewarded with the first flash of what she suspected was a rare smile. Pointing, she said in a quiet voice, "See the pale bands of lighter and darker gold in the fur around her throat? That tells how many pups she's carrying: one, two, three, four. A good solid litter! Gryphounds these last generations have been lucky to conceive and bear only one or two—or more and more often, none at all."

Thought of a future world without the majestic solitary creatures winging their golden way over the white-capped mountains brought an instant tightening to Ravenblack's throat. But she forced herself to smooth the thought away, to let the feeling ripple through her and past her like wind rippling through grass.

Ravenblack ran her hands over the animal's belly, feeling restless movements from pups eager to see daylight. "From the size of her, you'd think the whelps would come out big as fullgrown hunting dogs, right?" A slight nod from the girl. "But most of that is amnion and fluid—lots of fluid to protect the wings as they form, though they emerge tight-folded against ribs and spine. When they unfurl again, that's when the pups leave, one by one launching from the rookery into cold mountain air."

In Ravenblack's mind, Falkon's voice overlaid hers, as he explained the same things to the grubby raven-haired urchin he'd rescued from the streets of the wealthiest city in the realm. She remembered her surprise at discovering a gryphound's wings were covered in pale wisping golden fur rather than feathers, as most lowlanders thought. She wondered if the Magicker's little page had thought the same.

Standing, she said, "Come, let's give the mother-to-be her rest. She'll need it before tomorrow is done, or I don't deserve my title as Keeper."

The Houndskeeper slept later than she'd intended. She drew on her customary leathers and ranger's boots with careless haste, noting on her way out the chamber door that Netta must've stopped the night before to retrieve the ruined feasting finery. The gold buttons and jewelry were gone from the vestibule. Ravenblack imagined her old nurse staying up through the night, hunched in her private chambers near the small hearth, straining her ancient eyes over thread and needle in the service of the difficult lordess she'd cared for from childhood.

The residential chambers seemed strangely silent as Ravenblack made her way swiftly down the sloping passages toward the kitchens. An absentness tinted the air, an empty quality to the rooms she passed and to the torch-lit passageways.

A first since coming to live in Hounds Keep as a child, Ravenblack found the main kitchen hearth unlit and empty. "Netta? Gart?" she called out, answered only by her own echo.

More puzzled than alarmed, she strode through the great hall. Feasting dishes had been stacked and the hay swept the night before. There should've been at least a trio of maids scrubbing wine stains off the ancient stones, refilling the torch fuels, beating the ancient tapestries, clearing ashes from the enormous hearth. Growing more unsettled by the minute, Ravenblack began to run, the muffled thud of her bootsteps ringing in the soaring cavern as she rushed past Falkon's portrait at the end of the row of illustrious Keeper predecessors.

Heavy clouds had gathered, ready to dump their first truly winterweight burden of the year. But the yard was empty as the hall, the stables too. The Magicker's fine-bred lowland mount was gone—not surprising, since Ravenblack had expected the man to be on his way at first light if he wanted to clear the pass before snowfall sealed it for the season—but the Keep horses' water buckets were low, their grain troughs empty. Ravenblack's steed whickered as she neared his stall, thrusting his velvety muzzle into her palm. She turned, intending to fetch him some grain, when she caught sight of a bare ankle thrusting from the adjacent stall.

She knelt in the straw beside the prone body of her stable boy, a trustworthy child who loved the horses under his care like a Keeper loves her gryphounds. His snores and the steady pulse in his wrist proved he lived. After her first flush of relief, the sight of an empty wine cup in his hand momentarily made Ravenblack want to kill him after all.

She threw a horse blanket over the sleeping boy and went to find Gart. Her steward always knew what was going on, and something was definitely going on.

Gart was sleeping.

No, not sleeping; Gart was unconscious, and no amount of shaking or slapping or shouting pierced the thickness of his slumber. Netta was the same, slumped over her sewing needle near the fire, a half-empty glass of what had been heated wine sitting near her left elbow. The maids snored lightly in their chambers, and the cook and her husband, and the doddering House accountant who old Falkon said had been ancient even when *he* came to Hounds Keep as a boy. Ravenblack was slightly embarrassed to find her head armorer's unclothed form draped over the equally unclothed laundress in the woman's modest chambers—the household details Gart blessedly spared his lordess!—and everywhere, everywhere she went, she was met with silence, and slumber, and the dregs of the previous night's wine. The wine Ravenblack had not touched, but at least a cup of which had, as was custom during a host-feast, been served to every member of her household from steward to stable boy.

She lifted the laundress's dented tin cup and sniffed. Nothing smelled out of the ordinary: no herb or diluted tisane added to the mix. Not even a trace. Only sorcery could've accomplished so complete a task and left no hint of its passing, no evidence. It would wear off; sorcery was a fleeting manipulation of energies, unsustainable for long without a Magicker nearby. In intense bursts and close proximity to the caster, magicks were deadly. But ensorcelled wine, served by the dozen pages of a greedy lordling from over the mountain, would have a diffused effect. Already the sleepers' limbs were moving, their feet lightly kicking and their arms twitching, like people swimming back from the land of dreams.

But *why*? Ravenblack asked herself, a single question with so many parts is wasn't a single question after all but a symphony of questions ringing in her skull at once, all funneling into the one word until that word ceased to have meaning as she took a headcount of all her people, made sure everyone was present and safe and warm and well, if completely insensate. *Why*? Was it some prank, some petty retribution for interfering with the lordling's training methods? Was it simply a lesson, a challenge to the Queen's Houndskeeper, a warning to stay out of the Magicker's way at court as his services grew increasingly indispensable in the war with the over-ocean King? *Why... why... why...?*

Other than livestock, only Ravenblack, though sheer blind luck and fortunate timing, remained standing at the Keep. Ravenblack, and... the gryphound.

Heart pounding louder in her ears than her boots on the winding stone stairs, the Houndskeeper thundered upward, upward, the hewn rock ringing under her heels. Forgetting to calm her mind, she burst into the rookery, the wildness of her entrance causing a great flapping of the gryphound's mighty wings and setting off a chorus of mewling wails from the three pups nuzzling their mother's golden-furred barrel of a chest.

The sight of the pups swept all else from the Houndskeeper's thoughts. The love flooding her, the pride filling her up and suffusing her blood came partly from the mother gryphound, but partly from Ravenblack too. She'd stood in for this gryphound's colony these last months, had spent countless hours changing hay and stroking the feathery fur and looking deep into the golden eyes. She was as much family as a gryphound would ever know once it left the rookery, once it unfurled its bronze-gold wings and launched itself at the sun.

Blinking back tears, Ravenblack reached for the nearest pup. So unbearably tiny! It had been a long time since the rookery had seen a birth. She'd nearly forgotten that for the first few days, a creature who'd eventually stand taller than the Queen's mounts, whose wings unfurled would blot the sun and strike terror into the hearts of ill-doers, could fit in the palm of a woman's hand.

Ravenblack set the pup beside its two siblings, stroking each in turn, her fingers trembling with a fiercer love than her skin could contain. She looked around for the fourth pup—a runt, perhaps, and smaller than his brothers and sisters? It had happened before.

But there was nothing.

Ravenblack frowned, counting again the rings on the mother gryphound's furry neck. One, two, three... yes four. Definitely four. In all the Keepers' written records dating back five hundred years, there'd never been a litter whose number did not match the mother's rings.

Closing her eyes, Ravenblack strove to empty her mind of its myriad clamorings. Smooth mountain sky, chill and blue and perfect. Empty. At peace.

An image replaced the one behind her eyelids. Not starry night—this particular gryphound's customary mindscape—but whiteness, nearly blinding whiteness on all sides, fat flakes falling, a smattering of darker shapes strung in a thin line like a broken necklace dropped, its beads unraveling in the snow.

The view receded, as though Ravenblack herself lifted upward into the sky, like she possessed the powerful wings of a gryphound, the keen sight of a creature who could spot a gaudily-dressed Magicker's retinue snaking through the narrow snow-filled pass back over the mountain a fathom below.

Ravenblack opened her eyes, certain in the fibers of her soul that the Magicker had stolen the fourth tiny gryphound and was nearly through the snowy pass that would seal him off from her until spring, by which time the pup would have died without his mother to nurse him, nor his Keeper to record his passing after he was gone.

Cursing, Ravenblack cinched her saddle tighter, furious with herself for having been so clumsy in readying her horse, so *slow*. When had she gotten so soft? It was easy to forget, nestled in her cozy mountain aerie between peak and pass, that the world still ticked and rolled and turned below. As the Magicker had reminded her, war was coming.

Beyond the sheltered portions of the Keep proper the wind was bitter. Locals claimed one could taste winter in the mountains. Glad for her battered warcloak, Ravenblack rolled the acrid flavor of cold on her tongue. Though only late morning, heavy snow-clouds made it seem closer to evening. This time of year the mountain saw little sun even on a good day. By midwinter the darkness would be complete.

But Ravenblack's mount was a sturdy creature of hardy mountain stock, his coat thick, his blood warm. They soon caught sight of the procession: single horse and rider cloaked in the heavy exotic furs of some over-ocean animal; two wagons and a handcart dragged by the Magicker's dozen or so near-identical pages, harnessed into teams like oxen at the plow and staggering under the weight. At least the man had the wealth and foresight to provide them warm wool clothing. The retinue's lack of guards wasn't surprising; what fool would mess with the Queen's Magicker?

"You, stop!" shouted the Keeper. A sudden gust of wind snatched her words, swept them away up the steep side of the pass with falling sleet. "Magicker!"

This time her voice carried across the hardening ice. The Magicker wheeled his mount to face her, man and horse under the shaggy furs looking like a single mythical over-ocean beast from sailors' tavern tales. As she neared, Ravenblack saw the guilt in the Magicker's face, residing alongside the scorn and no small measure of defiance.

The children eased from their harnesses and came to cluster around their lord out of instinct or training, or perhaps simply fear of the rough, raven-haired Keeper, fear of her big flat sword and of her huge steaming horse with its enormous shaggy hooves capable of walking over the snow they struggled through up to their knees.

Ravenblack managed through teeth clenched tight with fury, with unseemly loathing and dangerous, banishment-producing thoughts: "Give back what you've taken."

Wind whistled through the crags like a wordless tune through a veteran soldier's broken teeth. For several long heartbeats, the Magicker simply stared at her, his ring of mop-haired attendants like small pale mushrooms growing around the base of a rotten tree. A finger of ice colder than the mountain air, colder than the frozen mountain soil, snaked up Ravenblack's spine at the thought the pup may already be dead, abandoned in some crevice between ice and rock, or tossed over a cliff's edge en route to the narrow pass.

But then the Magicker nodded. With the toe of his boot, he kicked the page nearest his horse. "Go, boy. Get the Keeper what she's come for."

The page slogged ungracefully through the churned snow to the nearest cart. Stepping over the empty harness, he unlaced the heavy canvas covering. Aware of the lowlanders' eyes on her, Ravenblack slid from her mount and joined the boy, that ice in her spine infecting her veins, freezing her blood in a way the chill mountain air never did, even in the middle of winter. She reached for the canvas, hating to see her fingers tremble for the second time that day, trying her best to empty her mind, to make of her fears and thoughts and loathings a simple clear blue sky, with harmless clouds wisping at its edges.

With a flick of her wrist she tore the canvas free. She stared without immediate comprehension at the jumble beneath. She blinked, telling herself those were *not* tears, and the jumble resolved into ancient tapestries from the sitting rooms in the residential chambers, and into silver plates and flagons Ravenblack ate and drank from every day, and into gem-encrusted ceremonial daggers from the Keep's library, and on top, a handful of gold buttons, and the circlet of a twisted golden torque, the weight of which she still remembered chafing her neck.

She searched the flat eyes of the silent page. "Where is it?" she said.

When he didn't answer, she drew her sword, and ran lightly over the ice to the next cart. With three hacking strokes she slashed free the laces of the canvas over the next wagon. More silver, more gold. More tapestries and even some of the silks and linens from the guest chamber bedrooms… but no tiny newborn gryphound with eyes still closed, curled smaller than a woman's fist.

A few quick strides brought her to the Magicker, his pages scattering like rats before a stableyard cat. She lifted her sword, ready to plunge it upward into the man's gut. He raised his arm and invisible energies swirled between them, pressing her back.

"Thief," she said.

"I took nothing you need to get through the winter, did no lasting harm to your people. But war is expensive. Every House must contribute to the cause."

Ravenblack saw it in an eyeblink: the man was an opportunist, and a greedy one. He knew Hounds Keep would be cut off from the realm for the winter, stuck on the other side of the pass, protecting the Queen's mountain borders with regular patrols and the help of generations of wild, solitary gryphounds who called the peaks home, sharing their aeries with a small number of humans who revered and loved them. He probably even had some sorcery prepared, ready to blast the precarious shelves of snow building hourly at the top of the peak, to send it crashing down into the narrow cut, thousands on thousands of tonnes of ice and rock. By the time the pass thawed he'd have used his new wealth to buy favor at court, to convince the

Queen of his indispensability to the war—might even have had opportunity by then to have proven the truth of his assertions.

Ravenblack's muscles strained, shaking against the tremendous invisible force holding them in check. Past the teeth rattling in her head, she gritted, "Return what you stole, lordling. I have no idea what treacherous magicks you used on a gryphound in the throes of whelping, nor how you managed to escape the rookery with your head still attached to your shoulders, but I want that pup."

Confusion flitted across his face. He twisted in his saddle, sweeping both arms up so the massive shaggy hide slid from his shoulders. The pages clustered behind him cowered like one creature, all but one dropping to their knees in the muddied snow and pressing their foreheads to the icy ground. "You," he said, hands poised midair as though he would choke the child from a distance again. "I should have guessed. Come here."

Ravenblack felt the pressure against her arms ease, and slowly lowered her sword as the child stepped over her fellow pages, one foot dragging after another. No fear showed in the girl's face, no defiance or supplication. No wariness or anger or joy. Only emptiness.

Ravenblack recalled the quick flash of a smile the night before in the rookery, and wondered if it had been even rarer than she'd known.

When the child reached the Keeper, she fumbled under the bulk of her layered wool tunics, finally drawing out a small bundle of golden fur. The pup was still warm from resting against the girl's ribs, still at peace from having fallen asleep to the beat of the child's heart.

Ravenblack accepted the tiny sleeping ball with one hand, tucking it into the neck of her tunic where it slid down, rousing briefly to wriggle into a more comfortable position near the pit under her sword arm.

"The girl will be punished," said the Magicker. "Severely. Very severely."

Recalling the punishment for spilling wine in a host's hall, Ravenblack's stomach churned. Only one in a thousand humans could've entered the gryphounds' rookery without the escort of a Keeper. Only one in a hundred thousand could've left alive. She was one such, and this strange, silent lowland girl was clearly another.

"No." The Houndskeeper looked up into the man's face, hating feeling so small in the snow beneath him, so helpless against his sorcery and his cruelty and his greed. "Give her to me."

He laughed, short and hard. "Give you a daughter of my House? You're mad."

Daughter. How had she not seen it before? She studied the raised faces of the kneeling pages. Their lips were blue, their lashes dusted with ice, and a couple showed signs of frostbite, but one to the next to the next was as alike as brother to sister to brother. "These are your children? All of them?"

"Sorcery is a dangerous art, and hereditary. Casualties are high, the power tempered like your steel. Only one can inherit my House."

Casualties. The way he stared at the girl when he said it made Ravenblack feel sick again. And it was true: never did the realm boast more than one Magicker at a time. Without looking away from him, she whistled for her mount. Patient, well-trained, he clopped up behind her over the ice, until his warm breath ruffled the loose hairs straying from her coiled braids.

"Girl," she said. "Climb up onto my horse. He's big, but he'll stand still. And you don't strike me as someone afraid of large creatures." She quirked her lips into a smile, wondering if it was her imagination that she caught the flash of a responding grin from the corner of her eye.

The lordling too ignored the girl, wholly focused on Ravenblack. "This close, I could crush you both with a flick of my wrists, send you choking to your knees, squeeze until your throats collapse. The Queen wouldn't banish me if I told her the gutter lordess from over the pass tried to abduct my own daughter."

"I'm sure that will be a comfort," said Ravenblack, sheathing her sword and swinging up behind the child in one smooth motion, "when the dozen pieces of your corpse are scattered over these peaks, carried there by dint of mighty golden wings, gripped tight in the bloody claws of big jointed paws."

She allowed herself to look away at last, having seen reflected in his eyes the swirling shape she'd sensed overhead, the mighty golden beating wings and swish of leonine tail. And another. And another, until several huge silhouettes circled, stark against the winter-white sky.

Her mount wheeled under the slightest pressure of her knees. Ravenblack felt the child gripping the saddle in front of her sag into her warmth and strength. The tiny gryphound resettled under her scarred leather armor between them, blind and helpless, its wings curled tight like fuzzy little cabbage leaves against its spine.

"You'll not get your gold back," the Magicker shouted above the whipping wind. "I have your tapestries, silks, and silver. I'll bring this mountain down behind me before you see any of it again."

Ravenblack twisted to look at him. But his attention was riveted on the wheeling forms overhead, five now, six—more full-grown gryphounds than Ravenblack had ever seen gathered in one place.

"Keep the gold," she said, shifting her weight in that perfect way to let her horse know to head for home. "Keep everything else. I have all I need."

KING'S SHIELD: A TALE OF THE WORLD OF RUIN

BY ERIK SCOTT DE BIE

LUETHER THE SUMMER CITY—RUIN'S NIGHT—961 SORCERUS ANNIS

Ovelia Dracaris first met the prince as a squalling bundle of anger wrapped in crimson swaddles and weeping for his ancestral city in turmoil around him. Many expected him to bring peace, but Ovelia dreaded his coming.

"Your son, my Lady of Winter," said the midwife. "A healthy, strong son for the thrones of both our cities." Her mahogany face beamed with fearsome pride.

The midwife extended the babe toward its mother, but Lenalin Denerre nô Ravalis, Princess of Winter and wife to Paeter Ravalis, lesser Prince of Summer, flinched away. Pale as bone, Lenalin waved toward Ovelia instead.

After a slight hesitation, the midwife gave the babe into Ovelia's war-shaped arms. The young prince was so terribly fragile, Ovelia momentarily feared she would break him against her steel hauberk. The worry fled as soon as he rubbed his face against her white surcoat. To the daughter of the King's Shield, who had never wanted a child of her own, he fit well. Perfect.

"Lena, your child is beautiful," Ovelia said.

In truth, the babe was a wrinkled, purple mass of poorly-fused flesh, his tiny fists balled in frustration, his mouth wide in a regal O of displeasure. Still Ovelia smiled.

"Shall I send word to His Majesty, your father?" the midwife asked. "He'll want—"

"Leave us," Lenalin said. "All of you! Except Ovelia—she can stay."

The woman looked dubiously at Ovelia. "But Lady—"

"Away, summerblood," Lenalin said. "Or must I summon warders to dismiss you?"

The woman left as instructed, as did the wetnurse after a reassuring glance from Ovelia. A babble of expectant voices rose, but the door sealed off the words.

"At last." Lenalin fell back amongst the sweat-drenched bedclothes, exhausted. "Did you hear her call it a boy already? When it's just born?" She made a disgusted face. "Gods of Winter, these summerborn are *obsessed* with what's between one's legs. Even a *child.*"

Ovelia nodded. In Tar Vangr, children did not become "he" or "she" or "they" until they took names and chose how they wanted to be. The midwife calling the child "he" had predisposed Ovelia to think of it in those terms. It seemed... unfair.

"I wanted to do this back home with Maure," Lenalin said. "But instead my *good husband* wanted me here amongst his snakes with their flicking tongues. Don't let anyone in."

The bitterness in her voice made Ovelia shiver. "Even your father?"

Lenalin scowled. "The council hears Cassian's last plea today. I wish my mother were here, at least, but the Winter King and Queen must support their allies."

"The Ravalis are your kin, Lena—far more than mere *allies.* Is Paeter at the council?"

"Politics," the princess said. "That and he can't stand me."

Ovelia bit her lip. Lenalin had confided in her often as to their unhappy marriage bed. Did Paeter not know what he had? What others coveted so badly? What Ovelia herself—

"It's enough that you're here, Lia." Lenalin sighed. "Sit with me, won't you?"

"Of course, Highness."

They sat, the princess and her warder, in that room that stank of blood and sweat, as the prince's cries subsided to a plaintive mewling. His mother had not held him—not even once. Lenalin breathed heavily as she stared into space, hands curling into tight fists and out again.

Ovelia well understood her frustration. Paeter had insisted that his son be born in his ancestral homeland, no matter that the Children of Ruin had laid waste to its surrounding lands and even now camped outside its mighty gates. Skyships could still dock at Luether's high-city despite the siege, but without land- and sea-bound supply lines, the city would fall in time.

The Winter King Orbrin had not only agreed to the prince's request but flown his entire royal family to Luether on the skyship *Heiress*, named for Lenalin herself. The princess thought it madness, but Ovelia understood the logic: Orbrin meant to show support for his beleaguered allies, the Ravalis, as they tried to convince their fellow Luethaar Bloods to accept northern aid against the barbarian hordes. Just as the union of Lenalin and Paeter meant to bring an end to the centuries-long feud between Denerre and Ravalis, the Winter King sought an alliance to reconcile Tar Vangr and Luether.

Alas, days of bickering at council had come to nothing, while the Children's inhuman gibbering kept the residents of Luether awake at all hours of the night. Even if they could not breach the gates, the barbarians seemed unsettlingly present. Ovelia felt secure but not safe inside the walls of the mage-city. *Trapped.* How much worse must Lenalin feel? Alone, far from home, bearing her first child? At least Ovelia could be with her.

The babe squirmed in Ovelia's arms and cried. "Lena, did—did you want to hold him?"

"Ugh, get it away." She pressed her hands over her face. "Fetch me a drink or sweetsoul or a knife to cut my wrists. A babe's the *last* thing I want."

"He's hungry," Ovelia said. "And you sent the wetnurse away."

"Old dead gods." Lenalin groaned. "I did my duty already, didn't I?"

"Your Highness."

"Oh, *Your Highness*, is it?" Lenalin sighed and sat up. "Give it here, then."

Clinking, Ovelia knelt and put the babe in Lenalin's arms. She did so with the greatest of care, fearful the princess might drop the child in her weary indifference. With some relief, she saw Lenalin's face brighten—it seemed the magic of a child touched her just as it had Ovelia. Smoothly, Lenalin slid the blanket down to expose one white breast. She shivered a little when he began to suck, then sighed. Ovelia felt self-conscious, kneeling there in armor as the princess exposed herself. Her eye settled on the porcelain basin.

Ovelia started to rise, but the princess caught her hand. Her bright blue eyes sparkled with unshed tears. "Don't leave me," Lenalin said. "Now that this is done."

"I wasn't," Ovelia said. "I thought perhaps some water—"

"That isn't what I meant," Lenalin said. "Now that I've given Paeter his child, you—what you must think of me." She looked away to hide her wet eyes. "You and Regel both."

"The King's Shadow? I'd be surprised if he had a feeling one way or another in that cold heart of his." Lenalin winced and Ovelia's eyes widened. "You don't mean—you and Regel?"

"Oh stop," Lenalin said. "And before you give me that look, he's been on missions for the King since Paeter and I married. He…" She hung her head. "He didn't take the news well."

Ovelia bit her lip to avoid saying what immediately rose to her lips— that neither had *she.*

Rather, she closed her fingers around those of the princess. "I'll never leave you, Lena," she said. "No matter whom you marry or how many princelings you bear."

"He's not so bad." Lenalin looked down at the child at her breast. "I should name him. The Luethaar do that, yes? Name children?"

Ovelia nodded. "You said Paeter would name a boy 'Cassian,' after his uncle the king?"

"Silver Fire burn my *husband's* wishes," Lenalin said. "He chose politics over his woman and his child, so he has no say in naming his son. Agreed?"

Ovelia suppressed a thrill of joy at that. "As you say, Highness."

"Darak," Lenalin said. "After my great-greatfather. Thus I name him."

"Lena," Ovelia said. "I—" She kissed Lenalin gently on the cheek. "I'll never leave you."

"Never?" the princess asked.

"Never." Ovelia kissed her again, this time on the lips.

Startled, Lenalin met Ovelia's eyes. Surely she saw how much Ovelia wanted to kiss her again. That she had *always* wanted to kiss her.

"Lia," Lenalin said. "I—"

Voices shouted loudly outside the door, and Ovelia pulled away before it shoved open. She tensed for an attack, but relaxed when she saw her father leading the three warriors in mail. Syr Norlest was tall and crimson of hair like his daughter, but his skin was much darker—the burnished complexion of full-blooded summer. An anxious frown split his warm face. The King's Shield had one hand upon the leather-wrapped handle of his sword and carried a bundle of clothes in the other.

"Syr Norlest!" Lenalin covered herself, but the red in her cheeks came from her temper, not any sort of shame. "What is the meaning of this?"

"Father." Ovelia inclined her head. "Pass in peace—" The ashen look on his face slew her words before she could finish the blessing. "Something has happened."

"Yes." Norlest chewed his lip, as he always did before he had dire news.

"What is it?" Lenalin asked. "Out with it!"

"Blood Vultara has betrayed us," Norlest said. "The council was a trap, and Cassian Ravalis lies dead, along with much of his Blood. Ambushed and slaughtered."

The wetnurse wailed in terror at the threshold, prompting Norlest's honor guard to draw steel, but the woman only sank to the floor in a faint.

"Old Gods!" Lenalin hugged little Darak close. "My father! Where is he? Is he slain?"

"Nay, Highness, he is well." Norlest raised his hand. "King Orbrin took a slight wound, but I was warding him. I left him at the *Heiress* and came to find you."

"Who else?" Lenalin asked. "Who else is there?"

"Demetrus, the King's brother. Prince Paeter. Other Ravalis. I—" Norlest hung his head.

"What?" Lenalin asked coldly. "What is it?"

"Your mother, Highness," Norlest said. "I could not protect her and the king both."

Horror filled her, and Ovelia pressed her hands over her mouth. "Gods," she said.

Lenalin, however, reacted with cool detachment. After that initial outburst of worry for her father, the king, she became the Princess of Winter she was born to be. She rose from the bed, Darak cradled protectively. "We're going then?"

"Yes, Highness," Norlest said. "I'm to escort you in all haste. Can you walk?"

"Yes." Lenalin wavered for a heartbeat, then stood steady.

"Good." Norlest thrust the bundle of clothes at Ovelia. "Help her dress. We need to go."

That said, Norlest drew Draca—the fabulous bloodsword of their lineage, with its wavy, flamed blade of red steel and hilt shaped like a dragon of legend—and signaled through the still-open door. The midwife came back in, half-carrying the languid wetnurse, as did three hooded Luethaar servants. The room suddenly filled with people. Norlest projected an easy confidence, but Ovelia could tell he was afraid. Old gods, *she* was afraid.

Lenalin gave Darak into the wetnurse's arms so the servants could dress her. As they worked, the princess stared emotionlessly ahead. Ovelia held Lenalin's hand for comfort, and the princess squeezed back. "The barbarians can't fly. We'll be safe in Tar Vangr."

"My mother is dead," Lenalin said. "I cannot—"

Ovelia nodded. Her own mother had perished bearing her, but she'd had nearly twenty years to grow accustomed to the loss. "It will be well," she said. "Somehow."

Darak squalled. The wetnurse offered the child her breast, but surprisingly, Lenalin cut her off with a glare. "I will feed my own child."

The wetnurse bowed, and Ovelia felt a little touch of pride despite everything. Lenalin was so very strong, in her way.

When they were finished, Lenalin took Darak into her arms and rocked him to grudging silence. Then she turned to Norlest. "Ready," she said.

"Ready." Norlest called to his men. He turned. "We—"

Ovelia saw the danger before anyone else. Shadows gleamed from the surface of the Dracaris bloodsword in her father's hand. The warning magic of Draca—attuned with the power of the Perfect Warder—showed shadowy outlines of an ambush. Norlest saw it too, but too late.

Ovelia would never forget that moment.

From beneath his loose robe, one of the servants drew a caster: a horrible Luethaar weapon like a bow laid cross-wise on a firing mechanism that held multiple quarrels. He loosed with a deafening *crack*, drowning out Ovelia's warning cry. From three paces, he could not miss.

Norlest had not borne the office of Shield of the Winter King more than twenty-five years for vanity's sake. The quarrel struck him full in the shoulder, but it hardly slowed him. He charged forward, Draca slashing. The assassin cried out in pain, and they went down in a tangle of limbs and steel. The caster fired again, and Norlest jerked straight as a rail.

On the other side of the bed, another servant lunged for Lenalin and Prince Darak, but the midwife threw her considerable bulk in his path. The point of a knife burst out the back of her neck. She fell, choking and scrabbling at the servant. He stabbed her again, this time in the chest.

"Admirable," said a gravel-shredded voice that chilled Ovelia to the bone.

The leader of the assassins stood before her, drawing all her focus. Dimly in the depths of his hood, she saw an awful black leather mask stretched tight across the man's face.

Terrified out of her wits but without hesitation, Ovelia lunged at the knife-wielding servant as he went for the midwife again. The sudden ferocity caught the man by surprise, and his blade scraped off the plates of Ovelia's hauberk. She caught his wrist and drove his own thin blade into his gut. He blinked and sank down onto the blood-stained bed. Darak wailed behind her as Ovelia stood and faced the leader of the traitors, armed with only the assassin's dagger.

"Admirable," the man said again. "I've no time for the games of foolish girls, however."

He raised his left hand, which bore a silver gauntlet of cunning aspect. The air around his fingers distorted as with heat. *Magic.*

"Lena," she said. "Run—"

Magic slammed into Ovelia and closed around her like a fist. When the sorcerer closed his hand, the force crushed breath from her body. Her chest burned and her vision crumbled.

"Stop it!" Lenalin cried. "Release her!"

The masked sorcerer gave her an ironic look. "As you command, Highness."

Waving his hand, he crushed Ovelia first against the floor, then against the ceiling, then hurled her into the wardrobe in Lenalin's chamber. Her body screaming, Ovelia gasped and choked and fought to stay awake. The sorcerer stood over her, his eyes bright and red. The barbed gauntlet on his right hand crackled with flame to match.

"Lia!" Lenalin cried. "Lia—"

Darkness fell.

Ovelia started awake to the sounds of a screaming child. When she wiped at her face, her fingers came away sticky with blood.

First, Ovelia saw Prince Darak, swaddled in crimson, mewling on the sweat-stained bed. His tiny fists were balled up as though around the hilts of tiny daggers. He wanted to fight the forces arrayed against him but could not. She felt much the same at the moment.

She saw a man slumped against the wall, most of his body turned to ashen ruin. Ovelia recognized the man by his Ravalis attire: he was one of the men who'd come to kidnap the princess, slain by the sorcerer. Why kill his own man? The assassin was still twitching, and could not have died long ago.

Finally, she saw her father lying at the foot of the bed. She wondered how he could have fallen asleep. Even the spreading pool of blood seemed perfectly in place. His open eyes, however, made her heart skip. Ovelia crawled to him on hands and knees and put a shaking hand to his brow. She didn't understand.

Shadows wafted from Draca, which lay by Norlest's hand. She wrapped her fingers tight around the leather-wrapped handle, and the bloodsword's warm magic infused her, awakened to the power in her blood. The sword pulled her toward the doorway, hungry for the kidnapper's fading magic, and she realized she could follow them if she moved quickly.

Blood smeared the sword: Norlest's blood and that of the traitor he'd died fighting.

Died.

The world focused on Norlest's face—his sun-brown skin made pale by bleeding. Horror rose in Ovelia's chest, but she swallowed it down. She didn't have time to mourn—not if she wanted to save her princess.

Or should she save the *prince?*

She had a choice to make: take Darak to the *Heiress* or follow after the sorcerer and try to get back Lenalin. If she fled with the prince, it would be too late to save Lenalin. She could not do both: she could not fight a sorcerer and carry a babe. They would all die.

Behind her, Darak mewled piteously, and Ovelia heard an answering sob from the next room. The wetnurse had hid under a table, somehow left alive in the attack.

"You." Ovelia stepped forward, Draca pointed at the woman.

The woman cried out and scrambled away but slipped on blood in her panic. The sticky gore got on her face and she wiped vainly at it.

Ovelia wrenched the midwife up by the collar. "Look at me," she said. "Look."

The woman's chest heaved and she moaned, but she met Ovelia's eyes.

"Do you have a name?" Ovelia asked. Most summerborn did, unlike Tar Vangryur.

The wetnurse nodded. "Fala," she said.

Ovelia noded. "You are loyal to the Ravalis," she said. "To Darak Denerre nô Ravalis?"

Fala nodded.

Ovelia bit her lip, struggling to ignore the voice inside her that called her a traitor. But the longer she put off this choice, the less likely either path would lead to anything but tragedy.

She gave herself three seconds. The first to fear, the second to quash that fear, and the third to make the choice.

"Do you know where the skyship dock is?" she asked.

Ovelia trembled as she stalked down the halls of Castle Luether, fully armored, carrying her father's shield and Draca. Her heart hammered hard in her chest, and she could feel every thud between her ears.

The walls around her echoed with the screams and clashing steel of battle. Bodies littered the corridors, a few sheathed in the gray mail hauberks of Blood Denerre soldiers but most clad in the warmer attire of citizens of the summer city. Many lay where they had stabbed each other, brothers in face if not in spirit. The conspiracy to bring down the Blood Ravalis must have run deep and wide. Hundreds had died and thousands more would die this day.

Ovelia tried not to think about the decision she had made. If she did, she would go mad. She focused on Draca's humming magic, praying to the old gods it would lead her to Lenalin.

Shadows flowed from the sword to warn of an attack just around a corner, and Ovelia pressed herself against a wall. Two men ran past, cackling, but these were not from any civilized mage-city she knew. Grotesque scars distorted the face of one man and he had no nose but only slits for nostrils, making him resemble some kind of serpent. The other had thrust shards of iron through his eyelids, propping his bugging eyes open. They smelled of blood and hate.

Ovelia had never seen one up close, but she knew the men for Children of Ruin: barbarians who roved the land outside the mage-cities, born of the crumbling world itself and devoted to advancing its destruction. They worshipped at the altar of destruction and existed only to bring utter desolation to any who dared carve out order amongst the chaos. They had laid siege to Luether for years, hungry for its downfall in honor of their mother: the World of Ruin herself.

Why were they here? Had Vultara forged an alliance with these monsters?

Pressed against the wall, Ovelia clenched her fingers tight around the bloodsword's hilt. She might be able to ambush the barbarians, but what if they wounded or killed her? What would become of Lenalin? On the other hand, if those men came upon Fala and the babe, they would kill them quickly and brutally. It was not too late to go back for them…

No. Ovelia gritted her teeth. She had made her choice.

The barbarians hurried right past her. After a five-count, Ovelia pushed on, trying to ignore her screaming doubts.

Draca grew warmer, leading her toward the battlements of Castle Ravalis, and soon Ovelia climbed the open-air spiral steps that ascended the massive ziggurat. The throne room of the castle stood high above the city, open to the city's eternal fair weather and looking down upon the two-tiered city spread out before it. Huddled against the hot wind, Ovelia gazed out over high-city Luether, floating on three massive discs of mage-glass stronger than steel. Buildings lined the glass streets and tiny folk bustled about in agitated, huddled groups. From a distance, it looked so normal—hardly like a war zone at all.

Only when Ovelia peered through the transparent streets to the smoky low-city on the ground level did she see evidence of the invasion. The great south gates stood open, one door blasted apart and the other ajar. Hordes of men and women clashed in the streets. War machines moved among them: great rolling and striding beasts of metal and gears that vomited flame and sent storms of casterbolts through ranks of foes. Many of them, however, hobbled and stuttered, unleashing their devastating payload on friend as much as foe. *Sabotage*, Ovelia realized.

Also, she saw teeming waves of thousands of barbarians clustered outside the walls.

Luether had already fallen—it simply had not realized it yet.

Over the wind, she heard the *slik-slik-slik* of an ornithopter overhead. A small craft swooped from among the clouds, three concentric silver power rings turning around it as it flew toward the battlements. Mask's escape, she thought. Ovelia hurried up the last few steps.

There stood the ragged, masked man before the throne at the height of Luether, his back to her and his arms flung wide as if to absorb the sky. Magic dripped from his hands: thorny green and black vines of liquid power that dissolved on the stone and left a sickly gray patina. He floated a few fingers' breadth off the dais, the air beneath his toes distorted with magic. The sorcerer overflowed with power, infecting the area with a foul gray haze.

Trembling, Lenalin sat on the other side of him on the wide throne of the Summerlands. Her eyes flicked to Ovelia, but she did not react other than a tiny inhaled breath. The sorcerer was saying something to her, but Ovelia could not hear it over the wind. Then he turned his head slightly to address her, and she could hear him clearly.

"Welcome, Dragon's Daughter," he said. "Kindly point that sword away."

"No." Ovelia put both hands on the sword and held it before her like a talisman.

The sorcerer shrugged. "Witness Luether's rebirth, under the Queen Who Never Should Have Been." He gave Lenalin a mocking bow. "Her Majesty."

Upon her head he'd placed the Coronet of Summer, a beautiful work of goldcraft set with rubies that glowed crimson in the setting sun. Fresh blood stained its burnished surface—it had dripped two spots of red on Lenalin's pale brow.

"Tell me your name," Ovelia said. "So I may know who brought Ruin to Luether."

"So dramatic." The sorcerer faced her fully. "I did not do this—I am simply taking advantage of the chaos the Vultara have wrought. And you may call me Mask."

Lenalin slipped from the throne to run, but Mask waved his silver glove and the same force that had knocked Ovelia senseless slammed the princess back in the seat. Ovelia gasped and took half a step forward before she could catch herself.

"I did not expect you to follow *me*," the sorcerer said casually. "I see the Blood of Dracaris can be foresworn."

"Never," Ovelia said. "I swore to protect her."

"To protect the Blood of Denerre," Mask said. "She is but mother to a prince. Do you not owe *him* your devotion? But instead you abandon him to die."

Ovelia pointed Draca at his face like a lance. "Is your tongue your greatest magic?"

"Hardly." That made the sorcerer laugh. "You think all that steel will avail you?"

He turned the blackened gauntlet on her, and Ovelia braced for waves of flame. Instead, her armor—breastplate, vambraces, greaves, all of it—suddenly heated as if in a smithy, searing her flesh. She had to drop her father's shield as it grew too hot to hold. Draca, on the other hand, seemed to grow *cooler* rather than warmer. It drank in the magic like a sponge, and the heat in Ovelia's armor waned. As quickly as it had flared up, the armor cooled once more.

Mask banished the flames with an angry growl. The pilot of the ornithopter appeared, shouting to Mask, and the sorcerer plucked him up with the power of his silver glove and hurled him at Ovelia. The hapless pilot dashed her bodily to the roof then rolled off the edge, screaming.

Mask floated off the roof, his power shaking the open-air throne room. The magic tore hunks of stone from the roof and sent two at Ovelia, one after the other. The first she managed to duck but the second slammed into her with dizzying force. Her armor absorbed most of the impact, but her body still went numb. Without the armor, that would have shattered her bones. She dropped Draca and grabbed up her father's shield just in time to block a third stone. The battle-worn steel groaned but held. Her whole body shook, about to collapse.

It was then she realized Mask had wanted her to lower the sword.

The sorcerer roared in pain and anger, and Ovelia's heart skipped when she saw Lenalin stab him with the Coronet of Summer. He held it away, though his left hand was impaled on a tine, twisted harmlessly wide. He wrenched the crown from her hands and flung it aside, trailing blood as it flew. Mask glared at her in outrage, his mask boiling with green fire.

Seeing Lenalin about to die, desperate strength surged through Ovelia. She picked up Draca, lunged forward, and drove the blade into Mask's back. Blue power exploded, throwing them both aside.

Stunned, Ovelia lay for a five-count, then shook her head to clear it. She crawled to where Lenalin lay stunned but whole. Ovelia crouched over the princess, brandishing Draca.

"This is your choice, Princess of Winter!"

Mask floated above the throne, magic arcing from his wide-flung hands. His cloak had all but torn away in the wind, revealing an emaciated body wrapped in black leather. Sickly green magic streamed from his mask, and he collected it in his hands like fistfuls of rotting intestines.

"Live and die as less than you could be," he said. "The world crumbles regardless."

He raised his hands and the power arced around to stab into the castle below them like threshing talons. Where the green magic struck, the stones grayed and crumbled, rotted away as by a thousand times a thousand years.

"In time, Daughter of Dragons," Mask said. "You will wish you had not won this day."

Then the sorcerer flew away, boots trailing smoke, as the castle stirred beneath their feet.

Ovelia pointed the coughing Lenalin toward the ornithopter. "This way," she said.

She helped Lenalin into the passenger seat and climbed behind the controls. The hapless pilot had left the mage-engine engaged, and Ovelia had no trouble slaving the controls to her will. She'd flown such a craft only once before and not well, but at least she remembered how.

Lenalin mumbled something about blood that Ovelia didn't catch, but she didn't have time to ask. Under her guidance, the ornithopter lifted up and the silver rings started to spin.

They pulled away, and Ovelia watched Castle Ravalis collapse like a great cake melting in the heat. Dust swirled as the rock cracked and slid apart. Ovelia had seen the place evacuated before she climbed to the roof, but it still made her heart ache to watch a thousand years of history and art tumble to ruin. The legacy of Blood Ravalis crumbled before her eyes.

"Blood fails," Lenalin said. "Such is the way of ruin."

Then she buried her head in Ovelia's neck and wept.

The Luether skydock fairly buzzed with activity. Word had spread of the invasion, and the surviving rich of the city were fleeing as quickly as possible. At the center of the dock stood King Orbring Denerre, welcoming as many folk aboard the Heiress as the skyship could carry.

Ovelia's heart lightened to see him. "There! Your father is waiting."

Lenalin stared out the window, seemingly oblivious.

They landed and Ovelia made it a few paces before she realized Lenalin had not followed her. She stared out at the setting sun, arms crossed. Ovelia took a deep breath.

"Lenalin," she said. "I—"

"Princess." A man appeared out of the crowd. He wore a cloak of deep gray, the hood pulled low. Black stubble coated his strong chin and his dark eyes cut like knives.

"Regel," Ovelia said, hardly able to breathe.

The Winter King's shadow nodded, his dark eyes betraying nothing. In his arms, he bore a bundle wrapped in a red blanket. It made a giggling sound. "Your child, I think."

"My son." Lenalin took Darak and pressed him to her breast.

"How—?" Ovelia could hardly breathe. "How did you find him?"

"I found a dying summerborn woman," Regel said. "She protected him to the last."

"Thank you, Regel." Lenalin glanced at Ovelia, then nodded. "You are a loyal servant."

Tears welled in Ovelia's eyes, and she turned away so they would not see her weep.

THE LIONESS
BY ANYA PENFOLD

"The *arena*?" Mother repeated, her eyebrows rising almost to the edge of her headscarf. "Linnie, is it *safe*?"

"I don't mean you're not capable," she added, while Leodinae twisted the worn fringe of the tablecloth between her fingers and wondered if she should have saved her surprise visit until sundown, "but you've done too much already. Five years' danger, just to keep bread and cloth on this table. *And* you lied to me about the Malik's entrance requirements. I found out. And to *them*, about your age—"

She winced as the door banged open. Leodinae sensed, rather than heard, Callie's slippers marching over to slam down a basket, in a way that was obviously meant to be rudely loud. She managed somewhat better with the water-jug.

"The arena," she repeated, her lip curled.

"Mother, I won't be ring-fighting," Leodinae said, ignoring the glowering gangle of limbs that had somehow replaced her little sister. "I'm an—" instructor would barely be believable, "a sparring partner. The money's good," she added, her calm tone slipping a little.

"I hear the money *is* as good as you can get without any kind of skill," Callie sniffed.

Leodinae was surprised when her mother's palm slammed down on the tabletop.

"Carilabelae Al-Beriac, you will not speak to your sister like that!" she snapped. "Linnie is back hale from the war, and you will be grateful for it. We *all* will. We'll have a proper breakfast. Let's see; figs, and cheese…" She rose from the table and turned, muttering, to the cold-store set into the heart of the thick-walled adobe apartment.

Leodinae exchanged an equally chilly stare with her sister.

"At least you're *not* a gladiator," Callie allowed, after a moment. "They're vulgar. Especially the new crop, their posters are up by the fountain already! There's one, the Lioness, she's *supposedly* one of the Hundred, but if the artist's accurate, her father was an Efreet. Her hair's *scarlet,* and she looks like a prostitute—"

Her voice faltered as their mother's head whipped around. "I don't mean the Temple girls! Or the classy ones, with their hair up in a waterfall-over-the-rocks. I mean the—"

"That's enough, Callie," Mother said sharply. "Listen to yourself, sometimes. If she's one of the Hundred, Linnie fought beside her when the Young Malik's army took down the Ghoul-Malech." Then, more gently, "Linnie, is this… Lioness… a friend of yours?"

Leodinae looked at her hands, almost wishing she'd told the truth, but mostly hoping very hard that no telltale, dyed strand had escaped her headscarf.

"I might know her to see her," she muttered. "The Hundred isn't the number we started out as, you understand. It's just how many of us were left, after…"

There was silence, long enough for the warm loaf to be cracked open and smeared with honey, and the dates and figs to be finished. One look at the cheese told Leodinae it had seen better days, a fine allegory for the family finances. Only her mother ate it.

"I should be getting along," Leodinae said, feeling awkward. "My letter of introduction won't do much good if I'm late."

It was another lie. She'd enrolled three days previously, not wanting to bear good news to her family when it might turn out false, have to watch her mother pretend not to be disappointed. Imagining how she'd be welcomed home had sustained her through the weeks of recuperation after the fight against the Ghoul-Malech's tomb-raised army. She'd bled too much to be fatally poisoned, the physicians had said — just — and the fever had mercifully blurred her memories of the actual battle.

Now, of course…

"You're *five years* late," Callie said, in what was almost a reasonable tone. Caught off-guard, Leodinae glared at her. "When I was your age—"

"When you were my age you could barely read or write, and you probably can't do better now," Callie snorted. "Pappy *paid* for your education. If you'd just studied, you could have got a job *here*, and we could have—"

"That's *enough*," Mother repeated, but Callie was already up from the table and storming to her chamber. This time Leodinae heard the tiredness in her mother's voice, although she managed a smile. "You *will* be back for dinner, Linnie?" she asked. Leodinae, already squirming with guilt, found it impossible to say no.

The problem with Zarakene, Leodinae told herself as she stomped the streets of its capital, was the way everyone, from the gods and poets down, both celebrated every aspect of life and found it shameful. She'd once assumed it was the way everywhere, although she'd heard since that in the northern *kingdoms* many harmless enjoyments, from dice to dancing, even *wine,* were *sin*, forbidden. She didn't think she'd like living there, quite apart from the cold that, allegedly, made the very rains freeze. Still, though the Games were one of Sarafanda's three "jewels of civilised life," her mother's polite horror didn't *wholly* stem from concern for her safety.

She should have expected such a reaction. Her cohort had been provincials, all, and sighed over the dancers and gladiators of her city in the same breath they condemned its decadence. She'd had some short, vicious fights over it before she'd learned it was meant in good humour. Mostly.

Recalling this brought home that she was the sole survivor, not just of her cohort but of her entire contingent.

Thinking about her family was no comfort either, now. Better to face front, especially with the great curve of the coliseum wall ahead. She had five days until her opening bout, and she still had no idea who her opponent would be.

She hoped it wouldn't be a fellow nobody, as the arena guards stepped forward and she raised her sleeve to show the pass-braid, have her presence chalked on the wall. It wouldn't be someone *famous*, of course, but if an established fighter picked her out, it might show faith in her.

The changing-room was crowded with half-dressed flesh that would have mortified her, prior to military life. Leodinae pushed her way to a bench, easing her passage with palms against bare shoulders and an open-lipped smile. Given to *strangers*. Mother would have palpitations.

She was only halfway into her ill-fitting practice-wear when a gong was sounded. She barely remembered to snatch off her headscarf.

The novices lined up in the passageway outside. Leodinae glanced, a little curiously, towards the eastern archway. Beyond lay the arena; her first step onto the white sand would be at the spring ceremony. If that was marred by river-fog, which closed the Games for winter, and often climbed as high as the Malik's palace, nobody below the aristocracy would even see the opening bouts. It would be an inauspicious beginning.

Everyone else probably cared about that. Try as she might, Leodinae couldn't.

She rocked on her heels when someone jabbed her in the collar bone.

"You," said a guttural voice. "Dreaming of glory already? *Ha.*"

Leodinae faced front, her mortification increased when she found herself staring straight into a milk-pale cleavage, *mostly* hidden behind sheer silk and chain-mail. She looked up at the thin lips of what could only be the Ice-queen. Helm-covered from cheekbone to crown, her pale colouring still gave her away.

"Follow me, Fire-hair," the fighter snapped, already turning away westward. Leodinae had to double-time to keep up.

"Who've you trained with?" the Ice-queen demanded over her shoulder.

"I—uh."

It was difficult not to stare. The northerner's step lacked the sashay learned by every toddler in Zarakene, but her determined plodding sent ripples up her thighs that the leather britches couldn't quite conceal. Leodinae was tantalisingly sure the effect might continue up and under the front of her mail surcoat. She tried looking up, away from the surge and quell of those wide buttocks, but only discovered how the Ice-queen's hair, pulled into a yellow queue through the top of her helm, wagged in time to them…

"The, uh, instructors. I've only been here three days—"

"Who *before* that?"

"Fifth cohort of the Sublime Contingent of the—"

"Sword? Spear? Flail? *Tell* me you weren't cavalry."

"Sword," Leodinae replied, as meekly as possible, "and spear. Ma'am."

The northerner snorted.

At least the Ice-queen allowed her to select weapons weighted to her preference. Leodinae was dismayed to find they weren't to spar in the practice yard, with the others, but in a smaller room beyond. She set her guard, and was nonplussed when her opponent merely circled around it, weapons down.

"Why this?" The Ice-queen stroked a strand of her hair, frowning. Leodinae hoped her own face didn't betray her feelings. Hair was *personal*.

A northerner mightn't know that. Especially a famously-*aloof* northerner.

"The— my mentor suggested I look, um, distinctive. Ma'am."

"Like me?" The question was followed by a brief smile. In a movement, she had her helm off, queue and all, revealing surprisingly deep-set eyes and a scalp as bare as any respectable Zarakene man's.

Leodinae gulped, to her embarrassment. The fuzz on the woman's head looked just as pale as her plume, and soft as…

"Fight bare-headed, rattle your brains in a season. What we do here is not just *show*."

She felt her tongue glued to her teeth, and the Ice-queen sighed. "Snip snip, glue it to your helmet," she said. One smooth movement replaced her own helm and, without any change of inflection, she added, "Now, guard."

It was strangely freeing, as always. There was no consideration outside the swing and feint and hammering of strike and counter-blow — no *time*, nothing but now — but your thoughts could drift atop this dance, if you knew how. Leodinae noted the Ice-queen had spent considerable time in Zarakene, to master the swaying, twin-weaponed mode of combat. When a strike that started as a sweep suddenly lanced straight at her, she realised, too, it wasn't her only style of fight.

Leodinae had survived the assault on the Ghoul-Malech's citadel, but as morning became afternoon she felt increasingly hard-pressed.

Eventually, as she'd feared, her right arm numbed and drooped.

"Show me," the Ice-queen ordered. When her demand was met only with open-mouthed panting, she took Leodinae's right hand and eased back the leathers to examine her forearm.

"Yrch!" she spat, recoiling. She growled a curse that sounded like *zoercherey*, before leaning in to run gloved fingertips up and down Leodinae's forearm. "Does that hurt?" she asked.

"No," Leodinae admitted. She couldn't feel *anything* there. "My arm just… gives, sometimes. It's why I took the Malik's discharge. If it gives here, I might die. If it gives in combat, that puts my *shield-comrade* in danger—"

"Hmph." The Ice-queen's fingertips explored a minute longer.

Leodinae told herself that the tingling was nothing more than the strange sensations around the scar's edges. Except it was mainly in her spine and loins.

"First bout, gauntlets only," the northerner announced. "Bare arms. Let them *see*." She flexed the arm, ignoring Leodinae's grimace. "Low trick, hitting you here. Good excuse. Have you thoughts on colours?"

As if both were merely matters of fashion.

She rolled her eyes at Leodinae's blank stare. "Yellow. For the 'Lioness.' Over the leather — shows the blood." She paused, her hand still wrapped around Leodinae's wrist. "Time to dine. We eat together?"

Leodinae tried desperately to appear star-struck, not love-struck. Then, heart sinking, she remembered her prior engagement.

"I can't," she said, regretfully.

The Ice-queen regarded her a moment. "Sweetheart?" she asked, shaping the word carefully. Her grip on Leodinae's arm slackened.

"Family," Leodinae muttered. "It's been five years…"

The Ice-queen seemed to brighten.

"Yas, family is *goot*," she announced. Then, clasping Leodinae in an embrace that smote her nose with her mail-clad bosom, "Maybehaps next time?"

Despite the nosebleed that came on in the bath-house, Leodinae could have danced all the way home.

Her mood soured when she saw her sister, hauling water-jugs to the fountain.

"Let me help," she offered.

For a moment, as Callie turned, Leodinae remembered the last time they'd gone for water together. Callie a moist-eyed lasso around her waist, herself explaining that she had to go and be a soldier now, because father was *dead*—

"It's about time," Callie sniffed.

All Leodinae's hard-won calm fled when she was around her little sister.

"None of this is *my* fault!" she hissed, conscious that any drama opened all ears.

"You *left*!" Callie whispered back, seemingly equally aware. "If you'd stayed—"

"Signing up was the best coin I could make," Leodinae said, grimly. "I would've *needed* money to stay in school, money we wouldn't have had for you. Scholarship still costs, Callie. Candles and coloured chalks… and the rest. Mother says you have the talent, I'm happy. But even if I did too, we couldn't afford it for us *both*."

She felt rather pleased with how she'd said it.

"If you'd stayed, you could have *helped*," Callie glowered.

"Helped with *what*?" Leodinae growled. "Those sigils in your sand-tray this morning? Those are *bad* signs, Callie. They were on the tombs that—"

"They're necromancer signs!" Her sister straightened, and came nose to nose with Leodinae.

"Necromancy got father *killed*."

Callie wasn't so readily cowed. "It didn't," she spat. "Pappy was sold a worthless scroll — a *lying* scroll — that told him the wrong tomb to raise from. We could've found out who did that, if you'd stayed around to *try*—"

"Why didn't you ask for Mother's help, if you really believe that?" Leodinae demanded.

Callie sneered. "Mammy cuts men's *hair*, now. Did you think we lived off thrown crusts?"

"Apparently you'd prefer that, as long as we fund your education," Leodinae retorted.

It was a long, silent climb back from the fountain.

Dinner wasn't much better. Mother had gone out for *ghoshi* and Callie's sour expression when she scooped out goat-meat indicated it was another extravagance. She was silent for the rest of the meal, leaving Mother to pepper Leodinae with questions, about her quarters, her schedule — mercifully *not* about the Lioness — and about her service.

"Their letters never said where you were, only where you had been," Mother sighed, in tones Leodinae heard as accusing. "We knew you were safe, they never sent the grave-coin…"

Between that and Callie's glowering, Leodinae found more reasons to eat with her fellow gladiators in future.

Mother had other ideas. "You'll be here for the evenings, Linnie?" she asked, after Callie had stomped off.

"We do have a curfew…"

"It's for Callie," she continued, determinedly. "She doesn't know, but—"

"She knows you barber," Leodinae sighed. "She doesn't approve, either." She regretted it at once.

"Pssht," her mother sniffed, surprising her. "No trade for a maiden or a wife, true, but a *widow*? No." She lowered her voice. "I'm training in needle-painting, Linnie. In the evenings. You see? Your sister thinks I've taken Haran Al-Carmalel as a sweetheart—"

Leodinae choked on her flat-bread.

"I had to think of the future!" Mother protested, in a whisper. "Callie's schooling won't pay off for years. What if you had come home injured? You still might. Accidents *happen*, Linnie."

Like father's.

"It's not that," Leodinae protested. "It's just… the thought of you and that *tax-collector*."

She received a long, level look.

"You *are*," she blurted.

"I'm not," Mother said, sounding prim. "I'd have to give up barbering. But he'll overlook the needle-art—which would pay better. *If* I'm established before I make… further decisions…"

Her tone was firm, but her fingers twisted in her lap.

"I'll see what I can do," Leodinae sighed.

Seeing her mother's relief only made her feel worse.

"It'll be so good, for you and Callie both," she smiled. "Scholarship makes for few friends…"

Their father's legacy, Leodinae reflected, cropping her own hair in the privacy of her cell. Both Callie's lack of friends, and the secrets they were all keeping from each other. Or was that fair? Necromancers were a tolerated necessity, like tax-collectors, and, even without Callie's nonsense, Father hadn't meant to do anything rash. Older graves were often mis-marked.

Anyway, all she could do about it now was work hard, hoping to make up time she'd wasted when she was too young to realise it.

Hard work was easily found. The morning's gossip announced her first opponent as the Gholem, long-past champion and low-level villain since. It was auspicious, but Leodinae had no illusions regarding the outcome. The man was built like an elephant's hind-leg, and rumoured to have been the Old Malik's head eunuch. She would lose, hard, and hope her pluck entertained the crowd. If the Gholem chose to humiliate her, instead, her next bout would open to jeers. Few careers survived that.

She faced her opponent that afternoon. He said little, swiping in a steady, mechanical fashion with a wooden version of his signature spiked club. Leodinae dodged and feinted, gradually realising the giant expected her to come up with a complementary style. There would be no helpful hints here. She had kept her arms bare; the right was ignored until the very end, when a merely-glancing blow rocked her to her knees.

The Gholem grunted, "Tomorrow," before turning towards the bath-house.

Leodinae followed, wincing. Then, feeling rather daring, she sought out the Ice-queen.

She was disappointed when the woman's welcoming smile wasn't followed up. Instead, the northerner spent most of the meal looking at her bowl, while Leodinae racked her brain for something to say and tried not to dread going home.

She was barely inside the apartment when her mother hurried out. Callie huffed, having deduced she was being chaperoned, and spent the evening with a wedge beneath her door, ignoring her sister's half-hearted attempts at conversation.

With hindsight, Leodinae wished she hadn't declared that Callie had "better not be raising ghouls in there." It probably hadn't helped.

Three more days seemed to set the pattern. Wordless sparring with the Gholem, a brief, breathless respite in the bath-house, a solitary dinner, and then a silent homecoming. Callie's quiet, behind her wedge-closed door, seemed resentful. Leodinae didn't seek out the Ice-queen again, feeling stupid, and guilty. *Mother* was putting off her own wants, after all. She tried to cultivate her fellow novices instead, missing the banter of service. Her success was minimal.

The pattern changed on the eve of her bout. Leodinae had brought her leathers home, needing to patch a rent opened during the day's practice, and something to do except *sit*. She nearly shrieked when she glanced up to see Callie standing in the corner.

"*What?*" Leodinae snapped, heart pounding.

"Nothing," her sister mumbled, looking at her hands. "Um. The Lioness. *Is* she a friend of yours?"

"No," Leodinae said evenly. "This is part of my job."

"What is?" Callie seemed distracted. "Never mind. I need a letter delivered. *If* you'd care to."

Leodinae stared. "To the Lioness?"

"No!" Callie stamped one slippered foot. "To the Gholem. The posters say the Lioness got called out by the Ice-queen, that's her next bout. And everyone knows the Ice-queen's got a kill-promissory hung over from last season."

"What's this letter about?" Leodinae demanded, trying to look like she knew all this. Her stomach lurched. Was *that* why the woman had barely met her eye over dinner?

"It doesn't involve you!" Callie protested, looking miserable. "Linnie, please. I swear, it won't bring you trouble. Just slip it into his dressing-room, or such. I can tell you everything. *Later.* Please?"

Leodinae had the no in her throat, when Callie gabbled out, "Peace, it's for someone at school. I mentioned where you work. His uncle, well..."

"Subverting a fight gets me *executed*, Callie! Right there on the sands." Leodinae realised she had her sister backed against the wall. She didn't even remember rising.

"It's *not!*" Callie snivelled. "It's... he wants an assignation, that's all."

"Huh." Leodinae stepped away, shaken by how Callie cowered from her. "Then what's the Lioness to do with it?"

"If she's your friend, you'd want to see her last bout, not be delivering messages," her sister stammered. "The last *good* bout. Not the one where..."

"*Oh...*" Leodinae breathed. "Oh, Callie. I'll deliver it."

Her sister wouldn't look at her. Chastened, Leodinae would have blurted out the truth, except Callie fled to her room the instant the scroll exchanged hands.

Leodinae slipped out early, deciding she could dump the letter in the Gholem's message-cubby on her way in. She had a costume to finish mending before tomorrow, and a lot of things to *not* think about meantime.

Spring arrived clad in mist, but it was clearing even as the Temples' trumpets died away. Leodinae flexed near the end of the jittery, silent queue of novices. The opening pair entered the arena... and left, quickly, one borne on a stretcher. She hoped it was for show, but the physician's expression suggested otherwise.

The crowd's "roar" had barely risen above a murmur.

The queue shortened, rapidly. Soon enough, the guards called her name.

She raised a hand in greeting as she entered, no longer expecting much response. The stands were still half-empty, but as long as she performed... and didn't *trip...*

The Gholem emerged to a muted cheer, and bore down on her the moment the gong sounded. His expression wasn't the impassive one

Leodinae recognised, but a blazing-eyed grimace she presumed he had put on for show.

Until his first swing.

This was nothing like what they'd practiced. He was furiously fast, seemed genuinely *furious,* and it was clear more than her career was at stake.

Trying not to panic, Leodinae let him back her toward the arena wall. *Mustn't* be too obvious. The white plaster would take a gouge from that club, but it would slow his swing — *if* she feinted away in time.

Her back struck something solid, and she let her expression slacken. The bait was taken, the Gholem's club flashed out. She was midway into the toe-touch that would take her up and out on the other side of his swing when the club rebounded, sparks showering from where it struck solid stone.

For a terrible moment, memory overran reality. A liplessly-grinning lich, corpse-fire guttering sparks in its eye-sockets as it loomed over her. Leodinae cringed… then the image collapsed, leaving her transfixed in the path of Gholem's return-swing.

Something changed in the Gholem's expression. He snatched at his club mid-flight, grasping it further up the haft. The spiked head, as large as her own, whistled harmlessly past her midriff.

Then the haft smashed against her maimed forearm, and she buckled to the sand.

Leodinae was vaguely aware of being half-carried from the arena.

"*Why*?" someone was repeating. She belatedly realised it wasn't her.

"Why what?" she rasped.

"Why defile my ancestor's tomb?"

That struck a chord, somehow.

"I haven't," Leodinae croaked.

"Tonight. You wrote to mock me with it!"

Callie. Leodinae hoped she hadn't groaned the name aloud.

"It's not from me," she protested. "I just—"

"You *signed* it! 'From the Lioness'!"

The awful moment. "I can't write," Leodinae muttered. "S'why I had to sign up."

She was surprised by the Gholem's laugh.

"Or me," he agreed, sounding rueful. "But... *someone* threatened—"

"I don't think so." At least her brains seemed to be working again. "I think... *they*... warned you. They just used my name because I..."

"Fought the Ghoul-Malech," the Gholem grunted. "Of course. My apologies for trying to kill you. But... maybe they *meant* me to. One of the Hundred, *here*... I would be helpless without your aid!"

"Er," Leodinae croaked, realising his intentions.

She might as well have been arguing against her mother.

The necropolis was on the shade-slope of the city, but the afternoon air was heavy. The Gholem, still dressed for combat, didn't seem to notice, but long skirts over Leodinae's leathers didn't help matters, and her headscarf prickled against her shorn, sweating scalp.

If the Gholem *had* been head eunuch, it was a significant step down. His family tombs were near the heart of the necropolis' sprawl. Leodinae's spine prickled when she realised that the largest, signifying a Grand-Vizier, had identical year-markers to those of the Ghoul-Malech's citadel.

His Grand-Vizier. Whom someone was trying to raise.

Whom the Gholem was heir to. *Had* the letter said what he claimed? If she'd confessed to being the Lioness, would Callie have told her?

The tombs around her were all chalked, faintly, with horribly-familiar sigils.

"Let's rub these off," she whispered, hoping it might do some good.

She was surprised when he helped.

Encouraged, Leodinae followed as he entered the Grand-Vizier's tomb. Sigils covered the statue-bases here, too, barely visible in the gloom.

It was disconcerting to bear nothing more than the staves Zarakene allowed. Thankfully, necromancers' powers were weak until sunset...

She was shaping a warning when a voice said, "caught you."

She backed into the shadows, heart racing, but it was someone else screaming, crying that he'd never get away with it, promising to raise pure spirits against his coerced ones.

Callie.

A figure entered, aura'd by unholy light. No, two figures, one holding the other, with a dagger to her throat.

"Your spirits won't rise, *madam*, because your spells are removed," the necromancer spat. "A shame you didn't put your faith in the living."

Leodinae felt sick. Beside her, the Gholem moaned in terror.

The necromancer turned his head, revealing a face she recognised from her childhood.

Something was moving at her back, too, stone come to life. She'd missed one of the statues. Before she could scramble away, a cold column was pressed into her palm.

A spear. She hefted it, and remembered how it had gone at the Ghoul-Malech's citadel, only with a different hostage.

And this time, she'd have to throw with her *left* hand.

She faced front, with all she had, and lanced her father's friend through the shoulder.

It was enough. He shrieked, releasing her sister. The Gholem, seeing him as mortal after all, charged, bellowing.

Mercifully, Leodinae fainted before witnessing the result.

"*Linnie,*" someone hissed. "Linnie. What happened to your *hair*?"

"On my helmet, for the indifference of the crowd," Leodinae muttered, realising her headscarf must have slipped off. It was another moment before she realised who she was talking to.

There was a long silence.

"You *are* the Lioness," Callie said flatly. "You *lied.*"

"And you lied about the letter," Leodinae retorted. "Some favours you ask."

"I had to get the Gholem here," Callie snapped. "He wouldn't have come for *me*. I was trying to keep you out of it!"

"Despite needing back-up," Leodinae pointed out.

"I did *not*!" Callie pouted. "I don't know how he removed *all* my sigils so quickly. I've worked on them every night…"

Leodinae had just decided to keep that to herself when a new thought struck her. "Wait. You've been climbing out the window? While I was *there*?"

"I just wanted a witness," Callie sighed, ignoring her words. "Show that pappy's 'friend' really was a monster. Show *you* I don't just *make things up...*"

Leodinae sighed too. "You do, though. We both do. Let's go home and tell mother a lie about where we were, shall we?"

The Gholem was gone. Leodinae avoided looking at the pulp he'd left.

Mother had not taken the disappearance of her daughters well. Leodinae could hear her lamentations from down the street. So could the neighbours, who added their own mutters of disapproval as she and Callie hurried through the lamp-light. But it was Haran who met them at the door, and had the most to say about their lack of consideration, until Mother cuffed his head and told him to let them inside.

There were hugs and tears, and Callie fobbed Mother and Haran off with the most outrageous lie Leodinae had heard her tell yet. She didn't argue it though, not with her sister sitting against her for the first time in five years.

Of course, four at the table left Callie little choice.

Leodinae discovered her second bout felt unimportant, after that. Win, lose, be jeered out of the arena... as long as she came out alive, they'd muddle along. Even if she didn't, the family Al-Carmalel now seemed on the cards. Mother and Callie would be all right.

It wouldn't stop her trying to be around for them, however, and she'd been studying the Ice-queen's moves *very* hard.

This bout was greeted with far more enthusiasm. Leodinae felt her fear leave her, allowing her to twist and dart and feint without thought imping-ing on her at all. She was at the top of her form, shedding the Ice-queen's feints like a fountain throwing leaves into the air.

Abruptly, she was dropped by a sweeping-kick, and found a sword-point at her throat.

"Goot. *Close*," she was told. The Ice-queen's eyes glittered behind that helm. "You have things to learn, maybehaps? I can show..."

Leodinae found herself swept up into a kiss.

The crowd loved it as much as she did.

It was after dark before she and the Ice-queen—hand-in-hand, and wreathed in veils—braved the streets. Leodinae took a roundabout route home, since all established gladiators had to pretend to anonymity. She tried not to feel nervous as they drew closer.

"My sweetheart, Haran," Mother said, once they were welcomed. "And this is my younger daughter."

Leodinae blinked at the sight of Callie standing against the wall, as shyly as a child. Mother smiled proudly as she added, "She's in training as a mage, like her father. My *first* husband."

The way her hand touched Haran's as she said it indicated a second marriage was indeed on the cards.

"*Zoercherers* do not wed, in my land," the Ice-queen growled. "They are killed."

Leodinae cringed.

"As are women who take women as sweethearts, I believe," Mother answered lightly.

"Yas," the Ice-queen shrugged. "Is why I'm no longer there. Problems?"

"No problems," Haran said mildly. "Except, with only four seats, who's to sit in whose lap?"

THE HERO OF ITHAR

BY SARAH HENDRIX

"I think he put that there just to annoy me," J'hell groused as they rode towards the town square.

Tirel, her husband, chuckled as they stopped at the object of her irritation. It was a statue, cast in bronze, of a young woman in full armor, her long unbound hair flowing artfully down her back and shoulders. She held a sword ready as she looked across a non-existent battlefield.

"Well, it's the only road into the square," he said.

J'hell glared. "Bad enough they have to put the thing here, but just look at it."

Her husband cast an appreciative glance at the monument. "I don't see anything wrong with it." He knew it annoyed her but J'hell was usually too frustrated to voice exactly what it was that bothered her.

His wife growled. "Of course you don't see anything wrong with it."

Tirel raised an eyebrow in speculation. "Well, I don't think I ever saw you just standing there looking around." He was about to say more but she punched him hard on the arm.

"That's not what I meant." She pulled her mare up next to the statue. "Just look at it." At her husband's perplexed look she snarled. "It has breasts!"

"Well so do you."

"Do you ever remember seeing breasts when I was in the field?" she said as she pointed to the armor cupping ample breasts on the woman. "Gods above and below, that's the sort of thing that get soldiers killed. An enemy's sword wouldn't slide off. It would punch right through! Anyway," J'hell continued, "why would they put something like that on a warrior figure? It's not like you can tell who has breasts and who hasn't under all the padding."

Tirel snickered. "That's what was bothering you about it?"

"You'd think the artist never saw a woman in armor before. It's not like I didn't stand about in the armor at the Chief's house for hours on end in every pose imaginable for a week." The town Chief had offered to display her armor once she had settled on the farm. She had taken him up on it without question knowing plate mail would be useless around horses and cows. If she needed it for ceremonies or to impress the locals she had simply to show up and put it on.

"He wasn't very impressed with you when you met," Tirel said quietly.

J'hell rolled her eyes. "I wasn't impressed with him either." She remembered the day the thin little man dressed in clothes completely inappropriate for travel showed up in town. Of course it had been during planting season and she couldn't simply leave the team to turn over the field. His biting remarks at her tardiness and snide comments about everything from her armor, hair and face had left her biting her lip raw. He spent a week of her time sketching and grumbling about his vision of the project before he left with a folder full of sketches and notes. She was glad she didn't see him when the monument arrived nearly a year later. He probably would have left with bruises around his neck.

Because she was busy on the farm, she didn't come to the square often. No one had informed her of the monument's arrival but she knew something was up when the town chief began to plan a huge banquet. She was more annoyed when people from the surrounding villages began to arrive. Some of the King's advisors had even showed up. But when the monument was revealed, she had to sit and feel the humiliation rise while everyone else ooohed and ahhed and complemented her on the likeness.

J'hell didn't even think it looked like her. Tall and lithe, the woman on the monument was a sharp contrast to J'hell's short, stocky frame. The long flowing hair was nothing like the retired warrior's short curly locks. And although the youth of the figure didn't bother her, the look of innocence turned her stomach.

"That one would be dead in her first battle," J'hell snarled.

Her husband shrugged. "Besides the 'oh kill me now' breast armor, what else would have killed her?"

"The sword," she replied without hesitation.

The weapon in question was a long thin blade decorated with thorned vines and tiny flowers. The hilt barely fit the woman's hand.

"Something like that would snap the first time I blocked a thrust." J'hell paused, and patted the short sword on her side. "Then there's the hair." She turned to her husband. "Did you ever see my hair like that?"

At his shrug she continued. "Not only would it catch in every part of your armor, it would be too easy for an enemy to grab."

"So that," Tirel gestured at the statue, "is a death trap."

She nodded. "I feel sorry for anyone who thinks you look like this after or even before a battle."

"Well it's improved the volunteer rate for the King's Guard here at least."

J'hell snorted. "Yeah, but anyone who joins from *here* knows what they are getting into. I won't sugarcoat what life is like while you are in the guard."

Once she and Tirel had retired to his parents' farm here at the edge of the kingdom, they had insisted on creating a training program for those who wanted to join the King's Guard. With help from the local militia, they set up a weekly training session. Anyone was welcome to sign up, and learn skills necessary for survival in the field.

J'hell clucked to her mount and turned it away from the monument. "But no use arguing about it. Can't change the damn thing and the chief is waiting."

"Ah yes," it was Tirel's turn to snarl. "The yearly parade of the Hero of Ithar, complete with a festival and a thousand ways to kill off the guest of honor."

"It's not that bad," J'hell tried to soothe him.

He gave her a startled look. "Oh sure, the town is crowded with strangers. The food is shipped in from all over the kingdom. The town guard is never prepared enough and often ends up screwing up something. I have no idea what they would do if we actually had an attack. And the one person in the world I'd never want to live without is the center of attention." His training as one of the Prince's bodyguards always made him edgy during the festival.

He reached over for her hand. J'hell grasped it and gave it a firm squeeze. "That's what worries you most." She smiled as they rode on. "I don't think you have much to worry about. The worst that's happened in seven years is that stupid monument."

"You look beautiful," Tirel said. He smiled brightly and leaned in for a kiss.

J'hell sighed and leaned her head on his shoulder for a moment. The truth was she hated being the center of attention. It was part of the reason she had retired here, far away from the capital. Being the Hero of Ithar was exhausting for a single evening, and she couldn't remember how she survived doing it day after day. "Thank you," she whispered.

While she didn't think she was beautiful, she was at least presentable. Over the years, she had developed the talent of wearing clothing other than armor and wrestling her hair into something other than a mess. Tonight she wore a dress made from a material that was a higher quality than most women of the village could afford but cut in a simple and practical style. Her unruly curls had been tamed to frame her face. A light application of powder subtracted a few years and wrinkles from her features.

She and Tirel sat at the high table just under the shadow of the monument along with the town chief and the council. The children were off with her mother-in-law or chasing the dogs that continually hung around the town. The Chief had already given his speech. The town elders would take turns talking to the crowd before it was her turn. Once that was over, the feast would begin, along with the drinking. At some point, they'd be able to escape and head home.

She looked across the square identifying familiar faces and strangers. Since this was the seven year anniversary of the battle of Ithar, the scattering of people of importance was a bit stronger although there was no one she was familiar with. They sat at the table to the right, just a level lower than the main. To the left sat the chiefs and mayors of the surrounding towns and villages. The rest of the square was filled with tables from local homes spread out in an unorganized sprawl.

The scent that arose around them was mouthwatering. Most of the homes in town had been preparing for days. The bakery fires had burned steadily for days baking breads, rolls and desserts. Animals specially selected for slaughter were butchered, buried in pits, split over slow fires or baked in ovens. J'hell was looking forward to some particular sweet and savory dishes that she only tasted on occasions like these.

Earlier a group of musicians entertained the crowd with songs. After the speeches they'd regain the crowd's attention. Once the food was consumed, most of the tables would be cleared and the square would be filled with dancers. As the night progressed, things would become wilder, but nothing more than some public drunkenness. Overall, J'hell supposed it would be another quiet evening.

She sat straight and tall, barely listening to the words of the council. The words drifted into a monotone as she remembered other festivals and speeches. The oldest member of the council stood and began his speech when the screaming began. J'hell stiffened, eyes scanning the crowd as silence fell. The people at the edges, nearest the road into and out of town began moving towards the middle of the square. In a moment the trickle became a flood of bodies, moving away from the disturbance.

Tirel grabbed her shoulder getting her attention. She hadn't realized she had stood up. "Sit," he whispered.

She slowly lowered herself into her seat, but her hands still reached for weapons she decided to leave at home this night.

"I'm going to tell the others to keep calm," he said as he nodded to the table of nobles. "Stay here."

She nodded as he moved to whisper to the Chief and the others at the high table. Before he moved very far away her attention was taken by a group of heavily armed men forcing the town's people before them like cattle.

There were more than twenty armored troops surrounding a mounted man. The troops were wearing heavy chain, and carried swords or maces. They marched in unison moving like a well trained unit. Unlike the other troops, the mounted man was only lightly armored, but wore a flamboyant helm making him impossible to identify from this distance. The troop moved slowly, allowing the townspeople to move before them but not around them. They spread out as they reached the square, flipping tables out of the way, scattering food, drinks and the occasional dog or cat. To their credit most of the residents moved away without panic. J'hell tightened her lips as the crowd pressed closer to the main tables.

The militia captain, sitting beside her, started to get up. J'hell stopped him. "Just sit," she hissed. "Now's not the time for a fight."

He glanced at the crowd then back at her. "My troops."

"Are either captured or dead," she told him coldly. It wasn't the first time she had to say those words and when she moved here she had hoped never to say them again. "Either way you can't help them right now."

The captain squeezed his eyes shut a moment and nodded. Although he did sit, he was tense ready for a fight.

J'hell glanced around making sure the rest of the table sat calmly as the troop approached. She knew from experience that keeping at least a semblance of calm often made the difference between a few lives lost and a slaughter. She watched the crowd and acknowledged every frightened glance with a nod. It calmed many as she saw the frightened looks drain away to determination.

Finally the crowd could be pushed no further and the troops stood at wary attention. The mounted man pushed further as the crowd parted before him.

"Where is the Hero of Ithar?" he called out as he pointed to the statue. "I would have words with her."

J'hell noticed the chief barely shake his head. "She's not here."

The man mounted on the horse laughed. "Of course she's here." He reached up and took off his helm. "Is this not the anniversary of the overthrow of the Lord of Ithar? Is this not where the great Hero took leave of her position? What hero wouldn't attend her own feast?"

He pressed his mount further into the crowd. As the details of his face became clear, J'hell felt her heart drop. The lord of Ithar had been mad. Convinced that he alone would be the next king, he conscripted most of the countryside, forcing anyone strong enough to wield a weapon into joining his army. With the help of his religious leaders he led a holy war against his neighbors. With a few victories, his troop numbers swelled making it impossible to put up a defense.

When her kingdom came under attack, J'hell found her troops playing a cat and mouse game against the larger army. Guerrilla tactics kept the larger company at bay but she knew it wouldn't last. When word reached her that the lord himself was commanding the troops set against her, she devised a plan to take him out. It had succeeded, but the lord's son Chriv, escaped.

From what she knew, this man was much more deadly than his father. And he was here seeking revenge.

"Give her to me and I'll leave this town in peace," Chriv yelled. "Resist and I'll burn it to the ground."

J'hell had no doubts that he would and once again started to stand, but the captain grabbed her arm. "We aren't giving you up," he hissed. "If there's anyone here who can outsmart him, it's you."

It had taken every trick she knew to outsmart the Lord of Ithar. She had been young then and willing to try the riskiest of plans, desperate to save the lives of her troops and her kingdom. She was twenty years older now; injuries that healed ages ago ached when the weather changed. Her sword dances looked impressive, but they no longer held the strength or the speed she once had. Except for a few, most of the people around her weren't trained for combat. She'd have to wait for an opportunity.

Chriv raised his hand in a silent command. His troops began pulling women from the crowd. Then he pointed his raised hand at the statue. "So be it. Bring me anyone who looks like that."

Chirv's troops swarmed the square and separated the children from mothers and the men from the women. Anyone looking remotely like the statue was brought before the lord's son, who now sat at the head table enjoying the remains of the meal. His troops had taken one look at J'hell and dismissed her. She joined the other women near the chief's house under heavy guard.

As another young woman was presented, Chriv shouted, "No that's not her. She's a vicious warrior, not a little girl." He threw a goblet at the soldier. The girl was escorted to the group of women. Another was brought forward.

J'hell stood at the back of the group where the shadows were deepest. She watched as the girls were brought before the Lord's son and he rejected them. Eventually his patience would wear thin.

"J'hell," Abret, the chief's wife, whispered nearly in her ear. "What should we do?"

J'hell didn't turn. "I need a distraction," she told the older woman. "And the keys to the house."

She felt Abret's breath as she exhaled sharply. "When?"

Another girl was rejected. The pool of younger women was startlingly small. "Soon." She felt the cold metal of a key placed in her hand before the woman's presence disappeared from her side.

J'hell slowly made her way to the door, whispering instructions to the more responsible and level-headed women on her way. The whispers passed quicker than she did, and a wall of the tallest women in the town stood before the door when she arrived. Although she was partially out of sight, she still moved carefully and slowly. She slipped the key into the lock and cringed when it clicked open.

The sound of wailing drifted to her ears and the guards turned their attention to the sound just long enough for J'hell to open the door and slip inside. From there, she made her way to the library where her armor hung. She began unlacing her dress, hoping to the gods that the chief had salvaged her under-padding as well.

It had been a while since she had dressed herself, and a few of the straps needed adjusting before she was confident nothing was going to rattle itself off. Luckily the chief had seen that the joints were well oiled and the small repairs she had asked for had been made. She buckled the belt that held her sword, then pulled on her helm.

The chief's house had several doors, and she made her way back through the maze of halls to one that would open up at the side of the group of women. At best, it would give her an unobstructed charge at Chriv. At worst, she'd be captured immediately. She grasped the handle of the door with a little prayer and pulled it open.

"...has to be here somewhere," raved the lord's son. "She has to be!" Chriv stood on the table, overshadowing the rest of the young women before him. Some knelt on the ground crying, while the others clutched each other in terror. Chriv swung a heavy mace high over their heads. "Tell me now, before I smash you all to a bloody pulp."

"Enough," J'hell shouted, surprised her voice and lungs still remembered how to produce such volume.

The lord's son froze, and he slowly lowered his mace. He straightened himself before he turned. J'hell felt a flutter of nerves as the man's eyes fell on her. He glanced at the monument then back to her, confusion furrowing his brow.

She took that moment to charge, pulling her sword as she dashed across the open space between them. Swinging at his legs, she hoped to wound him and be finished.

Chriv moved quickly, jumping just high enough that her blade swept through the air. He landed and hopped down to the ground as J'hell spun to face him again. He was younger, faster and had a heavier weapon. On most occasions that would give him an advantage, but J'hell wasn't going to give him room to close in. She danced away, keeping her small shield up, and slid beside the monument.

Chriv snarled and rushed her, swinging his mace. J'hell stepped aside and let the weapon crash into the bronze statue with a resounding clang.

"Bitch," he hissed as tightened his grip.

"I think your father said that, too," J'hell said, "right before I ran him through."

Rage flared in the man's eyes and his face turned red. He raised the mace again and stepped towards her, swinging. He was in enough control to not hit the statue again, but his swing went wild.

"Your father was a damn fool, and so are you," she shouted.

Chriv rushed at her again swinging wildly, his mace striking the statue again, but this time, his heavy weapon remained wedged in the metal.

Without hesitation, J'hell's well-placed thrust ended his life. She turned to the troops who stood in shocked silence. "Drop your weapons now or die."

It wasn't surprising that most of them surrendered but a few put up a fight. A few of the town's folk were injured but none severely. Once the town was back under friendly control, J'hell stood with the captain and the town elders.

"Good work," the captain said. "I thought for sure you were a goner."

She chuckled tiredly. "Luckily, Chriv wasn't that smart. Otherwise he would have realized that no forty-year-old woman would look like that."

"Speaking of which," Tirel said. "Your statue is a mess."

The bronze statue was battered where the mace had struck it. The sword had been shattered and the woman's legs had cracks where the casting had shattered. From the looks of it, the thing would have to be taken down before it fell over.

"We can have it rebuilt," the chief offered. "More to your likeness if you'd like."

J'hell ran her hand through her short, curly hair and smiled. "No, I think I like it just the way it was."

GOLDEN

BY TODD MCCAFFREY

"How does this sound? 'It can never be stressed sufficiently: to anger a dragon is to die. To steal a dragon's gold is to die, to covet a dragon's mate is to die. Death by dragon is swift but not painless, usually involving flames which can melt steel.'"

"I think you could have stopped with the first sentence, Daddy," Golden said. "The rest are merely illustrations of how to anger a dragon."

"And you forgot to mention challenging a dragon to a joust," Elveth said.

"If I mention that then you'll get fewer jousts and less gold," Simon replied. "I thought the idea was to create more challenges."

"The *idea* is to get more gold," Elveth corrected testily. She smiled at her daughter, adding, "Golden isn't getting younger and she'll need a hoard of her own." Her smile faded as she added pointedly, "You're certainly not getting any of mine."

"Of course, mother," Golden said demurely. When Elveth wasn't looking, she shot a look toward her father who shrugged sympathetically.

"Your mother left you quite a nice pile, if I remember," Simon said.

"That's because I killed her," Elveth reminded him waspishly. She flicked a finger at her daughter. "You're not to get any ideas, little miss gold scales."

"Yes mother," Golden replied, dipping her head and avoiding eye contact. Elveth was the sort of mother who would *literally* rip your head off if she got too angry: Golden had seen it once and needed no reminders—in this she was like her mortal and human father.

In most other things she was the exact replica of her mother. Only where Elveth was a mottled copper color when a dragon, Golden was pure gold—hence her name. Even when born, she had a beautiful head of fine golden hair and there was no contention over her name.

"She is Golden because she is my gold child," Elveth had said and Simon had wisely kept silent, particularly as, according to his studies, he was the first human dragon-mate to survive through the rigors of a childbirth with a head still upon his shoulders.

Simon and Elveth had often conversed on their daughter's coloring: Simon was convinced that it was protective in nature while Elveth held to the old dragon lore that color predicted flame.

"A pure gold like that will mark the hottest of fires," Elveth had declared with much warranted maternal pride.

At the time, Golden had yet to have her first molt and was still clinging to the forlorn hope that she was not a dragon but, rather, a normal human child. She loved her father as fiercely as all girls—perhaps a bit more so because of her draconish heritage. Simon, because he loved his daughter, hoped that her wish would come true but deep down he was convinced—and secretly relieved—that she would molt and turn into a dragon when she was of age.

There were tears all around when that day finally came and Golden found herself molted into the slim body of a young dragon princess.

"Oh, my dear, you are so beautiful!" Elveth had cried with tears of joy.

"I'm a dragon!" Golden had cried with tears of despair.

"You shall live forever," Simon had said with tears of relief.

"As a dragon!" Golden had wailed. "I don't want to be a dragon!"

"Well, you are," Elveth had snapped, her copper color eyes warming dangerously.

"Ixnay on the agon-dray," Simon had muttered warningly to his daughter.

"But it's true!" Golden cried, flouncing out of their small house and accidentally destroying the staircase, the good dining table, and three large iron pots.

When they had found her later, she was lying on her mother's hoard in the deep cavern that was hidden behind their house.

Elveth growled and looked ready to change but Simon put an arm on hers. "She must have a terrible headache."

"Golden, how do you feel?" Elveth asked, primed by her mate.

"My head feels like it's going to explode!" Golden had cried.

"Oh, dear! It's all the magic going around," Elveth had said sympathetically. She turned to Simon. "I should go out and kill more mages to ease the pain of my po0r little girl."

"Now, dear, we've had this conversation before," Simon told her soothingly. "The evidence is that magic flows from the sun. The mages merely tame and use it. Ridding yourself of them leaves more magic to pain you."

"At least I've got my gold," Elveth said, moving to join her dragon daughter in the huge pile that spilled from its mound in the center of the cavern. She turned back to smile at her mate. "And I've got you to thank for it."

Simon blushed but said nothing.

"How's that, mother?" Golden asked, her talons digging deep into the pile and spilling it over her like a torrent of pebbles—although these pebbles were mostly gold doubloons mixed with the occasional broken crown or necklace.

"Well, it was your father who realized that knights and princes would wager much to fight against a dragon," Elveth said, glancing slyly at her mate. "And so he arranged it and I've been successfully ridding the countryside of useless knights and worthless princes."

"But I thought Daddy was—"

"Your father, a knight?" Elveth asked with a laugh. She eyed Simon thoughtfully. "Well, he *is* of the nobility or he would not be a suitable consort for one such as myself but he was a squire when we met and much more scholarly than most." She smiled at him. "The bashful boy was completely taken with me after I'd scorched that useless knight of his into mere ash."

"Sir Girwhed was noble and brave," Simon said in defense of his long lost knight, "but he would not listen to my counsel."

"And that was?" Golden prompted, lifting her snout through a pile of treasure and letting it spill to either side.

"I told him if he fought the dragon, she'd burn him to a crisp," Simon said with a shrug.

"See!" Elveth cried, giving her mate a look of adoration. "He's one of the smartest humans I'd ever met."

"Of course it took a while for our courtship to mature," Simon reminded her.

Elveth laughed long and brassily. "Yes, I recall telling you every night that while I enjoyed our conversations, I was never going to be foolish to transform into a woman just so you could kill me."

"Actually," Simon said, "I seem to recall endless nights of your telling me how quick and painful my demise would be."

"Only after you beat me at chess!" Elveth said, her expression slipping.

"And then she changed into human form," Simon said with a smile that bordered on a leer. To Elveth, he added, "I always knew that you'd be the most beautiful of women."

"Flatterer!" Elveth chuckled. "And, of course, well, Golden dear, you came along."

"And now I'm a dragon!" Golden cried. "And I'll hoard gold and flame useless knights to ash just to build my hoard !"

"And it had better never get bigger than mine, missy," Elveth added warningly.

"Of course, momma," Golden replied shyly.

"How's your headache?" Simon asked.

"Better."

"Then maybe you can change back," Simon suggested.

"Change back?" Golden repeated in wonder. "How do I do that?"

"Close your eyes," Elveth told her. "Close your eyes and think your wings away. Think your pretty scales gone and your beautiful slitted eyes turned back into small golden round orbs. Feel your hair on your shoulders and your body shrink as you become a mere human shape."

It took more coaxing but in twenty minutes, Golden was once again in human form.

"Later, dear, we'll teach you how to build clothes," Elveth promised as Simon lent his daughter the jacket he'd worn just for the occasion.

That had been the beginning of dark days all around.

"Well, I'm learning a lot," Simon had quipped when challenged to find the good in the emotional stew that was two dragon-queens in the same house—one daughter of the other.

Golden would wail about her mother, Elveth would shriek about her daughter, and Simon would spend most of his time trying to perfect his flameproof armor and—naturally—work on creative ways to keep one or the other from escalating things into a firestorm.

"The house is made of wood!" Simon had cried hopelessly at the beginning of their first mother-daughter, dragon-dragon spat.

Not long after the ruins were made of ash.

A year later, Simon was saying, "I didn't know your flame was hot enough to melt brick."

It had been Golden's flame which had reduced their second home to glowing glass slag—much to the surprise of all.

Simon had taken to spending much time in the village tavern—they knew nothing of his home life; thinking him merely a farmer with a wife and daughter but to no avail. It had ended the night Golden had run into the inn crying and a copper dragon had flamed off the roof.

Simon had, at least, earned much respect from the villagers when he'd stood up to the copper dragon and had sent it packing.

Of course, as he knew, the whole family was shortly packing to find some new dwelling—not just because of Elveth's flame tantrum but also because the villagers decided that they were better off without the services of a farmer who spoke to dragons.

They settled many hundreds of miles away in an entirely new kingdom far in the south where, after not too much time, Simon had begun convincing princes in other lands that their greatest glory lay in challenging a flaming dragon in a duel to the death.

Simon also learned much of the ways of daughters and mothers from those willing to share their knowledge—and there were many—and grew more and more despairing for the survival of not just his dwelling, or his hide but of his family.

It seemed like it would all end when Golden, just barely fifteen and far too young for a dragon to go a-roaming, fled the house in a flaming huff which set the far mountains alight.

With the flames marking a clear path back to their home, Simon knew that he and Elveth would also have to move or face uncomfortable questions and other such things—like pitchforks.

"Pitchforks won't hurt me!" Elveth had exclaimed when Simon brought them up.

"I, on the other hand, am not so sturdy," Simon reminded her. She had not been so distracted by the loss of her daughter as to consider the impending loss of her husband unworthy of her concern and so, as Simon had urged, they fled for healthier parts.

Fortunately, Simon was a wise man and had their destination long-planned—when living with two strong-minded dragons, it was practically inevitable that one way or the other they would find themselves relocating—so, even though her family fled in her wake, Simon had the comfort of knowing that Golden would know where to find them.

They were settled into the cold, wet north that was safely far away from their other homes for over two years before Elveth started pining for her missing daughter.

"She's old enough to take care of herself, dear," Simon had staunchly assured her—trying to believe the words that he'd been telling himself for the past twenty-four months.

"A dragon isn't mature until her fiftieth year!" Elveth cried.

"You were forty-five when you ate your mother," Simon reminded her.

"Exactly!" Elveth said. "I'm glad you take my side in this, Simon. If only you had been quicker, she would still be with us."

Simon wisely kept silent. The only result of his reminding his dragon-wife of her part in their daughter's departure would be to have her grieving over the ashes of her husband… and, doubtless, complaining that *that* was her daughter's fault.

When Elveth had finally dissolved into a flood of heart-broken tears, Simon said, "There, dear, we'll find her. She'll be back, you'll see."

"She'd better," Elveth hiccupped, pushing herself away from her husband, her eyes slitting as she speared him with her gaze. "After all, it's all *your* fault."

"Yes dear," Simon had said wisely. He then excused himself on the grounds that he needed to get some water. He did not say that he intended to douse himself in it for protection. He was away long enough that Elveth was asleep when he returned, her human body slumped in her chair, head on the table. With a sigh, Simon gently pulled the chair back, lifted her up, and carried her to their bed.

He was still drying himself off, having covered her in their blankets, when he heard wings rustling. He dropped the towel and tore out the front door.

Out of the darkness a golden-haired girl emerged hesitantly.

"Daddy?" Golden asked in a small quiet voice.

Simon raced to her, grabbed her and twirled with her in his arms, his head pressed firmly against her shoulder, his tears flowing unabashed. "Baby!"

They stood, entwined, for the moment that was forever. Then, because even eternity must end, Simon pulled away from her.

"Are you staying?" he said, glancing back to their newest home and wondering how to manage the re-union and its aftermath.

Golden shook her head and her fine blonde hair shimmered around her like a gold waterfall. "I can't."

Simon heard another noise rustle in the darkness and quickly pushed her behind him, ready to defend her with his life.

A small, dark-haired, green-eyed woman shrank back from his motions.

"This is Erayshin," Golden said, grabbing his arm and pulling him to a halt. She beckoned with her other hand for the girl to approach.

"Is she—?" Simon asked, his eyes wide in fear.

Golden shook her head.

"Does she—?"

"Yes," Golden said. She gestured again for the girl to join them. The girl stepped forward. She was smaller than Simon, short, and lithe. Her eyes were on his daughter. They flicked to him with worry and then back to Golden with determination. Golden's voice hardened as she said, "They wanted her to marry a prince and she didn't."

"She saved me," Erayshin said, her voice fluid with words learned far away.

"He brought a dowry," Golden said, her voice filled with the sharpness and longing that Simon had first heard so many years before from his dragon wife—the voice of dragon lust.

"There have been twelve more," Erayshin said. An impish look crossed her green eyes and gave Simon the distinct impression that the foreign girl was just as devilish as his daughter.

"I've got a rather nice hoard," Golden agreed.

"I asked to come here," Erayshin said, giving Simon a frank—and somewhat terrified—look.

Simon had rarely seen that look but he knew all the muscles that caused it. He waved to his daughter. "Why don't you let me talk with your friend for a bit, Golden?"

"I need to stretch my wings," Golden said agreeably.

"There are some nice places to the north—the far north," Simon suggested.

"Thirty minutes?" Golden asked.

"That would be plenty," Simon agreed. His daughter smiled at him, waved at her friend and walked off into the dark. Not long after a beautiful gold dragon erupted into the skies above them and raced away northwards.

"She's been gone two years," Simon said in the silence.

"I met her about six months after," Erayshin said, moving closer to him so that she could look up into his eyes in the gloomy dark.

"My wife—her mother—is inside, sleeping," Simon said, waving toward the house. "I'd invite you in but... well, Elveth is jealous."

Erayshin smiled. "So is your daughter."

"She learned it from the best of teachers," Simon told her with an answering smile. A moment later he said, "Will there be a prince who claims your heart?"

"Will there be a woman who claims yours?" Erayshin responded. When Simon shook his head, she nodded. "I came to ask you how you managed."

"It will be easier for you," Simon told her. "Without a daughter to argue with, all you'll have to—"

"There will be a child," Erayshin said, her hand going to her belly. "I wanted to know —"

"A child?" Simon interrupted in amazement. "How?"

"Golden told me: 'Where there is a heart, there is a way'," Green said. "It took her many months but we found a way."

"The child is *hers?*" Simon cried.

"Ours," Erayshin said. Her smiled turned inward for a moment. "Just once, she became a male."

"I must write of this," Simon said, preparing to run back to the house for pen and paper.

"Please," Erayshin said, reaching forward and touching his arm for the first time. "I must know—how, what, how—?"

Simon put his other hand over hers. "You have to say yes if you say anything," he said, glad to have this one chance to share his hard-won knowledge with someone. "You must be silent when you want to scream, be obeisant when you want to fight—"

"I can do that," Erayshin said, trying to sound certain.

"You should be ready to move often," Simon warned.

"She has a hoard , we know where to go," Erayshin affirmed.

"And you must never stop loving the both of them," Simon said finally.

"How do you do that?" Erayshin said as they heard wings in the distance flapping back toward them. "She's been gone all this time—how did you—"

"And you have to love them more than life itself, love them enough to let them go when they need, love who they want," Simon told her. He moved and brought her close against him, wrapping her into a tight embrace.

Erayshin looked up at him, her eyes wet with tears. "Will you forgive me? For taking her love from you?"

Simon shook his head, his lips quilting upwards. "You could never do that. I will honor you."

"For what?"

"For the courage to love her."

The wings hovered near the forest, stopped, and Simon turned them to face the darkness.

Golden rushed out into the light, paused fearfully, and then rushed into their open arms.

Twenty minutes later, Simon returned to his home, pausing just long enough to watch the gold dragon and her rider wheel overhead and then disappear into the dark night.

He sighed and quietly entered the house, went to the bedroom and crawled into bed with his wife.

Elveth nuzzled against him and murmured sleepily in a combination accusation and comfort with a plain meaning: Where have you been? I missed you.

"Golden came back," Simon told her softly. She tensed against him. "She has a partner, a hoard , and a home."

Copper-colored eyes opened and peered up at him.

"They are with child," Simon said, choosing his words as carefully as always. "You're going to be a grandmother."

Elveth was silent for a long while, her eyes closed tightly. When she opened them again, tears streaked from them. "There has never been a dragon who knew her grandchild!"

Simon leaned forward and kissed her tears away. "I know."

Elveth was silent for a moment, then snuggled herself against Simon.

"She's a good child," Elveth murmured before turning to face him directly. "Let's make another."

Simon, wisely, said nothing.

SHARP AS A GRIFFIN'S CLAW

BY RHONDA PARRISH

Where I come from they say there are a finite number of souls and after death each goes to a great repository to await another vessel to fill. By that reasoning, if one were to live forever, they would encounter the same souls over and over again...

I recognized her the instant I heard her. The sound of her resonated with me, its vibrations thrumming through my entire being. I ached, *ached* to see her, to touch her.

"*Bayne*," I said telepathically to my companion. "*Bayne, the bard. I want to hear her.*"

He shrugged off the whores who clung to him like stalactites and swaggered across the tap room to the corner where the elven bard sat. The nearby fireplace cast shadows over her face, her hands and the stringed instrument clasped between them, and when she sang her voice was as sultry and ethereal as the smoke which drifted from the fireplace to cloak her. She sang a story from another age, another era. Ugly truths made beautiful by the music of her instrument.

Once, in a land far darker than this, on a plane ruled by demons and devils, there was a love so beautiful, deep and transcendent that it was destined to tragedy, as all pure things are. A love between a swordsmith and her forge imp.

Her name was Abira and she could fold and twist metal like taffy. Banished from living with her own kind she'd come there, to the darker plane, bringing with her something more valuable than gold or silver: secrets and skill. She alone knew the secret of smelting metal that shone silver and bright rather than dull and black. Customers travelled for weeks to seek her, for her blades were light and strong with edges sharp as a griffin's claw.

In truth the credit for her masterpieces was only partly hers. Without her imp, who was especially talented at manipulating temperature, her furnace couldn't possibly have held the perfect heat so consistently. The hammer strikes upon the metal were all hers, but its heating and cooling controlled by Teyat.

He was an ugly misshapen creature, even for one of his kind. Squat and bumpy with blotchy olive skin and a voice like the hiss of red steel dropped in water. He had three eyes, yellow and cat-like, which spanned his forehead, two back legs, strong and powerful as a hare's, and a pair of forelegs so short he couldn't scratch the back of his own neck.

The swordsmith was no great beauty either. Her ebony hair was frazzled from the constant heat of her forge, cut short, just beneath her pointed ears to keep it out of the way, and her skin, where it wasn't covered by her great leather apron, was pocked and scarred from sparks and burning debris. Ugly as they were, still, the half-elf and the imp created dozens of beautiful ways to kill.

Each morning when she entered her forge she would call into its shadows and the imp who lived within would set the coals alight. At the end of each work day she'd put her tools away and blow the imp a kiss. "Try to miss me," she'd say facetiously.

Tongue oozing sarcasm he would answer "I shall dwell in darkness until your return," and douse the coals.

What started as a business arrangement grew over time into something much more. Like the folds in a piece of steel, their relationship developed, layer after layer, until one day the imp found from the time Abira blew him his kiss at the end of the day, until the next morning when her voice warmed the forge once more, he was not just alone, but lonely. He missed the sound of her moving around the forge, her scent, the sight of her bathed in sweat and colored by flames.

Love is not a common thing for imps who are, by nature, selfish and mischievous creatures. In this Teyat was no exception, yet, as the years passed, he was eventually forced to admit-to himself if to no other-that he had fallen in love. In love with a mortal, no less.

The bard didn't sing the story, but spoke it softly, accompanying herself with the lute. The background song added to the tale, locking my attention in, pulling me to her. I felt as though she were playing for me. Only for me.

"*Heard enough?*" Bayne asked, looking from the bard to the bevy of women, all warm and desperate for his company and the coins it brought.

I hadn't. I wanted to curse him for interrupting the tale, for demanding my attention for even a moment, for distracting me from her. I wanted to explain that I recognized her. That I *knew* her. But I didn't. That would take too much time, lead to too many questions. How could I explain? How to make him understand?

"*Not yet,*" I said, my voice in his head deliberately cold and casual.

He shrugged once more and raised his empty mug to a barmaid indicating he wanted another, then gestured to one of the whores. She scurried over like a mouse and tucked herself under his arm, pressing her body against him and giggling. Her perfume cloaked Bayne and I both, flowery and insufferably sweet. Nothing like hers…

He worked harder than ever to make her happy. He honed his skills at manipulating temperature and soon he was able to heat or cool any metal to any degree within less time than it took for her to speak it. He began to anticipate her desires—so clearly it was as though he could read her thoughts. Their blades became even more impressive. Lighter, stronger, sleeker.

Men began to look at her differently. Now they came to the forge not only to contract but also to court her. The man who could make her his wife would find himself rich beyond measure. Not only could her work be hired out as she had been doing, but also if a man could control her, he could outfit an army with her weapons. An army such as that would be powerful. Unbeatable.

She spurned the advances of all those who entreated her, saying only her skills and not her soul was for sale.

Abira sold to noble and ignominious alike. To humans and demons, to wise and foolish. She had a trove of treasure that grew day by day, as she armed the men who fought one another. The land drank up their blood and she drained their pockets. Over and over again. She knew if she were foolish enough to let man become too strong, to take over the land, eventually there would be peace, and if there were peace there would be no need for a swordsmith. So it was in her best interest to keep things chaotic. Evenly balanced. So she scaled her prices so that no man, however rich, could afford more than a handful of her blades. No man could gain too big an advantage.

Then things began happening to the men who visited her forge. Unfortunate accidents. One would sit upon a stool only to have it suddenly become red hot and burn their breeches to ash within the second it took them to leap from their seat, another would pick up a hammer, playing with it casually while flirting with Abira and have it turn so cold it would fuse with their palm, requiring great care and warm water to separate them.

After one such incident, as the injured suitor limped out of the forge with a bandaged hand Abira turned on Teyat, fury flashing in her forest green eyes. "Teyat, you threaten my business!"

"And you," he shouted, carried away on a wave of jealousy toward the man who had dared to stroke Abira's cheek with his knuckles, "You, threaten my heart!"

The words, so honestly and passionately spoke, shattered something within Abira's heart and she looked at the imp, dirty and hunkered down among the coals in her furnace. The only creature, the only man, she'd ever known who hadn't wanted anything from her but her company. Who never asked for more than her voice. Misshapen and broken he was, but no more than a lump of ore waiting to be forged and as she looked at him she saw, for the first time, his beauty.

From that day on they were inseparable. Inseparable and in love.

People talked. People talked, and whispered and laughed. The half-elf and her imp lover. None had ever heard of such a thing, and yet, there it was. Right before them.

Sounds of love interspersed the ringing of hammer on steel within the forge, and those who made the mistake of entering without knocking soon came to regret it. It was unnatural, they said, but Abira's business boomed. As her connection to Teyat blossomed and grew, so too did the quality of their work. Soon they could communicate without speaking, and work together without thought. The metal became like clay beneath her hammer and she worked it into ever more intricate and marvelous forms. Her wealth grew and grew, and she and Teyat were happy.

So happy that before long she'd pat and rub her belly when no one was looking, humming softly under her breath.

And then came the wizard.

"There's always a wizard isn't there?" Bayne said, smiling down at the girl under his arm. "And they are always evil, aren't they?"

She laughed and burrowed herself deeper against him, muttering something unintelligible and unimportant. Bayne pushed his bone white hair back, out of her face, and leaned over to kiss her. I tried to ignore them. To ignore the irritation that flashed through me at the continual interruptions. The girl would say whatever she thought Bayne wanted to hear, at least for as long as he was paying her, but he should know better. He'd had enough experience with magic users that he should know how easily that power can corrupt. How often even those with the best motives go bad and how horrible it can be when they do.

I expected more from him.

But he was distracted by his whore and it wasn't worth pursuing. Not now. Not while she was there. Right there. So close I could almost touch her...

The wizard had a proposition. A deal Abira couldn't possibly say no to. He offered to teach her how to imbue her blades with magic. How to make them even more powerful, more beautiful. In exchange she would make him a handful of automatons, metal creatures he could animate to do his bidding. He wasn't asking for an army, so Abira couldn't see how this would hurt their business, quite the contrary. She discussed it with Teyat and he agreed, and so the seeds of their destruction were sewn.

Abira worked hard with the mage, learning the magical runes she needed to work into the blades, memorizing the words she needed to speak to wake the magic and coax it to do her bidding. She frowned over the pages he showed her. Spells written in languages long dead, spelled out in pictures and scratchings none but those of the craft could understand.

Teyat watched her face grow pale, and though her belly became more round, the rest of her became sharper, more pointed, as weight dropped from her day by day. She did not eat, she did not sleep. She bent every ounce of her will toward learning, toward understanding. This. This, she said, was the thing which would make her famous, rich beyond dreams and, more importantly, it would bring her the kind of power even money cannot buy.

Eventually understanding dawned. One afternoon as she squinted at the page by the light of the fire, the words suddenly made sense. The sounds didn't twist her tongue into a rune, instead the magic dripped like honey from her tongue.

She forged the mage's automatons and sent him on his way, and true to his word he left with her the spell pages she'd need to craft her blades, to make them sing with magic.

Then she became obsessed.

"Don't you see?" she said to Teyat one evening when he begged her to come to bed, to step away from the forge, to rest. "Don't you see? A handful of these swords and we can make her a queen! A ruler of man and beast."

"Her? You're so sure."

"I am," Abira nodded, her eyes feverish, her face flushed from hard work. "I am. We can give her everything we never had, Teyat, my love. We can give her power, and acceptance. Never will she be mocked or called half-breed or forced to work for another. No one will dare. No one."

And Teyat understood how important those things would be to their child—the child of an imp and a half-elf. How could such a creature ever achieve understanding or happiness without such an advantage? Besides, he loved Abira with all that he was, and so he kept the furnace temperature just right, and when Abira fell asleep slumped over her books or her tools, he didn't wake her and ask her to bed, but covered her with a blanket as best his undersized arms would let him, and kept the forge warm for her.

Wizards aren't easily parted from their power, not even shreds of it, and so it was with this one as with all others. He'd tricked Abira. Though the spells he'd taught her were real and true, they took their power not from the ether, not from the world itself, but drew upon life force.

The child was born dead. Perfectly formed with the shape of her mother and her father's eyes, the girl was still and silent as she slipped from Abira's body, and no amount of steel or spell could give her breath.

Abira bled so heavily that Teyat brought a midwife, a demonic woman with tiny hands and immense horns upon her head, who stopped the flow of blood but told the imp his love could never be with child again.

They wept, the broken couple, holding one another, huddled together in their bed. Outside random stones melted yellow and liquid as egg yolks and the falling rain turned solid as Teyat's control over his gift faltered.

I didn't want to hear this part of the story but I couldn't leave. I had to stay there, where I could see her, where I could hear her. I wondered, did she know I was there? Could she recognize me too?

They tried to take comfort in one another but could not; could not because so many dreams had been shattered, and even the pleasure they'd found in touching one another was tainted by thoughts of what it had once led to, and what had been taken from them. Only by destroying the wizard could they find peace and perhaps happiness with each other once more.

The imp and the half-elf forged a plan. She would craft a sword. The ultimate blade. Her masterpiece. And with it they would hunt down the wizard and take their revenge.

Abira was a skilled swordswoman—you don't spend a lifetime crafting weapons without learning a thing or two about wielding them. Coupled with Teyat's magic, that ought be enough to buy them revenge.

Abira forged a blade. She etched the magic runes the wizard had taught her upon the metal before forming it, knowing the steel would remember their shape even after she pounded them invisible. She worked day and night on the sword. Pouring her blood and sweat and tears into it. Each hammer strike resounded through her core and she drove her pain into the metal time after time after time.

Finally, eventually, she held the sword. Though it was perfectly balanced, honed and straight, it wasn't a lady's weapon. It didn't have a filigreed guard or visible engravings. She'd crafted it to kill; it needn't look pretty while doing it.

It was a two-handed beast, nearly as long as she was tall, with a simple leather-wrapped pommel and a divet in which she embedded the hinged and hollowed out ruby which held their child's ashes. It would have been impossible for her to wield if not for the enchantments she'd placed upon it. It was lighter than it had a right to be, for one, and helped to hold itself up though a slight levitation spell. When she practiced with it, it moved like an extension of her body.

She looked fierce, and frightening, and when Teyat watched her wielding the sword in the light of her furnace, her shadow elongated and twisted across the walls, he shivered. This was not the woman he'd fallen in love with, and though he loved her still, he also feared her, and feared for her. She'd changed. No longer apart from the world around them, she was like every one of her clients. Single-minded and bent upon destruction. Teyat knew then how their story was going to end, as he watched the tears and sweat roll off her body, but his heart wouldn't let him do anything but see it through.

He didn't know, I thought. Not then, he didn't. He knew it wasn't going to be a happy ending, to be sure, but he had no idea just how much he was going to be made to suffer. No idea at all.

The bard's voice was whisper soft as she continued, and most of the taproom patrons quieted to listen, many leaning forward to hear her better. Her lute's sound turned softer, more like sobbing than music, and as I listened I knew. She recognized me. She knew I was here and a mixture of shame and happiness swept through me.

She knew. She knew.

Finding the wizard wasn't difficult, the land was not overly large and the mage was well-known to all within it. Teyat sat upon Abira's shoulder for the whole trip there, and once they arrived it was no challenge at all for him to burn the front door to ash. Before they could enter they were met by the automatons Abira had crafted for the mage, but Teyat flash heated them until they glowed with it, then just as suddenly caused them to cool. The metal they were forged from exploded from the strain, showering them with splinters and shards.

Abira was safe beneath her armor, but not Teyat. Not the imp.

He felt the metal, colder than ice, bury itself in his belly. The momentum knocked him off Abira's shoulder down onto the ash covered stone floor. His breath rushed out of him in a gush and left him flailing his arms in panic while the bottom half of his body lay still; twisted and bleeding. He struggled to breathe, his lungs burning with the effort, while the searing pain in his belly blossomed to fill his entire being. Finally he sucked in breath, and stars erupted behind his closed eyes, then all he knew was the fire in his belly where the metal had penetrated him. He struggled with his stubby arms to grasp the wound but couldn't reach.

And then she was there.

Abira pressed her palm against his injury and within two beats of his heart her hand was coated in his blood. Hot, warm and so dark a shade of red as to be almost the color of cold coals, it pumped from his body with every heartbeat.

"Go on," he gasped, hoping she would think his motives honorable, that he only wanted her to avenge their daughter, but in truth he didn't want her to see him like that. Bleeding and helpless and dying. The smell of blood and shit filled the air and he could feel tears of despair pricking the back of his eyes. "Go on."

"I can save you," she said, and he felt the warmth of her tears as they fell upon his cheeks.

"No."

"I can. I can cast you into the sword—"

He looked into her face, tearful and grey, scared and angry, and he nodded. At least he would still be with her, and the pain would stop. The pain would stop.

The spell which ripped him from his body and cast his consciousness into the sword rent the skies with its power and great torrents of rain poured down and washed the tears and blood from her face. She kissed his broken body once more and stood, the massive sword held tight in her hands.

"*Are you ready?*" she thought to the blade she wielded, to her love.

"*Yes,*" he thought back, sending the words into her mind telepathically.

A magical extension of the connection they'd already forged over the years of working and loving together. *"Oh, yes. Let's dance."*

What the bard didn't say, because she couldn't, was how that fusion felt. The magic ripping through flesh and bone, pulling spirit, mind and soul from its body and infusing it with the steel. How the imp's body bucked and twisted on the ground, back arching impossibly before flopping back, lifeless, onto the stone.

She couldn't say because she wasn't there. She wasn't. But I was.

The wizard's home looked larger than it was, a feat he accomplished with magic and mirrors. They charged through it, shattering glass as they went so it couldn't distort their perceptions, couldn't deceive them.

Abira used Teyat's pommel to demolish an especially large mirror which hung at the end of a short hallway in the upstairs of the wizard's home. The glass rained down, tinkling like crystal tears, and revealed behind it a door. Abira turned the handle and, before the blade could stop her, stepped through.

The wizard looked up from where he'd been bent over a book as they entered. Pointing a finger at them and a fist-sized ball of flame came soaring directly at Abira's face.

Teyat saved her.

Even from within the sword he could control temperature and he froze the ball as it flew toward her. By the time it connected with his blade it was a ball of ice, not flame. It exploded against him and fell in a thousand pieces to the floor at their feet.

Abira made short work of the wizard then, but wizards are sly creatures, more than capable of causing destruction even after their bodies have been relieved of their heads.

It was as they were leaving, flush with satisfaction, struggling with loss, vengeance, and Teyat's new form, that it happened. Abira stepped on a loose floorboard, one she'd managed to miss on the way in, and before she could blink the trap was sprung.

Finger-sized darts sprang from secret compartments all around them. From the walls, the ceiling, the floor. They filled the air like a swarm of bees. The majority stuck, quivering, in the wooden surface opposite of where they'd come from, or *ting*ed off her armor like hail stones. Thinking the battle done, she had removed her helmet, and several darts hung from Abira's face. Some were embedded deep in her flesh, while others clung to her skin, barely hanging on.

There was naught but silence for several long seconds, and then Abira screamed. She screamed and screamed, losing control of her mind she opened a telepathic channel and shared her agony with Teyat. He felt the river of pain she was riding. Knew how the poison in those darts made her blood burn like molten metal, felt it melt away all her self-control, all that she was.

This was the sort of heat he could do nothing to stop. Nothing to control.

He saw her memories, the happy thoughts she tried to cling to, the first time their daughter had moved within her, him screaming "And you threaten my heart!", her blowing him a kiss, the mage's head soaring through the air. He felt her grapple with them, try to hold onto them, to draw comfort from them, and fail. He felt her agony flare white hot and burn them away. Every memory, every happy thought swallowed by the burning, the burning, the never-ending burning.

He couldn't stop the burning, but he could stop the pain.

"Fall onto me," he screamed in her mind, as loud as he possibly could in order to be heard over the torrent of pain that wracked her. "Fall! Fall! Fall!"

And she did.

He was so big, so long, that it was awkwardly done, her falling on him, but done it was. He entered her, becoming hot and wet with her blood, went into and straight through her. He pierced her lungs, her heart, and exited out the other side and when finally her agony stopped, her love was inside her and the remains of their daughter pressed tight against her chest.

"I shall dwell in darkness," he said. "Until your return."

The bard let the story end there. She lowered her lute, bowed and accepted the applause and coins that were her reward for a tale well-told.

I didn't know what to feel. Hollow and lost, mostly, hollow and lost.

I wondered if the bard knew who she held.

I did.

I recognized her the moment I'd seen her. My love, my Abira. Her form was wooden now, and rather than ebony hair she was crowned with tuning pegs, but I knew her. Each time the bard had run fingers over her strings I'd envied her. Envied her ability to touch her, to play her, to make her sing. Once upon a time I'd had that ability. Once upon a time it had been I, not a bard, who was her partner.

It could be again, I thought, then looked at her strings. I looked at her strings and thought of my blade. Sharp as a griffin's claw. I admired the finish across her body, sleek and perfect, imagined it rubbing against my pommel, hard and unforgiving. I thought of the hinged gem that had been embedded in my pommel generations ago, of having to explain its loss.

The bard slipped off her stool, unstrung Abira and carefully packed her away in a case. I watched her every movement, torn between fear and desire, then she hooked her arm through that of the older man she'd entered the tavern with, her father judging by their similar appearance, and smiled up at him. She picked up Abira's case and started out the door. Out of my life. Again.

"*Bayne,*" I said in the mind of the man who wielded me.

"*Hmm?*"

"*I need—*" I need what? I need you to follow her? I need to see her? To hear her? To feel her one last time? I need to be with her? All true, all of them.

"*Teyat? What? What do you need?*"

"*Nothing. Never mind.*"

A NIGHT IN
NEW VEROSHTIN
BY CASSANDRA ROSE CLARKE

The war was changing.

That was what Lieutenant Raza told Salima during the debriefing. "They don't want us fighting battles the way we used to," she said from behind the big mahogany desk where the politicians had shoved her after the Battle of Anausi. It was a nice office, tapestries hanging on the walls and a window that looked out over the harbor, where the supply ships sailed in. But it was still an office.

"Yes, ma'am." Salima didn't need to be told this. None of them did. The war had been changing for awhile, and not just in the usual sense of the fronts shifting. A whole lot of sitting around in camp, smoking and drinking and watching the light shows from the magicians as they practiced their devilry out in the wastelands.

"But that doesn't mean the Realm doesn't still have need for you." Lieutenant Raza reached into a drawer and extracted an envelope and set it on the desk. Creamy paper and the Realm's seal, blood red wax with the imprint of a snake coiled in on itself. Salima's heart fluttered.

"We're shipping out?" she said

Lieutenant Raza hesitated. "Not exactly. *You're* shipping out."

"That doesn't make any sense."

"As I said, the war's changing. Our way of fighting isn't the best tactic anymore." Lieutenant Raza nodded at the envelope. "But your talents can still be put to use. Open it up."

Salima peered at the lieutenant, suspicious. They'd fought side by side in

Salima's first battle, nearly ten years ago in Jirima. One of the last true battles of the war, not a drop of magic anywhere. Unlike Salima, Lieutenant Raza had trained for it in the citadels, the second daughter of a powerful nobleman. She was destined for leadership, and even at Jirima Salima had known that. But Lieutenant Raza had cut down an enemy assailant before he could kill Salima, and that had been enough to prove her worth as a soldier. But ten years was a long time ago. People changed. Just like wars.

"Go on," Lieutenant Raza said.

Salima slid the envelope over the desk. The paper felt like silk beneath her fingers. Enchanted paper, then. The magicians had their tendrils everywhere. She broke the seal and slid out the assignment. The ink shimmered in the sunlight pouring through the windows.

When she had finished reading, Salima set the assignment down on Lieutenant Raza's desk and looked up at her.

"Are you kidding me?"

Lieutenant Raza smiled. Her hair was already streaked with gray. "No."

"This isn't what I trained for." Salima gestured at the assignment. Anger burned up inside her. "This isn't—this is bullshit. It's murder."

Lieutenant Raza gazed at her from across the desk, her expression dispassionate. Her placidity just made Salima angrier.

"Do you agree with this?" Salima snatched up the assignment and waved it in the air. "Do you really think this is better than what we've been doing for the last century?"

"Shouldn't that answer your question? No war should last a century."

"Tell that to the Zyani!" Salima slammed the assignment down on the desk. "They keep coming at us! And we keep pushing back. But this—" She shoved the assignment hard enough that it swirled up into the air in a delicate arc "—this is nothing. This is a drop in the ocean. You think an empire like the Zyani will be bothered by this? You fought them. You know how relentless they are."

Lieutenant Raza rubbed her forehead. "We're battle sisters, Salima. And that's a bond I'll never forget, even here at headquarters. But if you don't take this assignment, the Realm will strip you of your warrior status."

All the breath went out of Salima. She slumped back in her chair. Lieutenant Raza wouldn't look her in the eye.

"You wouldn't dare," she hissed.

"No," said Lieutenant Raza, "I wouldn't. But this isn't my decision. I'm giving you orders that were passed down to me. Take the assignment, Salima. You're one of the best fighters out of Camp Kotor and I'm not letting them get rid of you so easily." She slid the assignment back over the desk. "Memorize these instructions so the paper can incinerate."

Salima stared across the desk, past Lieutenant Raza, out at the harbor dotted with white ship sails. Her hands were shaking with fury. Stripped of warrior status. They'd actually do it, too. It'd happened to more than a few good fighters the last couple of years. They'd send her to live in one of the inland villages, force her to hunker underground when the magicians swept through, raining desolation on the landscape. They'd take away everything that made Salima *Salima*.

She reached across the desk and picked up the assignment. The writing swam in front of her. She read through it again, a dull ache throbbing in her chest. She read it a third time. A fourth.

And then, the paper erupted in her hands, licks of gray flames that didn't let off any heat. The assignment burned away until it was nothing but a pile of ash in her lap.

"Very good." Lieutenant Raza stood up and Salima did the same. They shook hands across the desk as if they were just officer and soldier, like they'd never been battle sisters at all.

"Good luck," Lieutenant Raza said, and Salima said nothing.

Veroshtin had been destroyed twice during the course of the war. Twenty years ago it had still been a major choke point, but the front had shifted, as fronts were always doing in this war, and Veroshtin evolved into a place of neutrality. It looked the part, too. Salima would never have guessed this had once been a war city as she walked down the narrow, winding sidewalk toward the public gardens. They'd rebuilt fast. Something to do with magic—she remembered learning about it from her commander. The aftermath of the second magic attack had made it easier for Realm magicians to rebuild.

Now it was a city that tried to make you forget about war. The sun was warm and bright and shone on the white stone of the buildings. Pomegranate trees dropped red blossoms over the road. Women in stylish, extravagant dresses walked arm-in-arm with gentleman dandies, their laughter spilling up into the air.

The rich of both sides always found ways to ignore the war. They migrated to neutral cities like this one and lived side by side with their enemies, feigning civility.

The gate to the gardens appeared up ahead, twisting silver metal that glinted in the sun. Salima pushed it open and stepped through. Hibiscus flowers bloomed in garish colors. The air smelled sweet, like honey. She followed the path around, her hands tucked into her pockets.

Look for a horse, the instructions had said.

A damned horse. There were no horses here. No way they could even fit along the paths, which were narrow, intended for human feet. The gardens were emptier than Salima expected, given the warm sun, and people kept their distance from one another, voices hushed as if they were in library or a temple. Bees buzzed past; butterflies sent flickers of color wheeling through the air. Salima stopped at the center fountain. It was a sculpture of Raluma, the Goddess of War, only here her flaming sword spouted water instead of fire.

Salima glanced around, squinting against the glare of the sun. No horses. She moved along the path, following it around to the other side of the fountain.

She stopped.

A woman sat on one of the nearby stone benches, stitching an elaborate needlework. She was almost finished; most of the needlework was draped over her lap, revealing the design.

A golden horse, rearing up on its hind legs.

Salima's heart pounded. Stupid of her, to think it would be an actual horse—but she was a warrior, a soldier. She wasn't meant for this kind of nonsense.

She pulled her hands out of her pockets, not sure what to do with them. The woman hadn't looked up from her stitching. Salima took a deep breath. Funny, how she was almost more afraid of this woman than she was of riding into a battle. But with battle, you knew what to expect.

Salima had tucked a knife into her boot, even though the instructions had said to come unarmed. It was a small consolation for a woman used to full body armor and a pair of swords.

She walked over to the bench. The woman kept stitching, her hand moving up and down. The thread glinted. Salima stopped.

"Have you ever been to Lisadar?" she asked, feeling stupid.

"I have. Although I had a dreadful time." The woman finally looked up. Her expression was clear and guileless. "Have a seat," she said, and patted the bench beside her.

Salima sat down. Her heart hammered away. The woman folded up her needlework and slipped it into a satin bag at her side. Then she folded her hands in her lap and looked over at the fountain, her head tilted, her expression calm and pleasant.

"You can call me Amanza," she said, in the airy voice of a noblewoman making small talk. "How much do you know?"

"Enough to know I'm not supposed to talk about it."

Amanza laughed. She glanced over at Salima, her eyes flashing. "Of course. I meant how much do you know about the plan? For getting you in?"

Salima shifted her weight. Looked down at her hands. "Nothing. The assignment told me to meet you. Told me who I would—told me the target. That was it."

Amanza stood up abruptly and offered her elbow. "Let's walk," she said. "It's much easier to chat that way."

Salima hesitated. She thought of the last battle she'd fought in, up in Sondirra. The Zyani'd brought in magicians and turned the tide of the fight within the span of a heartbeat. Salima had ran through the madness, sword swinging wildly, her armor slick with blood. It was the only thing she knew how to do, even though, in that moment, it had been utterly futile.

Magic. Magic had brought them to this.

"Are you coming, darling?" Amanza asked.

Salima stood up and accepted Amanza's arm. They strolled along the path, the sunlight dappled and soft as it filtered through the trees.

"A lovely day, isn't it?"

Salima grunted a reply.

"I hear the weather will be turning soon." Amanza stepped onto a narrow path that wound more deeply into the copse of flowering trees. "I hate to say goodbye to summer, but alas."

"Why are you talking about this?" Salima growled.

Amanza looked over at her. She blinked once. Still guileless.

"Because there were ears in the main garden." She looked ahead again. The path was shady here. Concealed. "We wouldn't want to be overheard."

Salima sighed, fuming. "This is bullshit," she said. "I know what I'm supposed to do, just let—"

"You don't know how to find the target," Amanza's voice was still melodious and soft, but there was an undercurrent of sharpness to it that made Salima pay attention. "And even if you could find him, it wouldn't do to run in like a barbarian and slice his head off." She smiled pleasantly. "This isn't the Battle of Chamirra. It requires finesse."

"The Realm hired a soldier."

"This isn't a soldier's job." Amanza stopped and pulled her arm away from Salima and turned to face her. She was soft at the edges, in the way of wealthy women. If Salima were of a mind she could leave her battered and bleeding on the path without even having to pull her knife. But this woman was her superior, in the strange twisted way that things had become.

"Then why did they call me in?"

Amanza watched her for a moment. Drops of sunlight moved across her face. When she spoke, her lips formed the words in perfect enunciation, a weapon sharper than any blade.

"Because you know how to kill."

She turned and continued on the path. "We don't have time for this," Amanza called out. "I need to explain things to you."

And so Salima followed after her. Because even in this upside down world, that was what it meant to be a soldier. You did as you were told, for the good of the Realm.

"Tomorrow night." Amanza said when Salima was at her side. She didn't take Salima's arm again. "Tomorrow night, you will accompany me to the opera. *The Tragedy of Makemi le Raya*. Have you heard of it?"

"Don't exactly have time for operas on the front."

Amanza smiled as if the acidity in Salima's tone didn't faze her. "No, I imagine you don't. I have a private box where we can view the performance. It's closed off." She paused. Their footsteps shuffled against the worn-down stones of the path. "It's also right next to the private box where Duke Finbarr l'Jailo will be in attendance."

Hearing the name aloud struck Salima hard in her chest. The woman spoke the Zyani vowels without slurring them, as if she'd been speaking Zyani her entire life.

"There is a scene in *Makemi le Raya* where Makemi faces the warlock Palaron. It's customary for theaters to create a spectacle for it. They're always trying to outdo each other."

"Okay."

They walked together, their footsteps falling into synch. Amanza spoke in a soft voice as she explained the particulars of the assignment. The opera. The private boxes. The spectacle. And Salima's mission, a single task that she had done a million times on the battlefield. But in the context of an opera, it wasn't war. It was murder.

Amanza fell silent when the finished. The path curved into a clearing with a statue of Mataka at its center. A crown of fresh flowers lay upon her head. The goddess of fertility. Raluma's twin sister. Destruction and creation, created in the same womb.

They stopped in the clearing. Flower petals from the tree blossoms showered around them.

"Do you accept the assignment?" the woman asked.

Salima looked at the statue of Mataka. Her heart thudded. "Do I have a choice?"

"Yes."

"No, I don't." Salima had never payed much attention to Mataka. It was always Raluma whom she prayed to in times of darkness. But she didn't think Raluma or Mataka would look upon what they were discussing here with favor. "If I say no, they'll strip me of my warrior status." She turned to Amanza in a flush of anger. "I'll be nobody."

Amanza stared back at her, eyes clear.

"This isn't honorable," Salima said. The words came out in a rush. "This isn't the way to wage war. The books of Raluma explain the proper strategies. Always march directly at your enemy. Don't hide in the shadows. Lay out the terms of engagement." Salima glared at Amanza. "Have you ever even read the books of Raluma? Do you know anything about what it is I do?"

Silence fell around them like the leaves.

"About what it is all of us do? All of the soldiers marching on the Zyani? You don't, do you?" Anger spiked in Salima's bloodstream. She curled her hands into fists. "You live in this city, rebuilt out of *magic*, of all things, and you let the Zyani in and you wear your silks and your jewels, and you sip your tea in the afternoon and dine with your friends in the evening and the entire time, people are dying for you. I've seen soldiers with their intestines spilling around their feet, and they kept fighting until they died. I've seen soldiers dissolved by the Zyani mists. What have you seen?"

Amanza's eyes glittered in the sun. She stood very still. Salima breathed hard. Her blood was up. One quick movement, one strange noise out in the trees, and she'd have her knife out, ready to fight.

But when Amanza spoke, she did so softly, in a voice that she probably used on children or frightened animals.

"I was a child when the Zyani attacked Veroshtin the second time," she said. "One of the first to be evacuated—no doubt because of my status. Thousands of poorer children were swept up in the attack, an injustice I think of everyday. You ask me what I've seen? I've seen this city turned to glass by Zyani magicians. I was taken to a house nestled in the foothills of Veroshtin Mountain, and when I heard the sirens on the wind, I crawled out of the window of my room and ran to the lookout. The attack had already begun. A wave of light, pouring through the buildings." Amanza's voice did not waver, although her eyes glistened with tears. "I heard the screams even up in the hills. You've heard screams on a battlefield, but what I heard were not the screams of soldiers. They were the screams of children, of old men. And slowly the screams transformed into a chiming. Glass clinking against glass."

Salima was struck dumb. She couldn't have spoken even if she'd had something to say. Amanza reached up and expertly wiped the tears from her eyes before they fell.

"After the attack," she said, still speaking softly, her gaze fixed on the statue of Mataka, "when they went in to clean out the city, they found that the bodies were too heavy to move whole. And so they shattered them. An entire platoon of soldiers—our soldiers—swept through the city with clubs, breaking people into pieces." She lifted her chin and turned to Salima. Tears no longer sparkled in her eyes. There was a fierceness to her expression that Salima had seen in the faces of a million soldiers during her ten years fighting in this century-long war.

"Then the wizards came in," Amanza continued, "and they used the magic trapped in those fragments of people to rebuild. This city we're walking though is not a city. It's a mausoleum. Everything is pieces of the dead."

Salima's stomach twisted. Her breakfast from that morning churned around and for a moment she was afraid she would lean over and vomit on the path. For a moment she was afraid she would be the weak one. *Everything is pieces of the dead.* She glanced up at the trees dropping their flower blossoms to the ground. At the statue gleaming in the green-tinted sun.

"No," she whispered. "That's—an abomination. An affront to Raluma. They couldn't possibly—"

"It was the only way," Amanza said. "We couldn't leave the city destroyed.

We couldn't let the Zyani have their victory." She stepped closer to Salima, and Salima resisted the urge to pull away. "This man you say we're murdering," Amanza said, "is the Zyani's most powerful magician. He doesn't fight. He only develops spells and incantations to pass on to the lesser magicians, the ones they send into battle while he tours the neutral cities. You think I enjoy living side by side with our enemies, with the monsters who slaughtered thousands of innocents?"

Salima was struck dumb by the quiet fervor in Amanza's voice.

"I hate it," she hissed. "They say the neutral cities help us maintain our civility. But even magic is wiping that away now. L'Jailo comes here in the guise of a duke to relish his victory. When we kill him, we will kill the thing that has turned this war uncivilized."

Salima's face burned. The trees pressed in around her like a prison cell. Trees that had once been people. The thought twisted up inside her.

"I will collect you at sunset this evening," Amanza said. "Hide your weapons carefully."

Then she gathered up her skirts and strode down the path, leaving Salima alone with her horror.

A woman in a red ball gown stood on stage, her hair falling over one shoulder in a boundless pile of curls. She was singing. Her voice carried over the audience and up into the private box where Salima sat beside Amanza, who held up a pair of viewing glasses to her eyes. She had not looked at Salima once since the opera began. The performance seemed to have been going on for hours, for days, but they still hadn't reached the moment of spectacle that was to be Salima's cue.

The music changed abruptly, the tone going dark and frightening. Salima's heart thudded. The woman was still singing, but a man crept onstage behind her, dragging a heavy warlock's coat. Palaron, the opera's villain—Salima had been able to figure out that much. The rest of the story was a mystery to her. Weeping women, endless death, a lost love—whenever she thought she'd grasped onto the individual pieces, they would slip away. She was too anxious to try and grab them back.

She still wasn't sure she was capable of this assignment.

Amanza dropped her viewing glasses into her lap. She leaned in close to Salima and whispered in her ear, "It's almost time."

On stage, the warlock held a fake knife to the throat of the singer in the red dress. She struggled against him, the cymbals clashing, the drums pounding. The music sounded like Salima's heart.

Amanza leaned forward, not bothering with the viewing glasses. She smiled, almost as an afterthought, almost as if she didn't realize she was doing it.

A plume of smoke erupted on stage, stained green from benign magician's fire. Actors in dark cloaks and demon masks swarmed onstage, and the music was trilling and throbbing and terrifying.

"Go, soldier," said Amanza without turning away from the performance.

Salima stood up. The woman's voice had, in that moment, sounded so much like that of Lieutenant Raza's that the opera slipped away, and she was not standing in the private box of a Veroshtini noblewoman, but on the battlefield, surrounding by the burning landscape and the rush of Zyani soldiers and the acrid tang of magician's fire smoldering in the distance. She acted by rote, pulling the knife that had been concealed in her boot—the same knife she had taken with her to the park. It was the only weapon she needed. She pulled aside the curtain on the side of the private box. Her head was buzzing. Her palms slicked with sweat. Behind the curtain was the stone wall separating the boxes. There was a door in the wall, freshly cut. In the dim light of the theater you could barely see the lines.

Salima grabbed the loop of metal meant to serve as a handle. She pulled the door open. On the other side was a curtain, the same rich blood-red velvet as the curtain she had pulled aside.

She stopped. Her breath was coming short and fast, the way it never did before a battle. Before a battle, her fear manifested in other ways: as outbursts of anger, as a slow-gnawing anxiety in the pit of her stomach.

Raluma forgive me, she thought. She didn't want to have the right to battle stripped away from her. If she did not do this, her whole identity would be washed away. Lost at sea. It did not matter if she thought she was capable or not. Like a good soldier, she *had* to be capable.

She slipped through the curtain, and stepped into Duke Finbarr l'Jailo's private box.

Her appearance did not go unnoticed, but Salima moved quickly, with a cold detachment she never felt on the battlefield. A man sitting at the left of the Duke saw her first, and gave a squawk of surprise that was drowned out by the cacophony on stage. Salima slit his throat. Blood gushed over her hands. The Duke's two guards turned, charged toward her, but she stabbed one in the throat and grabbed the other's sword and whirled it around, slicing him at the weak place in his armor, under his arm. He fell bleeding, clutching his side. She drew her knife across his throat too.

That left only the Duke.

He was screaming, but, as Amanza had promised, his cries blended in with the riotous music and the screaming of the demon-masked actors onstage. He pressed himself against the balcony, hands held up in front of him in surrender, babbling at her in Zyani. She stepped toward him.

This was cowardice. He was not a soldier. Soldiers did not plead for their lives.

But then she saw the magic gathering around his fingers, his veins glowing red-gold. The back of her throat burned. He wasn't trying to surrender, she realized with a shudder. He was preparing to attack.

The war is changing.

She did not stop to think. She only acted. Her knife flashed, blood gushed, Duke Finbarr l'Jailo slumped forward. The magic dissipated, leaving a scent like burning metal on the air. Her eyes watered. She dragged him back into his seat, drew her hands over his eyes to close them. Not even a Zyani magician should have to face the Netherworld with open eyes. She wiped the knife on the leg of her trousers, on one of the few clean spots. Blood squelched in the carpet. She pulled the curtain aside and stepped back through to her own box.

Amanza had lifted up her viewing glasses again. Some of the smoke from the stage had drifted up to their box, little wisps of gray clouds. A change of clothes sat on Salima's chair. A vial of some magician's unguent which would wipe the blood from her skin. Another with bubbling liquid which would dissolve her clothes into mist, the way she'd seen her fellow warriors dissolved on the battlefield.

"I barely heard a thing," Amanza said without turning away from the performance. "You did excellent work."

Salima was cold all over. A true soldier would not have done what she just did. A true soldier understood that battle could only happen on a battlefield.

Lieutenant Raza had told her that the Realm would strip her warrior status if she hadn't complied. But yet her warrior status had been stripped from her regardless, the moment she had crawled through that space in the wall and killed those men in an opera box in a neutral city.

It seemed she was capable after all.

Onstage, the curtain dropped, and the audience broke into thunderous applause. It sounded like the war cannons of the battle of Jirima, ten years ago, when Liutenent Raza had saved Salima's life. A warrior protecting a warrior.

But now Salima understood: that world of that battle had been a facade, an imitation. It was a spectacle to hide the realities of the true hundred-year war, the war that waged in the shadows.

Now she had seen it, and she knew no warrior would ever save her life again.

AUTHOR BIOGRAPHIES

STEVE BORNSTEIN has been in the military, traveled to distant lands, and held the sorts of jobs you watch shows about on the Discovery Channel. Currently, he spends half his time on a big iron island in the middle of the ocean. He lives in Central Texas with his wife and four feline overlords, and enjoys making it up as he goes. Somewhere in the midst of all this he finds the time to put words on the screen. His short stories have been published in several anthologies alongside the likes of Rachel Swirsky, Erik Scott de Bie, and Mercedes Lackey. He's currently working on his first full-length novel, set in Ed Greenwood's Hellmaw setting. His infrequently-updated blog can be found at stevebornstein.com.

CASSANDRA ROSE CLARKE grew up in south Texas and currently lives in a suburb of Houston, where she writes and teaches composition at a pair of local colleges. She holds an M.A. in creative writing from The University of Texas at Austin, and in 2010 she attended the Clarion West Writer's Workshop in Seattle. Her work has been nominated for the Philip K. Dick Award and YALSA's Best Fiction for Young Adults. Her latest novel is *Our Lady of the Ice*, out now from Saga Press.

ERIK SCOTT DE BIE, SF/F author and game designer, has been joyously writing about women in practical armor since his first novel *Ghostwalker* came out in 2005. He has published work in the Forgotten Realms, Iron Kingdoms, Golarion, the Traveller universe, and numerous original settings such as the World of Ruin (see his contribution herein). His most recent novels include *Shield of the Summer Prince* (World of Ruin book 2, 2015), *Priority: Hyperion* (Summer 2015), and *Blind Justice* (December 2015). He lives in Seattle, on social media (facebook.com/erik.s.debie, @erikscottdebie), and at his website: erikscottdebie.com

KRISTY GRIFFIN GREEN is 33 years old and lives in Orlando, FL with her husband Linden, her daughter Susannah, and her cat, His Imperial Majesty Joseph Norton, Second Of That Name, Emperor of These United States and Protector of Mexico. She spends entirely too much time making her imaginary friends go on adventures. Her other hobbies include making papier-mache masks, decorating tiny hats, and learning Victorian flower code. She has never, sadly, hand-forged a sword.

AMY GRISWOLD has written several Stargate Atlantis and SG-1 tie-in novels, including the Stargate Atlantis Legacy series (with Jo Graham and Melissa Scott) and *Stargate SG-1: Murder at the SGC*. With Melissa Scott, she is also the author of the Victorian fantasy/mystery novels *Death by Silver* and *A Death at the Dionysus Club* from Lethe Press. She can be found online at amygriswold.livejournal.com and @amygris.

SARAH HENDRIX is a queen of Chaos. She herds cats, works as a personal assistant for Jennifer Brozek and handles promotions for Apocalypse Ink Productions and Evil Girlfriend Media. Spare time finds her writing, beading, editing and knitting. To complete her love of all things unorganized, she has two cats, two teenage boys and a fiancé. You can find her work in books from Dagan Books, Lakeside Circus and Abyss and Apex. You can follow her online at shadowflame1974.wordpress.com, or @shadowflame1974.

CRYSTAL LYNN HILBERT lives in the forgotten backwaters of Western Pennsylvania and subsists mostly on old trade paperbacks and tea. A fan of things magical and mythical, her stories tend towards a peculiar blend of high magic and Eddic poetry. You can find her latest stories "Oath Breaker Priest to an Almost God" in Betwixt, "Dawnsong" in Spark, and "Glittering; Guttering" in Capricious. Her poem "Little and Red" has also appeared recently in Apex. If you're feeling particularly brave, a monster masquerading as her sleeps at http://cl-hilbert.tumblr.com/

CHRIS A. JACKSON is a sailor, writer, and gamer; nautical and RPG tie-in fantasy came naturally for him. His *Scimitar Seas* novels won multiple gold medals from Foreword Reviews Magazine, and his Pathfinder Tales novels, *Pirate's Honor, Pirate's Promise, and Pirate's Prophecy* have received high praise. His non-nautical *Weapon of Flesh* trilogy has become a Kindle bestseller, spurring the continuation *Weapon of Fear* Trilogy. He's also branched into contemporary fantasy with *Dragon Dreams*, set in Ed. Greenwood's world of Hellmaw. His recent short works also include *Sweating Bullets*, in the *World of Shadows* Shadowrun anthology. Drop by Jaxbooks.com and sign up for his mailing list.

MARY ROBINETTE KOWAL is the author of *The Glamourist Histories* series of fantasy novels. She has received the Campbell Award for Best New Writer, three Hugo awards, and the RT Reviews award for Best Fantasy Novel. Her work has been nominated for the Hugo, Nebula and Locus awards. Her stories appear in *Asimov's, Clarkesworld,* and several Year's Best anthologies. Mary, a professional puppeteer, also performs as a voice actor, recording fiction for authors such as Seanan McGuire, Cory Doctorow and John Scalzi. She lives in Chicago with her husband Rob and over a dozen manual typewriters. Visit maryrobinettekowal.com

When **ERIC LANDRENEAU** first tasted escargot he was naked under the Cretan sun. Well, he was naked because it was hot, and he was a baby, and it wasn't escargot, just a snail, but it really was in Crete. Many years later he is a speculative fiction author daylighting as an optician in the 'burbs of Portland, Oregon. Connection? You'll have to build a quantum computational engine to know for sure. He has had short stories published here and there across the web and in print, including Kaleidotrope, The Rejected Quarterly and Title Goes Here. Stories of his will also appear in the anthologies Putrefying Stories Vol1 from Rampant Loon and Outliers of Speculative Fiction from L. A. Little. His self-published fantasy novel "BREAK! A Tale of Cursed Blood" is available through Amazon and wherever you buy e-books. His next book, a dystopian sci-fi adventure-comedy-spoof, will be out sometime in 2016. Promise. You can find out more about Eric and his stories at: http://ericlandreneau.wordpress.com/

WUNJI LAU has been wordslinging for his supper for most of his professional life, which has been sufficiently long to allow the use of the phrase "kids these days" without irony. He's been a Braille translator, game designer, technical writer, and science writer, and currently helps design software, technologies, and educational materials for the blind and visually impaired. Wunji lives in Indianapolis with his wife Sarah and baby daughter High Duchess Ellen Diane Squirmster of the Unicorn Smoothie Palace.

TODD J. MCCAFFREY is a US Army veteran, a cross-continent pilot, a computer geek, and a *New York Times* bestselling author. He feeds his weirdness with books, large bowls of popcorn, and frequent forays to science fiction conventions. He is the middle son of the late Anne McCaffrey and is proud to list among his credits eight books written on Pern — including five collaborations. His near-future AI thriller, *City of Angels*, will be published in May by Wordfire Press. The short story *Golden* is the first of many fantasy stories in a world of shape-shifting dragons. His website is: http://www.toddmccaffrey.org

RHONDA PARRISH is driven by a desire to do All The Things. She was the publisher and editor-in-chief of Niteblade Magazine for eight years (which is like *forever* in internet time) and is the editor of several anthologies including (most recently) *Scarecrow* and *C is for Chimera*. In addition, Rhonda is a writer whose work has been in publications such as *Tesseracts 17: Speculating Canada from Coast to Coast, Imaginarium: The Best Canadian Speculative Writing* (2012) and *Mythic Delirium*. Her novella, *Shadows*, whish is set in the same world as "Sharp as a Griffin's Claw," will be out later this year. Her website, updated weekly, is at http://www.rhondaparrish.com

ANYA PENFOLD has been writing since she was old enough to find her way around a BBC Micro, such a dismayingly long time that she has floppy disks older than some of her colleagues (and also, really needs to clear out some cupboards). She writes science fiction, fantasy, weird fiction and horror, and also paints, draws and practices subsistence wine-farming (weather and day-job permitting). She doesn't have any pets, but she used to have a cat. He was an antisocial, co-dependent grouch, especially when he got old, and she misses him too much to ever try to replace him. As well as *Women in Practical Armour*, she has a short story in the 2015 edition of *Outliers of Speculative Fiction.*

MARY PLETSCH is a glider pilot, toy collector and graduate of the Royal Military College of Canada. She attended Superstars Writing Seminars in 2010 and has since published multiple short stories in a variety of genres including science fiction, horror, and fantasy. Mary lives in New Brunswick with Dylan Blacquiere and their four cats. Visit her online at www.fictorians.com.

ALEX C. RENWICK lives and writes in the collective shadow of only slightly volatile Pacific Northwest volcanoes. Some of her most recent stories appeared in *Alfred Hitchcock's Mystery Magazine, Postscripts, ELQ,* and *The Exile Book of New Canadian Noir.* Her short fiction collection *PUSH OF THE SKY* (written as Camille Alexa) got a starred review in *Publishers Weekly* and was an official reading selection of Portland's Powell's Books Science Fiction Book Club. More at alexcrenwick.com.

DAVID SZARZYNSKI is: an attorney, sometimes author, lifelong Fantasy fan. Born in the Midwest, escaped to San Francisco. Has a cat, thin rimmed glasses, and a distaste for craft beer and irony. Disillusioned man. Prone to exaggerations: inventive without creativity. Enjoys grammar, but like a bad cook, burns it. Verbs nouns, occasionally.

JUDITH TARR's first novel, *The Isle of Glass*, appeared in 1985. Her new novel, *Forgotten Suns*, a space opera, was published by Book View Café this spring. In between, she's written historicals and historical fantasies and epic fantasies, some of which have been reborn as ebooks from Book View Café. She has won the Crawford Award, and been a finalist for the World Fantasy Award and the Locus Award. She lives in Arizona with an assortment of cats, a blue-eyed spirit dog, and a herd of Lipizzan horses.

EDITOR BIOGRAPHIES

ED GREENWOOD is an amiable, bearded Canadian writer, game designer, voice actor, and librarian best known as the creator of The Forgotten Realms® fantasy world. He sold his first fiction at age six, and has since published more than 300 books that have sold millions of copies worldwide in over two dozen languages. He was elected to the Academy of Adventure Gaming Art & Design Hall of Fame in 2003. Ed has judged the World Fantasy Awards and the Sunburst Awards, hosted radio shows, acted onstage, explored caves, jousted, and been Santa Claus (but not all on the same day).

Ed's most recent novels include *Spellstorm*, a Forgotten Realms® novel from Wizards of the Coast; *The Iron Assassin*, a steampunk novel from Tor Books; and *Your World Is Doomed!*–the first release from The Ed Greenwood Group, and the book that launched his Hellmaw setting. His upcoming books include *Death Masks*, a Forgotten Realms® novel from Wizards of the Coast, and *Between My Usual Murders*, *Cadis Telluris*, and *The Whispering Skull*, all from The Ed Greenwood Group.

GABRIELLE HARBOWY is a San Francisco-based writer and editor of fantasy and science fiction, with a background in classical piano and percussion, and a degree in Psychology from Rutgers University. She has edited for publishers including Pyr, Circlet Press, Paizo, and Apex Magazine, just to name a few, and has been Managing Editor at Dragon Moon Press since 2008. In 2014, she edited *The Complete Guide to Writing For Young Adults Volume 1* for Dragon Moon Press. She is a multiple-time Parsec Award judge and served on the Andre Norton Award jury in 2016. Her writing has appeared in several anthologies, including *Carbide Tipped Pens*, edited by Eric Choi and Ben Bova for Tor. Her first novel, *Hellmaw: Of the Essence*, is out in Spring, 2016 with The Ed Greenwood Group, and she has a Pathfinder Tales novel forthcoming from Paizo. You can find her on the web at gabrielleharbowy.com, or on Twitter at @gabrielle_h.

ALSO CO-EDITED BY
GABRIELLE HARBOWY
AND
ED GREENWOOD

When the Hero Comes Home
When the Villain Comes Home
When the Hero Comes Home 2

KICKSTARTER LEGION
BACKER ACKNOWLEDGMENTS

GAUNTLETS

Anonymous (x2)
Eric Staggs
Maha Saedaway
liftUPlift.com

PAULDRONS

Anonymous (x3)
Sarah Yost
Mike Hampton
Nathan Duby
Lewis Phillips
Henrik Lindhe
Adriano Varoli Piazza
Michael Lorenson
Normandy Helmer
Bianca Samaniego
Rufus Orsborne
Jessie Kwak
Chrtistian & Jess Kelly-
Madera
Mark Brown
Amanda Shore
Zombie Orpheus
Alexandre Maki
Peter Thew
Kenny Soward

Brian Quirt
Dana OShee
C.E. Robertson
Dominic Franchetti
Robert N. Emerson
Charisse Baldoria
Sifer Aseph
Belisarius
Jamieson Hoffman
James Arnold
Ana Mardoll
Brian Quirt
Sheryl R. Hayes
Rebecca Turner
Alex Conall
George Gibbs
Laurie
Michael Parker
Giana Tondolo Bonilla
Cliff Winnig
summervillain
Joel Thorne
S. Cuypers
Patricia Farnan
Mary Dickenson
Jeanne Kramer-Smyth
Beth Cato
Kelly Harrison
Shanna Germain

E. Catedral
Sara Watts
Wendy Westerduin
Jennifer Jamieson
Pauline Martyn
Tehani Wessely
Laura Christensen
Andrew Fleisher
Dwarven Ale
Nicole Lavigne
Eric Wagoner
Emily Fodor
Anne Petersen
Cybele O'Brien
Phil Cardenas
Adam Winnett
Chris Brant
Tone Berg
Katharine
Kieron Briggs
Erin M. Hartshorn
Ceri Stokes
Clinton Macgowan
Stephanie Folse
Echo Mae
Tracy Kaplan
Graeme Gregory
Cristella Bond
Kerry Beck

Jeffrey Bradshaw
Ann Tucker
Lucy Jefferies
Alan Cohen
Emery Shier
Michael J. Sullivan
Jennifer Howell
Bethany Jenkins
L. van Rijn
Jason Vrooman
Carolyn Rogers
Danielle Maiorino
Bridget Kiely
Roy Romasanta
Alana Joli Abbott
Ed Matuskey
Géraldine Zenhäusern
Jon Lasser
Seth Johnson
C.E. Robertson
Caitlin Hughes
David Perkins
Terren Lansdaal

CAP

Anonymous (x3)
Sharon Wood
Benjamin C. Kinney
Mark M Matthies
Gavran
Liz Grzyb
Erika Kuehn
Christopher Rodgers
Wendy Hammer
Sheena McFerran
Jonathan Dean
Jessie D. Foster
Alex S Bradshaw
Brad Roberts

Martin Hecko
John McKim
Sarah Mendonca
Browncoat Jayson
Jo Good
Simon Law
Chris McKenzie
Laura Woods
Jason Clark
Jen Edwards
Weenie_Tot
Francesca Frezza
Catherine Schwartz
Kelly Babcock
Jamie Bair
Dan Summers
Jeffery Davidson
Chris Barili
Jill Savage
Jennifer Young
Andreas Larsson
Erin Thompson
Lawerence Hawkins
Veronica Ramshaw
Sylvia Pellicore
Jenny Barber
William Ord
Daneen and William
McDermott
Song Palmese
Carolyn Reid
Roxana Steckline
Yara T. Reca-Vargas
Rebecca Smith
Rebecca Smith
Melanie DeMore
David Bowden
Impossibilis
Frank Wales
Paige Liberski

Eric Brooks
Allie Parker
chuu mong
Corie Weaver
Myles Braithwaite
Jennifer Albert
Cameron Russell
Mark H. Walker
Lisa Schaefer
Almudena Pumarega
Arroyo
Danial Watkins
Tim Voves
DCQ
David Mark Brown
Jenni Juvonen
Sarah Van Voorhis
Hisham El-Far
Samantha
LT Douglas Ivey
biscuit
Brenda Mercer
Margaret Chiavetta
Sarah Tupper
Ecogrl
Daniel Phelps
Stephen Ballentine
Wright Johnson
Peter Smith
Sara Gaines
Gwen Whiting
Woodrow Hill
Anya Penfold
Megan Sage
Katherine Malloy
Chris Matosky
Pat Hayes
Rudy
Susan Sutton
Sean Hagle

Amy Brennan
Iliyan Svetoslavov Iliev
imogthe
Carol Townsend
S. Ben Melhuish
Naomi Twery
Justin Jones
Janet Vandenabeele
Michelle Brenner
Jean Marie Ward
Mandy Small
Kathleen Hanrahan
M B
Joachim Fermstad
Eric Slaney
Jeromy French
Joseph Hoopman
Sarah Uhl
Shane Donovan
Shawn Pfister
Nitari Windrider
John du Bois
Veronica Ramshaw
Andan Lauber
Misha Husnain Ali
CGJulian
Russell Ventimeglia
Grace Gorski
Nathan Seabolt
Stephanie A. Cain
Chad Brown
Bill Emerson
Jack Lee
Mainon Schwartz
Mark W. Bruce
Joe Block
Emma Levine
Juliet Ulman
Belinda Marsh
David Jones

Paul M. Lambert
Tim Marsh
D. Moonfire

MAIL SHIRT

Anonymous (x2)
Doug Blakeslee
Andrew Wilson
Sean Forbes
Otomo
Lindsay Steussy
Jere Manninen
Richard Hunt
Ragnarok Publications
(J.M. Martin)
Ross Andrews
Katrina L. Halliwell
Donald J. Bingle
Eric Bakutis
Chris and Meagan Eller
Josh & Stephanie English
Patti Short
Marta da Costa
James Ballard
Alban Lorimer
Chris Jameson
Amanda Armstrong
Fraser Gerrie
Tracey F. Poist
Mike Rimar
Misty Massey
Jeffery Mace
Jerusha Achterberg
Ryan J. Smith
Ethan Schlenker
Katherine Gohring
Benjamin Hausman
Peggy Jurado
Jeffrey Jones

D Franklin
Laura Wilkinson
Marianne
Elizabeth Reesman
Tonia Brown
Caitlin Bonnette
Keira Marti
Emily
Django Wexler
Dusty Toboleski
Babs K Crump
James Fearnley
Annie
Rhonda Parrish
Annie Bellet
Tony Thompson

BREASTPLATE

Anonymous (x11)
Timothy W. Long
Rebecca Enzor
Claire Fletcher
Cassandra Kehoe
Kim Pittman
Meg Winikates
Nathan Clark
Daniel Galli
Elizabeth Buchan-
Kimmerly
Michael Green
Cassie Stirpe
Michelle Barratt
Kerry Ann Liddick
Michael Sims
Kaleigh Mathers
Matthew Montgomery
marcus arena
Lindsay Johnson
Rick Marson

Camille Griep
Christine A. Cooney
Barton Perkins
Neal Frick
James Vernon
Sarah Mijts
Stephanie Shena
Kat
Leandrie Duvenhage
Kayla Valderas
Michael Reilly
Carolyn Fritz
Elizabeth Kite
Amanda Johnson
Robert Sjoblom
Kimbrely A Vickers-
Dunning
Christophe Loyce
Lisa Rabey
Nik Rode
Pawel Daruk
James Crouch
Emily Murphy
Miria
Margaret St. John
Donald Hopkins
Randy Hall
Wei Jiun Lim
Elias Puustinen
Keiji Miashin
Kristina Torri
Mike Selinker
Kacky Andrews
David Kinney
Heather Roulo
Tom Wright
Ryan Garcia
Aneirin Pendragon
Linda A. Bruno
Angel Leigh McCoy

Wendy Gill
Thomas Keyton
Eric Menge
Belinda Draper
Rhiannon Raphael
Tanya Emmert
Mark Ferrer
Virginia Ellen Dixon
Kathryn Hunt
Raven Oak
David Dalrymple
Mary Law
Elizabeth Guizzetti
Marcus Juergens
Christopher Pitner
Jesse Ozog
Stephen Milton
Are Gunnar Aarø
Trisha Suhr
Krys Earles
Megan Turcotte
Lim Ivan
Katherine Little
Cathi Falconwing
Alan Paulsen
Ken Brady
AnaMaria
Jan Trybula
Ken Mencher
Dave Robison
Nicole Cook
Trisha Stouffer
Emme Hones
Cecilia Tan
Michelle Muenzler
Christopher Dunnbier
Kelly J. Cooper
Cat Wendt
Jinnapat Treejareonwiwat
Kimberly wilson

Mythoard
Danielle Gembala
Terry Weyna
Ashford Privette
Tone Milazzo
Eric L Wills
Samantha Press
Susan Collicott

VISORED HELM

Anonymous (x4)
Charity Tahmaseb
Lenhoff Family
Monika Holabird
Sally Novak Janin
Keith Strohm
Anthony R. Cardno
Tammie Webb Ryan
Jennifer Levine
Kimberly Bea
Monica Marlowe
Caraig
Meredeth Beckett
WolfieAK
Chris Volcheck
Mara Taylor
John Werner
Veronica Young
Megan Parsons
Melissa Katano
Amanda Helstrom-White
Tony Montuori
Elizabeth Allen
Phillip Bailey
Marie Brennan
Elizabeth Janes
Cleo Maranski
Jessica Flores
Sarah Stewart

Eva
Robert Abrazado
Albert P Tobey
Karen Enno
Ali Meacham
Brittany Kalten
Jaime Kirby
Elspeth Payne
Senji
Rhel ná DecVandé
Audrey DiFelice
Katie Roman
Amanda Johnson
C. Keeler
Chris Callicoat
Desiree Scudder
Justin Shepard
Vasilios Hoffman
Jim Cox
Dianna Smith
Joe Monson
Michael Hanscom
Mark Cockerham
Erik J. Meyer-Curley
Jessica Meade
Frazer Porritt
Alex Chevallier
Brett Washam
Shiri Sondheimer
Ludvig Carleson
Warren Charleston
Colin Ferguson
Mike Miller
A.Perez
Scott Maitland
laufeyjarson
Lynati
Erin VanDenEng
Steve Acheson
Don, Beth, & Meghan
Ferris

Kit Russell

PATENT OF NOBILITY

Anonymous (x3)
Tristen Warner
Marit Freya Pollei
Stuart Denyer
Jennifer Brozek
Tove Heikkinen
Jason Mical
Megan Beals
Ann Shilling
Sarah Troedson
Mistress CrankyBadger
Tabitha Reau
Carolina Edwards
Erik de Bie
Porter Wiseman
Anne E
Emma Clarkson
Amanda Cook
Caroline Pate
Leo Huang
Rachel Sasseen
Charles Parks
Patrick Pilgrim
Rosemary Warner
Debra M Williamson
Zoe Lewycky
Vivienne Jones White
Katharine Bond
Jennifer Haden
Felicia Fredlund
Ceallaigh MacCath-Moran
Jessica M Rivera
Aaron Gordon
Cheryl Dyson
Andrew Hicks

Richard Novak
Paula R. Stiles
Carmen Marin
Suebuzz
Shamine Athena King
Jenny Dybedahl
James Lucas
Megan Struttmann
Matt Hill
Calvin Sauerbier
Erika Brink
Samantha Goodfellow
Scott James Magner
Loree Parker
Anika Tenou
Pandem
Andrea Brandt

KNIGHTS OF THE REALM

Jenna Miller
Sebastien Blouin
Adrian Collins
mrmike
Heather ONeill
Sean Brooks
Matthew Walker
GriffinFire
Terry Adams
Carmen Christgau
Annafel
Kat Gordon
Sorck
Stephanie Schellin
Michael Grafton
Kathy Hillman
Sean Dillon
Kate Kuchler
Betty Morgan
Peter Clines

QUEEN'S CHAMPIONS

Matt Gambardella
Christopher Cates
Rissa Lyn
Chris Warack
Artur Valverde
Ingrid Emilsson
Darmys Asagiri
August Grappin
Brian Barnsley
Christie Fremon
Tiffany Jayde Gontczaruk
John S Costello
Brad Roberts
Mudd Law

MARK OF THE BLOOD QUEEN

Lynne de Bie
Yankton Robins
Philip Layfield
Sir James Watkins

DUCAL ORDER

K. Helbling
Kevin & Janna Morgan
Carl and Sarah Landreneau

LADY'S FAVOR

Christopher D. Muñoz
Abigail Schor

CLOTH COIF

Amanda Crowder
Brian S Blicher
Nicole Montgomery
Arkady

ALL-FOR-ONE

Katie Techa
Myon
Jaime Mayer